THE ROLLESBY CHRONICLE

THE ROLLESBY CHRONICLE

Ron Pallas

The Book Guild Ltd
Sussex, England

This book is a work of fiction. The characters and situations in this story are imaginary. No resemblance is intended between these characters and any real persons, either living or dead.

This book is sold subject to the condition that it shall not, by way of trade or otherwise, be lent, re-sold, hired out, photocopied or held in any retrieval system or otherwise circulated without the publisher's prior consent in any form of binding or cover other than that in which this is published and without a similar condition including this condition being imposed on the subsequent purchaser.

The Book Guild Ltd.
25 High Street,
Lewes, Sussex

First published 2000
© Ron Pallas, 2000

Set in Baskerville
Typesetting by
SetSystems Ltd, Saffron Walden, Essex

Printed in Great Britain by
Bookcraft (Bath) Ltd, Avon

A catalogue record for this book is
available from the British Library

ISBN 1 85776 418 8

To my wife, Erica

CONTENTS

Preface ix

Part I (1340–1345)

1 Sluys, Flanders – June 1340 3
2 The Sea Battle 8
3 Castor Manor 16
4 Growing Up 22
5 Springtime 28
6 The Homecoming 34
7 The Contest 40
8 Captain of the Guard 51
9 Norwiche – The Encounter 60
10 Norwiche – The Market and Other Affairs 76
11 The Constable's Prize and an Eventful Journey 86
12 A Matter of Life and Death 94
13 Seeds of Change and Political Intrigue 106

Part II (1346–1356)

14 The Battle of Crécy 121
15 The Aftermath – Calais and Beyond 137
16 Titchfield Abbey 142
17 A New Life 150

18	The Manor of Portchester and a Trip to Winchester	157
19	The City of Winchester and Palpitations	163
20	The Miracle!	170
21	Growing Prosperity	182
22	The Black Death	195
23	An Illusory Tranquility	205
24	Social Upheaval and Family Tragedy	216
25	The Marriage	230
26	'The Willows'	247
27	Reunion	256
28	A New Start	268
29	Marky	279
30	Jessica	289
31	Royal Celebrations and Gascony	300
32	The Second 'Chevauchée'	308
33	The Battle	321
34	Epilogue	328
	Sources	333
	Glossary	335

PREFACE

The Rollesby Chronicle is a family story set in the Middle Ages. The action takes place primarily in fourteenth-century England but also follows the armies of the 'Black Prince' campaigning in Flanders and France, portraying graphically all the tension, excitement and horrors of Crécy and finally, the battle of Poitiers in 1356.

The book focuses on the development of two brothers, Thomas and Paul, both highly gifted but born into poverty; the eldest distinguishing himself as an outstanding warrior and leader, the youngest becoming an extremely successful wool merchant, or 'brogger', who eventually founds a powerful, cloth-making dynasty.

Many fascinating aspects of the early and mid-fourteenth century are authentically portrayed: a society of wealthy nobility and clergy, frequently – but not always – abusing their power and privileges at the expense of the poor, the peasantry, workshop labourers, or the conscripted soldiers. We witness village life on 'demesnes' in Norfolk and Hampshire, and glimpse into the more comfortable manor houses and monasteries. Commercial activities in major cities like Norwich, Winchester and Salisbury are vividly brought to life: the dynamism of the markets, the craftmens' workshops, labourers at work in fullers' and dyers' premises by the riverside. We see the beauty of cathedrals and churches, impressive guildhalls and other fine buildings contrasting dramatically with the poverty and squalor of some side streets and workers' cottages. We feel the ominous presence of castles, garrisoned troops, the lawlessness and brutality of life in the streets, the corruption of some clerks and officials.

The reader also experiences the fear and horror of the Black Death as it sweeps through the countryside, devastating life in the villages and cities, leaving a third of the population dead in its wake. The people are powerless against it, have no idea what it is or what causes it. Innocent individuals or minorities are falsely blamed as being responsible; greedy or corrupt officials use the charge of witchcraft to falsely accuse and burn their innocent victims at the stake in order to misappropriate their wealth or settle a score.

Within this colourful, emotional and action-packed background, we follow a major part of the lives and passionate loves of Thomas and Paul as they strive to survive and move out of their poor circumstances, building a better life for their families, both impacting positively and dramatically on their environment in the process.

The Rollesby Chronicle Family Tree

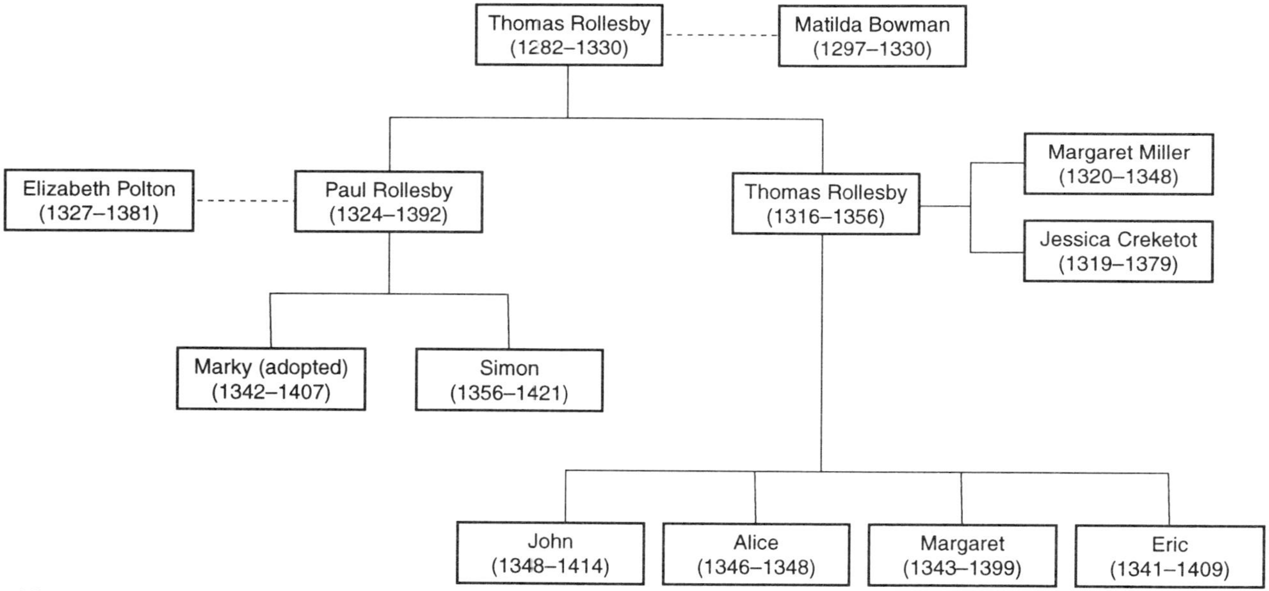

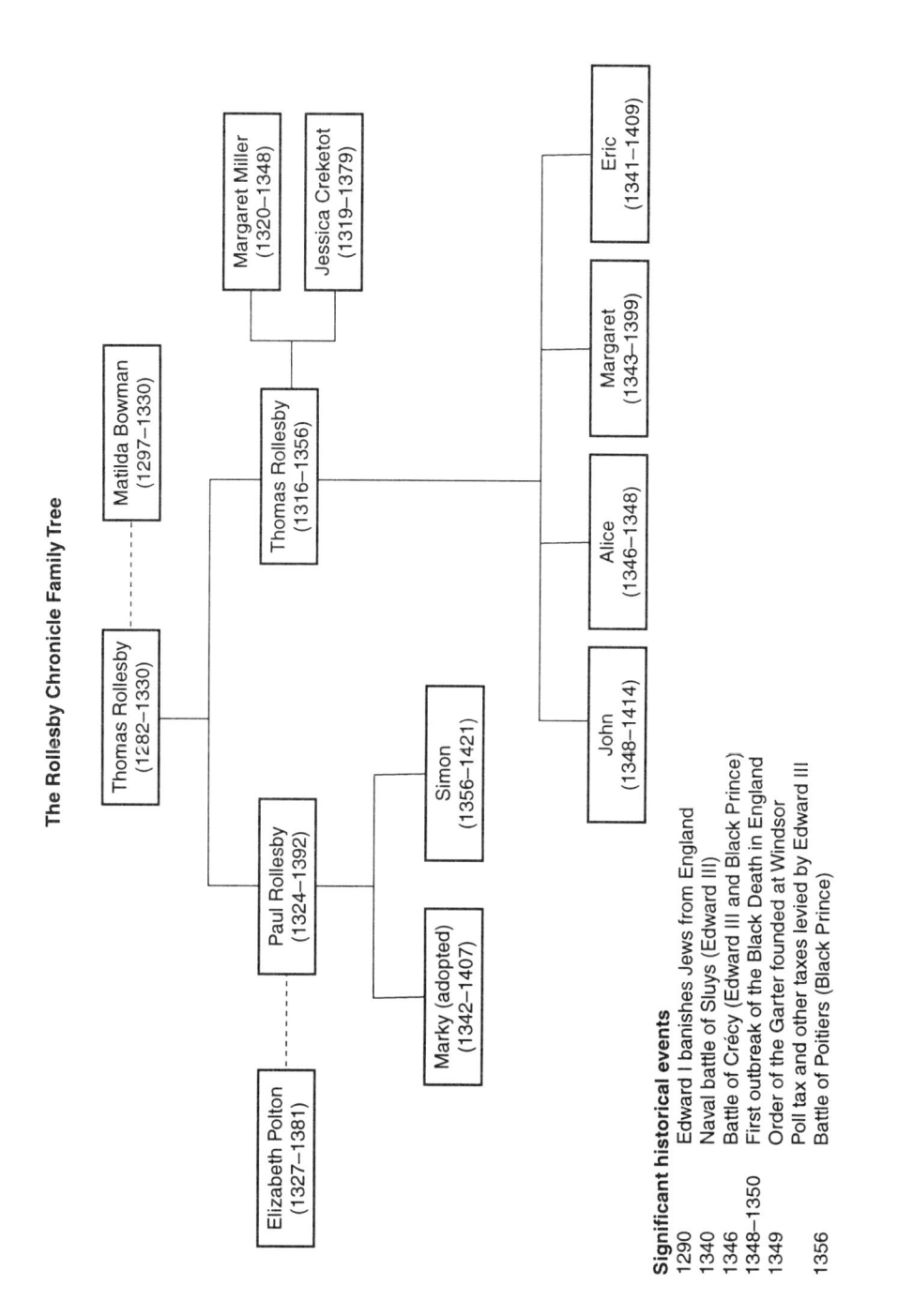

Thomas Rollesby (1282–1330)
Matilda Bowman (1297–1330)
Elizabeth Polton (1327–1381)
Paul Rollesby (1324–1392)
Thomas Rollesby (1316–1356)
Margaret Miller (1320–1348)
Jessica Creketot (1319–1379)
Marky (adopted) (1342–1407)
Simon (1356–1421)
John (1348–1414)
Alice (1346–1348)
Margaret (1343–1399)
Eric (1341–1409)

Significant historical events

1290	Edward I banishes Jews from England
1340	Naval battle of Sluys (Edward III)
1346	Battle of Crécy (Edward III and Black Prince)
1348–1350	First outbreak of the Black Death in England
1349	Order of the Garter founded at Windsor
	Poll tax and other taxes levied by Edward III
1356	Battle of Poitiers (Black Prince)

PART I
(1340–1345)

1

Sluys, Flanders – June 1340

Tom narrowed his eyes and looked along the rows of French ships bathed in the glow of the setting sun. They were about two miles away, due east, and appeared to be chained together with large planks between each ship. It looked as if there were probably three rows completely blocking the harbour mouth, and he could just make out some movement between the glistening shields on the bows and gunwales of some of the larger ships in the front rank, gently bobbing up and down in the slight swell. He started to count the ships in the first line, and gave up after reaching a hundred and fifty or so.

Good God! he thought, there must be at least a thousand in total. His thoughts were broken by the sudden activity of the crew hauling down the sails of the brigantine, and the harsh grating sound of the chains as the anchors were quickly lowered.

'Come on, Tom,' one of the vintenars shouted, 'we're going to eat now, and try to get some sleep before the action starts tomorrow. If you don't hurry, those buggers will scoff the lot.'

Tom smiled, knowing that the vintenar's main concern was his own stomach, although to be fair to him, ever since they had met at Orwel haven, Bob Kirton had been both friendly and respectful as far as Tom was concerned. He seemed to be aware of Tom's awesome reputation as a cool thinking, outstanding archer, which was not so surprising since in the last four years Tom had won every competition he had entered within a radius of twenty miles of his home village of Stokesbye, in the manor of Castor.

'Thanks, Bob, I'm on my way,' he called back, and picking up his longbow and quiver of arrows, made his way to the galley area of the brigantine.

Vespers turned out to be half a loaf of rye bread, salted herrings, some cheese and some fruit, all washed down with two measures of good ale. Not at all bad, Tom mused, especially when one included the two pence per day paid by the king. It was a lot more than he could earn at home both from his smallholding and his trade as a bowyer and fletcher. The people at home couldn't afford to buy his top-quality longbows or arrows, and he was more or less obliged to provide the lord of the manor with his requirements virtually free of charge as the 'fine' he had to pay in return for the land he inherited at his parents' death in the year of our Lord, 1330. But he would take his vengeance tomorrow on those 'Frenchies', by God, he had vowed, if it was the last thing he did.

He had just passed his fourteenth birthday as the French raiders stormed his village. He and his younger brother Paul, who was not quite six years old, had been fishing at the time of the attack. What he saw inside his house on his return would live with him for the rest of his life. His father had been hacked to pieces and parts of his body were scattered all over their tiny cottage. His mother's naked body lay on the rush floor by the hearth. After raping her, the raiders had cut off her breasts and slit her stomach open, leaving her to die in a pool of her own blood. His grandfather, the father of his dead mother, Matilda, arrived shortly afterwards and led the sobbing Thomas away from the carnage and prevented Paul from going inside the cottage. Other survivors of the village removed the bodies and helped clean the house out, so that the two brothers had at least somewhere they could later consider as their home.

Tom's grandparents looked after them initially – they lived in a neighbouring hamlet that the raiders hadn't found – and it was from his grandfather that Tom learnt the bowyer's craft. But Tom soon saw that his grandparents would not be able to support them for long. They had barely enough food for themselves, let alone two hungry, growing boys. Tom knew where his father had buried what few savings he had, close to a large chestnut tree in their small garden, and the money paid for the burial fees for his parents and enabled him to replace the chickens and the cow that the French raiders had taken with them. By working on the smallholding that his father, a villein, had managed to buy over the years from the lord with hard-earned money as a carpenter and wheelwright, and helping his grandfather to cut and prepare the yew tree branches he used for longbows, and the ash tree branches for the arrows, Tom managed to provide sufficient food and income to support himself and his young brother. Due to his father's standing in the community and the fact, as Tom later learned, that his father had fought the raiders with the ferocity of a cornered wild animal, killing at least three of them before he himself was finally overwhelmed and hacked to death, the lord granted Tom ten years to pay the 'fine' for his inheritance, and to find the cash to pay his charter of manumission that gave him his freedom from serfdom. Tom's lord also agreed to find employment for Paul within the demesne on his twelfth birthday.

Every free moment he had, Tom would take the longbow he had fashioned for himself and practise in the fields outside the village. By the time he was eighteen, he could hit targets the size of a man's head at a range of three hundred yards. He had also grown to be an extremely powerful young man, standing a little over six feet without his boots, and was viewed by the young ladies of the village as the most eligible and desirable bachelor of the neighbourhood!

He also made sure that his little brother Paul could handle a bow with great skill, and each year provided him with the right weapon for his stature. He was almost as accurate as Tom, at shorter ranges of course, but even at this age, it was clear that there were other things in life that were much more important to Paul.

There were sixty archers, fifteen crossbowmen and five men-at-arms on board, excluding the three vintenars leading the archers, the crew of twenty, and ten horses in the brigantine's hold. Each group of soldiers kept together and had little or no contact with the others. The archers did not particularly like the crossbowmen, and neither of them had anything in common with the men-at-arms who came from a completely different strata of society – from the world of lords, knights and other wealthy landowners or commercial enterprises.

After their evening meal, most of them continued to drink what ale was left over – the men-at-arms their wine – and laughed and joked to hide their nervousness concerning the following morning. Bob Kirton asked Tom if he would like to join a dice game, but he declined, saying he wanted to check over his weapons and then get some rest. Tom had no intention of losing what little money he had in a game of hazard. He always checked his longbow before a contest and tomorrow was going to be a very special one which he hoped to survive.

It was a pleasantly mild, early summer evening and Tom managed to find a reasonably quiet spot close to the helm. He took off the nocks at the end of the bow and untied the bowstring, examining it carefully before coiling it up and putting it in his jerkin pocket. He didn't want it getting wet or damp during the night because that could seriously reduce the range of his shots.

He also checked each arrow, making sure the peacock feather flights were in good order, and then, finally, sharpened the long dagger he always carried in his girdle. Satisfied that he was now well prepared, he settled down on the deck hoping to get a few hours sleep before daybreak.

Sleep was not easy that night! He had not been in any sort of battle before and he had certainly never killed anybody. From the age of fourteen, ever since his parents had been brutally slaughtered, he had sworn revenge on the French and tomorrow was going to be his first chance. He was not afraid of being wounded or even killed, but hoped he would survive and be able to return to his beloved Margaret.

She was the miller's daughter from the neighbouring village of Ormesbye. They had met at a local archery competition, and it really had been love at first sight. Margaret was the most beautiful girl Tom had ever seen in his life: a tall, slim brunette, with the face of an angel and the sexual hunger of a devil. He didn't have a chance. They didn't 'have' to marry, but Tom knew himself and enough about procreation to decide he had better do it quickly – not that it was a hardship!

He was able to afford the marriage 'fine' and Paul, now sixteen, was well established in the Castor demesne and quite able to take care of himself. In fact, Paul now lived in demesne property, close to the manor house, so Tom and his new bride were able to live alone in the Rollesby cottage, which thanks to the miller's dowry, had become the best-furnished cottage in the village. Within only two weeks of his marriage, however, the lord's steward summoned him to the manor house, complete with his weapons and food for two days, since the king was raising an army to fight the French and needed the best archers he could find.

Tom had felt himself torn between two forces – he dearly loved his wife but he could not disobey the king's command, and as he explained to a tearful Margaret, he had vowed to avenge his parents and this was the chance he had been waiting for. After a passionate farewell, Tom had promised her he would return as soon as possible and that she should not worry.

Once he was at Castor, a barge at the manor house took him and eight other archers through the canal to the River Burre and then on to Yermouth where they were joined by others, including the men-at arms. They overnighted in a tavern close to the quayside, and the following morning were led on to the brigantine which a few hours later sailed down the coast to Orwel haven, anchoring there amongst a mass of other ships. After five days of waiting, the brigantine set sail due east within a total fleet of around two hundred and fifty ships.

In spite of all these thoughts and the inevitable apprehension of the next morning, Tom fell into a sound sleep.

2

The Sea Battle

Tom awoke at dawn, suddenly conscious of a flurry of activity around him, both on the brigantine and on all the other ships anchored nearby. He and all the other yawning and stretching soldiers were ordered to assemble immediately with their weapons in the galley area where bread and ale were being served. He quickly fitted the bowstring, satisfied himself that the tension was just right, hooked the bow over his right shoulder, adjusted the quiver over his back, moving it round to the left side of his body just behind the scabbard hung on his girdle, and moved quickly to get something to eat.

It was at least a little warmer close to the galley, amidst the mass of bodies reaching for the bread and ale jugs. One of the men-at-arms was shouting at them to get a move on with their breakfast and go to the foredeck area as soon as possible. In the meantime, the ship's crew were busy hauling up the two anchors, unfurling and setting the sails, and the brigantine, rolling gently in the swell, began to move forward.

The five men-at-arms grouped themselves on the edge of the forecastle and ordered the vintenars to arrange their archers facing them in three groups of twenty men each, and the crosbowmen to stand together in the middle. The archers were mostly young and simple country men, mustered at the king's command from the south-eastern shires, without any previous experience of a military engagement, and it took quite some pulling, pushing and shouting until they were in any semblance of order, standing awkwardly facing the armoured knights. The crossbowmen, on the contrary, as professionals in the permanent employment of the Earl of Suffolke, were in position within seconds of being given the command, and they watched disdainfully the mêlée around them.

Bob Kirton had made sure that Tom was standing next to him, feeling somehow that it helped give him some more authority over his inexperienced group, which almost to a man knew and respected Tom from the various archery contests in which they had participated. They all knew he was the best archer on board, and also a man you did not quarrel with, if you were wise! The crossbowmen, who did not know him, had recognised that in some almost indefinable way this tall, powerfully-built young man carried a special sense of authority with him, and were intrigued to know why.

When at last, everybody was in position, the leader of the knights, who Tom later discovered was in fact the earl himself, began the briefing:

'Knights, yeomen, freemen and villeins, listen carefully to what I have to say. You will shortly have the chance to deliver a blow for our good King Edward, England and God against our arch-enemy Philippe of France. We have in front of us a fleet at least three times larger than ours, which has been reinforced with galleys from Spain, and we believe their troops on board also include crossbowmen from Genoa. We are clearly outnumbered and the French probably believe we don't have a chance, and I want to tell you why that couldn't be further from the truth, provided each and every one of you fights for the honour of your country, your families and the glory of God, our father in heaven, who will surely help us to defeat our brutal enemy. I am sure many of you here have lost loved ones in the frequent raids the French have made on our coastal towns and villages, and now you will soon have the chance to avenge your dead and strike a mighty blow against this evil race.

'I know the quality of my crossbowmen and I am told that we have some of England's best longbowmen also on board,' – the archers shouted their approval on hearing that compliment and after waving his hands for silence, the earl continued, 'and you will need every bit of your skill and courage today, and God's help.' On hearing yet another reference to help from the Almighty, Tom's thoughts began to wander and he no longer registered what the earl was saying.

He had an inner respect for some powerful, guiding force that, although he did not understand it, he felt instinctively exerted an influence on nature and the affairs of man, but felt sure that mankind itself must not rely or count on help from this force in times of trouble or difficulty. His parents had once told him how they had struggled to overcome the bad harvests of the year before Tom's birth and the following year. Villagers all around them had simply starved to death, but his mother's careful housekeeping and his father's determination to find ways to provide for his family, travelling miles when necessary, looking for work and additional food, had saved them. Nobody had helped them. They had survived as a result of their own efforts, only to be brutally slaughtered fifteen years later! Maybe it was right what the village priest had to say about the Almighty. He seemed to have little mercy on the sufferings of people and could take terrible vengeance for the sins of mankind, although Tom had always found his parents to be good and kind people, always prepared to help others. He sighed and decided this was something he would never understand. The French had killed his parents, and that he intended to avenge personally if he could!

The earl had now finished his speech, and one of the other men-at-arms began to shout out orders. Tom's group was sent up to the forecastle with ten crossbowmen, and the other two archer groups were each allocated one side of the boat, with a small reserve of five archers and crossbowmen at the stern. Some crew members, in the meantime, began to distribute further supplies of arrows, which they stood upright in large wooden boxes, within easy access, behind the three main groups of archers, and also stacked halberds alongside for their use if necessary. The crossbowmen took care of their own additional supplies, which included the windlasses they used to draw the bowstring into position. Tom looked back at them and grinned as he thought he would be able to fire at least six arrows to one of their bolts, which he noted were tipped with goose feathers.

While all this activity was taking place on board, the English ships swung round to a south-westerly position to avoid having the sun directly in their eyes when they attacked, and manoeuvred into a formation of four squadrons. The larger ships formed the centre squadron and contained men-at-arms and archers, and were also furnished with slings to catapult large stones and packs of lime, with the main body of archers in squadrons positioned at each side. The fourth squadron was held in reserve at the rear, mainly comprised of a strong force of additional men-at-arms.

As the English fleet was moving into position, taking every advantage of a fresh breeze from the south-west, French priests were busily leading Mass on the huge Spanish galleons and the great ship *Christopher*, captured from the English the previous year, all anchored and chained together in the first line.

It was at about nine o'clock that the king's flagship gave the signal to attack at full speed. Tom's brigantine was on the extreme left of the squadron that had taken up position on the right flank of the English main force, close to a large ship, the Mary Céleste. In his position on the forecastle, he had an excellent perspective of the English fleet bearing down on this vast collection of huge

French ships, grouped closely together, looking like a massive wall of castles towering above the sea and the smaller English ships.

At about five hundred yards from the French front line, 16,000 English voices, almost to a man, took up the cry of 'England and King Edward', and then the catapults released a hail of stones onto the French ships, breaking down some masts and rigging, and killing hundreds of French troops as they fell on the decks. At a signal from the men-at-arms behind them Tom and his fellow archers on the brigantine released their first hail of arrows onto the nearest French ship. Almost simultaneously, English arrows and crossbow bolts from every English ship in the three squadrons clouded the sky and fell on to the waiting, already badly damaged ships in the French front line. The longbowmen quickly reloaded, adjusting the elevation slightly as their ships drew nearer to the French line, and fired again and again, releasing almost 100,000 arrows in less than two minutes, with the crossbowmen placing their bolts more selectively, but of course, much more slowly, than the archers, in this first phase.

Tom could now see the effects of this initial bombardment much more clearly. Bodies were strewn all over the decks of the French ships and were hanging over the gunwales or floating in the sea, with arrows sticking out almost obscenely from all parts of the corpses. For whatever reason, they had waited for the English initial bombardment to stop before they countered, but it had been too late. This opening attack had been so devastating that a large proportion of the French soldiers – at least their more lightly clad archers and crossbowmen – had already been killed or wounded. Tom had already used eight arrows in this opening encounter, and after the initial excitement and nervousness had passed away and the targets were becoming clearer to identify as the brigantine drew nearer and nearer, he paused to wipe the perspiration from his brow, and look quickly around him.

It had not been totally one-sided. He saw that four of his fellow archers and one of the crossbowmen had been hit, with at least two of them killed on the spot, including the friendly vintenar, Bob Kirton. A voice behind one of the men-at-arms called out urgently. 'Get those men in the rigging quickly before we engage!'

Tom snapped out of his brief reverie, took quick aim and fired. One body fell screaming into the sea. He fired twice more, claiming a victim each time.

'Try for that tall man-at-arms close to the forward mast! He's directing all the others,' the voice again commanded.

Tom spotted him at once, with the sun glinting on his breastplate. He took careful aim, squaring himself as best he could to counter the movement of the ship, sighting a spot on the aventail, the chain-mail covering the throat, hanging from the basinet with an open visor. He held his breath and fired. The arrow pierced the man's throat, passed through to the other side and pinned him to the mast. He slumped immediately, blood spurting out of the hole from the fractured jugular vein, and hung there like a speared fish.

'My God, bowman, what an incredible shot! What's your name?'

'Tom, my lord. Tom Rollesby!'

'Good, Tom. Pick out any other men-at-arms you see until we collide, then grab one of those halberds behind you and follow me onto that ship!'

Tom was able to wound one more of the French men-at-arms before the brigantine crashed into the French ship directly ahead and towering over them. The crew threw out hooks on chains and other grappling irons, making the brigantine secure to the French ship, and the English men-at-arms, followed by Tom and twenty or thirty other archers carrying halberds, their bows slung over their backs and also armed with a motley collection of daggers and knives, prepared to board. A covering fire from the remaining archers and crossbowmen enabled the English to scramble up the high forecastle and turrets of the French galleon, fighting their way onboard. From then on, Tom found himself in the most dangerous situation of his life. French soldiers, some better armoured than others, were attacking them from all sides. Tom had not used a halberd before, but seeing a soldier with a raised sword, about to swing it down on him, made him a quick learner. He nimbly jumped a half-pace to one side, pushed the spike of the halberd quickly into the soldier's stomach, twisted it and pulled it out in time to take on the next one. And so it went on for what appeared to be an eternity, but in reality was not much more than about twenty minutes.

Suddenly, it was all over. A half-dozen or so remaining French soldiers threw their weapons on the deck and asked for quarter. Panting with the exertion, Tom looked around to reassure himself that nobody else was lurking about the ship waiting for the opportunity to slip a knife into the back of an unsuspecting English soldier, and reported back to the man-at-arms who seemed to have adopted him that all was clear.

'Good, Tom!' he exclaimed. 'Get the rest of the men up here as quickly as you can.'

A similar scene was being enacted more or less across the whole of the front line. After fierce skirmishes on each French ship, some of them had been sunk by divers boring holes under the waterline. The English forces were taking prisoners and preparing themselves for a further attack on the second line of moored ships.

The archers and crossbowmen formed up on the captured French ships. In some places a passageway had been cleared between them, and smaller English vessels passed through. Then the attack began on the second line of French ships. After a hail of arrows and bolts, the English archers and men-at-arms stormed the anchored ships and this time boarded them much more easily. There was only a little resistance and scores of enemy troops could be seen jumping overboard, most of whom were drowned. By now, however, it was getting dark, and it would have been madness to continue the attack. On top of that the English troops were exhausted and needed time to rest and prepare themselves for the final battle, so the order was given to withdraw back to their own ships for the night, leaving small groups of guards on the captured vessels.

It was only once back on board the brigantine that Tom realised that some of the blood on his clothes was his own. He had been lucky, however. An arrow had merely grazed his right arm, and he had a slight nick from a falling sword on his left calf, just below the knee. Nothing that some salt water couldn't quickly fix!

After vespers, the man-at-arms that had fought alongside Tom took him to one side and asked him many questions about where he came from, his family background, how he came to handle a longbow so well, what he wanted to do in the future, and so on. Tom answered them all honestly and with respect, knowing that the man-at-arms was a relative of the Earl of Suffolke, and therefore a wealthy and powerful landowner, a knight of the shire with responsibility for probably a score or more of manors.

Finally, Tom looked the lord firmly in the eyes and asked him why he appeared to be so interested in him. A smile hovered briefly on the face of the knight who replied: 'Tom, you perhaps don't realise it, but you are a very unusual man, particularly coming from your background. You are not only the finest bowman I've ever met, you fight like a lion even though you have never had any other weapon training, and from what I have seen, you are also very intelligent and a natural leader. It would be a real pity to waste your talents. I know you are an excellent bowyer and fletcher, but there is so much more you could do, I now know it. Go and get some sleep, and after our final assault tomorrow – I'm sure it won't last very long – ask for Sir William Fastolfe, lord of Castor. I want to talk to you concerning your future.' Before Tom could ask any further questions, the knight walked away with the easy assurance of the nobility.

'You seem to have made a big impression with Lord Fastolfe,' one of the crossbowmen commented, grinning from ear to ear at Tom's confusion. 'I can't say I'm surprised though. He's a great soldier and respects military talent and courage. I thought I was pretty good with this baby here,' he pointed to his crossbow, 'but what you did out there with that bloody longbow was almost unbelievable. Who taught you to shoot like that?'

Tom curtly replied that he had taught himself, and moved quickly away to be on his own to think about what the lord had said and the possible implications for the future. Ah, well, he thought, let's wait until tomorrow. A lot can happen in the meantime. And he was right!

In spite of the day's events, including the conversation with the lord of Castor, after thinking about his beautiful young wife Margaret for a few minutes and how much he missed her, how much he longed to hold her in his arms once again, feeling her soft warm body close to his, Tom sighed deeply, closed his eyes and within minutes was fast asleep, stretched out between the bodies of a score of snoring archers.

Shortly before daybreak, he was shaken awake by one of the archers alongside him.

'Come on Tom, wake up! We haven't got much time,' he whispered urgently.

Instantly alert, Tom saw movement all around him as the archers reached for their weapons, fixing the bowstrings and silently checking that everything was in order. Within a minute he was ready and moved into position forward with the others, straining to see if he could spot any movement in the French lines as daylight began gradually to replace the damp darkness around them.

The third line of French ships was a little too far away to make out any detail, but his attention was suddenly drawn to something floating in the water close to the brigantine. God, it's a body, he thought as it drifted closer. Then he saw another, and yet another, and twenty or thirty yards away, a score or more turning and gently rising and falling in the early morning tide. He could hear his fellow archers whispering to each other as an increasing number of bloated and mutilated bodies could be seen all around them. As the sun began to rise, they shaded their eyes with their hands and squinted towards the broad harbour mouth and the black-looking sea along the coast. It was horrific! As far as the eye could see, hundreds – no, thousands – of dead French soldiers were floating in the sea, carpeting the surface between all the ships of the two armies, and beyond.

'Not a pretty sight, I know, but we are not finished yet!' one of the men-at-arms commented, standing alongside Tom. 'Hopefully not many of us will be joining them today,' he added wistfully. Tom shivered slightly at the thought, and deliberately turned his mind to the scene he had witnessed at the cottage in Stokesbye barely ten years earlier to steel himself for this final attack.

'Not if I can help it,' he said coldly. 'When do we make a move?'

The man-at-arms looked sideways at him and smiled slightly. 'I expect the signal any moment now. We'll then move forward onto the ship we captured yesterday, and give the central squadron covering fire as they advance and begin boarding the third line of French ships.'

And that was exactly what happened. Two or three torch arrows were fired from the king's ship, followed by the war cry of 'King Edward and England', and Tom with the rest of the archers, crossbowmen and men-at-arms swarmed forward onto the other ship. As they took aim and prepared to fire the first salvo, they saw that there were now fewer French ships anchored than on the previous day. During the night, at least thirty or forty had slipped away to safety to fight another day!

It was quickly over. The remaining French troops seemed to have little desire to prolong the battle, and surrendered within the first two hours. It was a resounding victory for the English force. In all they captured around two hundred warships and more than thirty barges, with minimal losses in their own fleet. More than 25,000 French soldiers were killed or drowned, with a corresponding loss of fewer than 4,000 in the English forces.

After landing in Sluys, the English army rested in the town and neighbouring countryside, waiting for reinforcements from England before moving on to Ghent. Part of the original English force were relieved, and returned home. Among them were Tom and Sir William Fastolfe, lord of Castor.

3

Castor Manor

The demesne of Sir William Fastolfe covered all the land enclosed by the rivers Burre and Thurne, stretching up to Winterton on the coast at the northern extremity, and down to, but excluding, the port of Yermouth to the south. There were about a score of villages within the area which included Tom's village of Stokesbye, Ormesbye where his wife had once lived, the lakes around Filbye and Rollesbye, and several dozen hamlets scattered across the entire area. Wild boar and deer were to be found in the woods and forestland, and the rivers and lakes teemed with fish, which encouraged a large variety of wildfowl to breed in the surrounding marshlands.

Most of the villages had good arable land around them, ideal for corn, barley, oats and rye, and a relatively large choice of vegetables and fruit. Cattle also thrived in the common and demesne pastures, which included large flocks of long-woolled sheep located mainly in the surrounding marshland areas.

Until the encounter with Sir William at Sluys, Tom had never before met the lord of Castor, with virtually all of the demesne's affairs being managed by the reeve, Stanley Pettit. Sir William, Tom later learned, only busied himself with important cases of breaches of the law, leaving the rest to the local sheriff and his own reeve. He himself spent most of his time hunting, jousting, courting the most attractive ladies in the demesne and beyond, and maintaining his political connections to parliament and the court of King Edward.

Tom's brother, Paul, had first come to the manor house in Castor four years earlier, a few days after his twelfth birthday, as had been agreed shortly after that terrible day when his parents had been killed. His grandfather had taken him to the reeve, 'Mr Stanley', as he was known to the demesne villagers, and reminded him of the promise that had been made. Paul was then led away by one of the manor servants for the beginning of a completely new way of life.

Fortunately, he was used to working hard. From a very early age he had helped his brother Tom with the household chores, not only cleaning and keeping the house in order, but looking after their only cow and the chickens, and working on their smallholding. He had in those early years grown into a strong, sturdy boy, well able to fend for himself, and even then had a keen eye for a bargain. Tom used to smile inwardly at the way his younger brother would negotiate the exchange of eggs or a pail of milk, or a cheese with other villagers or visiting hucksters in return for whatever articles they required or he could bargain for, sometimes selling them or exchanging them later for other items of even more value. He was very young, but almost always got the better deal.

Paul was taken to the kitchen-house, which adjoined a relatively low, round tower, and since it was midday, joined most of the other manor servants who were already seated at a long trestle table in the courtyard outside, just starting their main meal of the day. Even young Paul, in spite of his usual self-confidence, was a little overawed at this first meeting with what seemed so many (there were about fourteen) servants, all working for the lord. Nobody took much notice of him, as Nellie the cook's assistant introduced him as young master Paul, the new kitchen-helper, and got them to make room for him at the table. They were all hungry and had little time to spend talking to the most junior one of them all!

The first few months were not very easy for Paul. He had been born with an excellent brain, had got used to working closely with his elder brother Tom, and also to being able to use his initiative when it came to buying and selling provisions and other household items. Here, he was not ill-treated, but handled almost as a slave, having to spend the whole working day – and it was a long one, from five-thirty in the morning until nine o'clock at night – performing the most menial of kitchen tasks. After the morning Mass at six, the cook gave him a hunk of rye bread and a jug of ale, and shortly afterwards, apart from the main meal of the day for the servants at noon until vespers, shortly before nine in the evening, he was kept continuously busy collecting and cleaning vegetables, gutting and washing the trout or carp taken from the nearby fishponds, plucking chickens, ducks or geese and even peacocks on special feast days for the great hall. Then, following each meal, all the pots, saucepans, caldrons, dishes and platters, flesh hooks and other kitchen paraphernalia needed to be scoured, cleaned carefully and dried. The cook, Mrs Galston, and Nellie were the only ones to handle and prepare the various meats and spices, although Paul was allowed to help with turning the spit on the days there were great roasts of oxen or wild boar and other game. Sometimes as a special treat, Nellie would give Paul a slice of the roast when cook had her back turned, and could always be relied on to give him a jug of fresh milk each day, which he gratefully took and quickly quaffed, never failing however to thank her.

The first three to four months seemed to fly by, in spite of the long days and what Paul always considered as very short but, he had to admit, comfortable nights. He had been allowed to make his bed in a small alcove set into the kitchen wall, not far away from the great kitchen fire. He had to duck his head to step into it, but had enough room to put his boots and clothes on a large chest that stood at one end of the alcove, and could stretch out comfortably in his bed of clean, dry rushes, covered with a large sheepskin. The kitchen was always warm and dry, clean, running water flowing from the river into the fishponds near the barge house was only a few yards away, and he was never hungry for long!

He knew that it could have been a lot worse, and as time passed by and Mrs Galston could see that he was a good worker and could be relied on, she began to talk to him more and give him additional interesting tasks. She began by acquainting him with the herb garden, showing him the various cresses, parsley, mint, sage, rue, and explaining with which food dishes they were best suited, as well as the medicinal herbs that were also cultivated there. In time Paul became familiar with all of them, including the different types of mallow and nightshade, agrimony, and marigold, which Mrs Galston used for her special medicinal brews. Within a very short period of time, she only needed to tell him what was planned for the day's meals and how many guests were expected, and Paul would collect the necessary herbs. She used to discuss him with Nellie, when Paul was out of earshot, saying how pleased she was with him, and that he was the brightest boy she had ever known, and so polite. Nellie found it very easy to agree, although if she had been honest with Mrs Galston she would have commented on the fact that Paul was rapidly becoming extremely attractive and growing at an almost alarming rate!

Towards the end of Paul's first summer there, the reeve, Mr Stanley Pettit, was standing in the kitchen, quenching his thirst from a pitcher of cool ale, drawn for him by the cook, and he asked her how the young Rollesby was getting on. He was pleased to hear that he had settled in so well and told her that he had expected nothing less from a son of Thomas Rollesby and Matilda Bowman! He had known both of them and their families very well, and respected them as good, hard-working honest people. 'Paul's father,' he added, 'was the best carpenter on the whole demesne. And as for the eldest son Thomas, I've yet to find his equal when it comes to the longbow. You know, he practices outside his village every free hour he has, with a determination and energy that can almost scare you. I bet he's made sure that young Paul knows how to handle one too!'

'Go on with you, Mr Stanley,' the cook retorted. 'That's all you men seem to think about. Firing arrows, fighting and drinking too much ale.'

'Not just that!' Nellie commented, with a broad grin on her face, having heard most of the earlier conversation. 'You must be getting old, Mrs Galston.'

'Now that's enough of that from you, Nellie Smyth,' the cook replied immediately, feigning a severity that Nellie knew was not meant. 'Just have a little more respect for your elders, or the lord will hear about it.'

Nellie stifled her laughter, having had more than one encounter with Sir William, in which she had on each occasion extricated herself only with great difficulty from his amorous advances. She was about to say something when the reeve concluded the exchange by adding:

'You women always exaggerate about everything. In spite of what you seem to think about us, this one in particular has got to make a move and get on with some more work. We're just coming into harvest time and I'll soon need every pair of hands I can find. I know you won't like it, Mrs Galston, but that must include young Paul this year. I'll have him picked up at dawn next Monday and you will have to do without him for the next six weeks.'

The cook had taken a deep breath and was going to protest, when the reeve said: 'I've already cleared it with the master, and besides, it will give me a chance to get to know him better, since if he is as smart as you say, he will need to get some other experience beside working in a herb garden! Don't forget to tell him, Mrs Galston, about next Monday.' He then drained the pitcher of beer, wiped his hand across his mouth, walked out of the kitchen to his horse that was tethered by the gate leading to the vegetable gardens, and rode off.

It was a good harvest that year, and for the first week or so Paul returned late each evening to the kitchen, feeling completely exhausted. It was almost non-stop activity the whole day. As one group of villagers advanced steadily through one field of wheat after another, swinging their scythes expertly, almost in unison,

Paul followed with another group, gathering it up and tying it into standard-size sheaves that were later loaded onto large carts and taken to nearby barns for storage before threshing. The grain was then put into sacks and taken to the village miller for grinding into flour. During this whole process the reeve kept a careful check of all the grain produced, from which fields, carefully supervising the manor's share to be stored in barns belonging to Sir William, and the rest that was allocated to the villagers.

Some years earlier, the lord had sold off some holdings, each of approximately ten to fifteen acres, or a half virgate as it was called, to some of his tenant farmers to raise some badly needed cash quickly. Tom's father had been one of them, having managed over many years to scrape together just enough money for such an eventuality. The majority of the villagers, however, were either tenant farmers of sometimes even smaller plots of land, paying their annual 'fines' to the lord and tithes to the Church by using the wheat as the cash crop, or villeins with little more than small, simple clay and wattle cottages and small gardens if they were lucky, totally dependent on the lord for their livelihood. The villeins were totally managed by the reeve for the various tasks of the manor, depending on the season: ploughing, sowing, harvesting the crops of wheat, barley, rye and oats, haymaking, ale-making, moving the sheepfolds from place to place over the arable land, helping with the washing and shearing of both the lord's flocks and the village communal flocks that were principally owned by the tenant farmers and the local clergy.

In the larger villages like Stokesbye, Filbye and Ormesbye, for example, there were also blacksmiths, carpenters, tilers and millers' assistants, as well as a host of other small cottage industries like leather-making, spinning, weaving, fulling, bow-making and fletching, frequently carried out by the tenant farmers to supplement their meagre incomes from the smallholdings.

During his first summer helping with the wheat harvesting, the twelve-year-old Paul had greatly impressed the reeve, Stanley Pettit. He had noticed that Paul worked shoulder to shoulder with the older men, was always courteous and helpful, and only needed to be told something once. He also saw that he had initiative and was eager to learn as much as possible. Whenever he saw the reeve and there was a quiet moment, Paul would ask questions about fertilising the ground, the types of seed used, and a host of other matters.

'Well, young Master Paul,' Pettit said one day, 'I can see that I shall need to keep you busy all right. I'll see what other interesting jobs I can find for you.'

And he kept his word. For the next four years, in addition to his duties at the manor house kitchen, the reeve saw to it that Paul had sufficient time away to learn other aspects of the manor's activities. He had agreed with Sir William that the youngster had all the makings of a future reeve or maybe an even higher position at a later date, and so in spite of the protestations of the cook, and the disappointment of Nellie, Paul was frequently relieved of his kitchen responsibilities in order to be able to work elsewhere on the estate, even though he almost always returned in the evenings to the kitchen for vespers, and shortly afterwards, his bed.

On two afternoons a week, the lord had arranged with his chaplain that Paul should be taught to read and write, and learn his catechism, of course! This latter point had been insisted upon by the chaplain, and was the only area of learning that was to present Paul with significant difficulties.

4

Growing Up

The following two years were spent learning the practical aspects of running a sheep business, which was by far, Paul later discovered, the most profitable part of the manor's activities. Most of the lord's sheep were of the long-woolled variety which thrived on the lush pastures and marshlands of the demesne, which were mainly in two areas: around the lakes of Rollesbye and Filbye, and along the banks of the rivers Burre and Thurne. In all, Paul was astonished to learn that there were just over 10,000 sheep belonging to the lord, divided into six large flocks in those areas, excluding another 1,500 or so pasturing on the communal lands of all the villages.

In a short space of time he got to know the different shepherds and loved to watch the way they could work their dogs to move the sheep from one area to another, or collect the strays. Some just used to whistle with an occasional shout, others had a reed pipe, and the dogs then knew exactly what had to be done, and Paul could see how much they enjoyed their work and how they wanted to please the shepherd. He had first thought that it must be an easy job being a shepherd, with the dogs doing all the work, but 'Mr Stanley' insisted that he understand the full cycle of work from one lambing season to the next, and so he was 'entrusted' to shepherd Ned Giles, who came from Mautbye, to learn what had to be learnt.

Ned had been a shepherd all his life. His skin was bronzed from a lifetime of working outdoors in all weathers. His hair was beginning to turn grey (he was in his middle fifties) but he was as fit as many men half his age. There was not an ounce of spare fat on his lean but sturdy frame. His legs were slightly bowed, and he had the sort of rolling gait of the countryman used to covering long distances on foot. He spoke slowly, with the melodious drawl of the region, loved his sheep, and Paul could see how the dogs adored him, even though he was very strict with them. It was an unforgettable phase of his life.

It began in the lambing season when Paul kept Ned company

during long, dark nights in the shepherd's hut, which lay about a mile and a half south of Castor, set on a small hillock, not more than a mile from the river Burre. Here it was well-placed to oversee the sheep grazing on the lush pastures and marshland that stretched for many miles westward. As it grew nearer the time for lambing, Ned had been moving the flock from Stokesbye closer to Castor and his hut, and had let Paul slip off occasionally to visit his brother Tom when they were in the area. As it was, the reeve let him have the use of an old, grey mare called Betsy so that he could attend his lessons more easily with the chaplain twice a week, and Paul returned back to Ned as quickly as he could to help.

He had brought up a stock of candles from the manor at Ned's request, because as he was soon to learn, they were frequently going to be sitting up many nights in the dark hut, bringing weak, new-born lambs into the warmth, and feeding them with milk heated in large earthenware pots placed close to the fire. The ewes, heavy with lamb, had been sorted out of the scattered flock and penned around the hut to make it easier to reach them quickly if there were any difficulties. Due to Ned's expertise and care, most of the newly-born lambs survived, but they were a very tense couple of weeks, with little time to relax and talk about other things, and sleep had to be taken in odd moments. This was particularly hard for the young Paul, especially on those afternoons when he had his tuition with the chaplain, who frequently complained about the strong odour of sheep that he brought with him!

The dairymaids also visited them at daybreak each day to milk the ewes and make the fat, round cheeses that were to be stored in the manor buttery. Paul came to like the strong-tasting milk that helped to wash down the barley or rye bread the girls brought out with them, and enjoyed the banter that took place until they jumped up on the cart taking them and the milk back to Castor. The reeve also came by periodically to check on the progress of the lambing and the condition of the flock, watching out particularly for the first signs of murrain or other diseases that could decimate the manor flocks and herds.

One late afternoon, after the lambing was over, and they had a little more time, Paul had asked Ned about the various sheep diseases and how they could be treated. He had seen how they were marked with 'ruddle', a reddish-coloured powder, and also that Ned applied a sticky tar to cover the odd sore, but felt sure there must be more that one could do. But Ned had shaken his head, gazed out into the distance, and replied:

'Not really, Master Paul. The feed is most important and of

course you have to keep their hooves scraped clean as you know, or they will quickly become cripples, especially in this marshy land. But as far as I can see, for most other things, we are in the hands of the Almighty, or the Devil, depending on what you believe. If you would believe everything the priest in Mautbye has to say on the subject, you would live in terror of your life most of the time, hoping that by paying the Church tithes, and attending Mass regularly, your soul would be saved from eternal damnation. I'm sure there is much more to life than mumbling foreign words you don't understand in a dark, damp building, trusting that the Almighty will not strike you down suddenly dead for committing what the priest calls cardinal sins, or something like that. It doesn't make much sense to me at all.'

Paul then began to tell Ned about some of his earlier experiences with the chaplain, and that he really enjoyed learning to read and write English, to learn how to count, but had great problems with Latin, the language of the scriptures and the Church. He wondered what its value was in today's world.

Ned grinned, listening to the young Paul grappling with thoughts and concepts which were either beyond him or he had secretly rejected years before, and interrupted him at one stage to tell him about how his village priest had tried to treat an outbreak of murrain some years ago.

'It was like this, Master Paul,' he began. 'First of all, he called all the village together and told us we had to meet up immediately in the church. We then had to sing a Mass in honour of what he called the Holy Spirit and each of us had to make an offering of one penny. We all went outside and I and two or three others rounded up the sick sheep – there were about forty in all – and he read out to them verses from the Holy Bible and then sprinkled them with holy water. We all then sang a hymn, had to chant three times what he calls the "paternoster" followed by the Ave Maria, and finally, he made yet another collection!'

Paul was listening carefully to Ned, as he recounted the tale, slowly and deliberately. 'What happened, then, Ned?' he asked impatiently.

'Nothing at all, Master Paul, except within two weeks all the sheep were dead!'

Before Paul could ask any further questions, Ned narrowed his eyes and looked toward the setting sun, as he had spotted a movement in the distance. It was the reeve approaching them on horseback. Ned walked out to meet him and the two men chatted for a few minutes, then the reeve shouted a greeting to Paul, turned his horse away, and rode off in the direction of Castor.

'Well, Master Paul, you have to go back to the manor for the next couple of weeks. Two of the house servants are ill and the lord has got a big banquet coming off next week, and Mrs Galston needs you badly in the kitchen.'

'Must I really go right now, Ned?' Paul asked, looking him straight in the eyes. 'We were having such an interesting talk and I...'

'Yes, Master Paul, immediately! Now be off with you! You'll be back here again in no time at all, you'll see. By the way, keep what I told you to yourself. You have to be careful with those priests! And before I forget, watch out for that Nellie; she's got her eye on you, I'm sure!'

Paul was already in the saddle, and he turned to see Ned grinning from ear to ear. He blushed and stammered. 'Away with you, Ned! She's much too old to be interested in me.' And, a little confused, he galloped off to the manor, leaving Ned scratching his head and still grinning.

Once back in Castor, he tethered Betsy close to the barge house and ran round to the kitchen to greet Mrs Galston.

'Ah, there you are, Master Paul. I'm so glad to ... My goodness! What a smell! Have you been sleeping with those sheep or what?' And before Paul could say a word, she pushed a large linen cloth into his hands and pushed him towards the bathhouse. 'There's already some warm water in the tub. I don't want to see you again until you've had a good soak and got rid of that terrible sheep smell. I'll get Nellie to bring you some clean clothes.' He started to say he could manage alone, but the cook wasn't listening, as she was already on the way to the vegetable garden calling out for Nellie.

Paul went into the small washroom, quickly slipped out of his clothes and stepped into the tub and sat down, enjoying the warm water and having to admit that he really did need a good bath. It had been quite some time since he had had the last one! He was busy splashing the water over his shoulders and the rest of his body and didn't notice Nellie standing in the doorway, a change of clothes draped over one arm, watching him intently. Suddenly sensing somebody was there, he turned his head and saw her. A little embarrassed, he moved slightly to the edge of the tub, concealing his nakedness, and asked her to lay his clothes on the stool nearby.

'Why, of course, Master Paul, anything to oblige!' With which she made a mocking curtsy, laid his clothes on the stool and remained standing there, continuing to stare unashamedly at him.

'Nellie, would you mind going now please? I want to come out and get dried,' Paul said, becoming more uncomfortable each minute. 'Please,' he repeated.

'Are you sure you are quite clean?' retorted Nellie, moving closer. 'Mrs Galston is a real stickler for things being clean, as you well know. Here, let me give your back a good scrubbing.' With which she quickly stepped to the edge of the tub, took a small cloth hanging from a hook on the wall, and began to rub his back energetically, holding him firmly around the shoulders with her left arm, enjoying his obvious embarrassment. 'What a fuss you make, Paul. Goodness me, don't you think I've seen naked men before?' she added, leaning over him.

Paul didn't now know what to do, particularly as he was having to concentrate to stop an erection, as he was becoming aroused by her attention to his back and the sight of her ample breasts almost falling out of her loosely-fitting smock. Nellie knew exactly what she was doing and while she was rubbing his back and shoulders, almost imperceptibly had slowly been moving her left hand down his chest until her fingers eventually, as if by accident, brushed against the tip of his erect manhood. She felt his shudder and did it again, this time allowing her thumb and middle fingers to stay there and gently move the foreskin slightly downwards and then up again. She felt him grow even stronger and slowly began to move her hand a little faster with longer strokes. He was now trembling and she kissed him firmly on the lips, forcing her tongue into him as she guided his right hand into the top of her smock and got him to caress her breasts and finger her already hard nipples. She began to rub him almost in a frenzy.

Paul had begun to pant, trembling like a leaf, when suddenly he heard Mrs Galston shouting: 'Nellie, Nellie, where are you? I need you in the kitchen immediately.' He started, and pushed Nellie away from him.

'Stop, Nellie, stop!' he said, breathing heavily. 'You must go to Mrs Galston now, or she'll come looking for you.' Reluctantly, flushed and aroused, Nellie slowly moved away from him, pulling her smock up on to her shoulders and tidying her hair, looked back at him briefly, and without a word, hurried out of the washroom.

Paul stepped out of the tub, quickly dried himself, dressed in the clean clothes and walked slowly to the kitchen to resume his duties there.

Time seemed to drag for the next few weeks, and Paul did everything possible to avoid Nellie, feeling guilty when he did see her, and not knowing what to say. She tried to talk to him, but he blushed and more frequently than not stammered some sort of reply and got on with something else. He had earlier lain awake at night thinking about what had happened, or nearly happened, feeling a little ashamed that he had lost control of his emotions, but he had to admit to himself that it had also been one of the most exciting things that had happened to him. He had noticed how she looked at him, unashamedly and with a sort of longing in her eyes – or had he imagined that?

The first session he had with the chaplain after the washroom experience had not been particularly good. He could not concentrate, finding his mind wandering back to Nellie in spite of himself. The chaplain had in fact got very angry with Paul, and in frustration asked him if he was ill or something. Somehow, Paul managed to do just enough that afternoon to prevent a further outburst from the chaplain, and then thankfully returned to his kitchen duties.

Mrs Galston had also noticed that something seemed to be disturbing him and asked Nellie if she had any idea what it could be.

'Oh, who knows, Mrs Galston?' she replied easily. 'He's just growing up. They can all be a little difficult at that age. It'll pass off, I'm sure!' And they left it at that. And it did!

5

Springtime

Paul had been so happy when the reeve called by some weeks later telling him to report to Ned. It was coming up to sheep washing and shearing time and many extra hands were needed, including the lord's chaplain, who was there to supervise everything. The sheep were first driven to the fields bordering the River Burre, close to the traditional washing place where the water was clean and just the right depth. They were then pushed along a plank and into the river and kept there with long poles until they had swum and scrambled along for about fifty yards and were clean. Only then were they allowed to walk ashore, shake the water off themselves and get dry in the sun and spring breezes. When dry, groups were then led off to the large shearing shed where gangs of shearers were waiting. Careful tallies were taken by the reeve and the chaplain on the numbers of fleeces, making sure they were correctly sorted for quality before being baled and taken to the manor barn for storage.

It took several weeks for all the sheep on the demesne to be washed and shorn, and when Ned's flock was completed the reeve took Paul to help out at all the others. He learnt how to shear and soon was as adept as the most experienced. Mr Stanley also made sure that he understood all the points that had to be considered when it came to sorting the fleeces for quality. They were then baled into 'sarplers', and the sheep skins, called 'wool-fells', were also baled and stored in the manor barn, prior to being sold to merchants from the 'staple' town of Norwich.

Paul had overheard the reeve talking to the chaplain about the 'staple' and the ever-increasing level of taxes the landowners were having to pay both to the king and the merchants of the staple, and asked him about it.

'Goodness me, Master Paul!' he replied, 'I'll tell you more about all that when we spend time looking at the pricing situation of wool and the demesne's income from it, the other livestock and the crops and some other areas of revenue, not forgetting our many expenses, of course. There are plenty of other things to learn first, including your lessons with the good chaplain, which I understand have been a little neglected in the last few weeks, what with all the shearing that had to be done. So, my lad, be off with you now, and I want to hear only good reports on your progress the next time I talk to the chaplain. I don't have any more time to gossip, but we'll talk a bit more at the feast tomorrow night.' The reeve then rode off quickly in the direction of Castor, leaving Paul in deep thought, more determined than ever to learn the Latin grammar he hated, and everything else he could from the chaplain.

There was always a feast after the shearing was done, as this was a time of great celebration in all the villages. While the shearing was taking place, the women and children were all out in the fields collecting the bits of wool caught on the branches of the bushes and trees, which they would wash and card, later to be spun and woven at home by the women. Large quantities of ale were provided by the lord for each feast, as well as one oxen that was spit-roasted. The revelry usually went on until late into the night, and as a special concession, the reeve let Paul stay with the men when the women took the children back home to bed.

The villagers had noted that young 'Master Paul', as he was known overall, was being 'prepared' by the reeve for a high position in the demesne at some later time, and were ready to help him wherever possible, particularly as he not only worked very hard alongside them, but was always polite and courteous, treating them absolutely as his equal, which he considered they were anyway. That didn't stop the men from teasing him, though, from time to time, and on this particular evening they made sure that his ale jug was never empty.

'My, my, how he can talk, this young man,' Ned the shepherd commented. 'I'm sure he could charm the birds down from the trees if he really tried, and as for those milkmaids, you should see how they look at him! I tell you, if I hadn't been around I'm not sure what they might have done!'

All the men around him guffawed loudly, one or two of them making the appropriate lewd suggestions to the increasing embarrassment of Paul, who tried to protest, but his tongue was becoming too heavy, and he realised he was no longer seeing clearly. In fact, he was no longer feeling at all well, and decided it was time to leave.

Excusing himself, he eased himself a little unsteadily up from the bench where he had been sitting, stood up, moved away from the long trestle table and made his way, swaying from side to side, back towards the manor kitchen, and his bed, to the good-humoured merriment of all around him. As he got nearer to the manor buildings, fortunately close to the fishponds, his stomach finally rebelled against the quantities of ale he had drunk, and he wretched violently, bringing the whole lot up. He felt terrible for a few minutes. His head was still spinning, he had a pain in his stomach, and he could smell himself, and it was awful! Oh, God, he thought, I'll not do that again, and he staggered, falling in a heap fully dressed onto his bed.

When he awoke the next morning he was still not feeling too good. He had a headache and his stomach felt as if it didn't belong to him. Fortunately Mrs Galston was in a good mood that day and she gave him one of her special brews which did wonders in no time at all. Within a few hours he was more or less back to his normal self, and he went out of his way to make sure that the cook was pleased with his work.

The next afternoon was one of his scheduled lessons with the chaplain. After the statutory Latin grammar exercises, they began a long discussion on some aspects of the basic tenets of Christianity. The chaplain had originally been a monk at the Benedictine monastery of Burye St Edmunds, and had after some years been appointed as the abbot of St Benet's Abbey, near to the village of Thurne, but on the other side of the river just outside of the demesne of Castor. He had been accustomed at Burye to lead an extremely high standard of living by comparison with most of the rest of the population. Apart from the time spent on the normal monastic devotional activity, including library work, hunting and feasting were extremely popular pastimes!

When the Reverend Father Ignatius, as was his monastic name, went to the Abbey of St Benet as abbot, he found it was not quite so easy to lead the same lifestyle as before, since it was a much poorer abbey than Burye, and he was therefore happy to supplement his income as the chaplain for the lord of Castor. He spent most of his time in the Castor demesne, even though the 'demands' of Sir William were minimal, frequently accompanying the lord when he hunted, and visiting his own many mistresses who were scattered across the area. It was in his own interest to ensure that careful records were kept in the demesne, especially during the sheep-shearing season since a percentage of the sheep belonged to him, and he made sure that he also got his share of other livestock for the standard church tithes and fines. He also supervised carefully those church taxes paid by all villages in the Castor demesne that were collected for the Pope, and sent on to his court in Avignon via the Bishop of Norwiche – not before, however, a good ten per cent had been diverted to his own coffers!

He professed to have a great faith and love for the 'holy father', and diligently ensured that the maximum possible sums were squeezed from the villagers, 'in the name of God, our father in heaven', to quote one of his favourite phrases! Most of the priests in the demesne were little better and Father Ignatius was sure the bishop would also guarantee himself a significant share of the total sum.

Paul was to discover all this later on, but for the moment was deeply engrossed in the conversation. He looked intently at Father Ignatius in his loose black gown with wide sleeves, the cowl lying on his back, and continued to argue on the question of poverty and the position of the Church. He could still remember a sermon he had heard some years previously from a poor friar who travelled from village to village, and quoted some appropriate examples.

The chaplain tended to discount the stories in which Jesus had supposedly told people to sell all their worldly goods and give the proceeds to the poor, by claiming this was a typical exaggeration of the time to make a point concerning caring for the poor.

'Caring for the souls of these poor people is much more important. To save them from eternal damnation is the most important role of our mother church. May God give us the strength to continue our holy mission!' He looked piously above, as if he was sharing a message being transmitted to him from beyond, and continued. 'Our holy father himself, Johannes XXII, may God protect him, wrote in a recent papal bull, "Cum inter nonnullos", that to say that Christ and the Apostles were without any possessions or things of value is a perversion of the holy scriptures. That, Master Paul, is good enough for me and must be for you too! You must not believe all the rubbish that these wandering friars propagate. In my opinion, most of them are heretics and should be brought before the courts of the Inquisition to be tried and duly punished for their sins.'

This was the first time that Paul had heard about the Inquisition, and it prompted a further series of questions that Father Ignatius was only too pleased to answer. Paul listened carefully to the chaplain's replies and dutifully gave the impression that he accepted the various explanations, although deeply within he was somewhat shocked and felt it had little to do with the message of God's love that the friar had preached so passionately and eloquently, and had demonstrated practically in helping the poorest people in his home village of Stokesbye.

Satisfied that he had planted the appropriate seeds within the mind of the young Paul, the chaplain drew the afternoon's session to a close, sent him off to the kitchen, and rode away on his beautiful chestnut mare to visit one of the demesne's parishioners, badly in need of 'spiritual comforting'.

But Paul was learning that life was not as simple as he had previously thought. One could not always take the words of people literally and automatically believe that what they said was necessarily the complete or even the partial truth.

That year quickly passed, and true to his word the reeve continued to broaden Paul's experience in all matters concerning the complete running of the demesne. In fact, once he was fifteen, he was relieved of all kitchen duties, and was able to spend all of his time, apart from his sessions with the chaplain twice a week, learning all that was necessary.

As a special reward for his excellent progress, Mr Pettit also made it possible for Paul to take over a small cottage in a neighbouring berewick to Castor that became vacant at the death of a childless widow. Within two weeks he had repaired the thatched roof, patched the crumbling wattle walls, cleaned the inside thoroughly and made a comfortable home of it. A local carpenter made him a brand-new wooden bed, he was given a table and two chairs, and Mrs Galston made sure he had all the kitchen utensils he would need should he not be able to eat with the other servants at the manor.

There was also a large garden attached to the cottage, with a well and washing trough close by. Paul quickly made a small paddock for Betsy and the reeve got one of the manor labourers to make a simple lean-to, so that the mare had some shelter in bad weather, and a little shed at the back of the cottage to store hay and straw.

Paul was thrilled with his new status and worked even harder to justify the help and encouragement that the reeve had given him. In the dark evenings, he studied details of the manor accounts, helping Mr Stanley to anticipate what had to be collected from one or other of the local markets, alerting him to any special points that needed to be followed up or investigated. All stock was listed: grain, animals and other things, and Paul particularly enjoyed dealing with the complex sheep accounts. The total demesne flocks were carefully recorded under the headings of females (the ewe flock), wethers (the rams), hoggets (the two-year-old sheep or boars) yearlings and lambs. The totals at the beginning of the year recorded deaths, numbers sold and those given in tithe, and the balance was calculated at Michaelmas, the feast of St Michael on September 29, when the accounts were closed.

In parallel to these accounts, Paul also helped to put together the details of the wool production and resulting revenues and costs. He had learnt that a sack of wool weighed twenty-six stone and the average weight of the fleece of a long-woolled sheep was three pounds. Discounting the villagers' sheep that pastured on communal land, the lord's flocks of just over 10,000 sheep produced around 2,000 sacks which were then sold to the merchants at between four to six pounds per sack depending on the quality. Excluding the various tithes and royal taxes, the gross income varied between 8–12,000 pounds per annum, of which Sir William, when all taxes and other expenses were paid, received between 3–5,000 pounds! Then came all the other elements of the estate's income from other livestock, grain, rents and fines, etc. My God, Paul thought, what a fortune compared with my penny a day!

One day the reeve had confided to him that the merchants who travelled with their packhorses from one manor to the next were able to sell the best quality wool on the foreign markets for at least double the price they had paid for it. Then he laughed and said, 'We've got the wrong job, that's for sure! But we should be content with what we've got. There's many a poor soul that has got next to nothing and you don't have to look very far!'

Paul agreed with him, but had already begun to think about the inequalities and injustices around him and resolved that one day, he would do something about it!

6

The Homecoming

In all, Tom Rollesby had been away from home for less than two months. As a newly-married man he felt it was closer to two years and he yearned desperately to get back to his beloved Margaret, and also to make sure that all was well on their smallholding.

After landing at Orwel haven with a troop of archers and crossbowmen, Sir William Fastolfe insisted that Tom should first return with him to Castor manor before going home to Stokesbye. Tom reluctantly agreed, knowing he had little or no choice in the matter, but wondered what the lord had in mind. On arriving at the manor barge house he was delighted to be met by Paul, and the two brothers embraced with real affection.

'Thank God, nothing has happened to you, Tom!' Paul said, looking his brother over carefully. 'I wondered if we would ever meet again.'

'Don't you worry, little brother,' Tom replied, grinning broadly. 'They won't get rid of me that easily!'

'I'm not so little, Tom,' Paul responded indignantly. He stretched himself to his full height, flexing his biceps, so that his brother could see his well-muscled body. 'In a couple of years, I might even be bigger than you, you'll see!'

Tom looked at his younger brother and continued to smile. 'You know Paul, there's much more to life than being a large, strong man,' he retorted. 'You make sure that you use those brains you were born with. That will bring you so much more in life. Mark my words! I have heard you can read and write now, and that you almost know as much as the reeve already. Keep at it, Paul, you will see that it will be worth all the hard work. I only wish I were as clever as you.'

He then gently pushed his brother away, slapped him on the back, and told him he would get all the details about Sluys when they next met, but now had to go immediately to see the lord in the manor house. He turned, and then walked purposefully along the outside of the moat towards the drawbridge leading to the outer court. The guard at the gate, expecting him, pointed out the moathouse leading to the inner court and the great hall, where he would be taken to meet the lord.

Another guard at the moathouse led him up the steps to a parlour, and asked him to wait while he informed Sir William that he had arrived. Within a few minutes, the lord came to greet Tom, giving the impression that they were old friends, and took him by the arm telling him they should go into the hall, as he wanted to discuss something important with him. They sat at the main table which stood on a wooden platform at the far end of the great hall. Behind the table was a large tapestry almost covering the wall, and the long, narrow glass windows set in the two longest walls let in sufficient light for the daytime. There were torch holders set in the walls at intervals of about fifteen feet all around the large hall, and in the middle of the long wall facing south-east was a large open fireplace, with logs stacked on each side in readiness for the evening. Under each of the long windows were sitting areas and opposite the fireplace Tom could see a large cupboard filled with platters, goblets and other articles he couldn't quite make out, close by some trestles and planks which were stacked up against the wall. The floor was covered with clean rushes, but before he could take in any more detail the lord began to speak.

'Well, Tom,' he began, 'you are almost certainly wondering why I have brought you here. Before you start asking any questions, let me explain. Before we met at Sluys, I had heard about you as a result of your prowess with the longbow, and that was why I had you enlisted in the demesne's group of archers requested by the king. What I saw during the battle really impressed me. You are one of the most fearsome soldiers I've ever met, by far the best archer I've ever seen and in my opinion, a natural leader. You are probably not aware of that quality, but I could see how the others followed you immediately and did exactly what you said they should do. You still have a lot to learn in terms of combat with the sword and other weapons, but I don't see any problems there.'

Tom listened intently, a little embarrassed with the many compliments being showered on him, and wondered where all this was leading to.

'I am authorised by the king to pay all the surviving soldiers from the demesne the sum of two pence per day for this campaign, which in your case is twenty-two shillings and ten pence, and here it is!' The lord then handed over to Tom a small purse filled with money which he gratefully took, checking the amount carefully but quickly. The lord smiled at him and said, 'You are right to check it, but I'm assured by the steward that it's correct, and I'm sure it is.' Tom grinned and nodded. 'Tom, I would like you to work directly for me, here in Castor, here in the manor. I will have you trained to be a competent yeoman and if you make the grade, which I'm sure you will, you will be made the captain of my guard. Initially you will receive two shillings per week plus your keep, and of course more when you have successfully completed the training. You will see that there are also very comfortable quarters for you here in the manor and, from what I hear, also for your beautiful wife. Think it over carefully Tom, and I hope you will agree. I'm sure you will not regret it, but go home first and talk it over with your wife. There will be all sorts of arrangements to be made with your own smallholding – I would advise you to include your young brother in those discussions, and let me know your answer one month from today.'

'My lord,' Tom replied, hardly able to conceal his excitement, 'thank you for the honour and trust you bestow on me. I swear you will never regret it, albeit you will discover that I am by nature not only very determined but, as my wife tells me, of a somewhat stubborn disposition. I will of course, discuss this with Margaret, but I cannot foresee that she would object to such an opportunity. With your leave, I would like to return home immediately as I have been away now for more than two months!'

The lord smiled knowingly and replied, 'I can well imagine with such a beauty waiting for you at home, you would prefer to fly if it were possible. I cannot give you any wings, but I will lend you a fine stallion for the next four weeks. Look after him well, he is a fine horse and very fast. His name is "Lightning" by the way.'

The lord then called a servant and told him to take Tom to the stables to collect the stallion. He then called after them to go first to the kitchen so that Tom could get something to eat quickly while the horse was being saddled and made ready. And so Tom made his first contact with Mrs Galston, was carefully scrutinised by Nellie while he was eating some bread and a mutton broth that had been simmering over the kitchen fire, and within twenty minutes was galloping off on 'Lightning' on his way to Stokesbye.

True to his name, the black stallion seemed to understand Tom's urgency and galloped at an incredible speed across the fields and along the cart tracks, expertly guided along the most direct route. Margaret was waiting for him at the door, having heard the drumming of the hooves some way off from their cottage. She had heard that Tom was safely back in England, and was overjoyed to recognise him racing towards her on the most beautiful horse she had ever seen.

He sprang down from the stallion, tied him to a post close to the door and they fell into each others' arms. They both felt that the separation had been almost an eternity, and had difficulty containing their passion.

'Oh, let me look at you, my love,' Margaret sighed. 'It seems such a long time.' She gently pushed him a pace backwards and looked deeply into his eyes, wiping her tears of joy away with the sleeve of her summer smock. 'Were you wounded at all, Tom? Was it terrible to be in such a battle? Answer me, Tom, please. I want to know everything. I've missed you so, so much!'

'I'm just fine, my darling, and now feel all the better to have you in my arms again. I told you not to worry before I went away, and you can see that nothing has happened to me. I only had a couple of little scratches and you can't see them now. I'll tell you later about the battle. Let's go inside.' He gently gave her a slap on the buttocks, took her by the arm and led her into the cottage.

Margaret didn't need any persuasion for she had exactly the same thing on her mind as her husband. She pushed the door closed, pulled him urgently towards their bed and within seconds her smock and underclothes were at her feet and she stood completely naked before her husband. Tom looked hungrily at her, wondering at her incredible beauty, feeling himself stirring with desire. She took hold of his hands and placed them on her large, soft breasts, the nipples already hard and swollen.

'Oh, Tom,' she sighed, 'if only you knew how much I have been looking forward to this moment!' She moaned as her passion began to grow more intense. Tom's excitement matched hers, as her hands moved slowly down his back, working their way gradually under his doublet, around the tops of his thighs. She knew exactly how to stimulate his desire and slowly moved her fingers along his rampant manhood. She eased her right hand inside his breeches, took hold of him and began to caress the silky foreskin, moving it slowly up and down.

'Is that good?' she whispered, looking him full in the eyes, flushed with desire.

'Yes, my darling,' he replied softly, beginning to tremble slightly with expectation.

He quickly moved a hand down the smooth skin of her flat stomach and gently rubbed her, making her squirm with ecstasy to the point where she was on the verge of a climax. He stopped suddenly and pushed her down onto the bed. He stepped out of his breeches, pulled the doublet over his head, parted her thighs and entered her, completing the union they both wanted so desperately. Almost intuitively, they reached their climax simultaneously and lay twined together, panting, both lost in a total happiness and contentment. They spent most of the night making love, sleeping for an hour or two and then coming together with what seemed an almost insatiable passion until one or the other reached an orgasm, and then at dawn they both fell into a contented sleep.

Late the following morning they reluctantly got up, dressed and began to organise the day. While Margaret prepared a breakfast Tom fed Lightning and made sure that he was comfortable and at ease in the enclosed field close to their cottage, looking around briefly, checking that everything was in good order on the smallholding.

While they sat at breakfast around the small table close to the large window by the door, Tom recounted the events of his two-month trip, from the moment he left home until he sailed back to Orwel haven. He described the battle in detail, playing down his own role, but she well understood that it had been a brutal affair and that even Tom had been somewhat shaken by the extent of the slaughter. She took his hand and pressed it close to her bosom, sighing and saying in a very quiet voice:

'Oh, Tom, thank God you were spared and let us hope that it is all finshed now and we can begin a normal life together. It is so peaceful here and I know we can be so happy. We have everything we need, and I couldn't bear the thought that I might lose you.'

He felt a little awkward because he had not yet told her about the lord's offer, which he really wanted to take, and was not sure how she might react. He hesitated a moment and then came out with the whole story, hoping desperately that she would agree. He sat back when he had finished, watching her face expectantly. There was a long silence which Tom did not dare to break. It was almost as if everything had suddenly come to a complete standstill. Margaret then looked at him intensely and he steeled himself, expecting the worst as she began to speak.

'Tom, is that what you really want us to do?' she asked.

He nodded, saying, 'but Margaret, only if you come with me willingly. If you tell me it's not possible, I'll not accept Sir William's offer, and I mean that!'

She smiled knowingly. 'Of course you must accept the offer. I would follow you to the end of the earth if needs be.' She then stood up, moved round to where he was sitting and put her arms around his neck and sat on his lap. 'Give me a kiss, Mr Rollesby, and don't look so worried. We've got a month, you said, didn't you? That gives us plenty of time!' She had felt the stirring beneath her, and moved her right hand down to confirm her suspicions, playfully adding, 'Now, my love, keep still! You have something I want!'

In the following weeks they found a suitable tenant for their smallholding, greatly helped by Paul who had in the last year or so become very familiar with demesne affairs and of course, the people living and working there. Margaret also visited her parents in Ormesbye to tell them the good news, giving Tom ample time to make all the necessary arrangements for the move to Castor, which included hiring a large cart with two horses and a driver to carry their household chattels and other possessions to their new home on the appointed day. Once everything was loaded on the cart to Margaret's satisfaction, he helped her up onto Lightning and they rode slowly towards Castor, wondering what they could expect in the months ahead of them.

7

The Contest

True to his word, Sir William had instructed the servants to prepare the living quarters for Tom and his wife in two rooms which were opposite the barge house and part of the building complex around the manor house kitchen. Their accommodation was in fact built onto a small round tower which served as a storehouse for the guards' weapons and armour, including that of the lord. There was a bedroom with a large, beautifully carved wooden bed covered with several sheep fleeces. At the foot of the bed Margaret was delighted to see a long chest for their clothes, and alongside it on the far wall, two perches, one of which had an oil lamp on it which could by means of a pulley and a rope fixed to the wall, easily be reached for lighting or filling. The other one Tom later discovered was designed to hang his personal weapons on, including a hauberk of chain-mail. The main room had a large, open fireplace, complete with a trivet in front of it for hanging the various pots and pans for cooking. Other kitchen utensils were hanging from hooks on each side of it, and on a small table nearby, Margaret was overjoyed to find not only an assortment of dishes, platters, carving knives, spoons and drinking mugs, but also some fresh provisions. A larger table with four chairs was placed under a window overlooking the manor gardens and the floor was covered with clean rushes.

When the cart arrived two hours or so later, except for their bed, they were able to utilise most of the rest of their own household chattels, and spent most of the afternoon organising it all and familiarising themselves with the area around them, meeting the cook, Mrs Galston, and the rest of the lord's servants. Lightning was stabled nearby and the steward advised Tom to visit Sir William early the next morning.

He and Margaret sat in front of a cheerful, burning log fire until late into the night, talking about the future and their luck to have a patron and master like Sir William. Tom warned her that even though his lord had always been more than fair with him in his dealings so far, he had a doubtful reputation when it came to the ladies, and she should be careful if or when she should ever meet him. Margaret merely laughed at the seriousness with which her husband spoke on this particular subject, patted him affectionately on the arm, and said reassuringly, 'You need have no fear for me, Tom. I really can take care of myself, and I could never be interested in another man. You are the best thing that has ever happened to me, and I shall love you, only you, as long as I live!'

Tom gathered her in his arms and held her close to him, almost overcome with love for his beautiful wife. He led her gently to the bedroom.

The next morning after Mass, he walked around to the great hall to meet the steward who then led him to the private chambers of Sir William, who was expecting him. He was briefly introduced to the lord's wife, Lady Mortimer, who left them almost immediately, leaving Tom little time to appraise her other than seeing that she was a beautiful and seemingly delicate lady, with a presence that automatically commanded respect.

'Well, Tom, how are the quarters? Is your wife pleased with them?' Sir William inquired, smiling.

'My lord, they are wonderful, and my wife Margaret asked me particularly to thank you for your kindness and generosity. Please tell me what my duties are and how I can possibly repay you for everything you have done for us!'

'Oh, there will be plenty of time for that,' said Sir William. 'First of all you need a thorough training in all the arts and skills essential for a yeoman, and I shall be your helper there. If you are the man I'm sure you are, you will be ready to take over the position of captain of the guard within a few weeks, but it will not be easy, as you will see!'

'You will find me a willing pupil, my lord,' Tom retorted earnestly. 'I only want the chance to justify your faith in me. I will serve you faithfully as long as I live.'

'I'm sure you will Tom,' Sir William replied. 'But you will first need to demonstrate your value to the rest of my guard. They need to be reassured that you have the necessary qualities to be their leader. Apart from one of my crossbowmen who saw you in action at Sluys, the rest do not really know you, since I have recruited them from various parts of our country. So let's give them the chance to see what you can do with the longbow.'

And so it was arranged that on the following day, a Sunday, a shooting contest would take place at midday in the fields to the south, immediately outside the fenced gardens. A line of targets was set up at about two hundred and fifty paces from a rope that was stretched between two posts, driven into the ground twenty paces apart. Word had quickly spread around the manor and well before the start of the contest there was a crowd of the lord's servants and most of the villagers from the neighbouring villages of Mautbye and Filbye, including the shepherd Ned Giles who was standing next to Paul, who wanted to see his brother win the contest.

In addition to the twenty or so archers that were part of the lord's permanent guard, there was an élite group of ten crossbowmen, which included five specially recruited Genoese, who were considered to be among the best in the field. The soldiers, led by the lord and the chaplain, marched the short distance from the small round tower, out of the the manor house gardens and around to the fields to a position behind the rope. They were in two groups. First came the crossbowmen, who were all carrying windlasses in addition to their crossbows, with a quiver hanging down the left hip holding fifteen bolts, attached to a broad leather belt. They were also all wearing the standard green tunics of the lord's troop, underneath light 'cuir bouilli' jerkins, and marched with an assured pride. Tom was in the first rank of the following longbowmen, and even though not yet officially appointed to the commanding position of the troop, looked every inch the born leader he surely was. He had been given that morning the green tunic worn by them all, but like the other longbowmen, was not wearing the armoured leather jerkin of the crossbowmen. All the archers had their longbows slung over the right shoulder, with quivers holding twenty arrows hanging from a leather thong that passed over the right shoulder and down the back to the left side of the body where it was fastened to a girdle. They did not appear to have the same bearing and discipline of the crossbowmen, most of them coming from very ordinary, simple country families, but were all especially chosen by the lord for their prowess with the longbow.

Paul excitedly pointed out Tom to Ned, who had recognised him anyway from earlier descriptions he had been given by the hero-worshipping younger brother during the sheep-shearing season of the previous year. It had not been too difficult since Tom was by far the largest man in the entire troop!

Once the soldiers were in position, Sir William, wearing a magnificent cloak trimmed with squirrel fur over his chain-mail hauberk, and a great belt supporting his heavy sword and scabbard, the tip of which was just touching the side of the long, soft leather left boot, began to address them:

'Crossbowmen, archers, our good King Edward has decreed that at least on all feast days, we should practice this art to ensure that we are always in readiness to meet and overcome our common foe, the French barbarians, should they ever set foot again in our fair land. I shall make sure that my troop will be recognised as being of the very best in this shire and perhaps the whole country, and with the help of the sheriff and our good chaplain, Father Ignatius, will ensure that all males in the demesne over the age of sixteen years shall take part in regular target shooting.

'I know that all of you here before me are expert with either the crossbow or longbow, but even experts need to practise! In addition, I want to award the special prize of a fine sword to each winner among the crossbowmen and the longbowmen, and the overall best shot shall have the coat of mail that I am wearing as well as this baselard dagger.'

There was a murmuring of approval from the assembled soldiers, and Paul whispered to Ned that the coat of mail would have to be enlarged, for Tom would surely win it!

'Don't be so sure, Master Paul,' the shepherd replied in a low voice. 'There are some fine Welsh archers in the group, and I'm not sure if the best of all the longbowmen can outmatch those Genoese crossbowmen. I've heard they can hit a man at three hundred paces!'

Before Paul could comment, Sir William continued:

'The crossbowmen will begin, followed by the longbowmen, and then finally, the best man of each group shall compete against the other. We shall start at two hundred and fifty paces and finally increase to three hundred if necessary. Pray make the arrangements to begin, Father Ignatius, and may the best man win!'

A feeling of excited expectancy swept the crowd that had gathered to witness the contest, particularly as very few of them had seen the crossbowmen in action, and none of them had ever witnessed a contest between both types of weapon.

While Sir William was walking to a small platform set up close to the fenced gardens, especially placed for him and Lady Mortimer at about a hundred paces from the butts, the archers moved to one side whilst the ten crossbowmen took up their positions behind the rope, spanned their crossbows, placed the first bolt in readiness to fire, and calmly awaited the chaplain's command. The Genoese were in one group together alongside the five Englishmen, each of them convinced that the only real competition for the overall prize came from one of the crossbowmen within their own group.

The chaplain confirmed that each man had three shots only, and that on the lord's signal, he would give the command to begin.

A hush fell as Sir William raised his sword and the order to fire was given when he swifly lowered it. The men carefully took aim at the distant targets, adjusting slightly for the range and the gentle breeze, and almost simultaneously released their first bolt. There was an ominous hissing sound and then the ten bolts thudded into the butts within a fraction of a second of each other. A roar of approval came from the crowd as they could see that they were all on target. While the crossbowmen were working their windlasses to reload, men placed near the targets ran to the butts to signal the scores to the chaplain who carefully noted them on a specially prepared parchment before announcing the results: four bull's-eyes and six outers! An incredible score for such a range and the first shot!

The crossbowmen signalled they were ready for the second shot. The chaplain raised his arm for them to take aim, and then gave the order to fire. Once again all the bolts thudded into the ten targets and within a few seconds the results were signalled: six bull's eyes and four outers! The chaplain then announced that there were five men each with two bull's-eyes, and after identifying them, the remaining five with lower scores were ordered to stand to one side while the others prepared themselves for the final decisive shot.

The tenseness of the situation was felt by all of the watching crowd as well as the five remaining crossbowmen. For them it was not only the possibility of winning the coveted prizes but the prestige associated with it and the question of national honour. There were three Genoese and two English crossbowmen standing in line behind the marker rope, each wanting desperately to win. The chaplain raised his arm and they slowly took aim, waiting for the order to fire. There was a slight pause after the command, and then the five bolts were released. It was incredible! This time there were five bull's-eyes!

The crossbowmen looked at each other, grinning broadly, proud of their achievement. They wondered what would happen next to decide the winner. The archers standing to one side recognised the quality of the competition and most of them were talking and joking with each other to hide their nervousness. The chaplain walked up to where Sir William and Lady Mortimer were sitting on the platform, to agree with the lord how best to decide the winner while the manor house servants and the other demesne villagers excitely discussed the contest, many of them making wagers on the likely winner!

Shouts of approval and encouragement came from the crowd as

they saw the five targets being carried a further fifty paces back, carefully set up and the bolts being removed. As the chaplain began to speak, they quickly quietened so as to hear how it would be decided. It was quite simple. They would continue to fire at the new range, eliminating anyone who failed to hit a bull's-eye! At that distance it was an achievement to hit any part of the target, and all the contestants knew this only too well.

At the chaplain's signal, the crossbowmen took careful aim, holding their breath, waiting for the command to fire. Once given, the five bolts were instantly released and sped into the targets. There were only two bull's-eyes; one from the Genoese and one from an English crossbowman, the man who had been on the same ship as Tom at the battle of Sluys.

The two remaining men prepared themselves to fire again, feeling the growing tension of the situation. As the bolts were released it seemed that most people realised that it would be the final decision, and they were right. The Genoese scored a clear bull's-eye, whereas the Englishman's bolt lay in the outer ring. The first part of the contest was over. Marco Paulini was the crossbow champion, much to the delight of the small Genoese contingent!

It was now the turn of the longbowmen, and since there were twenty of them and there were only ten places at the firing line, it was clearly going to take some reorganisation. Meanwhile all the targets were reset at two hundred and fifty paces.

The chaplain, however, in spite of his ecclesiastical training and background, was an avid hunter and also a reasonable shot with a longbow, and he was well versed in the various procedures of an archery contest. Hence he quickly clarified how the next phase would be decided. He counted out the first ten archers and ordered them to take up their positions, explaining that the winner would be the man who, when he gave the signal to fire, was the first to place six arrows in the target. Should there be a tie at this stage, the total number of bull's-eyes would decide. The men prepared the first arrow, took aim and awaited the command. Tom was in this first group, standing on the extreme left, towering over the others, closely watched, amongst many others who knew him, by his brother on one side and Sir William on the other.

The command to fire was given. Ten arrows whistled through the air and thunked into the targets. Less than ten seconds later, Tom's second arrow sank into the centre of the bull's-eye, and the remaining four were also despatched with such speed and precision that it remained a subject of discussion in the manor for many years. Tom not only fired his six arrows long before all the others, but they were all packed into the narrow circle of the bull's-eye! Even Sir William jumped to his feet and applauded the incredible feat. The crowd were cheering wildly and Paul felt tears of joy trickling down his cheeks as he jumped up and down, shouting loudly with excitement, feeling so proud to be called Rollesby!

The remaining ten archers who had not yet participated, to a man (and that included two Welshmen) relinquished their opportunity to compete, knowing perfectly well that they could not hope to match Tom's performance. Tom grinned a little sheepishly and felt somewhat embarrassed by all the fuss. But the contest was not yet over. There was still the question of the overall champion to be decided.

While the crowd were still buzzing with excitement, and the archers were crowded around Tom, slapping him on the back and congratulating him, the targets were taken to one side apart from two of them that were set up at three hundred paces from the firing line. The chaplain signalled to Tom and Marco to take up their positions, while he prepared himself to explain how this final contest would be run.

The element of rapid firing obviously could not be included since an experienced longbowman could release at least six to seven arrows in the time it would take a crossbowman to load and fire one bolt. So it would have to be decided by range and accuracy. Each man would fire three times in his own time, and the best score would of course determine the winner.

Marco felt reasonably confident. He had earlier already placed two bolts into the bull's-eye at this range of three hundred paces and his opponent had yet to demonstrate he could even hit the target at all. We shall soon see, Englishman, he mused, who is the best shot.

Tom for his part had been practising for years at this range and knew that if necessary he could even fire further with reasonable accuracy by his standards. He also knew that he had to win this contest to make sure that he would gain the respect of all the men, including the crossbowmen. His thoughts were disturbed by the chaplain, giving the command to fire when ready.

He whet his finger, pointing it towards the direction of the slight breeze, made a slight correction to his aim and released his first arrow which winged its way across the field to drop with a resounding thud plumb into the centre of the bull's-eye. Seconds later, he saw that Marco had also achieved an excellent first shot. After the shouting had died down, while Marco was busy re-spanning his crossbow, Tom placed his second and third arrows on each side of the first one, not more than three finger widths apart. He then took a pace backwards and stood watching intently while Marco finished the spanning and prepared himself for the second shot. It was almost as good as his first and Tom knew that this man was going to be difficult to beat.

One could almost hear a pin drop as Marco, perspiration oozing slowly down his forehead, concentrated on his final shot. A roar went up from the crowd as they saw the bolt sink into the edge of the bull's-eye.

The tension was dramatic. Who would be the winner? Both Sir William and the chaplain walked to the targets to check the final result. Looking carefully at the placings, the lord could see that Tom had definitely won, but the difference between the two was not sufficient for all clearly to accept that Tom was the undisputed champion, which he explained to the chaplain in a low voice. It had to be a fair result, he made clear, but it must be an outstanding difference, and continuing in hushed tones, he told the chaplain what had to be done. The chaplain then called over two of the butt assistants, gave them their instructions, and walked slowly to the firing line while Sir William made his way back to his seat by Lady Mortimer.

Both Tom and Marco were looking at the chaplain a little anxiously, wondering who had won. The crowd was absolutely silent as the chaplain began to speak in a loud voice.

'Honourable guards, you both have demonstrated that you are the absolute champions of your individual arms and we are all privileged today to have witnessed the extent of your skills. The final result was so close that it was not possible to distinguish a real difference. It has therefore been decided to place the targets at three hundred and fifty paces, and you will each fire three times. May the best man win!'

There was a gasp of incredulity from both the crowd and the rest of the lord's guard. This was an unheard of distance. At such a range one could hardly see the target, let alone hit it! Arguments broke out concerning how the wagers would be settled if neither man scored, which was more than likely in the opinion of most. Tom and Marco looked at each other, shrugged their shoulders and began to prepare themselves for the greatest contest that had ever been run.

The chaplain signalled that Marco should make the first shot, and moved over to one side making sure that the rest of the guard were quiet and clear of the two participants. Everybody watched intensely, fascinated by the drama they were witnessing. The bolt was released and sped past the target, missing it by a finger's breadth. Marco's shoulders slumped as he realised he had not scored, and he was not able to conceal his disappointment as he began to re-span his crossbow.

Tom took his position, slowly drew the bowstring back to his ear, increased the elevation, took a deep breath, narrowed his eyes, squinting once more at the target which at that distance looked like a small coin, and released his first arrow. It soared rapidly to a height well above the target and then dropped into the centre of it. He lowered his bow slowly, apparently unaware of the excitement and cheering all around him, took a pace backwards and waited for Marco to fire his second bolt.

Marco's arms were trembling almost imperceptibly as he concentrated on aiming at the target. He corrected direction slightly, held his breath and fired. He missed again, the bolt just passing the other side of the target this time. He cursed under his breath, looking back towards Tom, hardly able to conceal the look of hatred on his face.

Tom took aim carefully, and fired his second arrow which struck the target close to the first one, grinned in the direction of his brother who had been shouting words of encouragement during the whole contest, and then stepped aside without looking at Marco.

The Genoese knew he had lost the competition but was determined to show them all that he could also score at three hundred and fifty paces. He was now much calmer, having nothing more to lose and wanting to preserve his honour and reputation, and his final shot struck the outside edge of the target. His fellow Genoese and the other crossbowmen cheered wildly, delighted that at least their arm had demonstrated its lethal ability at such an incredibly long range.

The chaplain called for silence and asked Tom to make his last shot. With the relaxed air of the champion he was, he took aim quickly this time and saw his arrow drop neatly into the target, close to the other two. Pandemonium broke out all around him. Nobody had ever seen such an archery feat. Even Lady Mortimer was moved and congratulated her husband on employing such a man. Sir William was delighted with the result. He had always been sure that Tom Rollesby would win but he was astonished at the extent of the skill he had just seen and proud to have Tom in his own troop of guards.

A servant passed the two swords and the dagger to him, and he walked down to his troop and the chaplain all clustered around the firing line area. He called them to silence, and commanded that Tom and Marco should come forward and stand before him.

'Tom Rollesby and Marco Paulini,' he began, 'you have both demonstrated that you are absolute masters of your art and have provided us all with an unparalleled display of your skill. What we have all seen today will be the subject of many discussions in the years to come. We shall always need men like you to defend our heritage and families from the attacks of our enemies, and the day will come, I am sure, when you will lead our brave archers and crossbowmen to crush our common foe, once and for all, in the territory that he has unjustly usurped from England.'

Sir William spoke in a powerful voice, and the crowd kept absolutely silent so as not to miss a word, understanding the importance of the occasion, and beginning to be a little concerned at some of the implications of his words.

'I know that our good King Edward, may our Lord and Master protect him,' he continued, 'will in the years ahead seek to recapture and retain what the false French King Philippe has stolen from us in France. I and the other lords of this land, with the help of men like you and the rest of my troop, will only be too proud to help him achieve God's purpose and destroy that heathen!' He paused to take a breath, almost carried away with the emotion of the moment, and acknowledging the cheers of his soldiers, already beginning to think about the booty they could win. 'But that will be another day,' he then added. 'Today we will celebrate the exploits of Tom Rollesby and Marco Paulini. It gives me great pleasure to present to you Marco this sword, and to you Tom, this sword and dagger as the overall champion. You will also receive this coat of mail I'm wearing, tomorrow.'

The two men took the highly-valued prizes with great pride, knowing that such generosity was a rarity, and Tom's respect for Sir William increased even more.

But the ceremony was not yet over. Sir William turned to the troop of soldiers who had moved to one side when the two winners had been called to stand before him, pointed to Tom, and then proclaimed for all to hear:

'This man, Thomas Rollesby, has proven himself to be a worthy leader of you all. I witnessed his exploits at the battle of Sluys, and you have all seen today that he is the complete master of his craft. I have decided that he shall be the captain of this guard and I command you all to obey him in all respects.'

To a man, the archers and even most of the crossbowmen cheered. Paul and the whole crowd went wild with excitement that such an honour should be given to one of their own, and surged forward to get closer to their hero, who wished the ground could swallow him up he felt so embarrassed. Sir William smiled, and asked the reeve and the chaplain to make sure that the villagers had some ale to drink later that afternoon, and that two oxen should be roasted to feed them all that evening.

Lord and Lady Mortimer then returned to the manor house, accompanied by the new captain of the guard leading the troop of archers and crossbowmen, who, with the exception of Marco, were happy to have Tom as their leader.

8

Captain of the Guard

In the weeks following the contest, Tom was kept busy by Sir William, learning all the aspects of his new position as captain of the guard. As he quickly discovered, this not only involved responsibility for the discipline and training of the lord's guard, including ensuring that the manor house and immediate surroundings were always well guarded, but he also had to learn how to handle with expertise the variety of other weapons that were stored in the armoury room of the round tower. Once the lord's hauberk that Tom had won was enlarged, he was also given a 'gambeson', a padded tunic stuffed with wool, to be worn underneath the coat of mail as additional protection, which served him well many times during his sword-fighting tuition with Sir William.

He also had to learn how to help Sir William into his full armour and to become familiar with all the various individual items such as the basinet helmet with aventail, the short cape of mail covering the lower part of the face and shoulders; the breastplate, the pauldron and couter covering the shoulders and elbows respectively; the cuisse for the thighs and the greave for the shins; the poleyn for the knees and the sabaton for the feet. It was Tom's responsibility also to ensure that the armour was in top condition, free from rust and always immediately available for Sir William in times of emergency.

Sir William's war horse armour was also kept in the round tower and comprised of a chanfron for the face, a crinet for the neck, laminated to allow movement, peytral plates for the chest, flanchards for the flanks and a crupper for the hindquarters. The stableboy who looked after the the lord's war horse and other horses, including Lightning, also fell into Tom's area of responsibility. In fact, he felt somewhat overwhelmed with it all initially, and at night when he returned wearily to his quarters, he frequently confided to Margaret during supper that he wondered if he would ever master it all.

It was a difficult phase for them both. Each of them had to get used to a completely different lifestyle. Tom had suddenly found himself responsible for more than thirty men, had to learn the strange-sounding names associated with armour and knightly warfare, and found himself sometimes almost fighting for his life during the intensive sword-fighting and other weapons training he received from Sir William. Margaret, for her part as the captain's wife, had to learn how to conduct herself with the appropriate degree of decorum with the manor house personnel and other demesne personalities including the chaplain, who had not failed to notice her great beauty, and run a completely different household.

However, they were able to help each other, and in spite of the host of new and difficult problems that had to be overcome, their love for each other grew stronger as time passed. Late one evening early in the year of 1341 as they sat warming themselves in front of a log fire after supper, Margaret looked intensely at Tom, and then confided that she was expecting a child, wondering how he would react. Her concerns were groundless. He appeared initially to be startled, surprised and then delighted. He stood up and drew her to him, holding her closely and stroking her long black hair gently.

'Oh, Margaret, my love, how wonderful, how wonderful.' He took her by the shoulders, moved slightly backwards, and with concern asked how she felt. Did she have any pain? When would it be born? She stopped him with her laughter and told him that he would have to be patient; she felt fine and it would be born in the early summer.

And so it was. On the last day of June, their first child, Eric, was born. He was a sturdy son with a loud voice and fair hair. A son to be proud of, as all the servants and kitchen staff said as they fussed around Margaret, almost overwhelming her with their attention. Even Sir William and Lady Mortimer came to visit her, and the bond of friendship between the two women in the following months grew as the lord's wife became a frequent visitor, loving to hold the child in her arms while Margaret busied herself with other household tasks. Within a few weeks, the openness of the relationship was such that they discussed almost everything with each other, and it was clear for Margaret to see how much the very young Lady Mortimer longed to have a child of her own, and how lonely she felt during the frequent absences of her husband, either active in the parliament of the knights in London or busy with other political affairs, visiting important families both within or outside the county. Margaret also learnt how much Lady Mortimer admired Tom, who in spite of his many responsibilities, spent as much time as was possible with his wife and child. She confided that her husband considered Tom almost as the brother he never had, and trusted him implicitly in all affairs. He had been astonished how in such a short period of time Tom had grown in confidence and ability. He was now running the guard with the greatest efficiency and able to handle a variety of arms with greater skill than the lord himself. He had proved himself to be an outstanding leader in spite of his poor origins and lack of education!

Tom had the trust and respect of the manor soldiers, even the Genoese (with the one dangerous exception of Marco who had never forgiven him for winning the contest) and was recognised throughout the demesne as 'the' voice of authority in matters of archery training and community defence. Not only did Tom help the various demesne villages set up regular archery practice arrangements and contests on feast days, but also, in careful cooperation with the community elders, supervised their defence arrangements. The greatest danger at this particular time was not so much the possibility of raids from French invaders but more the threat of isolated attacks on individual homes or villagers, or theft of livestock by marauding bands of outlaws. Fortunately they were not at all well organised or disciplined, but their lawlessness and brutality was a constant danger.

Tom had a certain sympathy with the circumstances of some of them who had been so poor, sometimes made destitute by the tax and tithe demands of greedy landowners and clergy, that they had found it necessary to steal food to survive, and he sometimes closed his eyes to the odd theft of a chicken from somebody he knew could easily afford it. But if any type of violence had occurred, particularly whereby women had been abused, he was relentless in tracking the culprits down with the help of some of the younger villagers and a small contingent of Sir William's soldiers. If Sir William was available, he would preside at the official judgement, which in the case of most outlaws led to hanging. In his absence, the sheriff from Norwiche or even the chaplain would officiate at these courts.

During this period Tom was happy to spend a little more time with his brother Paul, who not only lived close to Castor manor, but also frequently participated in the archery contests and to Tom's delight (he himself no longer took part in them) was often the winner. Furthermore, Paul's work with the reeve had given him an excellent overview of the total layout of the demesne, and a profound knowledge of the most competent people of each village, which was of great help and value to Tom. Paul was often a very welcome guest at suppertime, and his wit and charm, in spite of his young years – he was just over seventeen – never failed to entertain and amuse both Tom and Margaret. Paul, for his part, was so happy to be in the company of the only real family he had and loved, clearly adored the infant Eric, sensing even at this time that he might well be a kindred spirit!

Paul was often a talking point with Tom and Margaret when they were alone after supper, and the young Eric was sound asleep. Margaret had been surprised one evening by a remark of her husband's concerning his brother. Paul certainly had an excellent future in demesne management, Tom had commented, that was clear for all to see. Within the next ten years he could well take over the reeve's job, since Stanley Pettit was already over fifty, and his brother had the ability and ambition to move even further ahead, given half the chance.

'But, you know, Margaret,' Tom added, 'young Paul is a restive spirit, and I'm not sure he will be content to wait such a long time for his chance. He really is a born trader, and one of these days, you mark my words, he will be off seeking his fortune elsewhere. It's somehow in his blood, I know it!'

Margaret, who was by nature a more cautious person, couldn't imagine that her brother-in-law could possibly leave behind all that he had built up, what with such a fine future ahead of him in Castor. Tom had merely smiled, shaking his head slightly, and ended the conversation with the words: 'Don't you be so sure, my love. You'll see. One day!' He then took her hand in his, pulled her gently to her feet and held her close to him. 'But never fear, Margaret, you won't lose me so easily. You are going to have to put up with me for the rest of your life whether you like it or not!' He looked deeply into her eyes and grinned at her mischievous expression as she led him to the bedroom.

Early in the following year – Tom would never forget the day, a beautiful but cold March morning – Sir William summoned him to the great hall. He was standing in front of the large fire warming his hands, talking rather loudly to a man standing next to him, holding a silver goblet. Tom didn't know the man, but had heard from the guard that an important visitor had arrived the previous day to see Lord Castor.

He was a tall, thin man with greying hair and a pale face, and, Tom thought immediately, cold, cruel eyes and a narrow, thin-lipped mouth set in what appeared to be an almost permanent sneer. Tom greeted Sir William first, turned slightly towards the visitor, inclined his head as a token of respect and politely acknowledged him with the words 'My lord, welcome to Castor!'

Sir William gestured towards the stranger and introduced him to Tom as Roderick McSwine, Earl of Dunghall, a visitor from the province of Ulster, Ireland. Tom had no idea where Ireland was and at that moment was not particularly interested, having taken an instant dislike to the earl. He was certain that his lord had summoned him for a more important reason than meeting a stranger, and he was right.

'Tom,' he began, 'you have now been with us here in Castor for a year and a half, and in that relatively short time have never failed to demonstrate your loyalty to me and my family, and have carried out your duties as captain of my guard, both here and within the demesne, in the most exemplary manner. In spite of all the difficulties you had at first, I could see that of course, you never complained and learnt very quickly. You are also probably the best longbowman in this country of ours, and now few could better you with sword, axe, mace, dagger or pike.'

Tom began to get a little nervous hearing Sir William talk so solemnly about his activities, which he considered to be his natural duty and which for the most part he fulfilled with pleasure and pride, and wondered what was coming next. He need not have been concerned!

'You have now grounded a family,' Sir William continued, 'and my dear wife, Lady Mortimer, insisted that you should be adequately rewarded for the services you have already rendered, and we know that you will continue to perform for us in the future, giving you the security you so justly deserve for both yourself and your dependants. I have therefore decided to endow you with a lifetime payment of twenty pounds a year, in addition of course to your daily keep here in our manor.'

Tom's mouth opened but no sound came out, and before he could even stammer his thanks, Sir William waved him to silence.

'You love that horse I lent you, and it's quite clear that Lightning only accepts you as his master – he threw me last week before he'd gone ten strides! He now belongs to you, Tom.'

The slight trace of a tear welled in Tom's eyes, he was so overjoyed and taken aback with the extent of Sir William's generosity, and for the first time in years was at a complete loss.

Sir William was aware of his captain's discomfort, but had still not quite finished. 'Lady Mortimer shares my views entirely, and wishes you to accept this mantle as a token of her esteem.' He then walked over to a chest close to the fireplace, picked up the mantle and handed it to Tom with a smile.

It was a beautiful woollen Lincoln scarlet mantle, lined with fur and trimmed with squirrel. Tom held it over his arm not able to believe that it really was meant for him. As he was continuing to look at it incredulously, he noticed that there was a coat of arms embroidered on the back and before he could pose the question Sir William added quickly: 'Tom, you are admiring the handiwork of my dear wife, Lady Mortimer, who designed it and spent long winter evenings embroidering it. These arms will now remain with you and your family forever.' He began to point out the detail while the visiting earl looked on with a cynical smile on his lips. He explained that the tower represented the small round tower of Castor manor, the lion was a link to the king, and the longbow and arrow and the crossed sword and dagger were the weapons that were Tom's special tools of trade.

'Tom, I know you had little schooling, and I want you to understand that motto beneath the shield. It's in Latin: *'tutor et ultor'*, and means 'protector and avenger', and by God I cannot think of anybody who better deserves it! Now be off with you, I have a lot of unfinished business to discuss with Sir Roderick before he departs for London.'

Still not sure that it could all be real, Tom bowed deeply, thanking Sir William profusely for his generosity and kindness, acknowledged the visitor, and took his leave, impatient now to recount it all to Margaret.

'So, Willy, that's the famous longbowman Tom Rollesby, eh?' Sir Roderick commented in a bantering tone. 'For the life of me I cannot understand how you can be so generous and talk the way you do with such a peasant! The man can't even read or write, and from what I just saw can hardly express himself in a civilised way. You know you've got to keep people like him in their place, or before you know it, they might get fancy ideas in their head. If you're not careful, he'll expect you soon to help him to get a knighthood, and he would never fit in with us, now would he?'

Sir William smiled, perhaps a trifle condescendingly, at his wife's cousin, and began to explain the background, achievements and talent of his young captain to the arrogant earl of Dunghall. 'That man is a born leader,' he added, 'and I would trust him with my life. The fact that by an accident of birth he comes from a poor family, and is still not yet familiar with all our ways is perfectly understandable to me. Of course, he was completely taken aback with the events of this morning, and appeared to have lost his tongue. He is in fact an eloquent speaker given the chance, and although there is no question that he is a man of action, he is very intelligent. You should see how he has improved our defences here and across the demesne. And yet, in spite of his strength and size, his incredible fighting ability, he is one of the most considerate and gentle persons I have ever met. No, Roderick, he doesn't have our education – he never had the chance. But I could not wish to have a better captain for my guard than Thomas Rollesby!'

The earl, noting the emotion of Sir William, decided to change the subject, since it had nothing whatsover to do with the real purpose of his visit. As a distant cousin of Lady Mortimer whose father, long deceased, had once been governor of Ireland, it was quite normal that he should pay her and her husband a visit. He was a man of great wealth and influence in the county of Donegal, or Dunghall as it was known locally, whose noble position inherited from his father made it quite natural for him to participate in the king's parliament from time to time. He had landed at Yermouth, and prior to travelling on to London had decided to visit his English relative to see if he could interest her husband in his business and political plans, although he had no intention of putting all his cards on the table until he had sounded out Sir William a little more. The lord of Castor, for his part, did not feel particularly at ease with his wife's relative, but of course offered the hospitality that his position demanded. Other than small talk and drinking an 'aqua vitae' called whisky which appeared to be Roderick's preferred drink (he had presented him with a gift of two kegs of it the previous day on his arrival at the manor house), up until the conversation with Tom Rollesby that morning they had not discussed anything of particular importance. He knew the earl was a large landowner and also a very important producer of wool, but not much else, and was interested to hear what was really on his mind.

The earl began to talk about the activities of the 'staple' and the ever-increasing level of taxation that the king was demanding from the wool merchants, parliament and the church to support his efforts to build up an efficient, well-armed, well-trained army. He paused to see what effects his words were having on Sir William, and noting that he was more or less nodding in agreement, felt encouraged to continue. The previous year, he added, the taxes that had been traditionally one-tenth or one-fifteenth of the value of all movable property in the total shires and boroughs of the land had been increased to one-ninth. In addition to that, the parliament of March 1340 had agreed to a tax of forty shillings on every sack of exported wool. This, he added, is what you can expect with commoners in the parliament. The burgesses – the citizens of the boroughs or walled towns – didn't know any better, he said, and were too easily persuaded by the king. The earl called this scandalous and if it continued he felt it could destroy the wealth and power of the nobility.

Sir William was clearly also concerned with paying more taxes, but began to feel a little nervous with the way the conversation was now heading. When Sir Roderick began to criticise the king even more openly, commenting negatively on the various campaigns and forays into France and other territories of King Philippe, he intervened immediately, pointing out the successful episode at Sluys, Flanders, where they had enjoyed an incredible victory against a much larger French force, which also included Spanish and Genoese troops. He had been there and knew exactly what had happened and the role King Edward had played, may God continue to protect him.

Perceiving his host's loyalty and feelings towards the king, Sir Roderick backed away from this subject and began to talk in more detail about the activities of the 'staple' and the ruinous wool taxes. He pointed out that the taxes in wool and on wool had reached the stage whereby it was hardly worthwhile to be involved in the business as a producer. He had heard that a total monopoly of the staple was soon to be set up in Bruges, Flanders, with the English staple cities acting primarily as wool-collecting points. He was personally convinced that the major English merchants running the staple would be certain to use their enormous power to keep wool prices down, making the situation for the producers even more ruinous. He certainly intended to make his voice heard in parliament during the next session, and would lobby as many of the lords as he could on this issue, and trusted he would also have Sir William's support.

He was an extremely fluent and persuasive speaker, albeit with a relatively strong accent of his native Ireland, and Sir William, also considerably affected by the new taxes, agreed immediately to support Roderick in this matter. However, as the earl began to probe further, never actually mentioning the word 'smuggle', but hinting at possibilities to circumnavigate the official channels of collection with a few sacks, perhaps cooperating with interested Italian buyers, who were always interested in top quality wool, Sir William became increasingly uncomfortable. He agreed that he himself had good connections with several merchants both in and around the city of Norwiche, and his family knew the east coast shipping traders well, but he personally would not get involved in activities that were illegal. Much to the obvious annoyance of the earl, Sir William refused to discuss it any longer and switched the conversation to other demesne matters including the magnificent hunting opportunities of the area, suggesting finally that, although it wasn't quite the 'time of grease' when the bucks and harts were at their fattest, he would arrange a hunt for his guest on the following day.

And so it was by chance that Sir Roderick got to know Marco Paulini, who had been instructed by Tom to accompany the hunting party as a guard.

9

Norwiche – The Encounter

On the day of the hunt, a manor house servant sent by the steward called at Paul's cottage at daybreak to inform him that Mr Stanley was ill in bed, and that he should report to him immediately. Paul had already washed and dressed before the servant arrived, and after taking a swig of milk from an earthenware jug on the table, he quickly saddled Betsy, and a little anxiously, galloped off to see the reeve.

'Ah, there you are, Master Paul,' the reeve wheezed, still lying in bed, while his wife busied herself with the household chores. 'It didn't take you long to get here. Haven't you been to bed yet, eh?' He grinned mischievously.

'Of course, I have Mr Pettit,' Paul replied. 'I got here as quickly as I could to see what was up. How are you? Is it bad? Can I get you anything?'

'Goodness me, no, thank you, Master Paul. Mrs Pettit has made me her special brew and this chill, or whatever it is, should be gone in a few days, and I'll be as right as rain! But we badly need some supplies from Norwiche and I also want you to call in at the guildhall and make contact with Mr Jeffries, our wool agent, to make sure he makes an early call on us next month. See what you can find out about prices this year, so we can make our plans accordingly. We need ruddle, candles and I want to try out some different varieties of corn this year. See what's available in the market and bring back a dozen sacks or so.' The reeve had to stop for a moment, racked by a coughing and sneezing fit, which brought Mrs Pettit immediately to him, telling him to lie down and to go back to sleep, or he would never get better.

'Away with you, woman,' he called with mock severity, 'we are almost done now, and it's important business.' He smiled at Paul, shaking his head and muttered 'Women!'

'Now, Master Paul,' he continued, 'where were we? Ah, yes. You'll need four packhorses from the manor stables, and don't forget to take their feed with you. And get that brother of yours to give you a guard. I know you can take care of yourself but the roads are very dangerous. From what I hear there are several outlaw bands in the neighbourhood, and they'll steal anything they can lay their hands on. The steward will give you some money for the trip, and enjoy yourself in Norwiche, but be careful. Don't trust anybody you don't know, and you can't always trust *them.* By the way, I almost forgot. My memory is getting terrible these days. Cross the Burre at Stokesbye – you should know that well enough – skirt to the south of Acle and then head due west until you see the city. As you get nearer, follow the River Yerus round to the south and west of the city up to the gate of St Gyles and enter there. There is a good, reliable stable close to a chapel on the edge of some large fields. Ask for Henry Tyler, tell him who you are and he'll take good care of the horses and anything else you care to leave with him for only a penny a day. Ask him to direct you to the Mitre Inn, it's close to the market and the guildhall, where I'm sure you'll find a warm, clean bed, and the food is also very good. Tell the landlord, David Cook – he comes from a small borough to the south of us – that you work for Stanley Pettit of Castor, and he'll see you're well taken care of.' The reeve grinned at Paul, and gave him a knowing look. 'You'll need a day for each way and I reckon you should be able to complete the business in two to three days, so if you set off at daybreak tomorrow, you should be back by next Monday at the latest. I had wanted to do this trip with you as a special treat, but as you can see I'm bound in bed for the next few days. So be off with you, Master Paul, and keep a sharp watch out for those bandits!'

Paul rode quickly back to the manor house to talk to the steward about the arrangements he had to make for the reeve, not forgetting the money he needed, of course! The steward was an old man of at least sixty-five, known to everyone as Mr S. He was fiercely loyal to the lord and his family, and he had been in charge of the household for as long as any of the servants could remember. Mrs Galston had once told Paul that she had heard that he had been taken in by the family when he was a baby, and that there was some sort of family scandal attached to it, but she did not know the details. She only knew that he kept the most careful record of household expenditures and one always had to account for every penny spent or there was hell to pay!

Mr S listened politely to what the reeve had told Paul, noted the items that were to be purchased, checked his records of previous costs, counted out the sum of eight shillings and sixpence which he took from a small leather pouch, noted the sum on a large parchment sheet and asked Paul to initial the entry. He then handed the money to Paul and told him to take good care of it and return whatever was left when he came back from Norwiche. He instructed a servant to go to the stables and help the groom get the four packhorses ready for the following morning, making sure everything would be done so that Master Paul could leave at daybreak. In spite of his apparent severity, he liked Paul. Although he rarely showed any trace of emotion, he put his hand on Paul's shoulder and bade him 'God speed', instructing him to make sure that his brother made at least one guard available for the journey.

A little later, Tom listened to his brother's request and would have liked to have given him more protection, but could only spare one man at that time. He explained there were two groups out on patrol due to outlaw raids that had been made in the area, and another led by Marco Paulini had just left to escort an important visitor on his way to London. 'Make sure you take your longbow with you, Paul,' he advised him earnestly, 'and don't be afraid to use it if necessary. There is a particularly evil bunch in the shire from what I hear, and if you show any signs of weakness, they'll attack immediately.' He also took Paul to the armoury in the small round tower, and handed him a long ballock dagger in a beautifully carved leather sheath. 'And keep that with you at all times,' he said. 'Your life could depend on it!' He hugged his brother affectionately, told him he would also keep a lookout for him when he himself was out and about the demesne, and reminded him that he hadn't been to visit them for some time, and as soon as he returned from Norwiche he must come for supper or Margaret would not forgive him!

'How can I refuse an offer like that, Tom?' he laughingly replied. 'Without fail, I promise!' And he then left his brother to make the rest of the necessary preparations.

It was a cold, rainy morning when Paul, accompanied by one of the Genoese crossbowmen, filed out of the stable area, riding easily on Betsy, and leading the four packhorses tied one behind the other. Both men had been given some hot wine and bread for breakfast by Mrs Galston, and sufficient provisions for a journey to London and back, Paul had teasingly added! The cook had always had a soft spot for Paul as he well knew, and when he kissed her on the cheek at his departure, he thanked her for her kindness, promising to bring back a little surprise for her.

Keeping the River Burre in sight for most of the way to Stokesbye, and deliberately avoiding the wooded areas to the north, they stayed in the meadowlands Paul knew so well. The land was very wet, and he skirted the marshy areas, pointing out the various landmarks on the way to the initially very quiet Genoese crossbowman, whose weapon was already spanned and within easy reach. He identified the many types of wildfowl they saw flying close to the river or wading in the reeds, and as they passed the first of the several flocks of sheep they were bound to see on the way to Stokesbye and then Norwiche, he recounted his experiences with the shepherd Ned Giles and some of the others.

Paul learnt then that the Genoese soldier's father had also been a shepherd – in fact had given him the same name of Federico – and within a short time their relationship began to subtly change. By the time they reached Stokesbye, they were conversing like old friends, and Paul told him about his earlier life there with his brother Tom. The Genoese listened intently, occasionally asking the odd question in his lilting accent, and suddenly added how much he now respected Paul's elder brother. It had not always been the case, he had explained, since he and his fellow crossbowmen were initially far from pleased to be led by someone they believed to be a common bowman, particularly since they originated from what was considered to be an élite force. However, he continued, that soon changed as they saw how competent a leader he was, always perfectly fair in the handling of the soldiers, but at the same time insistent in his demands for good discipline and the highest standards of operation. But, he added, he was not at all sure about the loyalty of Marco, who hadn't been able to accept the contest results at all, and was always looking to see if he could find some fault or other as far as the captain was concerned. He never clearly expressed his feelings about Tom, he confided, but he sensed he somehow hated him. Federico shrugged his shoulders then, saying that he hoped he was wrong and they should perhaps change the subject.

At midday, two miles or so to the west of Acle, they decided to stop for a light meal and tether the horses under the shelter of a clump of pine trees on a hillside that kept them out of sight of prying eyes, and gave them a clear view of the countryside for several miles. The horses had had the opportunity to drink on the way and were content to munch from the bag of oats that Paul gave each of them, while Federico, ever watchful for any kind of movement around them, carefully sliced the cold meat the cook had given them and set it out on a wooden platter with large chunks of rye bread. He then took a gourd of wine from his saddlebag and waited for Paul to join him before starting to eat.

It had stopped raining an hour or so before they halted, the clouds had disappeared, and in spite of the nip in the air, as they munched a couple of apples Mrs Galston had also dropped into the saddlebags, they began to enjoy the effect of having well-filled stomachs and the warming rays of the early spring sunshine on their faces and damp clothing. Federico had been telling Paul about his childhood, and how his poor family had rejoiced when a local, wealthy and titled family had taken him on first as a servant and then had him trained to carry arms, and become expert with the crossbow. He had started to describe how he became a mercenary soldier and his earlier escapades when he suddenly stopped, and pointed to a track about half a mile from where they sat, drawing Paul's attention to some movement there.

A group of some fifteen to twenty people, mainly men, but he could also make out two or three women, were filing slowly away from them in a northerly direction. The sun glinted on the weapons carried by four men on horseback, and the other men were armed with longbows. Most of them were also carrying packs on their backs.

'Keep perfectly still, Paul!' Federico hissed. 'They must not see us. I'm sure they're outlaws.' They watched them until they were out of sight, and Federico gave a sigh of relief, adding that there were probably too many of them to handle if they had attacked as they looked to be a bit better organised than some of the rabble he had encountered more recently in the area.

Tom had told his brother a little about the activities of some of the criminals in the area, but had never gone into much detail, not wanting to alarm Margaret, even though he knew she was safe enough so close to the manor house. Federico filled in the blank spaces of Paul's knowledge. He explained that many of the outlaws were ex-soldiers who had returned to England without any booty, in spite of all the promises that had been made to them. Frequently, they had not received any pay at all from their masters, who pocketed the money granted by the king or parliament for their services. When they returned home penniless, sometimes wounded or crippled even, their families often could not help them since they had no money either. What little they had was frequently swallowed up by the tithes and taxes of greedy landowners, including many of the clergy, and so some of them became outlaws, stealing and sometimes killing to feed themselves and their families. Some outlaws were worse than others, Federico noted ruefully. Some of them seemed to take pleasure in causing suffering and were nothing better than brutal beasts. Not content with stealing what they needed, they tortured, maimed and killed their victims. Women were ravished. Babies were slaughtered. You could not imagine what some of your fellow countrymen were capable of doing to their own people even, he concluded. Federico was almost beside himself with anger at this stage, and Paul had difficulty in calming him down so they could continue their journey.

Both of them were in a somewhat pensive mood for the following hour or so, watching out carefully for possible ambushes or suspicious movements, but fortunately there were no encounters with criminals of any kind. As they drew nearer to Norwiche their mood became lighter. They felt less threatened and were able to use well-beaten tracks, frequently meeting or overtaking groups of people also on the way to Norwiche.

These were not just merchants or peddlars carrying their wares by packhorse or on their backs. It seemed that a cross-section of society was on the road: knights with their retainers and monks with their servants all mounted on splendid horses; peasants carrying baskets laden with vegetables or fruit, or sitting in carts drawn by oxen or a horse, laden with sacks of corn or bales of straw on the way to market. Sometimes they were accompanied by a travelling 'jougleur' singing an ancient ballad, or minstrels playing flutes, pipes, flageolets, dulcimers, viols, tabors and cymbals and other instruments that neither Paul nor Federico had ever seen before. They saw carpenters, weavers, dyers, tapestry-makers, haberdashers, friars, wounded soldiers and beggars, some of whom were terribly mutilated or blind and led by dogs. Paul was shocked to see one beggar with broken and deformed legs, crawling alone on all fours. Wooden blocks were tied onto his knees and his hands were looped onto two other wooden blocks with a sort of handle or bar across the back of his hands. Paul was so moved that he stopped, giving the beggar a halfpenny of his own money, while Federico, smiling and ever-watchful, looked on.

By mid-afternoon, they could see the city walls and towers of Norwiche, and following the river round to the west as the reeve had instructed, by late afternoon reached the gate of St Gyles. Within a few minutes of entering the city they saw the fields on their right hand side and had no difficulty in locating the stables belonging to Henry Tyler, close by a solitary chapel. Once the horses were taken care of (Paul also left his longbow and arrows with the stable owner, but Federico refused to be parted from his crossbow and windlass) they asked for the directions to the Mitre Inn and made their way diagonally across the fields in the failing light towards what Henry Tyler had described as the 'cathedrall churche'.

They had only gone about two hundred paces, Paul carrying a saddlebag containing clean underclothes, and a purse in his left hand and in the right his dagger, and Federico the windlass and crossbow hooked over his left shoulder, his right hand in easy reach of his sword, when Paul suddenly stopped, alarmed by a strange creaking sound. Federico immediately drew his sword and they both stood stock still, peering into the gloom around them, listening carefully. The noise appeared to be coming from a tree to their left and they moved slowly and cautiously towards it, alert for any kind of movement. As they drew nearer, Federico broke the silence with a chuckle, adding in an amused tone, 'It's nothing, Paul, just a corpse hanging from that large branch there.' He pointed it out with his sword. 'This must be the city hanging ground.' Paul shuddered a little at the thought. He'd seen it before often enough, but unlike many others hardened to the fate of the common criminal, he had never been able to come fully to terms with the brutality and horrible finality of it all.

Federico told him he was a 'romantic', when Paul explained this to him, and laughed again, and then said they should get a move on before it got any darker, or they would never find the inn, and he was tired and hungry!

Keeping the church of St Stephen's to their right as instructed, they crossed the deserted market-place. This was partially illuminated by lantern light shining through the windows of haberdashery and other stores where employees were busy cleaning up and preparing for the following day's trade. Light also came from the leaded-glass windows of several taverns, filled mainly with market traders and workers from the cloth industry and other small businesses scattered throughout the city. They walked briskly up the cobblestoned high street keeping watch for possible footpads lurking in the shadows looking for an easy victim to rob, and shortly came to Mitre Lane without incident. The stable owner had told them that they should follow this lane through a small colony of fullers and weavers cottages that were grouped close to the river, which flowed right through the city. They couldn't possibly miss the inn that was on the right-hand side.

They heard the raucous laughter before they saw the inn. It was a large, three-storeyed building set back from the road, with a large garden around it. A path led to a yard at the back and they could smell the stables from the front, where there were several other wooden sheds containing straw, animal feed, logs and other provisions, grouped closely by the kitchen door.

As well as the traditional symbol of a bush attached above the main door, another sign hung alongside with the name of the inn, 'The Mitre', painted above an illustration of a bishop's ceremonial headgear. Through the large windows on each side of the door they could see that the parlour was full and the flames of a log fire on the far side cast an inviting glow across the whole room. Paul pushed the door open and they stepped inside.

There was a momentary pause in the many conversations taking place as the inn guests stopped to look the visitors over, and once their curiosity was satisfied and seeing no threat, they continued as if Paul and Federico did not exist. Taking off their cloaks, they walked over the rush-covered floor to the fire to warm their hands and take the chill off their damp clothes. A few minutes later, seeing an empty table they moved over from the fire and sat down, waiting for the serving girl to take their order. Federico leant his crossbow and windlass against the wall behind his bench seat and Paul did likewise with his saddlebag, both of them then looking around at the motley collection of noisy guests, mostly getting rapidly drunk quaffing large mugs of ale or taking generous servings of steaming grog from bowls set on the plank tabletops.

Judging from the conversations the patrons were mainly travelling merchants or wool broggers who bought up wool and woolfells in small quantities for delivery to wool wholesalers. Paul was fascinated to eavesdrop a little and also interested to see that none of them was short of money, judging by the way they were consuming their drinks and generously tipping the serving girls, often slipping a free hand up their skirts at the same time! Some of them were also winning or losing quite large sums playing dice, and Paul wondered if one of them was perhaps a professional gambler, judging by the number of times he seemed to win. But that's their business, he thought. I have to work too hard for the little money I earn, and I'm not going to lose it that way!

His attention was then drawn to a man who was obviously wealthy, at least by the way he was dressed, sitting at the next table with his servant. A heavy, fur-lined woollen cloak trimmed with squirrel was carelessly lying on a stool next to him, and Paul could see that his doublet and tight-fitting hose were of a blue silk, the quality of which he had not seen before, and that his black, soft leather shoes had silver buckles. When he spoke, it was always with a great deal of hand movement, to the extent that one could not fail to notice the large-stoned rings on the pudgy fingers of both hands. Looking more closely at his face, the eyes, nose and tightly pinched lips reminded Paul of a hawk he had once seen, tearing a young rabbit to pieces, and he shuddered inwardly at the thought.

The man had ordered the best wine in the house and while the attractive young server was pouring it into his glass, Paul noticed how he was staring into the top of the girl's smock. As she began to move to serve the servant, he caught hold of her arm and pulled her back to whisper something in her ear. She immediately blushed and with extreme difficulty managed to disengage herself from the clutches of the licentious guest, put the wine pitcher on the table and fled in the direction of the kitchen.

What a swine, Paul thought and turned back to Federico who gave him a knowing look, also having witnessed the scene. Shortly afterwards, a man whom Paul assumed was the landlord brought a tray of food and set it down on the next table, exchanged a few polite words with the guest, came over to their table, and asked them what they would like to eat and drink. Before ordering, Paul introduced himself and Federico, mentioned the reeve's name and asked if they could stay at the inn for the next three or four nights. The landlord smiled when he heard Stanley Pettit's name, called out to one of the servers and told her to make sure the chambermaids got room eleven prepared and warmed for the two guests.

The meal was excellent – a game soup, followed by cutlets of wild boar served on bread 'trenchers', sweetmeats followed by fruit, all washed down with a good ale. While they ate, the landlord, David Cook, joined them for a while, pleased to talk about how things were in Castor and the immediate area. Paul was astonished and proud to discover that the landlord knew about Tom and how much he was respected even by those who had not met him personally, such was his reputation! David Cook in turn then began to tell them where he came from – a small village called Wulpet, in the hundred of Thedwardstre, within the shire of Suffolke. His father had worked in the brickworks just outside the village, and in fact had eventually become the foreman there, responsible for the day-to-day running of the business. To his father's great disappointment, he had no interest in bricks, finding himself much more at ease and happy working with sheep and wool in general. One day he had by chance met a Flemish master weaver, who had been travelling in the area, helping the local people improve their spinning and weaving techniques so that better quality cloth could be produced. The man was called John Kemp, he explained, and he was able to spend a few days with him, watching, listening and learning. It was fascinating and he learnt a lot. Quite a few weavers from Flanders had settled in the area in the following years he said, and one could see that the cloth industry would one day perhaps be even more important than the production of wool. He himself had preferred to make his money as a wool brogger, with a little bit of smuggling on the side!

Paul then asked him why he had given it all up and gone to Norwiche to run an inn. The landlord looked somewhat pensive and explained that it was a long story, and since it was getting late and they must be tired, he would keep it very short. Now that the visitors at the next table had gone off to bed, he could talk more freely, he said.

He had over the years developed a good business. He paid fair prices for the wool and had established excellent relations with smaller producers all over the county. For some people, he added, he had become too successful. Particularly in the shire of Suffolke, the abbey of Burye St Edmunds had more or less a monopoly of the wool business, and did not take kindly to any form of competition. The small farmers who had been happy to sell their wool to him were one after the other threatened with excommunication, accused of leading heretical practices and witchcraft, and made to pay high fines until they agreed to supply only the monks, at much lower prices, naturally! He couldn't blame the farmers and smallholders when they told him what had happened, but it was clear he couldn't survive against that sort of competition. Even if he had continued, he explained, it would only have been a matter of time before he would have been accused of something similar.

'They talk about doing God's work,' he hissed, 'but for me, and particularly with what I have seen here, they and their kind are more like disciples of the Devil himself! You probably saw that one with his servant who was sitting there.' He pointed to the next table and when they both nodded, he added, 'He's not a monk, but a bishop from Winchester. One of the richest men in England, they say, but a nasty piece of work, if you ask me. Just talk to some of the girls working here and they'll soon tell you what he's like! Anyway, to get back to your question, Paul, I had saved quite a bit of money and I left Wulpet with a group of merchants one day, who were heading for Norwiche, and decided to try my luck here. It's getting very late now and I can see you're both tired, so let me tell you the rest another evening before you go, eh?'

As interesting as it all was, neither man needed much persuasion. The strong ale had also taken its toll, and they thankfully took the lantern the landlord handed them and made their way upstairs to room eleven which was at the back of the inn. On the way to the room Paul asked Federico if he knew where Winchester was, and although not too sure he replied he believed it to be somewhere close to the south coast not so far from the haven of Southampton.

Pushing open the door of room eleven, Paul was delighted to see that a small log fire was burning and the room smelt pleasantly warm and dry. There were also two truckle beds, each with clean straw covered by a coarse linen sheet with sheepfells lying on top. Between the beds was a large chest for their valuables and on the walls behind the top of each bed were several wooden hooks, ideal for hanging their cloaks and weapons. What luxury, Paul thought, and both he and Federico quickly undressed, put their boots at the foot of the bed and laid tunics, breeches, stockings and underclothes on the chest. Paul extinguished the lantern, wished Federico a good night and they both pulled back the sheepfells and thankfully slipped into their beds.

With a start Paul realised he was not alone! A warm, smooth-skinned, shapely female body moved over to him, a hand was placed over his mouth and a voice whispering in his ear told him to relax and enjoy himself! Her other hand moved slowly down his muscular chest and flat stomach to his groin and began to caress him. In spite of his initial fatigue, he responded almost immediately. He reached for her breasts, stroking them and playing with her nipples until he felt them harden, tracing a pattern around them slowly with the index finger of each hand and then holding them between finger and thumb, he pinched them gently as she squirmed in ecstasy at his side. His own pulse quickening each minute, he rolled her on to her back and moved on top of her as she parted her legs, helping him to find her moistness. The penetration – his first – was exquisite. He rode her, first slowly and then as his excitement increased, almost with a frenzy until he suddenly ejaculated, releasing all the bottled-up passion of his young eighteen years. Gasping, with perspiration running down his back, he lay on her, caressing her face, gently brushing the long hair away from her eyes. Ever since the little episode with Nellie he had wondered what it would be like to make love and now he knew! The intensity of the experience had taken him by surprise, and he also couldn't remember ever before feeling so at peace as he lay there now, recovering from the exertions of the previous few minutes. He realised he didn't even know her name, and he had also completely forgotten about Federico in the other bed only two paces away from him. Looking over he saw that he didn't need to worry about his companion who was still busily engaged in very energetic activity with his unknown bed partner.

'What's your name? How come you are here?' he asked softly, but earnestly, sitting up and looking at the girl intently.

She smiled, put a finger on his lips, then both hands around his neck, and pulled him down to her and kissed him. 'You ask too many questions,' she replied teasingly. 'I'll tell you later, if you are a good boy! I can't believe you are finished already, not with this body here.' She investigated the sensitive areas carefully, until he responded as she had anticipated. 'Come here, give it to me now, slowly and with feeling.'

She held him firmly, moving under him in perfect rhythm to his thrusting, putting his hands to her breasts, using him as a tool for her pleasure. As she herself neared her climax, she reached for his groin, suddenly arched her back and began uttering muffled cries, spurring him on to his almost simultaneous orgasm.

A little later, she patted him on the face, told him her name was Rosie, and that she belonged to the house, and that she and her companion must leave now. She quickly got out of the bed, calling to her friend that it was time to leave, and like two ghosts they slipped out of the room, gently closing the door behind them. Paul turned over, and within seconds drifted into a deep sleep.

Early the next morning, Federico shook Paul awake, laughingly asking him how he had enjoyed the night.

'Now you know why the reeve was disappointed he couldn't travel to Norwiche this time, eh Paul! Come on, get up now! You told me earlier there was a lot to do and I obviously need to keep an eye on you, or goodness knows what you will get up to!'

Once dressed, they went downstairs to the yard and washed at the water trough, waiting their turn as they discovered that the bishop's guard and the rest of his retinue had overnighted in some of the outbuildings around the yard, and they too were making an early start. They caught the smell of freshly baked bread coming from the kitchen and hurried back into the inn where they had eaten the night before, their mouths watering in anticipation.

The bread was delicious, washed down with a jug of ale, and as they sat there discussing the pleasant surprise of the previous evening and then how they should go about their purchases, and when the best time would be to visit the guildhall, David Cook joined them briefly. He asked them smilingly if they had slept well, and seeing Paul's initial confusion, laughed, clapped him on the back and told him not to worry and that it wouldn't show on their bill when they left. It was all part of the service at the Mitre!

He told Paul, answering his question concerning the likely whereabouts of the wool agent Mr Jeffries, to go first to the guildhall and almost certainly somebody there would know how best to contact him. The main part of the market would be open on Thursday he explained, and so they had plenty of time today for other purchases and to have a look around the city. However he advised them to keep a watch on their purses as there were pickpockets everywhere!

Back in their room, Paul unlocked the chest, took out his purse from the saddlebag and fastened it with two leather thongs to a broad belt he wore over his tunic, also making sure his dagger was easily accessible on the left side. Federico adjusted his sword, and then, securing the chest, they draped cloaks around their shoulders, walked down the creaking, wooden stairs and pushed open the door leading into Mitre Lane.

It was just beginning to get light but there was already a great deal of activity around the cottages in the lane. The front doors were open, young children were scampering in and out, frequently being scolded for getting in the way as their mothers swept out soiled rushes and other litter with brooms made of bound twigs. It had been too dark the previous evening to see that there were also one or two workshops between the cottages, all backing onto a stream which flowed into the Yerus, the main river of the city. They could hear the sound of the mill not far away, supplying water for the cloth that was being pounded to thicken it and consolidate the weave. They glimpsed weavers at a loom in one of the workshops, throwing the shuttle backwards and forwards between the warp threads, while alternately raising and lowering them by means of pedals. Paul was fascinated by this new world of clothmaking, and began to understand better what the landlord had told him about the weavers from Flanders. They also saw women sitting by the main windows of their cottages spinning wool on hand-turned wooden wheels, which Paul had frequently seen before in the demesne.

Even though they had stopped several times to watch the various activities of the cloth workers, they soon came to the cobblestoned high street which was already thronged with people of all types. The taverns and alehouses with their brooms hanging out on the wall above the door to signify their trade, were already busy serving ale and wine. Street vendors were offering hot pies, chestnuts, stockfish and a host of other foods; beggars with horrible sores or mutilated limbs, dressed in rags, held out a hand whining for alms, looking hopefully and pathetically at the faces of the passers-by who generally ignored them; workmen with handcarts loaded with bales of wool or sometimes finished or partially finished cloth, pushed their way noisily past them; housewives with baskets, merchants with leather bags, travellers on foot, sometimes on horseback, friars and priests, were all making their way up or down the high street. There was hardly room to move at times, and Paul understood why the landlord had warned them about pickpockets!

Lower down, they passed some fine wooden beam and brick houses belonging to wealthy merchants and landowners, and nearby, the narrow-fronted entrances of bakers, butchers, fruit and vegetable shops, candlemakers, leather-goods shops, silver and goldsmiths, shoe, clothing and haberdashery shops and a host of others in the narrow lanes leading off both sides of the street.

Federico was also fascinated by these aspects of town life that were foreign to him, and although sharing the excitement and interest of Paul, nevertheless kept a permanent wary eye open for thieves or potential trouble of any kind. It was, however the smell of horse manure, decaying food and other rubbish which provided a strong motivation to keep moving! They caught a glimpse of the castle walls at the end of a side street on their left side, and then found themselves on the edge of the market square.

The guildhall of the society of wool producers and clothmakers stood at the far side of the square. It was an impressive stucco-faced, two-storeyed building, dominating all others around it. From a distance they saw the large, leaded windows of the main hall on the top floor and what appeared to be intricately carved cornerposts and other main timbers. As they got nearer, Paul's attention was momentarily diverted by a woman sitting with her legs in stocks and a sign above her which read: 'Caught giving false ale measures.' A group of people were standing around her laughing and jeering while some small boys were playing some sort of game behind her back. Federico urged him to go past since it was nothing to do with them, and they had more important business to attend to.

The massive oaken doors of the guildhall were open and they walked up the stone steps into a reception room where a uniformed attendant asked if he could help them. They were lucky. The agent Mr Robert Jeffries was well-known and was in the main hall with some friends and colleagues, and if they would be so kind as to wait in the reception room, he said, a servant would be sent to advise Mr Jeffries of the visitors below. While waiting for the agent, Paul walked around the large room, admiring the portraits hanging on all the wood-panelled walls, of, he supposed, famous merchants. He was admiring and commenting on the fine clothes of these gentlemen with Federico when a middle-aged, alert-looking man, walking with a slight limp and leaning a little on a walking stick with a silver nob on it came up to them and introduced himself as Robert Jeffries. Paul immediately explained who he and Federico were, where they came from and the purpose of their visit. Hearing Stanley Pettit's name, the agent smiled pleasantly and suggested that since they had several things to discuss, perhaps they should step out with him to a quiet winehouse nearby where they could talk in comfort.

The winehouse was in a narrow lane more or less behind the guildhall, set back in an attractive garden, almost concealed from the road by high evergreen bushes behind a stone wall. There was a guard at the gate to keep out unwelcome visitors, and he seemed to recognise the agent as he quickly opened the iron-barred gate and let them in. Once inside the building, a liveried servant led them to a small private room and they were quickly served with a pitcher of the finest Burgundy.

Seated at a highly-polished round table, Mr Jeffries raised his goblet, gave a toast to the king, and they began to sip the excellent, refreshing wine. Looking directly at Paul, the agent began the conversation. 'Now, young man, tell me about how things are going in Castor and what exactly does Stanley Pettit want?'

He listened carefully to Paul's description of the demesne's affairs, particularly the status of the sheep and timing plans for the shearing, nodding thoughtfully. He agreed with Paul that he would visit the reeve in the first week of April to confirm prices and arrange transport of the wool purchased. When Paul began to probe on current market prices per sack, the agent became somewhat defensive and suggested a price of 'probably around three to four pounds, depending on the quality.' He looked a little surprised when Paul smiled and told him firmly but politely that the Castor quality was worth at least double that amount, and they had already had enquiries from an interested Italian buyer willing to pay much more than he now offered. As anticipated, the agent then began to talk about the legal rights of the Norwiche 'staple', trying to throw Paul off balance, and was surprised when he was politely reminded that they naturally had great respect for the offices of the 'staple', but the producers were not obliged to sell to them. That may change one day of course, he agreed, but provided they duly paid their taxes, which they did, they could currently sell to whom they chose! He quickly added that they had always been happy to deal with Mr Jeffries and were sure that this year would be no exception, believing that in the following weeks both the market and the quality of the Castor demesne wool would enable him to increase his offer and still be able to enjoy a good profit for himself.

The discussion continued in this vein for some time, with arguments, counter-arguments and viewpoints being mutually exchanged, and the agent was astonished at the skill Paul used with his ripostes, wondering how someone so young could be so wise. Federico also, not involved in the discussion at all, had been listening carefully, and his respect for Paul grew accordingly.

Suddenly, the agent began to laugh in a good-natured way, clapped Paul on the shoulder, and told him he was sure they would come to an amicable agreement the following month, and he would look forward to seeing the reeve, and of course his most competent assistant, then. In the meantime, they should enjoy their wine, as he must shortly leave to attend a meeting with a few merchants at midday.

Mr Jeffries left some coins on the table and ushered them out of the room a few minutes later. As they were just stepping out of the main door, Federico stopped suddenly, held Paul's arm and pointed to three men walking towards the garden gate ahead of them. 'That's Marco there in front of us,' he whispered. 'I wonder what he's doing here of all places? And that tall, thin man with the grey hair looks like the lord that visited Castor a few days ago. I saw him leave with Marco and an escort shortly before we left.'

Mr Jeffries also stopped with his guests, and observed the men just passing through the gate, adding drily and quietly:

'I also recognise one of them. The short, fat man with the loud voice is none other than the rather infamous scoundrel, the count 'de Kessinger', frequently involved in political intrigues of one sort or another, and suspected of organising large-scale wool smuggling. You can't trust him as far as you can throw him, believe me! Never turn your back on that one!'

10

Norwiche – The Market and other Affairs

Mr Jeffries left them at the gate of the exclusive tavern, returning to his meeting at the guildhall, leaving both Federico and Paul wondering at the significance of what they had just learned. Marco Paulini, the leader of the escort from Castor, appeared to be on friendly terms with the visiting earl, supposedly on his way to London, and apparently they were both involved with a local aristocrat of extremely dubious reputation!

Paul concluded there was nothing they could do about it at that stage, and since the market was not open until the next day, they could spend a few hours looking around the city before returning to the Mitre.

Following the lane to the end, they discovered that it led into a wider street that rose steeply up to the stone walls of the castle, which, at the top of a hill completely dominated the city. Behind these walls they could see a very large, almost rectangular tower, rising to what Federico estimated to be at least thirty paces, built of ashlar blocks of stone. The walls had pilaster buttresses with long, narrow windows between them on each floor and a battlemented parapet at the top. Federico told Paul that it reminded him of castles he had seen in France some years previously, during his earlier service prior to joining the guard at Castor.

They walked round part of the outside walls to the heavily-guarded main entrance, passing a jail, a blacksmith's, an armourer's, a fletcher's shop and a cartwright's workshop in the process. This was also a very busy and noisy quarter of the city. What with hammering from the workshops, people leading horses pulling carts up and down the cobbled street and shouting at everybody to get out of the way, mounted soldiers trotting to and from the castle, it sounded like all the demons of purgatory and frequently Paul and Federico could not make themselves understood due to the noise. They were both nevertheless fascinated by the activity and what was going on in the various shops and workshops on the way. While they were looking in the window of a saddler's, close to the castle's main entrance, Paul happened to glance up at the sound of horses cantering past them and saw the three men observed earlier quickly enter the castle gates. He kept the information to himself, deciding to ask the landlord at the Mitre later in the evening a few questions about the castle and its occupants.

They then walked back towards the high street where Paul bought a present for Mrs Galston, a small, pretty silk scarf he knew she would like, and then since they both felt they had done enough walking for the day, they returned to the inn to relax before supper. Once back in the room, they lay back on their beds, and talked about the day's events, agreeing on a programme for the following day, which would focus primarily on the purchases Paul had to make in the market-place.

They had almost finished their supper when the landlord came to the table and asked if he could join them. He had brought a jug of wine with him and topped up their goblets. In his usual friendly, good-natured way he asked how the day had been. Paul recounted the experience in the guildhall, the visit to the tavern and the walk around the city-quarter by the castle. He chose not to mention the detail of the three other visitors, but mentioned that the agent had recognised a certain count 'de Kessinger' there, who apparently did not have too good a reputation. The landlord also knew him and said that he was the constable of the castle, acting on behalf of the king who owned it, and it was rumoured that the count was frequently involved in dubious political and business affairs. He apparently maintained good relations with the Bishop of Norwiche – they frequently went hunting together – who was himself the most important landowner in the city and the immediate area. David Cook had lowered his voice so as not to be overheard, telling them both that one had to be careful with 'such gentlemen'. They were extremely powerful and it was dangerous to criticise them openly, he added meaningfully.

They then talked about this and that until Paul reminded him about the previous evening and his promise to explain what really had brought him to Norwiche, and how he had become the owner of the Mitre. David Cook smiled, adding that he hadn't forgotten, but it would take a little time to explain it all. He raised his goblet, drained the contents and both Paul and Federico sat back in expectation as he began his tale.

It had all begun in Wulpet, he said. They would remember how he had been pressured by the monks of Burye St Edmunds to the extent that all his customers had been 'persuaded' to sell their wool only to the abbey. He saw that his business was ruined and wasn't sure what to do.

'There is in Wulpet,' he explained, 'a beautiful church called St Mary's. It is in fact a famous place of pilgrimage, with its chapel and shrine to "Our Lady of Wulpet", near to the renowned healing well. There is a steady stream of people from all over England and other countries that go to Wulpet to pay homage to "Our Lady" and the so-called miraculous waters. Sometimes when I wanted to think over a difficult problem, I went to a bench seat in the churchyard, in the shade on the north side, behind the famous chapel. And it was there that I met her.'

'Not the holy mother herself?' Federico immediately asked with bated breath.

Smiling broadly, David replied, 'Not quite, but a wonderful old woman, nevertheless!'

He told them that from the moment he saw Lady Alice, he sensed that this was a very special lady. She had obviously been beautiful in her youth and even now had a flair and sparkle that one rarely finds, even in people thirty or forty years younger. She had seen that something was troubling him and asked if he would like to talk about it. She somehow made it so easy. She listened carefully, and even just discussing it all with a sympathetic listener seemed to help him. She made him understand that there was so much in life, and besides, he was so young; such a setback he had just experienced was all part of the learning process in life. Adversity strengthened one. There was always going to be injustice in this world, and it was all the more bitter when it came from quarters from which one would and should have expected brotherly love and help. But unfortunately that was very often not the case, and she doubted if that would ever change, in spite of the hypocritical platitudes and promises many such people were famous for! She then told him about some of her experiences.

'She explained that her dialect – and it was true, she spoke in a lilting, musical way – was typical of from where she originated, Kilkenny in southern Ireland. She had been born into a titled family called Kyteler, with considerable land but little money, and at a very young age was betrothed to an old rich banker and moneylender of Kilkenny, called William Outlawe, whom she subsequently married. They had a son, whom they also called William, but shortly afterwards the elderly husband died, leaving the entire fortune to his son. Her own family then pressured her to remarry as quickly as possible, and once again it was another much older man. Ten years later he also died, leaving her a very wealthy lady.

' "On the one side," she commented sadly, "even though my first two husbands were much older men, they were kind to me and after they died I inherited a fortune which should have enabled my son and me to live in peace and comfort! But, unfortunately, fate seemed to be working against me. I no sooner remarried an attractive man more or less my age, than he suddenly became ill with a terrible wheezing cough and some weeks later died, leaving me with a broken heart and expecting a child. My son was growing up fast into manhood, I was about to have another child and I was surrounded by relatives who had more concern for my money than the well-being of my children or myself. In spite of my wealth, and you will find out yourself that there is much more to life than being rich, I was unhappy and felt almost trapped in a complicated business world that I didn't fully understand, with members of my own family – and other people – looking for ways to rob me of my inheritance. It was a very difficult time, believe me."'

Paul and Federico had completely forgotten about their wine and sat there totally absorbed in the drama the landlord was describing, sensing that what was to follow would be even more compelling. They waited impatiently for him to continue. They were oblivious of other guests sitting in the same room, who were all too preoccupied with consuming large quantities of ale, or gambling or flirting with the serving girls to take any notice of the three of them sitting in the corner.

The landlord had paused to gather his thoughts, searching for a name, and then he remembered. 'Sir John le Poer,' he said, 'that's the one. The name of her fourth husband! He was apparently about the same age as the widow. His wife had died in childbirth, leaving him with a baby badly in need of a mother. Not long after the birth of the two children, they had met and, the way things sometimes happen, they fell in love and married. Lady Alice told me that her husband managed the family affairs brilliantly and helped the eldest son, William, to take over the banking interests, making him a successful businessman in his own right, which caused considerable jealousy with other members of both her and his family. She explained to me that unfortunately success always seems to create jealousy, particularly among those of lesser talent, and when it leads to wealth, there will inevitably be people who covet it, who are prepared to go to any lengths to get their greedy hands on it, as she was to discover to her cost in later years.

'She added that she and her husband had fifteen good years together and it was early in the year of our Lord 1324 that on a cold winter's day he peacefully passed away.'

Paul, a little startled, realised that this was the same year he had been born, and wondered a little at the coincidence.

David continued. 'That was the year when the worst of all problems began for Lady Alice. Relatives, far from happy that she had inherited her husband's entire fortune, accused her of bewitching all her husbands, and took their complaint to a certain Bishop Richard Ledrede of Ossory, the local see, who subsequently condemned her as a heretic and a magician! This bishop, she explained, had not long been in Ireland. He was an Englishman from London, determined to bring the mania of "heretic hunting" and all the associated barbaric practices of some leading churchmen, to Ireland. She had been, she believed, the very first victim in her fair country. However, by comparison with some of her friends, she escaped lightly, helped no doubt by her position in society.

'It was a nightmare, she told me. At the time of her arrest and interrogation, a friend called Petronilla had been visiting her, and was also taken by force to the ecclesiastical prison not far from the cathedral. Her friend had been in the cell next to hers, and although she couldn't see anything, what she heard would remain with her for the rest of her life. She frequently woke up at night, bathed in perspiration, as if she could still hear the screaming as they relentlessly tortured her friend. It was if they were in purgatory itself, with the forces of darkness punishing the sinners of this world. They had ripped off her clothes and she heard some of the lustful comments of the tormentors as they fingered her naked body before they began to beat her and do other indescribable things.

'Petronilla had of course confessed eventually to all the charges made, after being tortured, and then flogged six times, and even named other people who supposedly had also been involved in a variety of heretical practices, including witchcraft. The old lady added that they then burnt poor Petronilla at the stake and did the same to several other people found guilty. Some were exiled or excommunicated, and their property confiscated.'

David shared the feelings expressed by Paul and Federico, sickened and appalled by what they had just heard, and explained what then happened to Lady Alice.

'An appeal was made to the court at Dublin, but she was neverless found guilty and her goods confiscated, but not before she managed to escape by bribing a jailer. She left Ireland with her eldest son, taking some priceless jewellery and money that had been hidden in their garden. But her problems were not yet over.

During the voyage to England, a storm drove the ship down the west coast and it eventually foundered on the rocks off Land's End. She was saved, almost miraculously, but her dear son was drowned, she believed – she never saw him again. Her money was lost but she still had her jewellery when she waded ashore, helped by a brave sailor who had risked his life to save her.

'The local people were extremely kind, and after a few days they arranged for her to travel with some tin merchants to a port called Helston, where she was able to board a cargo ship bound for Orwel haven. She then rode with a group of weavers from Flanders – who had left their own country hoping to use their skills in England and start a new life – who were making their way into the shire of Suffolke. A family called Deeks had relatives already established in Melforde where she stayed a few days, and then she went with another group a little further north and ended up in Wulpet. And that, she concluded, was how she happened to live in Wulpet, an anonymous wanderer, settling with the help of the rector Henry Foxton, into a friendly village community. Nobody knew her real identity, and by carefully selling items of her jewellery over the years, she had managed to lead a simple, relatively comfortable life in a small cottage in Rags Lane, as it came to be called, a stone-throw from where we sat as she recounted her life story.

'She is almost certainly dead, now, probably buried in some corner of the churchyard of St Mary's, with a carved tombstone carrying the name of "Alice" and perhaps a family name that will certainly not be Kyteler! She was truly a wonderful person, and she inspired me to leave and seek my fortune elsewhere, to try something completely different and to learn from the experiences of a much wiser person. The chance suddenly came for me to go to Norwiche, and I had accumulated sufficient money to buy this inn, which at the time was a lot smaller than today. And, as you can see, it's worked out pretty well.'

With that, he stood up and excused himself as there was still work to be done and he had been away long enough from the kitchen!

It was clear that David had also been moved as he told the incredible story of Alice, and what he had said had not been lost on either Paul or Federico. There were so many unknown, interesting places to see and so many possibilities to explore, Paul reflected, asking Federico if he knew where Helston was, and did he know anything about witchcraft? Federico laughed, and admitted he couldn't answer the questions, and that it was very late and perhaps they should go to bed since tomorrow was another day!

While they were finishing the wine the landlord had left on the table, they heard some people at another table talking about an archery contest taking place on the Friday morning at the town fields. Apparently, the constable had put up a prize of five pounds for the winner, and men from all over the shire were expected to participate, as well as some soldiers from the local garrison. Paul went over to them and politely asked if it was open to anybody to take part, and flushed in anger when one of them burst out laughing, pointedly emphasising that all 'men' were invited to participate. Paul was about to react more aggressively, when Federico took hold of his arm, smiled at the seated group of men, and pulled him away.

'Come on, Paul,' he hissed into his ear, 'they're not worth the trouble. We're not known here and I don't want to end up in jail tonight, or get stabbed in the process of showing these "gentlemen" that they should be more careful about what they say. Let's go back to the room as we agreed, eh?'

A little reluctantly, Paul allowed himself to be led away. While climbing up the creaking, wooden staircase, Federico grinned and commented on the fact that in spite of the calm manner he had, Paul was, unlike his brother, a bit of a hothead as far as he could see, and he more or less propelled the mildly protesting Paul into the room.

Once inside, Paul quickly calmed and agreed with Federico that after tomorrow's business was completed he would enroll in the contest since five pounds was more than he earned in a year, and perhaps he had a chance. He was at least determined to try! Federico had never seen Paul use the longbow and had no idea how proficient he was, but agreed that it couldn't do any harm to take part, since it looked as if they had more than enough time. They weren't expected back at Castor until Monday, so why not!

They both sank gratefully into bed and slept soundly until daybreak.

By early morning they were already making their tour of the market-place while stalls were still being set up. Fruit, vegetables, meat, fish, bread, milk, cheese and a host of other food items were loaded onto tables, stacked in baskets or barrels, or jugs, or hung up on rails. There was a hive of activity with all the accompanying noises. Cows, oxen, sheep, horses, pigs and goats were driven into paddocks, poultry was squeezed into large cages, protesting vigorously. Tools, household items, leather goods, iron implements, pewter tankards and mugs, carved wooden figures, cutlery, straw baskets, spices from the Orient, silk from France and Italy, rolls of locally-produced linen and woollen cloth; in fact, almost everything one could think of, was on sale. Paul was almost overwhelmed with it all, and had some difficulty in finding exactly what the reeve had requested.

Once located, it was also necessary to negotiate a fair price, and the stallholders soon discovered that Paul, in spite of his obvious youth, knew how to drive a hard bargain! He purchased the candles and ruddle first, agreeing to collect them during the early afternoon for transport to the stables near the gate of St Gyles. Various qualities and strains of corn were available, but he had to visit several stallholders until he was satisfied that he was buying the best. He arranged for them to deliver it to the stables late afternoon, where he would pay them cash on delivery. During one of his negotiations, he found that one of the farmers was extremely knowledgeable about wheat yields, and learned a great deal about how to improve the soil quality with lime and marl, the importance of ploughing to the right depth, and above all, making sure that the ground was well manured. Seaweed was also one possibility Paul had never before considered, but he then came to understand the value of animal dung and how one had to balance carefully pasture and arable land, ensuring there were sufficient sheep and cattle to provide the essential manure. He felt sure afterwards that if the reeve agreed, they might even be able to double the yield per acre, utilising the information he had just picked up. Federico couldn't quite share his enthusiasm, since the discussion had been a little beyond him, but agreed good-naturedly that if he could increase the amount of wheat produced as he had described, Mr Stanley was bound to be happy to do it.

Once all the business was completed, they decided they deserved some refreshment, and slipped into one of the many taverns around the market-place to eat a meat pie and enjoy a cool quart of ale. An hour or so later, Paul hired a porter to take the candles and sacks of ruddle in his handcart to the stables and they went with him to make sure nothing got lost on the way.

Shortly afterwards, the dozen sacks of corn were delivered, and while Paul was paying the farmer, an employee at the stables helped Federico stack them in a shed close to where the horses were stabled. Betsy heard Paul's voice and began to whinny and kick the stable wall, only stopping when he went to her, affectionately patted her neck and talked to her.

'My, goodness, Paul,' Federico called out, breathing heavily from the exertion of stacking the corn sacks, 'that mare of yours is worse than a woman. Just wait till you've got a wife to look after as well. You'll really have a handful!'

'Not much chance of that in the next few years,' he replied. 'I'm far too busy, and besides, I'm too young!'

Federico was about to remind him of their first night at the inn, when Henry Tyler appeared to see what was going on inside the stable. Recognising Paul, he relaxed visibly, and asked if everything was in order, wondering if he needed help. Laughingly, Paul replied that it appeared that his old mare was happy to see him again, but she would have to stay a day or so longer there with the rest of the horses, if that was in order with him, since he planned to take part in the archery contest the following morning.

He was quickly assured that he would be welcome to stay as long as he wished, and that any friend of Stanley Pettit was a friend of his. Paul also learned that he would need to enrol early on the morning of the contest – in fact the tent would be set up close by the stables – and they usually started at midday. If there were a large number of entrants, they would probably have a preliminary test one hour beforehand.

Paul thanked him for the information, and asked him for his longbow and arrows that he had stored, since he wanted to practise a little before darkness fell. Mr Tyler brought them for him a few minutes later, and accompanied by Federico, Paul walked out into the town fields, looking for a suitable, safe target.

They found an old, discarded target lying close to the city walls, which Federico set up while Paul paced out two hundred yards or so, signalled to Federico to move to one side, and took aim. He had been well-schooled by his elder brother years before, but had spent little time with the longbow in recent months. Nevertheless, his first shot sank into the outer ring of the target. He adjusted accordingly, and then fired three more in quick succession before walking over to Federico to examine the results at close range.

'Not too bad at all, Mr Paul Rollesby,' his escort commented, grinning broadly when he arrived at the target. 'It must run in the family. Your brother would be proud of you. You've got three bull's-eyes!'

Paul looked at the clustering and felt relieved that he was not as 'rusty' as he feared he might have been. Some things you never forget, he mused, although he had felt the strain in his forearms.

'I had a good teacher, Federico,' he confided. 'But I would just like to increase the distance a bit and try a couple more times, and if that works out all right we'll call it a day!'

His next shots at around three hundred paces were equally as good, and after retrieving the arrows, he slung the longbow over his shoulder, and accompanied by a pleasantly surprised Federico, they returned in high spirits to the Mitre.

11

The Constable's Prize and an Eventful Journey

They left the Mitre at daybreak on the Friday morning. Paul had settled the bill the evening before, explaining to David Cook that he wanted an early night because of the contest the following day, and they intended to begin the journey back to Castor immediately afterwards. He thanked him for his hospitality, promising that should he return to Norwiche, he would definitely stay at the Mitre, and should David ever be in the Castor area, to make sure to visit him. His cottage was not as luxurious, but he would always be welcome.

In spite of the early hour, they were not alone on the way down to the town fields. Some soldiers passed them on horseback, the iron-shod hooves clattering noisily on the cobblestones, and other obvious participants carrying longbows were also emerging from taverns on the way, walking purposefully in the same direction. It became quickly clear that there were going to be a lot of competitors trying their luck to win the constable's prize of five pounds, a fortune for most of them, and probably a host of pickpockets and other scoundrels also, Federico warned Paul, looking for likely victims!

The constable, Count de Kessinger, had been entertaining that week, amongst others, two 'commissioners of array', sent by King Edward periodically to review the status of the armed forces of the nobility. They not only checked the numbers of men-at-arms, yeomen, hobelars (mounted archers), the pike-men and the common archers, but also their arms and the general standard of their skills. The king, frequently needing well-trained fighting forces for his campaigns outside of England, did everything possible to encourage the regular practising of the martial arts among his earls, barons, knights and commoners. He arranged tournaments for the knights and ordered them to do everything in their power to establish archery practice in the villages and towns throughout their demesnes, and sent the commissioners to check this also.

The count wanted to make the best of possible impressions on the commissioners in order to enhance his relationship with the king, and had therefore arranged this contest with a prize that he knew would attract large numbers and almost certainly many men of quality. His men had already set up tents, roped off areas for spectators, erected the targets and built a small platform for the count and his visitors by the time that Paul and Federico found their way to the place of enrolment.

A notary supervising the recording of names and the locality of all entrants was astonished when Paul took a pen from the desk and wrote in his own details. None of the others up till then had been able to read or write, coming from peasant stock that was not at all educated. There was a long line of more competitors waiting impatiently to register with one of the clerks sitting at the long bench-table and he had no time to question Paul, who had quickly moved away from the tent with Federico.

Once outside, the duly enrolled participants were herded almost like cattle into a compound to await further instructions, at which Federico wished Paul the best of luck and joined the other spectators who were already beginning to arrive. Within an hour or so, the enrolment was completed, and something like two hundred and fifty archers were milling about, waiting impatiently for things to begin. Eventually, a guard captain approached and called them to silence. When he was satisfied that he had the attention of them all, he explained briefly that because of the high number of participants there would have to be a preliminary shoot-off. The method was quite simple. They would file out of the compound ten at a time. Two soldiers were posted at the compound entrance to control the numbers. The contestants should then take up positions at the firing line, which he pointed out to them. A soldier was standing at each end of the rope marking the firing line, with a group in reserve standing close by each of them. Each man, once in position, should fire two arrows only at the target in front of him. Anybody with two bull's-eyes would automatically take part in the next round; if nobody managed that, the man with the best score would be chosen; if nobody hit a target, that whole group would be disqualified and should go home immediately, give their bow to somebody who knew how to use it and take up spinning wool where they would be much better employed!

After the laughter died down, he added that the soldiers at the firing line would lead the finalists back to the tent and they should give their names to the notary, and then wait behind that tent for further instructions. The unsuccessful archers in each group would be directed away from the compound, and could of course watch the contest with the rest of the spectators if they wished. He then warned them that anybody causing any sort of disturbance amongst the spectators would be flung into jail immediately and flogged. He asked if there were any questions, and satisfied that his message had been clearly understood, after a slight pause, ordered the first ten men to take up their positions.

And that was exactly how it was run. Within two hours, the preliminary round was over and thirty men were chosen for the final round that was to begin at midday. Even though there had been some mild booing and catcalls at times, the overall standard was very good. One or two archers only failed to hit the targets at all, and several, including Paul, got two bull's-eyes. It was clearly going to be an open contest.

While they were waiting for the constable and his guests to arrive, the finalists were given a hot pie each and a jug of ale, served by some servants from the castle, while others were moving the targets back a further fifty paces, causing Paul to wonder at the extreme efficiency with which everything had been handled. Somebody had certainly spent some time working out the organisation of all this, he reflected. Not at all like the one or two local contests he had taken part in around Castor last year, which eventually were completed after considerable confusion and argument. Within the last few days he had learned a great deal about many things, realising that there was a whole new world outside of his demesne.

His reveries were abruptly disturbed by a fanfare of trumpets as the constable and his guests arrived on horseback, magnificent in their long robes draped over the flanks of powerfully-built 'destriers', the war horse of the lords. That of the constable was the most imposing – a magnificent white stallion which stood by the platform, pawing the ground, snorting and tossing his head, seeming to recognise the importance of the occasion and proud to belong to the royal keeper of the castle at Norwiche, one of the most important cities of the realm! Suddenly the whole atmosphere had changed. It was as if a flash of lightning had passed through the crowd and the waiting archers. Everybody seemed to be talking at once, conscious of the change and wanting to be part of it. The preliminaries were over and now the real contest could begin!

Helpers ran to the horses to hold the bridles while the lords dismounted and took their positions on the specially prepared platform, and once seated, were immediately handed a goblet of wine by waiting servants. The captain of the castle guard immediately got the attention of the finalists and explained how the contest was to be run. The spectators were stamping their feet to keep them warm, talking loudly with each other, impatient for the start, as the archers gave their bows a final check and the first ten filed out to take their positions. The constable stood up, drew his sword and held it up high as the signal to begin. There was a roar of approval from the spectators and the bowmen took aim and fired their first arrows.

From each group of ten, two were selected to go forward to the final shoot. When Paul took his position in the last group, Federico took a deep breath, almost imagining that he himself was taking aim, and concentrated on his target. It was a bull's-eye. Also the second and third shots, which were sufficient for Paul to qualify! Federico cheered with the rest of the crowd, who to a man appreciated good shooting.

It was now down to the last six, and as they took position, Federico heard an archer in the crowd nearby say to somebody who was dressed in rags at his side to make sure and keep an eye on whoever won, if he wanted a share of that five pounds!

'Maybe Peter will win, and that will save us the trouble,' the ragged man replied to the archer, who nodded and grinned in acknowledgement.

Federico wondered which one of the six was 'Peter', but since there was nothing he could do until the end of the contest, he concentrated on the final phase. Each man was to fire six arrows, with the top score winning. As the arrows began to thud into the targets, Federico saw that it looked as if it was going to be decided between Paul and a scarred, swarthy-faced, heavily-built man standing next to him. It was certainly going to be very close, and finally it was decided by the last arrow. Both men had five bull's-eyes, and Paul's last shot fell just outside. The powerfully-built, dark-haired man took careful aim and the arrow sped towards the target and dropped into the outer ring, at least a handsbreadth further out than Paul's! Federico whooped with joy, jumping up and down with excitement, delighted with Paul's victory. It had been close at the end but he had clearly won, and would soon be five pounds richer! What a day!

The captain of the guard led Paul, who was still trembling slightly, across the field to the platform where the constable was sitting with his guests. As Paul drew nearer, the constable stood up, smiling broadly, and opened his arms in a somewhat theatrical way to greet the winner, acknowledging the cheers of the crowd.

'By God,' the constable exclaimed in surprise when he saw how young Paul was, 'how can one so young handle a longbow like you? What is your secret, young man, eh?'

Paul flushed with embarrassment, not sure what to say, and managed to stammer something about his brother teaching him and that he had been lucky today to defeat all the others.

The constable then asked him what his name was and where he came from. When Paul replied, one of the guests suddenly said: 'Rollesby from Castor, you say? Are you a relative of Tom Rollesby by any chance?'

Looking at the man who questioned him for the first time, Paul realised with a start that this was one of the two men he had seen with the constable leaving the tavern near the guildhall and later entering the castle gates earlier in the week. 'He is my brother, my lord,' Paul replied respectfully. 'One of the finest men in all England,' he added, his back stiffening with pride.

'Well, well, constable,' the earl commented, looking at the count de Kessinger as he spoke, a sardonic sneer on his face, 'this really is an unusual family of peasants.' He turned to the two commissioners of array also present and added: 'That's a family name you should note for the future, gentlemen. His brother is certainly the best longbowman I've seen in my life, and is already a legend in Castor!'

The count, anxious to remain in the limelight, quickly called for his steward who handed him a leather pouch, heavy with the coins it contained. 'Paul Rollesby,' he stated in a loud voice, 'congratulations on your fine performance in spite of your young years. You have demonstrated today, with many others, that we have a large number of excellent archers in the area to preserve the traditions of skill with the longbow. Today, you were the best of all, and I am pleased to present you with the prize of five pounds, as promised. Inside this purse, you will find sixteen new gold florins and twelve silver groats. Make sure you put it in a safe place. It's a tempting sum!'

Paul took the purse, quickly checking the contents to the amusement of all the platform guests, and was led away by the captain after he had secured it to his belt. The captain congratulated him, adding that should he be looking for a post in his troop, he would be happy to take him in. Paul duly thanked him, and politely refused, but skilfully left the door open should he change his mind sometime in the future.

Federico slapped Paul on the back when they met, and although delighted with the contest result, was a little concerned about what he had heard while standing with the rest of the spectators. He warned Paul that there were enough poor people around who would like to get their hands on so much money, and they should leave for Castor as quickly as possible.

They made their way quickly to the stables, paid Henry Tyler the stabling fees, then loaded the four packhorses with the twelve sacks of corn, three sacks of ruddle and sack of candles. It was still light, and they wanted to get as far away from Norwiche as possible before nightfall. The horses were heavily loaded and they knew progress would be much slower than their journey to the city, and Federico was anxious to find a safe place to sleep for the night.

They had been riding for about half an hour, when suddenly four men appeared on the trail in front of them, two on horseback and two on foot. Both Federico and Paul quickly reined in their horses short of the men who were blocking the trail, and Federico, his crossbow at the ready, moved slightly forward, stopped, and asked what they wanted. The men laughed and one of them said: 'Just listen to him now.' The apparent leader separated himself from the group and brought his horse to a halt about five paces from Federico, while the two men on foot moved over further to each side, unslung an arrow, and threatingly slotted them onto their bowstrings, slowly making ready to fire if necessary. The leader, they saw, was in fact the swarthy-faced archer that Paul had narrowly beaten in the contest.

'Your friend is carrying something we want,' he said. 'Tell him to throw the purse with the money in it to one side, leave us two of your packhorses and you can go free. If you resist, we shall kill you both and take everything!'

Paul had also freed his longbow immediately on reining-in. He looked around carefully to see if there were any more bandits skulking nearby, and began to feel afraid, knowing that their lives hung in the balance.

Federico calmly looked the leader in the eye and said in a quiet voice, in a tone that made even Paul shiver: 'Signore, if one of your men makes so much as a move you are a dead man.' He levelled the crossbow and aimed directly at the leader. 'Maybe an arrow might hit me, perhaps kill me, but you signore will have this bolt in your heart. My friend behind me, as you well know, is also pretty good with the bow, and so if we are unlucky, we will only kill two of you, even though I believe it will be at least three. I am not going to discuss anything more. Ride away now, right now, you and all your men, or I shall fire.'

The outlaw leader, Peter, paled and realising that he had misjudged the situation, paused only for a second, then commanded his men to lower their weapons and follow him. Reluctantly, they obeyed, and turning off the trail, the leader began slowly to move away across a field, towards a wood that was about three hundred paces distant, followed by the other horseman and the two archers on foot. He had ridden about fifty paces, before he turned in the saddle and shouted out in fury: 'We shall meet again my friend, and then may God have mercy on your soul!'

Federico and Paul watched them move slowly out of sight, and then, spurring their horses, galloped as fast as they could with the packhorses, covering the next mile or so very quickly, and then slowed down to a steady pace, heading for Acle, keeping a careful watch to see they were not being followed. The sun was already beginning to set, but Federico was insistent that they should make as much ground as possible before darkness, because he was sure the outlaws would try again, perhaps trying to outflank them, and then ambushing them without warning. Paul's main concern was the packhorses. They were heavily-laden and breathing hard with the exertion, but he understood only too well that they must keep moving on.

When it was clear that they had not been followed, and it was dusk, Federico pointed to a wooded hillside on their left, and suggested they should make their camp there for the night. So long as they had no fire and kept quiet, they should be safe for the night at least, he explained. He led them carefully up the hillside and into the wood until they came to a small stream gurgling its way along a gulley leading down to the meadows below. They dismounted, let the horses drink their fill, crossed the stream, and walking parallel to the track far below, continued for a few more minutes until they came across a small glade. It was an ideal spot for the night, providing good cover on all sides and invisible from the track below.

Once the horses were tethered and munching contentedly from their feeding bags, the sacks were unloaded onto bracken Federico had gathered to prevent them getting wet and also to serve as beds for them both as well as protection from the wind. In fact, Paul commented, bearing in mind they couldn't light a fire, covered with their cloaks it made quite a cosy bed for the night, even though at Federico's insistence they shared two-hour watches until dawn.

Since they hadn't eaten the night before, they decided to enjoy a hearty breakfast to sustain them through the rest of the day, and with luck, they had reckoned they would be able to sleep in their own beds in Castor by early evening. Mrs Galston's salted pork with a rye loaf of bread they had bought at the city gate of St Gyles on the way out, washed down with wine, made a pleasant start to the day.

12

A Matter of Life and Death

When the four outlaws had left Federico and Paul with their tails between their legs on the Friday evening, they had returned to a temporary camp set up close to an old abandoned quarry, in the hills north of Blofeld. During the previous weeks, several small groups of outlaws had made their way to the area, and Peter – or Black Peter as he came to be known, had made himself the indisputable leader of the whole group, with a brutality that even by the standards of its members (escaped convicts, wounded ex-soldiers, thieves and a motley assortment of ruffians) was without equal.

There were more than thirty men and half a dozen women in the group, and Peter had organised them to ensure that the living quarters were satisfactory for the winter and there was an adequate food supply. He had also set up a system of lookout posts so that they could not be surprised by an approaching enemy. For weeks they had been terrorising the neighbourhood, stealing cattle, horses, food and anything else they could lay their hands on, and then returning to the well-concealed hideout. It was not too far from the city, giving the pickpockets an opportunity to spend a lucrative day or two in Norwiche, and also within relatively easy reach of several poorly-defended villages, berewicks and smallholdings outside of the demesne of Castor. They had made one or two sorties into the Castor area, but found it to be too dangerous for the effort, since Tom Rollesby had worked hard to improve the defensive systems of all the villages in the demesne, as well as organising regular patrols of his soldiers.

Black Peter was in a foul temper when he arrived back at the camp. Not only had he returned empty-handed, but there were no lookouts on guard – they were all sleeping off the effects of a drunken orgy in the absence of their leader! He almost went berserk with anger, and got his three companions to rouse all the sleeping men present in the collection of huts around the quarry and assemble them in the communal cooking area. He began by asking which men were due to be on guard that night, and when this finally became clear, he had them tied to nearby trees and lashed them mercilessly with a leather whip until they were unconscious. The women, hearing the screaming, dressed and went down to see what was going on. One of them, Bertha, found her man, his doublet torn to ribbons, blood dripping from his bare back and shoulders, slumped against one of the trees. She began screaming abuse at Peter, challenging his right to almost kill her man.

Realising his leadership was being questioned, he acted quickly. He smacked her viciously across the face, knocking her to the ground. He then pulled her violently to her feet, and holding her arms behind her back with one hand, ripped off her clothes with the other until she was naked, facing the crowd of leering men. Not satisfied with that humiliation, he seized her right breast and squeezed until she screamed, then threw her towards the now wide-awake group of outlaws, telling them to do whatever they wanted with her. Two of them snatched her away from the others and dragged her away shouting and screaming to one of the huts.

'Now listen to me, you scum,' he shouted, 'without me you would be lost and you know it only too well. If anybody doesn't accept me as leader, he is free to leave right now. But if you stay, you will do exactly what I tell you. Is that clear?' Nobody left, and it was clear the danger was over for the time being. Peter looked intently at each man, sent three of them out to complete the night watch, picked out ten of his better archers and foot soldiers and told them to come forward to him. He then sent the others away back to their huts.

Once they were alone, he told them to sit down around the fire that was still smouldering, and then explained what was to be done. He told them about the two travellers – one a youth and the other a trained soldier – omitting the details of the contest and the humiliation he had suffered at the hands of Federico. He made it clear that the men were wealthy, had four loaded packhorses as well as their own horses, and right now would be asleep not that far away. Taking his sword, he traced out on the ground their route from Norwiche, and where approximately they would be sleeping for the night. He knew they were heading for Castor, and his plan was to ambush them to the west of Acle. The place he had in mind was about three hours' ride from the camp, and they could easily be in position just after daybreak if they left within the hour.

He sent them off to collect their weapons, take enough food for two days, saddle up ten horses from the corral, and be ready to leave as quickly as possible. Satisfied with his plan, he sat down on a bench seat by the fire, stirred the embers and threw some fresh pieces of wood on them, waiting for his men to return. Revenge would be sweet, he thought, and grinned maliciously in anticipation of the following morning.

At the time that Paul and Federico were settling down for an early night in the hidden glade, Tom Rollesby was sitting with his wife Margaret in front of a log fire after their evening meal. Tom had not spoken much during the meal and was now staring into the fire lost in thought. The silence was broken by his wife, concerned with the unusual mood of her husband.

'What is it, Tom?' she asked. 'What's bothering you? You've hardly spoken a word all evening. Are you feeling unwell? Please tell me what's worrying you. It's just not like you to be so quiet!'

He looked up, smiled at his wife, and replied: 'I never could keep anything hidden from you, could I, my love? To be honest, I'm worried about young Paul. Ever since the early afternoon, I haven't been able to get him out of my mind. Something, somehow is wrong, I'm sure of it!'

Margaret then tried to reassure him that Paul was big enough to take care of himself, reminding him that he had also arranged an escort for him, and so surely Tom had no grounds for concern. He took her hands in his, looked down for a moment, searching for the right words, and suddenly in an intense way that at first alarmed her, fixed his eyes on hers, and said: 'I'm going to tell you something that I've never confided to anyone else before, and you must promise me not to repeat it to anyone.' He shook her hands gently. 'Do you promise? Do you promise before God that you will not tell a soul, Margaret? It is a dangerous secret, believe me.'

Thoroughly alarmed, she nodded, and said, 'I promise, Tom, may God be my witness!'

Looking a little relieved, he began to explain to her the secret known only to Paul and himself. 'You see, Margaret, I'm not sure I can understand it myself,' he said. 'Paul and I in our own way are extremely close. We are very different people, but somehow, in some situations, in a way I can hardly explain, we seem to think alike. It's almost as if we can hear the other one talking, even though we are far apart. It's in the mind, somehow, and when strong emotions are involved, it's clearest. We have talked about it before and feel that it must be some special sort of gift from God, perhaps. We know we cannot talk about it to other people, because you've seen yourself how priests and doctors behave here when they come across something they cannot understand or have never themselves experienced. Before you know what's happened they accuse you of heresy or witchcraft, and – thank God it's not yet been the case here – you are tortured and burnt at the stake, so I've heard. I'm not an especially religious man as you know, Margaret, but I'm not mad and I've never had anything to do with sorcery and witchcraft or the likes, may God be my witness!'

His wife pressed his hands with affection, and said in a hushed tone that she of course believed him, and her lips would be sealed. She would discuss this with no one. Inwardly she was astonished how eloquently Tom had suddenly expressed himself, almost as if he had an inner self that had more akin with a troubadour than the disciplined, orderly, soldier-like, yet kind and generous person she had known and loved these years. He was suddenly, she realised, talking more like the way his brother would discuss things when he was at their quarters for an evening meal, and reminded of Paul, she asked her husband when he was due back from his trip.

'I talked with the reeve this afternoon,' he confided, 'and he said he should be back by Monday at the latest, but if everything went according to plan, he could be home by tomorrow night or sometime on Sunday morning. If that were the case, knowing that the packhorses would slow him down, he may well have started the journey home already and is camping out on the way, so he can expect to get back late tomorrow night. Margaret, I'm sure now that he has already left Norwiche and is in some sort of danger. The reeve told me the route they would take, and I've decided to go and meet him.'

'Take some of your soldiers with you, Tom,' Margaret replied. 'If he really is in danger, you also may need help.'

He realized that the danger could only be from outlaws, and that if it was a band of them, some additional support was a sensible suggestion, so he agreed to get the lord's permission immediately, that very evening.

Tom did not tell Sir William everything, other than that his brother was returning with some valuable supplies from Norwiche, and what with the general outlaw activity that seemed to be getting worse at the present time, he would like to take a troop out to escort him back. Sir William agreed instantly and called for the steward to get two days' provisions for six men ready so they could leave an hour before daybreak. After thanking Sir William, Tom left to alert the men about the early-morning start.

He took two crossbowmen and three archers with him, making sure they all had swords and a javelin lashed onto the saddle. He knew them all well, and was satisfied they would be more than the equal of a force three or four times larger if necessary. He himself had his longbow slung across his shoulders, and as well as his sword and dagger, had a knight's mace hooked onto the saddle. Impatient to get started, they left the stables in darkness and for the first hour made relatively slow but steady progress, reaching Stokesbye by dawn. Fording the River Burre in daylight, they cantered towards Acle.

As Tom and his men were splashing across the Burre, Paul and Federico, with the taste of Mrs Galston's delicious salted pork still on their lips, leading the horses carefully down the hillside, had just reached the main trail. After checking again the loads of the packhorses, they mounted and began making relatively fast progress on their way to Acle which lay about seven miles away to the east. Federico particularly was somewhat nervous, sensing that their brush with the outlaws the previous day may not have been the last, and was anxious not to lose any time getting back to Castor. Paul, on the other hand, despite his initial fright at the confrontation, was in a good mood. He thought about the five pounds he had in his purse, the good purchases he had made, the new knowledge he had picked up in Norwiche. He had a little stab of guilt when he thought about the first night in the Mitre, but on reflection, it had been a very pleasant experience, he concluded, smiling inwardly. It was dry and looked like being a beautiful, early Spring day. The sky was cloudless, birds were twittering in the trees, ducks and other wildfowl were periodically winging their way across the trail towards the marshlands a mile or two away to the south, and the sun was rising in its full glory directly in front of them.

It was perhaps this latter situation that bothered Federico most of all. From time to time they had to shield their eyes with a hand to see what was ahead, making them very vulnerable to a surprise attack. He was so concerned that, in spite of Paul's protests, he insisted that they should discuss exactly what must be done should they be ambushed.

Black Peter and his men reached the planned ambush position just before dawn. One of his men had had to return to the camp because his horse had badly stumbled in the darkness and was lame. They were all tired, not having slept the previous night, but fear of their leader had driven them on. He had chosen a place about two miles west of Acle where the main trail passed through a small wood close to the village of Beyton. They could conceal their horses, position themselves on both sides of the track without being seen, and had an excellent view of the open fields and meadows to the west, the direction from which Paul and Federico must certainly come, as well as having the sun at their backs.

Once in position, he told them to make sure they kept awake and to wait for his signal to fire. He wasn't intending to make the same mistake again. There would not be any warning. Paul and Federico would have no chance to retaliate!

They had been waiting almost an hour when Peter saw movement in the distance, and immediately alerted his men with a warning whistle. The men ahead were still about half a mile away, but he was sure it was them. A few minutes later he saw clearly that he was right and they were approaching quite quickly, bearing in mind they had packhorses with them. As instructed, seven of the gang began to prepare themselves to fire at Federico, with the remainder concentrating on Paul. In a matter of a few minutes, Peter thought, it will be all over. Easy game! He grinned at the thought and how he would kill Federico if he was only wounded.

Federico had seen the wood from a distance and realising that it was a particularly dangerous spot, had arranged with Paul that at about three hundred paces from it, they should quickly leave the trail, stepping off to the left of it, and skirt around the woods, climbing up the higher ground, and then if everything looked quiet, make their way down towards Acle, coming onto the main track about half a mile ahead. Should they be attacked, he explained, Paul should wait for his signal, dismount, cut loose the corn sacks from the packhorses and send them off running while they stacked the sacks in front of them as a wall over which they could fire. And that was exactly what happened!

As the outlaws were watching their progress intently, and about to take aim, their quarry suddenly left the track and began cantering off up the sloping ground on their right. For a moment they were all stunned, until Black Peter roared in anger, 'Get to the horses quickly, you fools, or they will escape!'

For a few valuable minutes there was pandemonium and absolute chaos as the outlaws ran and stumbled to their tethered horses and prepared to give chase. Meanwhile, Federico and Paul heard the shouting and lashed their horses on as fast as possible, almost dragging the packhorses with them. But Federico soon saw that they were no match for the outlaws who were not burdened with supplies. Already the first bunch was beginning to reduce the distance between them, shouting and whooping blood-curdling battle cries.

'Quickly now, Paul,' Federico shouted. 'Dismount! We've only got two minutes at the most!'

As planned, they cut off the sacks, piled them up as a wall, whipped the horses away and took aim behind the sacks. 'If we don't kill them, they will kill us, Paul. Make every arrow count!'

Paul fired first at just over three hundred paces and missed. His next two shots were successful and two outlaws tumbled, badly wounded, out of their saddles. By the time the first one hit the ground, Federico's first bolt had pierced the heart of a third, and the two remaining outlaws veered away and went to join the second group led by Black Peter, who brought them all to a halt, just out of range. He was beside himself with anger and frustration. He had already lost three men, and although their prey could not get away, he knew only too well that this could be a costly battle. He was almost certainly going to lose one or two men more at least if he continued. One of them suggested they should settle for the six horses and call it a day while they could, and if Peter hadn't needed every man, he would have killed him on the spot. Seeing his fury, the rest kept quiet, waiting for him to tell them what was to be done.

In the meantime, while Paul and Federico were getting their breath back, and placing their arrows and bolts in easily accessible positions, laying daggers and swords close by, watching the outlaws as they planned the next attack, Tom Rollesby and his troop were only about a mile away on the track below them, and were approaching quickly, all unaware of the drama being enacted, except Tom himself who for the last few minutes had somehow picked up his brother's anguish, and had spurred his men on for more speed.

'Tom's near us, Federico, I'm sure of it,' Paul blurted out, while they were waiting.

'If that's the case, and I hope it is,' Federico replied, 'he'd better come soon my friend, for here they come again, and this time from two sides. May God protect us, Paul! You take the left, I'll take the right group. Get the archers first!'

Arrows began to thud into the sacks as Black Peter and his archers fired at the gallop, charging at full speed, screaming abuse. Three of the archers were hit, two fatally, and it looked as if Paul and Federico had won the day until an arrow fired by Black Peter sank into Federico's chest, penetrating the 'cuir bouilli' jerkin he wore, mortally wounding him. The outlaw leader, whooping in delight, shouldered his bow, leant over his horse's neck making himself an almost impossible target, drew his sword and leapt over the sacks of corn, slashing down at Paul while in mid-air. Paul managed to turn the blow with his longbow that was shattered in the process, and snatch the sword Federico had stuck into the ground nearby. While Peter was turning his horse, the three remaining outlaws reined in their horses, dismounted and took positions out of reach of Paul, who meanwhile had also drawn his dagger, and with his sword in the other hand, his face contorted with fury, was urging them to attack him so he could kill them. He had had no chance to see how badly Federico was wounded, but knew it must be very serious.

'Leave him to me!' Black Peter shouted. 'This one is also mine.' He dismounted quickly and approached Paul with drawn sword.

Tom Rollesby and his troop had noticed the six horses grouped together on the hillside and then, hearing the shouting, had turned off the trail to investigate. As they drew nearer, they saw the outlaw leader just as he leapt over the wall of corn sacks, slashing downwards with his sword. There was no time to plan an attack, and Tom, drawing his sword, spurred his horse on at top speed, waving to his men to fan out and follow.

The drumming of horses' hooves attracted Black Peter's attention as he prepared to attack Paul. Reluctantly he stepped back quickly, shouting at his men to mount, and ran to his own horse, but Tom got there first and sprang to the ground, running at the outlaw leader in fury. Before the other three outlaws could ride anywhere, two fell to the ground, struck by well-placed javelins, and Tom's men took up the chase of the one survivor, who desperately tried to escape, riding down to the woods, temporarily safe from arrow or bolt.

'Defend yourself as well as you can, you cowardly bastard! If you want to kill my brother, you will have to get rid of me first. Let's see how good you really are.' Tom forced the words out through gritted teeth as the two men circled, looking for an opening. There was fear in Black Peter's eyes as he measured up his massive adversary, realising he would not have a chance.

'How could I know he was your brother? I have a purse here, full of gold coins! Let me go before your men come back and they're yours.'

Tom shouted at his brother: 'You hear that, Paul? It's pathetic, isn't it? No way, you swine! On guard!' He lunged forward, driving the outlaw backwards with enormously powerful slashes of his sword, fixing him in the eyes, determined to smash him into the ground. It didn't last long, and a few moments later, there was a scream of pain as Black Peter, run-through, with Tom's sword emerging from his back, sank to the ground, spitting blood, his eyes rolling. He died almost instantly.

Tom pulled out his sword with a jerk, and wiped it on the grass to get most of the blood off it. Sheathing it, he walked quickly over to Paul to see if he was wounded or not. His brother was cuddling the head of the dead Federico, tears pouring down his face, sobbing bitterly.

'Oh my God, why did he have to die? Why? Why? Why? He was so good and gentle. He saved my life. Without him I would have been dead long ago.'

Tom, relieved that his brother was safe and not wounded, tried to comfort him, telling him that even though he himself was not a religious man, perhaps there was indeed a reason that God had spared his life. Federico as a good man would surely find peace with his 'maker', and he, Paul, must see that maybe he had been spared to perform some very special task for mankind.

But Paul was not to be comforted as he sobbingly told his brother about the contest he had won at Norwiche, and it was that alone that had attracted the outlaw's attention. It was his greed. Because of it, Federico had to die, and it wasn't fair. Tom, understanding the tension and strain of his brother's recent experiences, pulled him gently to his feet, drew him closely to him and patted him on the back, reassuring him that he most certainly was not responsible for Federico's death, and he must be thankful to have survived. The world has been rid of all this vermin, he added, pointing to the outlaws lying sprawled around the sacks of corn and beyond them, further out in the field.

His men returned at that moment with the body of the outlaw they had pursued lying lifeless, face downwards over a saddle. They were highly pleased with themselves and delighted that their captain and his brother were safe. Their pleasure was short-lived, however, when they saw that Federico was dead, and grim-faced they carried out Tom's orders to round up all the horses, and collect the bodies of all the dead outlaws and their weapons and bring them back to him.

Tom then sat Paul down on a corn sack, removed the arrow from Federico's chest and cleaned him up as best he could for transport back to Castor. An hour or so later, his men returned with all the bodies of the dead outlaws secured to their horses, including one who was still alive, having only a painful flesh wound on the side of his chest. They had also managed to round up the packhorses, including Betsy and Federico's horse, on which they had tied all the weapons they had found.

Seeing the one survivor, Tom realised his men would want revenge for the death of Federico and quickly took the initiative. He immediately took charge of the prisoner, ordering his men to search all the bodies for valuables, letting them keep what they found, including taking their pick from the assortment of weapons they had collected. Then, holding a dagger to the outlaw's throat, he called the men to him, saying: 'Men, I know only too well how you feel about Federico. I, too, since he saved the life of my brother. Vermin like this don't deserve to live at all. But let's use our heads for a minute. Maybe he could be of more use to us alive rather than dead.' Turning to the outlaw, he added, 'You must have a camp somewhere not too far away, and I want to know where it is, how many people there are and how it is defended.' He prodded his dagger a little into the side of the outlaw's throat, and added menacingly: 'Tell us now or I'll hand you over to these men, and then, may God have mercy on your soul!'

Looking at the soldiers fingering their daggers, the outlaw knew only too well what his fate would be if he didn't cooperate, and looking at Tom out of the corner of his eyes – the dagger prevented him from freely turning his head – he asked if his life would be spared if he told them all he knew.

'If you tell us the truth, I swear to you that I will do everything possible to persuade my lord, Sir William, not to hang you. It depends on you, but you have my word I shall do my best. If you try to escape in the meantime, I or one of my men will kill you, of that you can be sure. Well, what is it to be?'

The outlaw agreed immediately to help them, and Tom told his soldiers sternly, 'I have given my word! Don't forget that! Be patient and in a few days I'm sure we'll find booty enough to satisfy you all, as well as ridding ourselves of a dangerous nest of outlaws.'

Muttering in agreement, the soldiers carried out Tom's further instructions, loading the packhorses carefully, so that corn did not spill out of the damaged sacks, and when that and all other preparations were completed to his satisfaction, Tom led the long column slowly back towards Castor.

For most of the way, where the trail was wide enough, he had Paul and the prisoner alongside him. He wanted to keep an eye on his brother who was very quiet, still suffering from the shock of the outlaw attack and the death of Federico, and also question the captured outlaw on all the details of their camp. He learnt that there were several women in the camp, and when the outlaw begged Tom to save their lives and spare them from humiliation,

Tom began to feel that it was perhaps worthwhile to save this man's life – he seemed to have at least some values!

As they filed through the village of Castor on the way to the manor house, people came out of the cottages to look more closely at the commotion caused by so many horses. The children pointed at the bodies of the dead outlaws, trying to touch them as they passed by, shouting and cheering. The adults greeted Tom and Paul cordially, wishing them well, and, noting their bloodstained clothes, nodded in respect and appreciation, crossing themselves nevertheless, when the dead bodies passed by. Within hours, the whole neighbourhood was buzzing with excitement, full of rumours and exaggerated details of the dozens of men that their Thomas Rollesby and his soldiers had slaughtered. Everyone wondered when the hanging of the captured outlaw would take place!

Margaret heard the cavalcade as they were making their way to the round tower to deposit their weapons and lock up the prisoner, and she scuttled out from their quarters to see if all was well with Tom. She tried not to let it show, but whenever he was out on one of his 'missions' as he called them, she was always on tenterhooks until he returned. Hearing his voice instantly relieved her until she caught sight of all the bodies, the blood on Tom's clothes and the state of Paul – pale, bloodstained and walking as if in a trance.

'Oh, my God!' she exclaimed, holding her hands on the sides of her face, horrified. 'What's happened to Paul, Tom? Are you both wounded?'

'No, Margaret! We are both fine. It's just that Paul's a bit shaken up. Take him to our quarters, please, and take care of him. I'll be back soon and we can then talk more about it!'

While Tom went off to report to Sir William, his men moved the bodies out of sight and saw to the horses, unloading the supplies Paul had bought. Margaret led Paul gently but firmly back to their quarters, sending a servant to get some hot soup from the kitchen. Sitting him down on a chair, she went out into the yard to haul a jug of water from the well, quickly returning to clean his face and hands with the cold water, which helped to bring him back to his senses. Mrs Galston herself appeared with a bowl of soup, anxious to see how Paul was. Seeing and understanding Margaret's signal, she did not ask any questions, but fussed over Paul until he had finished the soup, and was content to see that some colour was coming back into his cheeks. The two women then led him protesting into the bedroom, insisting that he should rest for a few hours, and refused to go until they saw him settle wearily onto the bed, more or less falling asleep in front of their eyes.

Once outside the bedroom, Mrs Galston couldn't hold back her concern any longer.

'My goodness, mistress Rollesby,' she exclaimed, 'what have they done to that poor boy? He looks as if he has been to hell and back.'

'I think he has, Mrs Galston,' she replied. 'I don't really know more than yourself at the moment. I'll hear all about it from Tom later. All I know is that he must have been attacked by a gang of outlaws, and Tom and his soldiers must have got there just in time and killed them all – except one. They are all covered in blood and they brought back at least a dozen bodies from what I could see. It must have been terrible for the poor boy. When I learn more I'll let you know.'

Satisfied that she could do no more for the moment, Mrs Galston returned to the kitchen, leaving Margaret, lost in thought, waiting for her husband to return.

Sir William had listened intently to his captain's report of the events and had been delighted that Paul was unhurt, and was clearly saddened when he heard of the death of Federico, promising to give him a hero's burial in the manor house chapel. They also agreed between them that Tom should take fifteen soldiers and a levy of ten of the best archers in the surrounding villages to attack the outlaw camp in three days' time, and totally destroy it. Sir William gave Tom absolute authority to make all the necessary arrangements. He was happy with the ten or so horses that they had brought back with them, and expected there would be a few more when this new mission was accomplished. He had insisted initially that the captive outlaw should be executed, and it was with the greatest difficulty that he allowed himself to be persuaded to spare him, insisting, however, that the outlaw should accompany the attack on the stronghold, to ensure that it was taken with the absolute minimum loss of his soldiers. He also made Tom responsible for the outlaw's conduct both before and after the raid.

Sir William then called his steward, explaining briefly what had happened, and arranged for him to summon the reeve to take charge of the purchases that Paul had made, also alerting him to make the necessary preparations for the forthcoming military activity. The steward and Tom then took leave of their lord since they both had enough to arrange before the forthcoming raid; the captain of the guard being particularly anxious to return as quickly as possible to his quarters to check on the progress of his brother, unaware that many things would never quite be the same as they had been before!

13

Seeds of Change and Political Intrigue

Both Tom and Margaret were unable to sleep. After taking his brother back home late in the evening, they had talked into the early hours of the morning. He had begun by telling her more or less what had happened from his point of view, not wishing to dwell too much on the details, including what Paul had told him as they were riding back to Castor together. He explained that it was quite usual for someone so young and inexperienced in such combat to be somewhat shocked and to be concerned about actually killing for the first time. This was absolutely understandable, he maintained, particularly since as far as he could see his brother had probably killed at least five of the outlaws himself. Seeing Federico struck down before his eyes, someone who had become a real friend in their short time together, was finally too much. Paul was a sensitive person, he added, and he would need time to get over it. They both would need to keep a watchful eye on him for the next few weeks and help him over this difficult period. He would also talk as soon as possible with Stanley Pettit the reeve, he concluded, to make sure Paul wasn't left too much on his own.

Margaret had not said much, asking more questions than anything else, but she confided how alarmed she had been at the look on Paul's face when she first saw him, and how his eyes had somehow been focused on something she couldn't see.

'He appeared to be completely unaware of what was going on around him,' she said. 'Totally lost in thought, almost another person. It was terrible! I hope you're right about him getting over it!'

Tom took her in his arms to comfort her, and as he was slowly caressing her back in an attempt to soothe her worries and calm her, she moved closer to him, moving her hips up against him, until she felt the stirring in his loins. Then, kissing him passionately, she mounted him and they began to make love with an intensity that finally led to exhaustion and a deep sleep. Unknown to them both, their second child was conceived that night.

Two days later, as promised by Sir William, a special memorial service was held at the manor house chapel, in honour of Federico. He and Lady Mortimer were there as were all the soldiers of the troop, most of the household staff including the steward, the reeve and of course Paul, accompanied by Margaret. As the 'requiem aeternam' was sung, led by the chaplain, Father Ignatius, there was not a dry eye in the chapel. Sir William spoke a few words in an official 'laudatio', and as he looked at Paul, he signalled for him to also say a few words in honour of the man who had saved his life.

Making his way to the front of the congregation, Paul squared his shoulders, took a deep breath, looked at the mass of faces staring at him in the gloomy chapel, and began: 'My Lord, Lady Mortimer, Father Ignatius, thank you for giving me the opportunity to honour the name of Federico, whose devotion to duty and courage saved my life on more than one occasion in just the last week, when I had the privilege to get to know him as my escort, and then friend, on our fateful trip to Norwiche.'

He then briefly outlined the main events of the trip, including the archery contest he won, and the role that Federico played until his death at the hands of the outlaws. As he spoke, tears were coursing down his cheeks, and there was not a soul present who was not moved and astonished at the eloquence of 'young Master Paul'. Tom listened intently to his brother's words, spellbound, sad and yet proud of the wonderful quality of this spontaneous speech. People talked about it for weeks afterwards, and then of the final gesture, when Paul concluded by saying that if he had not thought so much about the prize money of five pounds, perhaps Federico may have been alive today, and he therefore, in his name, would donate this money for the well-being of the poor people in the demesne. With which, he walked over to Sir William and handed him the purse filled with the gold and silver coins he had won, begging him to use it in the way he had suggested. He then made his way slowly back to his seat, alongside Margaret.

There was a visible admiration and respect that emanated from all those present. If it had not been a place of worship, there would have been a wild outbreak of cheering and applause. The final words of Paul gave Father Ignatius the perfect link to complete the service, prior to the actual burial, illustrating that in a way, surely predestined by God the Almighty, the tragic loss of Federico, as well as serving as 'a lesson to all' had also brought sustenance to the poor.

Malicious tongues later discussing Paul's speech and his donation, wondering why Paul gave the prize money to Sir William rather than Father Ignatius, concluded that it was done probably to ensure that it actually was spent on the poor families of the demesne!

Early the next morning, Thomas Rollesby led out of Castor fifteen of his best men, accompanied by the captured outlaw, and picked up a further ten archers as prearranged with the elders of three neighbouring villages. The instructions were clear. The encampment was to be totally destroyed and burnt to the ground. All livestock was to be collected together and should be distributed evenly between the villages supplying the levied archers, with the exception of the horses – they were the property of the lord of Castor. All money or other valuables should be collected and would be divided equally between all the participants. The weapons would be handed over to Tom. All captured outlaws would be taken back to Castor and would be tried and sentenced by Sir William. He, Tom Rollesby, was in complete charge and his word was to be obeyed at all times. Saying this to his men, Tom looked at the levied archers in particular, and it was clear that nobody was going to question the point!

With the help of the captured outlaw, Tom outlined the position and layout of the quarry area and living accomodation, and the three watchmen positions. He also detailed the plan of attack, dividing his men into three groups: the outlaw, two archers and three soldiers were to accompany him; the other two groups of ten men, each comprising of six soldiers and four villagers, were led by a crossbowman. He and his group would take care of the lookouts and then support the two-fronted attack as best they could. Each of the main groups were allocated an area of huts they were to set on fire. They were then to pick off the outlaws as they came out to fight. Tom's final words were concerning the women in the huts – they were to be spared, in no way to be abused, and he would decide on their fate when everything was over. Satisfied that everything was clear, Tom gave the signal to move off to the assembly point near Blofeld, about two miles from the outlaws' camp where they would spend the rest of the day and night, to rest and prepare themselves for the attack at dawn on the following day.

While the Castor force was riding towards Blofeld, the Earl of Dunghall, Sir Roderick, accompanied by the Genoese crossbowman Marco – who had failed to return with the rest of the escort from London, deciding to work for the Irish nobleman – and the constable of Norwiche, the Count de Kessinger with a considerable bodyguard, were making their way to the castle at Richmond, in the North Riding of Yorkshire. Both the count and the earl had attended a brief session of parliament in London that had met to discuss King Edward's latest demands for financing his wars in Flanders and France, and were not very happy at the outcome. The king's campaigns at this time were not only costly but also not very successful. It appeared that the new taxes were just being poured into a bottomless pit, but in spite of this, a majority had voted to provide more money. The earl saw this as yet more wool taxation to be paid, and the count, whose personal friend, Nicholas de la Beche – previously constable of the Tower of London – had been humiliated by Edward a year earlier, was more interested in clandestine efforts to weaken the king's power than in helping him. The fact that the constable had been punished for failure to carry out his job properly – namely to ensure that the fortress and port were correctly manned for the defence of London at all times – did not interest the Count de Kessinger.

During this journey, when they had the opportunity to talk without being overheard, they gradually revealed more of their personal plans to each other, since they had discovered over time that they had a common hatred of the king. The count had explained to Sir Roderick that his friend Nicholas had earlier been a guardian to the king's eldest son, the young Duke of Cornwall (later better known as the Black Prince), who had lived some time in the London fortress. Through his friend he had got to know the young prince, and established quite a good relationship with him, which had enabled the count to remain well-informed about the affairs of state and the court. He had discovered through the prince that the king was planning to re-establish a Round Table of several hundred knights of the realm and he wanted to be among them, believing that his apparent friendship with him would ensure it. Now that the previous constable of the Tower of London was in disgrace, he was no longer able to maintain contact with the young duke, whom he expected one day would be king of England. Whenever the king was out of the country his eldest son carried the title of Guardian of England so his accession looked certain. What had earlier seemed to be an easy way to increase his influence and power with the royal household was no longer available and he had thus become a secret enemy of King Edward.

Although Sir Roderick's motive was purely that of financial gain, believing that another king would not continue the expensive wars outside of England, whereby weathy landowners like himself were having to foot even higher tax bills each year to finance them, he also did not like Englishmen at all! His family in Ireland had very close relationships with some powerful Scottish families, and since, apart from the Count de Kessinger, his veiled approaches to English nobility including the lord of Castor, had been singularly unsuccessful, he believed he could expect better support in Scotland, a traditional ally of the court of France.

The earl had planned a secret meeting with Edward's brother-in-law, David of Scotland, just north of the border, which he had not disclosed to the Count de Kessinger, whom he considered to be an idiot, merely using him and his escort as the safest way to reach Richmond, close to his real destination. He did not want to reveal the extent of his treachery at this stage, if at all, to the count, who believed that the real purpose of the journey was to increase the scale of his own smuggling operation, by involving a powerful relative of Sir Roderick's at Richmond into the network, before the Earl of Dunghall continued home by ship to Ireland. The Count de Kessinger was happy to provide the escort which would be more than repaid by his eventual share of what he believed would be a very large increase in the amount of smuggled wool that would escape royal taxation. That would not only be a smack in the eye for King Edward, he considered, but would at the same time be a welcome addition to his own personal, already considerable fortune!

By the time the earl and the duke had caught sight of the great tower of Richmond castle, rising majestically high over Swaledale, Tom Rollesby's troop had arrived at their assembly point and were beginning to set up camp for the night prior to the planned dawn attack on the outlaw's stronghold.

Once the horses had been fed and watered and were safely tethered out of sight in the small wood, and Tom had chosen where they would overnight, he called all the men to him, and went over the plan once again to make sure everything was clearly understood. He insisted that all weapons should be carefully checked and made ready for the pre-dawn departure, including the specially prepared torch arrows that were to be used to fire the huts. Watches were allocated, a meal was prepared, and they began to settle down to rest before the exertions of the following day. Tom kept the captured outlaw close to him to avoid any possibility of him slipping away during the night to alert his comrades, although Tom had already gained the impression that the man wanted nothing more to do with them!

An hour before daybreak, they were all awake and quickly getting ready to make a start. One man was left to guard the horses, and the prisoner, with Tom alongside him, led the group off, walking briskly out of the wood and up the hillside on the way to the quarry and the encampment, which was about two miles away. Walking in absolute silence they made good progress, greatly helped by the clear sky and the gleaming stars. Occasionally, a bird or mouse or some other small creature would scuttle off for cover, alarmed by the nightly intruders. At about five hundred paces from the quarry, they stopped, formed into the prearranged groups, and, guided by the prisoner and Tom, worked their way silently to the three lookout positions. It was easier than they thought. In the absence of their leader, Black Peter, there were only two guards snoring peacefully at their posts, and they died unaware of anything!

They moved along the two sides of the quarry gradually descending down to the rows of huts that fanned out in a crescent-like shape, following the line of the granite galleries. Long since abandoned, grass, bushes and trees had encroached on the more open side facing them, and in the distance they could just make out a corral for the horses, near the spot the prisoner had described as the cooking, eating and meeting area. Refuse and other broken implements littered the ground and a slight breeze wafted the smell of urine, excrement and horses towards them as they took up position. The horses were a little uneasy, snorting nervously from time to time but the breeze was in the wrong direction for them to pick up the scent of the intruders.

One group positioned themselves on the left flank, another on the right, so that the outlaws would be caught in a crossfire when they came out of the huts, while Tom took his men to the cooking area which faced the huts. In a nearby shed they found several bales of straw, which they quietly laid in front of the doors of each hut, and then returned silently to their positions, waiting for the sunrise. Within a few minutes, the first rays appeared and gradually the huts became clearly visible to them as the sun almost imperceptibly eased itself over the horizon behind Tom and his men. He prepared the torch arrows, using a flint-stone to ignite a handful of dry straw with which he and his men set fire to the pitch and cloth wound around the arrow heads and fired them into the straw piled in front of the huts.

They did not have to wait long. Initially the outlaws didn't realise they were under attack as they stumbled out of the huts, coughing and shouting, totally disorganised. Then they saw at least ten of their number sinking to the ground, pierced by several arrows and screaming in pain. Some of them took a chance and sprinted for cover towards the horses where they were picked off by Tom and his group who were waiting for such an eventuality. Others went back into the huts searching frantically for their weapons, hardly able to see for the smoke and some were overcome by the fumes or trapped by the blazing timbers and died horribly in a fiery inferno. Few of those that returned outside to fight lasted more than a few seconds before they fell, mortally wounded or killed instantly by the hail of arrows and bolts. The captured outlaw screamed at Tom to spare the women. Tom then immediately ordered a ceasefire, and advanced quickly towards the huts, his men alongside him, prepared to fire if necessary.

Survivors were told to surrender and their lives would be spared if they came out of the huts unarmed. There were only four people who came staggering out of the huts, with blackened faces and burnt clothes, begging for mercy. The rest had been killed or had been burned to death.

Suddenly there was silence for a moment and the soldiers and levied archers on the two flanks, whooping and shouting with delight at the victory, came running down from their positions, checking each hut where it was possible, and bringing the four prisoners to the captain.

On closer inspection, Tom saw that there were three women and a young boy, all in shock and shivering in the early morning cold, wondering what would happen next, but not really expecting any pity and fearing the worst. They were astonished to hear the massive soldier commanding his men to lend them cloaks, to feed them, while others were starting a fire to warm them. One of the crossbowmen was placed in charge of the four prisoners, while the rest of the troop began to collect and strip the bodies of the dead outlaws and dig a large grave for the corpses. There were at least thirty of them thrown into the common grave, and before the bodies were covered, Tom felt obliged to say a few words.

He began by saying that Sir William had appointed him as captain of his guard in the demesne of Castor, had given him as family arms the motto of 'Protector and Avenger', and by God he would do just that to keep the land free from murderous bandits and other rogues! He understood only too well that some people had turned to crime to survive in these difficult times, but that gave them no right to perpetrate some of the acts of violence and brutality that had occurred in the vicinity. Maybe, in the grave before them, there were some men who had once been good and honest, and had grown into bad and evil ways. He could not judge that, but ended by saying with all humility and sincerity, that the Almighty would know whether their souls should be saved or sent

112

into eternal damnation. He paused, added an 'Amen', and signalled the men to complete the burial.

Once the large, common grave was filled, the horses were rounded up by the soldiers while the ten levied archers shared out between them the cattle, poultry and other stored provisions they had found, and with Tom's permission began to make their way back to their villages ahead of the soldiers.

One of the women prisoners asked to speak with Tom for a moment and quietly informed him that she knew where the outlaw leader, Black Peter, had hidden a large sum of stolen money and jewellery. She had been living with him and said that the outlaw had buried it in a wooden chest under the floor of their hut that was now a smoking ruin. Leading him to the hut she pointed out the spot and he began to scrape away the soil and stones that covered it. They had in fact found very little booty and he was delighted when he saw what was stored inside the chest: hundreds of florins, groats and pennies as well as gold and silver rings, necklaces, brooches and several fine silver plates and ornaments – a fine prize for his men and a good sum for his lord!

After a meal, once everything was loaded on the horses they had rounded up, Tom took charge of the horse carrying the chest, and with the outlaw at his side, led his troop and the four captives back towards Castor. During the ride back, he talked a long time with the outlaw who told him about his earlier life, and what had led him to join Black Peter's group.

His father, he explained, had been a reeve on an estate owned by the Abbey of Burye St Edmunds in the shire of Suffolke. They had lived in the village of Stoke close to the River Orwel. His mother was long since dead due to an illness at his birth from which she never recovered, and in his childhood days he had been brought up by an aunt, living nearby in Neyland. From the age of twelve, he had worked with his father, learning the various skills to enable him one day to take over from him. One day their village was overrun by a raiding force of Genoese and Frenchmen and his father was killed while he was working in the cornfields some distance away from the village. He was only fifteen and too young to take over his father's job, and without his good influence drifted along, somehow managing to get enough work to survive. Like all the young men of the village, he practised regularly with the longbow and a few years later had been levied to take part in an expeditionary force of the king to fight in France. He had found himself in a group led by the Earl of Derby, and during a raid on the port of Le Tréport had been badly wounded by a crossbow bolt in the leg, managing somehow to survive and returned to England with other wounded soldiers. When it came to payment, nobody appeared to be responsible – the money was probably pocketed by some of the clerks, he added cynically – and he found himself barely able to walk, alone and penniless in Yermouth.

Coming from the countryside, he was able to find fruit and wild berries to help keep the hunger away, and managed to poach the odd trout or trap a hare or steal a chicken from time to time. Nobody was willing to give him any work, particularly as his wound was still troubling him, making it very painful for him to walk any distance. That was when he met Annie, he said, when she was travelling alone on her way to Norwiche to her sister, hoping she could stay with her for a while since she had no other family, her husband having been killed by bandits.

Even though she had nothing herself, apart from two or three pence which she shared with him, Annie helped him, cleaning and dressing his wound, using the juice from some wild herbs to cure the infection that had been giving him so much trouble. Before he could add any more, Tom asked him what had happened to Annie, and the outlaw looked over his shoulder and said, 'She's there behind us. The one who showed you where Black Peter kept his money!'

Realising that this must be a difficult and highly emotional subject for the outlaw, since Annie had been living with Black Peter, Tom apologized for the interruption and asked him to continue.

He described what a wonderful woman she was. Without her, he would have probably died or at least have lost his leg. He had asked if he could accompany her to Norwiche, since now his leg was better, he could at least offer her some protection on the way, and he had been happy to do that, since he had fallen in love with her. All had gone well until they had passed Acle, where they were attacked by Black Peter with four or five of his men. They didn't have a chance. They were about to cut his throat when she pleaded with the outlaw leader to spare his life. Understanding the situation well, he had agreed, provided she would live with him, and her companion would join his band. To save the life of each other, they both reluctantly agreed to Black Peter's conditions, and that was more or less the whole story. They had been in the camp for several months against their will, and only the death of Black Peter had given them an outside chance of perhaps one day being able to live together.

By now, they were close to the manor house, and Tom, realising that without Sir William's support he could do little, tried to reassure the outlaw that maybe there would be a chance for them both, but in the meantime he would have to trust him, even though he had to put him back into the prison cell for another day or so.

Once back and the horses stabled, Tom put the young boy in the care of Mrs Galston, took the three women to his quarters asking his wife to take care of them, and carrying the wooden chest under one arm, went to report to Sir William.

Sir William and Lady Mortimer had almost finished their supper when Tom arrived. He was immediately offered a pitcher of ale and asked if he was hungry. He thanked them profusely but added that his wife was busily preparing a meal for him. However, he needed to discuss an important matter first and hoped his lordship could spare him a few minutes.

Sir William was intrigued by the chest that Tom had put down by the side of the long table, but waited for his explanation. As usual, Tom played down the details of the attack, but confirmed that there were at least thirty outlaws less to trouble the demesne, and that he had returned with twenty-two more horses for his lordship! He then picked up the chest and opened it so they could see the contents. Lady Mortimer was thrilled with the silver plate and the beautifully modelled table ornaments, and it was clear to see Sir William's pleasure at the quantity of gold and silver coins, and the valuable jewellery. He immediately summoned the steward to put it all in safe keeping. Before the old man arrived, however, Tom asked Sir William to grant his soldiers a share of the booty, suggesting that perhaps each man should have a florin and two groats in recognition of the absolute success of the mission. Sir William immediately agreed.

'And what about yourself, Tom?' Sir William asked, with a twinkle in his eye. 'Without you, I doubt if we would have the half of what you have brought back, and all without casualties! Tell me, what would you like to have and it's yours!'

Lady Mortimer watched him a little anxiously, perhaps fearing that he would ask for the plate or the ornaments which she dearly wanted to keep, and they were both surprised when he replied that he had no need of more money, but had a little favour to ask. Knowing that he was in a relatively good position to negotiate he mentioned that he had four captives, and recounted the outlaw's story. He then went on to suggest a possible way to handle them, adding that if he were to grant the outlaw his freedom, he, Tom Rollesby was certain he would make an excellent addition to the demesne, and that the captive Annie would be an ideal wife for him. As for the young boy, who was without a mother, he could not think of a better solution than Annie to take care of him.

'And the other two women?' Sir William asked with a suggestion of a smile.

The captain looked at his master and then Lady Mortimer, and added that perhaps the manor house needed or could manage to take on another two servants, but his ladyship would know that best.

'My God, Tom,' Sir William retorted, 'what a persuasive fellow you are! You've won. I agree to all your suggestions, and my dear wife will certainly be happy to make the two new servants feel at home here, I'm absolutely sure!'

With which, Tom thanked Sir William, bowed to his wife and requested permission to return to his quarters and make the necessary arrangements. Sir William waved his acknowledgement and the household captain returned to Margaret, delighted with his handiwork!

And so it came to pass. The chaplain conducted the marriage service of John Dexter, the outlaw, and his bride Annie, and they settled down in a cottage found for them by the reeve, Stanley Pettit, who was delighted to have the services of a man with the knowledge and skills of John. Paul seemed to find a kindred spirit in the young boy that the couple adopted as their own son, and helped him more than anyone else to settle into the new surroundings and circumstances of the demesne. The other two captive women recognised immediately the advantages of working in the manor house for Lady Mortimer, and rapidly became her most loyal servants.

Early in the following year, Margaret gave birth to a daughter, who bore such a resemblance to her mother that it was natural for her to be given the same name. The child was not only the apple of Tom's eye, but also somehow in her initial helplessness helped Paul to recover fully from his earlier depression, and he almost became a second father to her. Margaret frequently commented to Tom that his brother seemed to enjoy so much the company of their daughter and the adopted son of the Dexters that he would surely make a wonderful father and should start to look for a suitable wife. Tom always laughed at her and told her to stop being a meddlesome matchmaker, for his brother was now old enough to find someone himself if that was what he wanted!

Paul himself had also thought about marriage, although he never admitted it to Margaret in the good-natured conversations that used to take place when he was a guest at their supper table, which was frequently! As much as he loved children, he somehow knew that Castor was not to be his home and he had to see much more of the world before settling down with a family. He engrossed himself in his work, making sure that he learned everything possible from the reeve, and within a year or so had even convinced him to try new methods of ground drainage and soil fertilisation to improve the crop yields.

While the affairs of the demesne prospered, due particularly to the efforts of the two brothers and the goodwill of Sir William and Lady Mortimer, other forces were developing that threatened it.

King David of Scotland had listened carefully to the ideas of Sir Roderick, the Earl of Dunghall, but explained that the truce he had signed with his brother-in-law prohibited him from taking active steps against Edward for the time being. He continued to maintain friendly contact with the French King Philippe and would indeed help him at the right tactical moment, he added, not knowing then how fate would treat him at Neville's Cross a few years later!

The earl in the meantime had returned to his home in Ireland, not wanting to be drawn personally into any of Edward's campaigns. He busied himself with his wool smuggling plans and activities when he was not totally besotted by whisky, using Marco Paulini to act secretly as his intermediary with the constable of Norwiche castle, the Count de Kessinger.

The count, for his part, continued to increase his personal wealth with ever-expanding smuggling activities, even going so far as to steal sheep from time to time. His 'agents' usually were more active in isolated areas far from Norwiche, but occasionally in the winter months made the odd foray into the Castor demesne, to please the count's partner in crime, the Earl of Dunghall. The Count de Kessinger also maintained a very active presence in parliamentary affairs, continuously seeking ways to curry favour from influential nobility that would help him to get closer to the king's eldest son. He had been present at his investiture when the king bestowed his son with the title of Prince of Wales in parliament, in May 1343, and subsequently invited him and his 'entourage' to a tournament he set up and financed at Norwiche. It was with bitter disappointment that he found himself not included in the select 'Order of St George' that the king founded in the following year, which was restricted to a mere two dozen leading knights of the realm. This further strengthened his resolve to subversive treachery.

The village life in the demesne of Castor and many other manors across the country appeared to continue its normal course, conscious perhaps of an increasing number of crimes of violence around them, but too involved in the personal struggle for survival to be aware of the political plotting and manipulations of the nobility or the implications of increasing taxation on wool and other items, or the long-term economic effects of the 'staple' monopoly. Most of the population lived in small communities, rarely, if ever, venturing into the towns or cities, working the land primarily for the benefit of a powerful minority: the lords and the Church. They were largely uneducated and not encouraged to think for themselves.

Some things were, however, beginning to change. Hard-working peasants had begun to own smallholdings, which gradually became larger and more important. Occasionally, from this background, a person like Paul Rollesby learned how to read and write, or a natural leader and warrior like Tom Rollesby appeared, each unwittingly beginning a process or processes that impacted dramatically on their environment, in spite of the ever-present comfortable and privileged establishment, fearful of any change that could challenge their position.

During the year of 1345, the king had ordered that 'Commissioners of Array' should travel through the whole country, noting men between the ages of sixteen and sixty who were fit to serve in a future army, particularly the best longbowmen. The names of Thomas and Paul Rollesby stood at the top of the list of the commissioner who some years previously had visited the Count de Kessinger and attended an archery contest in Norwiche.

PART II
(1346–1356)

14

The Battle of Crécy

Tom looked down at his brother, now sleeping peacefully under the cover of trees above the village of Crécy, his longbow, a quiver of arrows and a sword alongside him, lying amongst row after row of other archers, exhausted from the exertions and excesses of the last six weeks or so. He was also himself hardly able to keep his eyes open, but had made sure his men were all comfortable for the night, and was now sharing the first watch with two others. They were at least reasonably protected from the rain which had intermittently fallen during the long day's march, and this position was well-sheltered from the wind which periodically gusted over the hills and through the valleys around them.

He had promised Margaret that he would keep a close eye on his brother and do everything possible to protect him, little knowing what lay before them when they left Castor towards the end of June. It had all started so well! The sun had been shining on that morning as he took leave of his wife and family, which now included another daughter, Alice, born early in the year. Even his brother Paul had seemed to welcome leaving Castor for a new adventure. He had taken several months to get over the terrible events that led to Federico's death, immersing himself in the affairs of the demesne and spending what little free time he had with Tom's daughter and the Dexters' adopted son, Robert. In spite of the thought of war and what that involved, Paul was excited about the prospect of travelling to France and seeing another country. He was still only twenty-two – a couple of years younger than Tom had been when he left home for Flanders six years earlier – and felt that it was now time for a change of scenery. Tom had warned his brother that there was nothing romantic in such a campaign, but at the same time didn't want to alarm him unduly with details of what the reality could be, hoping that perhaps it might be a little different from the sea battle at Sluys.

The lord of Castor, Sir William, much to his own regret, was too ill to travel, and although confined to bed with a fever had insisted on fully briefing Tom before giving him his blessings and prayers for a safe return.

So, ten soldiers from the troop, a levy of fifty archers including his brother and fifty pikemen from the demesne, all led by Tom, travelled by barge from the manor house along the canal to the River Burre and then on to Yermouth. In all it took two days for the whole contingent to reach Yermouth, where the Earl of Suffolke's marshals met them before embarking three days later on ships bound for Portchester, where they were billeted in tents for another week as the army was being assembled.

The weather had continued to be kind to them and they were all fascinated to watch in beautiful sunshine all the preparations being made: the rows of carts filled with provisions, weapons (including tens of thousands of arrows), tents and tools, all lined up waiting to be loaded on to the barges and ships of all types anchored in the harbour area and along the huge estuary as far as the eye could see. There were at least 1,000 of them. The specially-erected paddocks in the fields behind them were filled with several thousand horses waiting nervously to be led onto barges or ships moored all along the jetties, sensing the general excitement and tension in the air. Finally, the men-at-arms arrived, resplendent in their fine uniforms, with their chain-mail hauberks and shields glistening in the sun, banners flying at the ends of their lances, sitting proudly on the huge destriers, followed by mounted yeomen carrying the helmets and other weapons of their masters and other helpers leading carts loaded with armour, spears and javelins.

It took days for everything and everybody to be taken on board – in all, almost 20,000 men, excluding the ship crews, and almost as many horses – but they eventually set sail early in July, heading due south for Normandy. In spite of the danger ahead, the sense of excitement and the spectacle of so many ships with their flags and pavises hanging on the sides was a sight that none would forget. It reminded Tom of his departure six years previously, although it had been on a much smaller scale, but then he shuddered slightly as he recollected some of the scenes he had witnessed at Sluys, pushing them out of his mind as he listened to his brother excitedly describing and commenting on the impressive departure. Surely this would be better, he hoped!

They had no sooner passed the Wight Island when a strong wind sprang up, whipping the waves into boiling masses of crested water, causing many of the men to be violently seasick. Not only that, but they were blown off course, driven west and obliged to ride at anchor for several days off the coast of Cornwall, only able to land at Saint-Vaast-La-Hougue, a small port on the Normandy coast, on 12 July.

It took five days for the army of 2,000 men-at-arms, 10,000 archers and 6,000 footmen, pages and other helpers to disembark and recover from the stormy crossing, before forming up into three main groups prior to beginning their long march. Tom's soldiers and the fifty levied archers were placed under the command of the Earl of Warwick, and the pikemen became part of the force led by the king and the Prince of Wales.

Looking back on those last six weeks, without being specifically told, Tom clearly saw that the purpose of this invasion had been to despoil France, to both provoke and humiliate King Philippe, by showing the people how incapable he was of even protecting them. It had been horrible! Both he and his brother had witnessed scenes of violence and depravity they could never forget. Small, prosperous villages and smallholdings had been looted and destroyed. Unarmed men, women and children had been slaughtered or perished in the flames of their homes which were all set on fire after having been sacked. Young women and their even younger daughters had been ravished, violently abused and left to die in and around the burning houses. They had both helped with the destruction, and although not participating in the many acts of wanton savagery and debauchery, and at times intervening to prevent some or other excess, Tom and Paul had become almost immune to the tragic scenes and suffering around them.

After strong resistance, they had captured and despoiled the city of Caen, because the inhabitants had refused to surrender, and amassed large quantities of booty to the delight of the English soldiers. Towns like Bayeux and Lisieux surrendered without resistance to avoid the fate of Caen. The army had then swung eastwards towards the French capital of Paris, laying waste everything before it, with only the River Seine between them and a much larger French army apparently waiting for the ideal opportunity to attack and destroy the English interlopers, but somehow never daring to take their chance!

King Edward had then given King Philippe the impression his army was going to advance around the southern suburbs of the capital, drawing the French army away to the east while he suddenly feinted to the north, crossing the Seine at Poissy under cover of darkness and heading towards Calais.

For the following week, Tom and his men with the rest of the English force had hurried as fast as they could, many of them laden with booty, up towards the River Somme, frequently in torrential rain, hoping to avoid the French army in hot pursuit on their eastern flank. It was not a flight of panic, Tom reflected; but the weather, their manpower losses during the whole campaign, illnesses, general fatigue and the knowledge that an infinitely larger army was close by, began to tell on the overall morale of his men. He had had to coax and even bully them at times to keep themselves and their equipment clean and in order. It had not been easy! And then they found all the immediately accessible bridges across the Somme had been destroyed by the French vanguard, and all known fords were either badly damaged or closely-guarded by large concentrations of French soldiers levied from all neighbouring towns and cities.

Their situation at that moment had looked desperate until a local official that had been taken prisoner, in return for his life and freedom, agreed to lead the English army to a secret ford at the hamlet of Saigneville. After a night of frenetic activity, the whole English army was prepared in readiness to cross the Somme at daybreak on St Bartholomew's Day, at a ford called Blanche-Taque. Tom, with his brother Paul and the remaining thirty-five of his archers and seven soldiers, were placed into the vanguard led by the Earl of Warwick, and provided support with several hundred other archers for a force of about five hundred mounted men-at-arms that charged across the ford, vastly outnumbered, to attack the French militia assembled on the other side, equally determined to stop their advance.

It was a savage and bloody encounter, and the outcome was uncertain for the first half hour or so. The English men-at-arms knew they had to cross the river and clear a way for the rest of the army or they would all perish miserably, but their French counterparts, well supported by crossbowmen, archers and foot soldiers, took a heavy toll on their traditional enemies. Tom had seen the danger in time and directed his group to concentrate on the enemy archers, with volley after volley of well-aimed arrows, until they fell back in disarray. At that stage, he led them across the river, where they continued to wreak havoc on the enemy forces, and, followed by others, forced a large section to retreat and then eventually run away to safety.

Once the position on the northern bank of the river was secured, the balance of the English force quickly crossed the Somme, spurred on by the king and the young Prince of Wales, forcing their way rapidly further north, making as much ground as possible between them and the main French army approaching from the east. Well clear of the river and the swampy fields, the English army reformed and the king led them along the tracks of the large forest area of Crécy-en-Ponthieu until they reached a good defendable position above the village of Crécy on the evening of 25 August, where they camped for the night, completely exhausted.

In spite of the circumstances and the dampness, Tom slept soundly at the end of his watch, and was awakened at daybreak by a marshal from the Earl of Warwick, summoning him to attend a briefing. Somewhat surprised and still yawning he made his way quickly down to a meeting place just on the edge of the tree line, overlooking a valley to the south and a river he later learned was called the Maye. The earl was talking to a group of men-at-arms when he arrived, and seeing that Tom was obviously ill at ease, beckoned him over and introduced him quickly to the noblemen around him.

'Gentlemen,' he began, 'this is the yeoman archer I was telling you about, Mr Thomas Rollesby. I had already heard about this man from a friend, the lord of Castor who unfortunately was too ill to join us, and had the pleasure to see him in action at Blanche-Taque. He is not only the best archer we have here at Crécy, but he fights like a lion and his men follow him without question. He is here because I want him to be responsible for all the longbowmen and pikemen on our right flank, and he will, therefore, with his men, play a critical role in this forthcoming battle. I am giving him absolute command over all these men and that is why he is here to take part in this briefing.' Then, turning to Tom, he gave him a green and white jerkin with the arms of the Prince of Wales on the front and back. 'Wear this over your hauberk and no man shall question your authority!' The earl then embraced him and the other noblemen shook his hand and welcomed him to the group. Within a few minutes he felt part of the planning group, listened carefully to the details of the overall plan, asked good questions, and was pleased that his own suggestions were accepted by them all.

After about half an hour, the earl left to join the other commanders, the Prince of Wales and the king to hear Mass, make their confessions and receive communion, as was the usual practice of the leaders before most battles. Tom, for his part, happy not to have been invited to join them, returned to the hillside where he had left his men and a large group of other archers, working over in his mind the various things to be done.

Paul was already awake and seemed pleased to see his brother and was delighted to hear that he had been so honoured to command around 2,000 archers and 1,000 pikemen, as Tom explained it all to him.

'My God, Tom,' he joked, 'they'll be making you a knight one of these days, if you're not careful.' They both laughed heartily as Tom playfully punched him on the shoulder, telling him to show more respect to his elder brother.

While the earl's marshals were busy rousing the sleeping archers and pikemen, calling the centenars and vintenars to them to get the various groups counted and organised, Tom took his brother down to the area on the hillside to show him where the archers and pikemen of the right flank were to be positioned and how the baggage wagons loaded with bundles of spare arrows and pavises were to be placed behind them in a line up to the back of the group of men-at-arms that would be led by the Prince of Wales. Shading his eyes from the early morning sun he pointed down the valley to the River Maye they could just see below them and explained that the rapidly approaching French army was expected to appear from there within a few hours and they had no time to waste with the preparations.

'Paul,' he added, 'I want you to take charge of all the arrangements for the waggons and the supplies. I must have a man I can trust to handle it. You can only have a hundred archers and pikemen as a defence should the French try to come up around the flank. I don't think they'll make it because of this wood here, and in any case we may need a bit more support from behind. You'll need to watch that carefully, and if things are really bad send a man up to the king's position for reinforcements. He's got about a thousand archers and six hundred pikemen in reserve back up there. Paul, I'm relying on you. Do you have any questions?'

The only question Paul had concerned their chances against a force that was rumoured to be more than 100,000 men, almost ten times more than they now had. Tom looked at his brother fondly and shook his head, saying he couldn't answer that question. The only thing he knew was that if they didn't fight with everything they had they would all die, and if possible he wanted to survive. He was also tired of what seemed to be an almost continuous use of force frequently against people not able to defend themselves. But in this case, all the enemy were well-armed, and if it was only in memory of their own mother and father, then by God, he would fight until he could no longer stand. He embraced his brother, told him to take care of himself and returned to his men.

The biggest problem he had, he knew, was the morale of the

men. They were all tired and hungry. Many were without adequate footwear, their soft leather boots being completely worn out by the long marches and some were even barefooted! Others were suffering with stomach pains due to eating unripe fruit they had found on the way, to ease their hunger, and most were, like himself, sickened with the brutality of the previous weeks. One of the suggestions he had made at the briefing was the need for a hot meal, since a full, contented stomach solves many problems, and it had been arranged that a meat and barley soup with rye bread and beer would be brought to their positions by mid-morning.

Grumbling at the shouting centenars and vintenars who had organised them into recognisable groups of a hundred archers and pikemen, almost 3,000 sullen-faced soldiers faced Tom as he stood before them. He could only see half of them, since the massed groups stretched back into the forest where they had camped for the night, and it took some minutes before it was quiet enough for him to begin. He knew he had to be short and to the point and told them immediately about the forthcoming hot meal which brought cheers from all. However, he added, they must first take up their defensive position on the hillside. He explained briefly where it was and how they should deploy themselves under the supervision of the centenars: a hundred pikemen to two hundred longbowmen. Then the protective pavises would be set up and the spare bundles of arrows would be distributed; only then would they be fed! Once that was done, they would be given more information. He ordered the centenars to take over and move the men to the designated position, making sure the archers kept their bowstrings dry since it looked like more rain again!

Marshals under the supervision of the Earls of Warwick and Harcourt had already roughly staked out the areas where the three main bodies of the men-at-arms would be stationed, and most of their horses had been taken to an area at the back of the woods close to the reserve troops, well behind the entire army, since the king had decided his knights should fight on foot. The longbowmen and pikemen were also divided primarily into three main groups, one in the centre and the other two on each flank, each group being more or less supported by the three forces of men-at-arms deployed behind them.

Tom saw that his brother had also been busy, since the line of baggage wagons were almost all in position by the time he had walked down the hillside to supervise the deployment of his archers and pikemen on the right flank. The fan-like formation was paced out, roughly a hundred yards or so long at the front edge facing south looking down onto the River Maye below, and a little more than fifty yards wide at the deepest part of the apex behind them, backing onto the line of wagons. The first three lines of longbowmen were formed into a sort of saw-toothed formation, positioned a yard or so between each man, with a gap of three to four yards between each row, with just enough space to enable two rows of foot soldiers to position their pikes between the archers of the first two ranks.

Grouped behind each of these 'saw teeth' were ten blocks of reserve pikemen and archers ready to rush forward to replace fallen comrades or to help them attack any enemy men-at-arms who had fallen from their horses. The balance of Tom's archers were then in more or less straight lines behind the saw-toothed formation, within the confines of the total 'fan shape', taking advantage of the sloping ground behind them so that they could easily fire over the heads of their comrades in front. Other pikemen and archers were also placed at stategic points around the total flanking position to prevent any enemy infiltration from the sides or rear of the formation.

Once his men were in position, all available pavises were set up in front of the archers and bundles of spare arrows were distributed, as well as spare pikes and halberds that were stored in the ten forward 'reserve' areas. Making a final check of the total position, Tom was satisfied that he could use his longbowmen optimally to focus on both the whole of the enemy front and also engage any advancing men-at-arms in a murderous crossfire; and the double row of pikemen should be able to hold back any mounted men-at-arms that attempted to attack the archers. He then gave the order for the men to 'stand down' and collect their food and drink from the waggons behind them.

He sent a messenger to the Earl of Warwick confirming their state of readiness and requesting any news of the approaching French army before joining his brother Paul whom he found sitting in one of the waggons, draining a jug of ale. Sitting alongside him, after finishing a large bowl of hot soup and wiping his mouth, Tom asked him how he now felt.

'Well, to be honest, I'm scared stiff Tom,' he replied after a long pause. 'Like everybody else here, I'm tired of all this fighting and I mean, what are we doing here anyway? How can we really consider this land belongs to us? We don't speak their language and the people here have been working this land for generations and don't need us. In fact you saw yourself how they fought at Caen to keep us out and I'll not forget for the rest of my life what happened there after we captured the city! If I should survive and somehow manage to get back home, I'm not saying that I'll take refuge in a monastery but I want to do something much more worthwhile with my life than killing and stealing from other people. What about yourself? How do you feel about all this, Tom?'

His elder brother looked down the hillside in front of them, taking in the beauty of the valley, the beech, oak and pine trees that covered the rolling hills around them. He sighed gently, and replied: 'Much the same as you do, Paul. I don't enjoy any type of warfare against ordinary folk and never will. Earlier it was easy to kill French soldiers when I thought about what they had done to our mother and father, as I told you earlier. I don't know the answers to your questions about why we are here, but we are with our King Edward and he is our lord and this land used to belong to England, so Sir William once said, and I believe him. I owe everything I have to that man. He's been good and fair to us both as you well know. Paul, I feel I have a duty to perform and even though in this case I don't much like it, I'm going to do it. Not only that, if we don't fight we shall all die and I'm responsible now for all these men here, and I'm going to do everything I can to try to win this coming battle with as few as possible of these basically good, simple men being killed. May God protect us both also, Paul. Take good care: and now excuse me, I still have a great deal to do.'

He jumped down from the waggon and began to talk briefly to groups of soldiers that were lounging on the grass, either eating or drinking, or sharpening swords or daggers, or trying to sleep for a few stolen moments. He understood their thoughts and misgivings, and gave words of encouragement to them all, before moving on to the next group. Paul watched his brother and marvelled at the way he cared for the men, seeming to know exactly what to say to his soldiers, and how they appeared to respect him. He oozed a confidence and energy that was somehow transferred to them as he went from group to group until he was out of sight, leaving Paul lost in thought, reflecting on what his brother had said.

Tom spent more than two hours with his men until a messenger returned, advising him the king had begun to make a tour around his army and could be expected shortly at their position, and so he ordered a trumpeter to sound the 'take position' fanfare.

It took more than ten minutes to get the men back to their right positions with the help of the extremely vociferous centenars. Tom called them all to silence as soon as they were ready, telling them to stay on guard since the king would shortly arrive. In fact he had no sooner made the announcement when King Edward appeared on a magnificent white destrier, accompanied by the Earls of Warwick and Northampton. The king, followed by his escorts, rode slowly along the front line and around the entire position, stopping every thirty paces or so to wish them all well, commending them to God's grace and mercy and challenging them to defend their own honour and country with the bravery he had witnessed so often in the last weeks. It was a simple message but was very well received by the packed ranks of archers and foot soldiers, who all heartily cheered him as he moved on to the next group.

Before riding off with the king back towards the army rearguard, the Earl of Warwick told Tom that scouts were following carefully the progress of the French army which was expected to appear in the late afternoon, and to keep his men well prepared! As soon as the royal party was out of sight, Tom called the centenars to him, briefed them on the commands and directions he would give, embraced each man wishing him God's protection, and told them to get all the men to relax in their positions, since they would all soon need every ounce of strength they could muster. He then called the trumpeter to him and walked slowly away carrying a pavise, his longbow and a quiver of arrows to a position at the extreme left and slightly forward of his total force of almost 3,000 men and the flanking group of three hundred dismounted men-at-arms, led by the young Prince of Wales.

Once established in the vantage point he sought, a centenar, as instructed, sent five archers and pikemen, all carrying extra bundles of arrows and a spare halberd or two, to take up position around their leader. There was hardly a man in the total force that would not have volunteered to join Tom and protect him, such was their respect and regard for him, and all eyes were momentarily on him as he stuck spare arrows into the ground in front and behind and supervised the positions of the small group around him. Then he sat down, looking towards the River Maye about half a mile below the sloping meadow, in the direction the French army was expected to appear.

The sun was now in a favourable position, making its way gradually towards the western horizon behind them, and Tom wondered if they really would fight that day, since the French would need time to organise themselves for an effective attack after a relatively long march, and it was already well into the afternoon. Surely, he thought, they would prefer to rest for a night and then do battle at a time when the sun would be in the eyes of the English army? Suddenly he saw movement and three horsemen made their way across the relatively shallow river, fanned out and cantered with some difficulty up towards the three main positions of the English army. They were scouts on their way to report to the commanders, and they began to shout that the French, with a huge force, were only a mile or so behind them, and were approaching quickly.

A few minutes later, a faint droning sound could be heard in the distance, and then the dull throbbing of hundreds of drums, with an intermittent blaring of trumpets, dulcimers, flutes and clashing of cymbals. It gradually grew louder, and then louder as the sound of the many instruments was augmented by hundreds of waggons grinding and screeching their way forward, the drumming of thousands of horses' hooves with the clanking and rattling of their riders' armour and weapons and the tramping and shouts of thousands of soldiers.

The English army by comparison was almost silent, listening carefully and somewhat fearfully to the ominous approaching sounds which were getting louder every minute, at times seeming to be all around them. Tom gave his men the trumpet signal to take their positions which immediately dispersed any sense of lethargy and set their pulses racing as they peered between the pavises, waiting for the appearance of what sounded like an army of demons on the move. The ground trembled slightly and then suddenly beyond the trees on the other side of the River Maye, a multitude of soldiers appeared: crossbowmen; pikemen; archers; mounted men-at-arms resplendent in their gleaming armour, lances raised high with banners streaming near the tips; squires; musicians; pages and servants crossed the river and stopped as suddenly as they had appeared when they saw the English army in formation at the end of the long meadow sloping up above them.

Incredibly, there was a moment's pause of near silence as if time had stood still while the two armies faced each other in confrontation, a silence suddenly broken by a large flock of crows, cawing furiously, that swept through the valley, passing over the leading ranks of French soldiers and heading west before quickly disappearing in the direction of Crécy village. Consternation broke out in the French ranks. Orders and counter-orders could be heard from many directions until eventually several thousand Genoese crossbowmen began to move forward uncertainly and form up as the vanguard of the French attack. Then there was a crash of thunder. The dark clouds that had been gradually gathering overhead released an incredibly heavy but short shower of rain.

It was so heavy that one could hardly see for two or three

minutes as the rain pounded down, making the already wet meadow even wetter and softer. The English soldiers could hear the squelching sounds of thousands of feet stepping in and out of the muddy ground as the Genoese crossbowmen stumbled with difficulty into a formation. Then, as suddenly as it had started, the rain stopped and the sun reappeared.

There was a renewal of the shouting and almost frenzied activity behind the packed ranks of the Genoese but the huge phalanx remained in position, the soldiers appearing to be arguing with each other, pointing up to the English positions and the late afternoon sun whose rays were slanting down almost directly into their eyes.

'Better them than us with that sun,' Tom murmured to himself and sent a messenger to his centenars, telling them all to remain in cover until his command, but to be ready for instant action.

Some mounted French men-at-arms began to move to the sides and behind the massive formation of crossbowmen, shouting and waving their swords at them, apparently urging them to advance up the hillside, and then eventually, after a long, shrill war cry, the Genoese began to plod steadily up towards the English positions. After about a hundred paces they stopped, shouted and then continued their slow advance. A hundred paces or so further they paused again, shouted once more and advanced until they were about two hundred yards from the rows of English pavises spread out to their left and right flanks and in front of them. They stopped, shouted again and then immediately let fly with their crossbows.

About 10,000 bolts thudded – for the main, harmlessly – into the protective pavises. The cries of some pikemen who were hit could be heard, and one or two horses tethered by the waggons and carts behind the English flanks also received painful wounds from bolts that dropped over the crouching archers' and foot soldiers' heads.

There were two blasts from trumpets across the English lines and the longbowmen stepped forward, clear of the pavises, and released volley after volley of well-placed arrows into the packed rows of Genoese, who were struggling frantically to reload their cumbersome crossbows. Before their second bolts were in position, almost a third of the crossbowmen were either wounded or dead, and as the unharmed remainder straightened up to take aim, a further 15–20,000 arrows rained down on them, decimating their ranks. In panic, they turned and began to run back down the hill, slipping and sliding to their own lines as arrows continued to fall onto them. Many in their haste threw their crossbows away. Furious

French men-at-arms, enraged by the cowardice of their own men, attacked them viciously with swords and lances, cutting them down without mercy. Meanwhile, the English longbowmen continued to fire into the mass of fighting Genoese and French knights, taking a fearful toll. Scores of heavily armoured men-at-arms were killed in their saddles, with arrows that frequently pierced helmets and breastplates. Wounded horses threw their riders to the ground, where they were often suffocated by bodies falling on top of them or by their own heavy armour pressing them into the mud. There were pitiful cries for help and screams from the wounded or dying along the whole French front. Within the first ten minutes of the battle, more than 10,000 French soldiers were slaughtered.

New lines of French men-at-arms were formed and as they stumbled their way through the piles of their own dead, trying to reach the English lines, almost all of them were mown down by the deadly fire of the archers. One wave after another was formed, surged forward and failed like all the others, and for the first half an hour, hardly a man was able even to reach the front ranks of the English formations. The few riders that got close were caught in a murderous crossfire that either killed the knight in question or so badly wounded his horse that he was thrown to the ground to be instantly killed by a pikeman or an English dismounted man-at-arms who moved quickly forward and then returned to his defensive position. The wet meadowland between the two armies was soon covered with a patchwork of blood flowing from the corpses, and badly wounded French soldiers and their horses, many of which were still writhing and screaming in the agony of their death throes.

There was a slight pause during which Paul sent pages and foot soldiers from the supply wagons to replenish the longbowmen with more arrows, and drag away the few dead within the English formation. Then the French onslaught continued, with group after group of mounted men-at-arms pressing forward. They stumbled and tripped over their own fallen troops, but still kept advancing. The archers wounded and killed them in their hundreds, and stricken horses pierced with arrows bucked and whinnied in terror, throwing their riders to the ground, where they were quickly despatched with pike or dagger. Some of the horses turned about and, in spite of their riders, plunged back down the hillside, often colliding with others trying to reach the English lines.

After more than an hour of continuous fighting, dripping with perspiration and almost breathless, Tom's group and the others began to feel the strain. The attacking French men-at-arms kept coming. The fallen were immediately followed by yet more and more until eventually, by sheer weight of numbers, they crashed through a section of the front line to reach the men-at-arms led by the Prince of Wales, and engaged them in deadly hand-to-hand combat. Encouraged by this first success, further groups of French mounted men-at-arms swarmed up the hillside, charging towards the hole in the centre of the English formations, and even though many of them were shot from their saddles on the way, a large number managed to reach their comrades, and, quickly dismounting, pressed forward with loud cries, slashing wildly with sword and mace.

The battle was now in the balance as the greatly outnumbered English troops fought desperately to defend their position, and Tom, seeing the danger to the young prince, led a group of his archers and pikemen to the central position, shouting, 'Edward and St George! To the king's son!' The Earl of Northampton had also diverted a number of his men to give further support to the hard-pressed Prince of Wales, and Tom found himself fighting shoulder to shoulder with the English nobility to prevent the king's son being captured or falling beneath the flailing French swords. His legs were trembling slightly with fatigue, but he marshalled his strength and fought like a man possessed. He was now close to the prince, who fell to his knees under the weight of his attackers, and saw how the royal standard-bearer straddled the fallen banner and stood before the prince defending him with a huge double-handed sword until he was able to scramble to his feet and resume fighting. The enemy knights came from all directions and everywhere the clash of steel on steel, and grunts and cries could be heard as sword and mace struck other weapons or hammered down onto shields and armour. As the armour-clad men-at-arms fought each other, English archers and pikemen darted between the groups, thrusting here and there with pike or sword or pushing daggers into the helmet visors or aventails around the throat area of French knights that had fallen to the ground.

Tom didn't have a shield, but carried a spear in his left hand which he put to good use, quickly stabbing a slow opponent or parrying blows from swords. He then wielded his own sword with enormous power, smashing each opponent that was prepared to face up to him down to the ground, leaving them then to the not-so-tender mercies of his own men. After what seemed an eternity – it was in fact less than twenty minutes – the gap in the English lines was closed and the French men-at-arms that had penetrated the central formation were finally dispatched, allowing Tom and his men to return to their own lines.

Paul had also not been idle in the meantime. Seeing his brother moving to the central position with a section of his men, he had immediately filled the forward ranks with men from the reserve areas to ensure a completely solid right flank of longbowmen and pikemen, and bullied the pages to keep up the supply of arrows to the archers, who kept up an incessant fire on new French formations being assembled lower down the valley.

In spite of the terrible slaughter of all the earlier attacks, one wave of French men-at-arms continued to follow another, flinging themselves against the re-formed English ranks, and each new assault suffered the same fate as all previous ones. Those that survived the deadly hail of arrows (and most of the horses did not) were killed when they reached the English positions. Those that managed to arrive on horseback, if not held at bay by the pikemen and knocked to the ground, fell from their rearing and bucking horses as foot soldiers slashed at the horses' underbellies or hamstrings, and were subsequently killed by men-at-arms or other foot soldiers. English pages also rushed out from time to time to retrieve as many arrows as they could, since their supplies were beginning to run out, ripping them out of wounded horses or dying men, or picking them up from the ground. The carnage was unimaginable!

At the height of these massive French attacks, Tom began to wonder if it would ever stop, even though he had virtually no time to think about anything other than 'kill the next one before he kills you!' Whenever he could, he picked up his longbow and tried to hit those that were leading the charges, and frequently noted with satisfaction that he had succeeded. He wasn't absolutely sure, but believed he may well have wounded the French King Philippe, since when he fell from his horse a large group of knights stopped to help him to his feet and escort him back to their own lines.

And then, as suddenly as everything had begun, just as it was getting a little dark, the attacks ended. Tom ordered a ceasefire from his formation, and his men leant on their weapons, their chests heaving, panting like hounds returning from the hunt, wiping perspiration from their brows, scarcely able to believe that it was probably all over and most of them had survived!

Looking down over the battlefield, Tom could just make out some movement below as the remnants of the shattered French army crossed the River Maye and disappeared into the forest on the other side of the valley to join up with the rest of the dispirited survivors that were beating a hasty retreat, making infinitely less noise than at their arrival some hours earlier!

My God, he thought, what a victory! But at what a cost! He shuddered and hoped that one day he might forget what he had done, and cast an eye over the masses of bodies that littered the whole hillside, hearing every now and then the muffled groans of the many wounded that were destined to die a slow and painful death during the approaching evening and night. He looked round to see if there was any sign of his brother, and with immense relief recognised him some hundred paces away, sitting down talking with a couple of pages.

Wearily, Tom made his way towards Paul, acknowledging the greetings and friendly shouts from his resting soldiers, inwardly happy that at least most of them appeared to have survived.

15

The Aftermath – Calais and Beyond!

When it was clear that all the remaining French army had retreated, the English soldiers gathered wood and made fires on the hillside above the battlefield, since it was getting dark and chilly, and squatted around them to celebrate the victory. Kegs of ale and wine were distributed and the soldiers sang lewd songs, drank and talked excitedly with their comrades long into the night before flopping down, totally exhausted, to sleep.

It was almost dusk when the king came down from the windmill from which he had observed the battle, to congratulate his son and the other commanders on their incredible victory and the bravery with which they had fought against the enemy. He had seen that the main hand-to-hand fighting had centred around the position of the Prince of Wales, and had spent anxious moments wondering if his son would survive the many furious French onslaughts. He was visibly moved when he saw that the prince was uninjured. The prince then commented on an unknown giant of a man wearing his coat of arms who had appeared from nowhere and fought alongside him and his standard-bearer at one critical time, dispatching the enemy with a force and determination he had seldom seen before, and then disappearing as quickly as he came.

'That will have been the yeoman archer Thomas Rollesby from Castor, Sire,' said the Earl of Warwick. 'He was also a pillar of strength at Blanche-Taque and I gave him the command of the right flank of archers and pikemen, which served us so brilliantly today as I'm sure we all saw!'

The young prince thought for a moment, noted that he must thank the man himself when he saw him again, and, pulling a ring off his left hand, bade the earl to give it to Thomas immediately as a token of his esteem and thanks. The earl took the ring, excused himself and left the royal group to find Tom.

Walking from fire to fire he eventually found Tom sitting with his brother in a group of his men, enjoying a pitcher of ale, listening with a grin on his face to the exaggerations of one of the archers concerning the number of Frenchmen he had personally laid low. Seeing the earl approaching, he stood up to greet him and was both astonished and moved when he saw the ring and heard the earl's explanation and congratulation. It was a massive gold ring, with a large, beautiful emerald set in it, and clearly worth a fortune. The men around gasped when they saw it glinting in the firelight and talked excitedly about its great value. They were clearly delighted that Tom had been so honoured. Paul was also pleased for his brother and talked with him through to the early hours of the morning about that and all manner of other things.

The following morning was a Sunday. Clerks were slowly working their way down the misty battlefield, recording the numbers of the dead and the details of the more illustrious nobility that lay there. A few soldiers were close behind them, scavenging for anything of value they could find, stripping the corpses of their armour and gathering up weapons that cluttered the ground. When the commanders returned from a Mass in the church of St Severin in the village of Crécy, after a hearty breakfast a large force of mounted archers which included Tom and at least a hundred men-at-arms was assembled to search the neighbouring countryside for any possible remaining groups of French soldiers.

They found evidence of the hasty retreat with waggons and carts of all possible descriptions abandoned in the many tracks leading north and east, and as they were making a sweep round to the south, they surprised a considerable force of levied French troops coming up from the Rouen area, making their way to a battle they did not know was over! Totally unprepared for the large force that suddenly swooped on them, their ranks were decimated in a few minutes and the few survivors fled back in the direction from which they had come, while the English force returned triumphantly back to Crécy.

The clerks had completed their grisly task of recording the numbers of the fallen, and the extent of the French disaster became clear. They had listed a total of more than 30,000 dead, which not only included the flower of the French nobility but also more than 3,000 knights and other men-at-arms. English casualties were slightly less than a total of 1,500, of which only a hundred and twenty were men-at-arms.

While his brother was out with the reconnaissance force, Paul and hundreds of other foot soldiers were busy digging large pits as mass graves for the dead. Before the bodies were covered over with earth, priests and other clerics that had accompanied the English army performed the funeral rites at the various open graves, signalling almost mechanically to the waiting soldiers when they should be filled in. Carpenters made large wooden crosses to mark the last resting place of the multitude of men that had died for their countries, and preparations were made for the army to move on as quickly as possible.

Paul understood only too well the extent of the victory but was appalled by the resulting carnage. He had talked about little else with his brother the previous night, and was resolved never again to take part in such a campaign, and if he survived, he vowed to make a completely new start somewhere else. During that Sunday he had talked at length with one of the priests, who was in fact a canon from the Premonstratensian Order in Titchfield Abbey, within the manor of Portchester. The canon was a good listener and realised that Paul had a great deal on his conscience and needed desperately to talk to somebody about it. After giving him absolution, he asked Paul what he had been doing in England before the campaign and was intrigued to learn that he was so well informed about sheep farming and other agricultural matters. Most importantly, the canon saw that Paul was highly intelligent, young, enthusiastic and full of energy.

The canon explained that the abbey possessed very large estates with many thousands of sheep as well as considerable arable land, although he confessed that the yields had been relatively poor in recent years, for whatever reasons. Paul then immediately asked him how the land was manured and other technical questions to which the canon replied he didn't know much about agriculture, but should he be interested there would always be a job for him on the abbey estates, and he would personally guarantee him a home in the village of Titchfield.

Paul told him he was interested, but explained his position at Castor and that he would first need to discuss it all with his brother Thomas to see how his obligations to the lord, Sir William, could all be handled. The canon did not comment but was inwardly pleased at the way Paul thought and his sense of responsibility. He said he would try to talk to Paul again before they reached Calais, and if not and he should return to England and was still interested, to ask for Canon Matthew at Titchfield Abbey.

Shortly afterwards, Tom arrived back at the camp with the large, jubilant reconnaissance force, and further food and weapon supplies they had collected from the French force of levied troops they had routed. It was beginning to get dark and frantic arrangements still had to be made to ensure that the army could leave at first light the next morning, so that it was only shortly before bedding down for the night that Paul had a chance to have a few words with his brother to sound him out concerning the canon's offer.

He was in a particularly good mood, and Paul was relieved that his brother told him not to be concerned since he was certain that Sir William would be satisfied with the sum of money he would receive, as their campaign in France so far had produced considerable booty. Not only that, he felt sure that the freed outlaw, John Dexter would be a good replacement for Paul on the demesne. The main thing, he had added, was that he, Paul, did what he felt to be right, and be prepared to take the opportunity that was being offered him. He had seen for some time now that Paul was restless and looking for a change, and so he had not been at all surprised at Paul's wish to go to Titchfield. Since it was near to Portchester, he concluded, they could still keep in touch. He then excused himself, explaining he still had some things to arrange for the morning and left Paul, telling him to get a good night's sleep and to be ready for an early start.

At dawn, after a light breakfast, the army moved off towards Calais in three bodies, fanning out in a broad sweep parallel to the coast and destroying everything in their path. Heavily laden with booty, on the morning of 4 September, the army sighted the busy French port and some hours later took up position before the main city gates. While heralds sounded a fanfare, a messenger from the king was admitted with a letter for the military governor and the army waited impatiently, most of them wanting nothing more than to return home while they were still alive.

Tom moved out of his formation briefly and had a word with his brother who was in charge of the hobelars escorting the fully-loaded baggage wagons. Looking at the high, crenellated city walls and towers and the broad moat that completely enclosed Calais, with large numbers of archers and crossbowmen peering down at them over the battlements, he confided that he doubted if the French would just let them in without a fight.

'It looks to me as if it'll take a long siege, Paul, and to be perfectly honest, I've also had a bellyful. I'm going to see if the Earl of Warwick will agree to us and our remaining men leaving here soon. I want to get back home to Margaret and the family, and I know you want to make a new start in Titchfield with that monk you were telling me about.' He then turned his horse about and calling over his shoulder, 'See you as soon as I can,' he rode quickly back to his position.

As Tom had anticipated, the military governor of Calais, a certain

Jean de Vienne, refused to surrender the city, and the English army began to make preparations for a long siege. The port was blockaded to prevent supplies reaching the French, and work began to set up winter quarters for the army, while ships regularly brought them reinforcements, provisions and more weapons including cannon from England.

Several hundred men were allowed to leave Calais, including the Prince of Wales and his entourage, to ensure the royal share of the booty was safely deposited in England and to keep parliament well-informed of King Edward's victories and future plans. The Earl of Warwick had granted Tom's request for him and his brother to return back home immediately on one of the empty supply ships, agreeing his men could follow on within a week or so. Thus they both sailed into Portchester in mid-September, 1346.

Tom made his way to Castor, with two horses and a waggon loaded with booty for Sir William, a handsome sum of money for himself and a chest full of dresses and other French clothes for his beloved wife. Paul, after an emotional farewell with his brother, struggling hard to hold back his tears as he watched him ride off, mounted his own horse. With his longbow slung over his shoulders, and well-packed saddlebags which included a purse full of gold coins, he sighed gently, and turned its head towards Titchfield.

At precisely the same time the two brothers were going ashore at Portchester, Marco Paulini was boarding a cutter moored at a quayside in a small place called Leape close to Bewley haven, to supervise the loading of forty bales of smuggled wool onto an Italian galley at anchor just offshore of the Wight Island. He continued to act as a secret intermediary between his master, the Earl of Dunghall and the Count de Kessinger. Marco played an important role as contact man with several important Italian wool buyers, and the galley he would shortly board was due that evening at high tide to set sail for Genoa. Little did he know that on his eventual return, he would be responsible for carrying a fatal disease back to the county of Donegal in Ireland.

That very evening, David, King of Scotland was eating his supper, a prisoner in the Tower of London, wondering at the fate which had led to his capture at Neville's Cross, and why he had allowed himself to be persuaded by the Earl of Dunghall and King Philippe of France to cross the border and attack the English!

16

Titchfield Abbey

The village of Titchfield was little more than two hours' ride west from Portchester, and as Paul later discovered, had its own busy port. After crossing the river he came into the top end of the high street and rode slowly down the gently sloping roadway until he reached the cobblestone market square, stopping at the Bugle Inn. It was a charming wooden-frame building, with white plaster covering the wattle between the large beams, and a gate alongside leading into a courtyard with stables. After tethering his horse to a rail outside a stable door, he slung his saddlebags over one shoulder, made his way to the front entrance and pushed open the door. Some fishermen were sitting at one of the tables, talking and joking with each other in loud voices, and two soldiers, one of whom had a black patch over one eye, were sitting at another drinking wine and playing dice. Their longbows, quivers and swords were leaning up against the wall behind them and judging by the pile of coins on the table and the drunken expression on their faces, it looked as if they had had some success in a recent campaign and wanted to forget it all as quickly as possible!

Paul was ignored by the fishermen but the two soldiers watched him intently as he went up to the publican and asked if he had a vacant room for a few days and a stable for his horse. The publican looked at the two soldiers over Paul's shoulder and asked if he would mind going to a small side room with him. Closing the door behind Paul, he excused himself. 'The least those two out there know about you the better! To be honest I wouldn't trust them as far as I could throw them, so be careful, young man and watch out for your purse!'

Paul thanked him for his consideration and was delighted to hear that he could have a good room and a stable for his horse for only two pence per day. He was led up some stairs to a room overlooking the square and the publican pointed out a large chest where he could lock up his valuables, and several wooden hooks on the walls for his weapons and clothes. 'When you go out though,' he concluded, 'it's advisable to take your sword and dagger with you. At the moment we have quite a lot of soldiers in the area just back from France, and some of them, like those two downstairs, are not to be trusted. So be careful.' He then went out to see to Paul's horse.

It was already late afternoon, too late to visit the abbey, Paul reasoned, so he decided to explore the village for a couple of hours while it was still light. He checked his sword and dagger, made sure his valuables were locked up in the chest and pocketing the key left his room, walked downstairs, and found a way out to the courtyard at the back of the inn. He wanted to see that all was well with his horse and to avoid letting the two soldiers inside see him leave.

The innkeeper had already stabled Blackie, a temperamental stallion that Paul had taken over in France, and was having difficulty getting his harness off when Paul appeared. Looking relieved on seeing Paul, he asked him to lend a hand since he didn't think he could manage on his own.

'Thank God you're here,' he added, breathing heavily. 'I reckon he would have killed me if you hadn't turned up. Is he always like this?'

'I'm sorry, I forgot to mention that Blackie can be a bit difficult with strangers. It's a good job you didn't try to ride him, I can tell you,' Paul replied. 'He didn't want to know me at first either!' He then soothed his horse with a few words, stroking his neck and muzzle gently, and taking the innkeeper's hand placed it close to Blackie's nostrils and held it there for a few seconds. 'Now,' he said, 'just move slowly at first, and he'll let you take off the bridle and harness without any problem. He's got to know you with me, and in future, just speak to him for a while, let him get your scent and you won't have any more problems, I promise you!'

Somewhat reassured, the innkeeper gingerly did as Paul recommended, gave Blackie a pail of oats, and closed the stable door, wiping his brow. 'Nobody will steal that one, that's for sure! I'll see to him personally in future and warn the stableboy to keep away from him. I see you're going out for a walk. Can I help at all?'

Paul thanked him for his kindness and said it wasn't necessary since he just wanted to look around to get the lie of the land and stretch his legs a bit, and that he should be back for supper before nightfall. Then, swivelling round on his heel, he walked out of the courtyard gate, turned left and began his first exploratory tour of the village.

He passed several small thatched-roof cottages and a larger house with a barber-surgeon sign hanging outside, and peering along the narrow lanes he crossed over, saw they were lined with cottages similar to those in the market square. At Church Street, he paused, deciding to take a look at the fine church he saw at the far end. There was a small haberdasher's shop on the left-hand side of the street between more small cottages, and directly opposite was a long, large building, with walls made of logs with clay and wattle between them. Two stone steps led up to a massive oak front door that had two large lead-panelled windows on each side of it. Standing on tiptoes Paul peered into one of them and from what he could see it looked as if it must be the communal village hall. He continued a little further down the street until he was facing the main entrance of the church and stopped to look up at the impressive stone tower rising above the porch. He saw three seagulls were perched at the top and appeared to be staring apprehensively down at him. Smiling as he saw a sea-monster carving above a pillar in the porchway, he pushed open the heavy door and stepped inside.

It was much lighter inside than he had expected. When he thought about the dark, damp churches he had visited in the Castor demesne, this was a pleasant change. The long nave stretching before him was illuminated by large stained-glass windows on all sides of the church, and his eyes were caught by the tall candles burning on the raised high altar within the chancel at the far end. He also then noticed that there were two or three old women sitting on chairs on the left side of the nave quietly praying, while masons and other workmen were working on a small chapel that was being built on the south side of the chancel. Moving closer, he saw coloured statues of the saints standing in niches around the chancel, which were also illuminated by sputtering candles around them, and noticed the familiar picture of heaven and hell over the chancel arch: a picture which had always given him some problems when he thought about its implications and the standard sermons of the chaplain and other priests at Castor!

His thoughts were disturbed by a light tap on his shoulder, and turning he saw a monk standing by him, dressed in a long, voluminous white robe.

'Can I help you, my son?' a quiet, friendly voice inquired. 'You must be a stranger here, I've never seen you before.'

'Er, no thank you father,' Paul whispered, a little startled. 'I've just arrived in the village and wanted to look and see what is here.'

'Very well, my son. Please feel free to visit me at any time if you have any questions or problems you wish to discuss. I shall be happy to oblige. My name is Brother Peter, by the way.'

'Thank you again, Brother Peter,' Paul replied. 'I won't forget.' Turning away, Paul walked back to the main entrance as the monk seemed to glide almost soundlessly towards the workmen.

Once outside, he took a deep breath before deciding to take a footpath to the right leading through the churchyard to join another pathway running alongside the river he had crossed earlier when he had first entered Titchfield. He walked briskly past more small cottages on his left and a building on the right close to the river, and seeing hides hanging on wooden frames outside assumed it was the tannery. Continuing a little further he soon came across a very large house with a spacious yard behind it with several stables alongside, flanked by a couple of small cottages on each side. Sniffing the air he realised it must be an alehouse and began to feel thirsty. However, he decided to wait until suppertime since he wanted to see more while it was light enough.

Then, hearing the sound of a water-wheel turning somewhere ahead, he hurried on, passing another bridge until he came across a large stone building that was in fact the village mill, owned by the abbey as he later discovered. From the mill, as he looked across the fields which were covered by grazing sheep, about half a mile away he saw behind long, high stone walls, the towers of a massive building that dominated the more hilly land to the north. 'So that's where the abbey is,' he murmured to himself. 'I'll take a closer look tomorrow and see what Canon Matthew has to say, if he's there!'

Turning towards the setting sun, Paul decided after a few minutes to return to the Bugle Inn following a track on his left that skirted a small wood and the houses of some some smallholders on a hillside, before veering round to the outskirts of the village. He had a good sense of direction and shortly found himself approaching the high street. He looked into the windows of one or two of the small shops selling household items, farming tools and implements, and leather goods, before strolling leisurely into the market square, crossing over by the market hall and entering the inn.

He was just about to go up the stairs to his room when the innkeeper suddenly appeared looking somewhat harassed and concerned.

'Mr Rollesby!' he almost shouted. 'I'm afraid we've had a spot of trouble. Those two soldiers tried to steal your horse. They went outside shortly after you left. I'd only been back from the stables about ten minutes, saw them go out and then heard a hell of a racket. Your horse . . .'

Before he could say any more, Paul interrupted him. 'What's

happened to Blackie? Is he injured? Where is he?' Without waiting for a reply he rushed to the stables with the innkeeper in hot pursuit.

'He's fine, Mr Rollesby, nothing really happened to him,' he called out to Paul reassuringly, trying to catch up. He stood behind him breathlessly as his guest went into the stable wondering what he would find behind the door, and was confronted by his black stallion looking at him with a quizzical eye.

'I tried to tell you everything was in order now but you were too fast for me,' the innkeeper said as he peered around the door observing the scene of Paul making a fuss of his beautiful horse. He was still not listening. He was so relieved that Blackie was still there and uninjured that he was unaware of anything else for a moment or two, and then, sensing the presence of somebody behind him, he turned and listened eventually to the innkeeper's explanation. He explained that in reality not much happened at all, adding that within the short time it took him to investigate what was going on, Blackie had evidently bitten one of the men on the arm and kicked the other so hard that he was lying on the stable floor screaming with pain and terror, expecting to be trampled to death at any moment. 'That's what I found when I arrived,' he added, 'and a couple of the fishermen I know well came round as well to lend me a hand. But it was all over by then. The soldier with the bitten arm dragged the other one clear and cursing and swearing, helped him to his feet, and they made off as quickly as they could, with the fishermen helping them on the way with a kick in the backside for good measure.'

Paul began to relax and, smiling for the first time since he returned to the Bugle, thanked the innkeeper for his help, gave Blackie a final caress along the side of his neck and muzzle, closed the stable door and accompanied the innkeeper back to the inn. Since the fishermen who had helped were still there, Paul thanked them all personally, and told them that they were all invited to supper with him that evening.

It was the best thing he could have done. The innkeeper went out of his way to prepare something very special: a pottage of leeks, onions and bread steeped in a meat broth, followed by roasted rabbit and pigs' legs all washed down with an excellent ale. There was even fruit and various types of nuts for those still a little hungry and a flagon of wine afterwards. Paul made himself some good friends that evening and flopped down wearily on his bed around midnight, sleeping soundly until dawn.

Shortly after sunrise, he led Blackie out of the stable and yard, turned left down the first lane he came to, and rode down towards the river until he picked up the track he had walked the previous evening. He then headed north towards the abbey. It took him less time than he had thought, since Blackie was eager for some exercise and within twenty minutes he was at the main gate, and rang the bell hanging outside. An old monk wearing a white robe shuffled slowly to the gate and asked Paul what he wanted. Hearing that he had been invited by Canon Matthew, he opened the gate immediately and after Paul had tethered his horse in the shade of the high front wall, ushered him to the main door, opening it by turning a large metal ring.

Once inside, the old monk led him to what he called the 'parlour' and asked him to wait while he looked for the canon. It took about half an hour before he appeared, for which he apologised profusely, explaining that he had been working in the library and Brother Martin hadn't known that. Looking Paul squarely in the eyes, he put his hands on his shoulders, and then said: 'Mr Rollesby, I'm so pleased you decided to come and visit us. But before we talk on other things, it's very early and you are no doubt a little hungry, so let's go first to the kitchen and see what the cellarer has to offer.' He requested that Paul should leave his sword and dagger in the parlour, 'Since you won't be needing those here,' and led him to the kitchen.

After a jug of fresh milk and a hunk of warm, newly-baked rye bread which Paul ate with great relish to the obvious delight of the canon, he nevertheless initially felt a little uncomfortable as he began a brief tour of the monastery and was introduced to some of the other monks, still not quite sure what he was doing there and what it would all lead to. However, once in the library he lost his shyness and was fascinated as he saw several hundred leather-backed books on the many shelves lining the walls, and monks sitting at bench tables near the windows, laboriously copying or illuminating the open volumes with the most beautiful of colours. The canon was astonished to see Paul looking over the shoulders of one of the monks and clearly reading the Latin script, and exclaimed with genuine surprise and pleasure: 'But you can read the Holy Script, Mr Rollesby! How wonderful! How can that be?'

He listened intently to Paul's description of earlier days in Castor and the many, difficult hours of tuition with the chaplain, and of his work with the reeve there.

'Truly fascinating, Mr Rollesby,' he concluded, and then invited Paul to follow him into the abbey gardens where they could talk some more.

Strolling slowly around the huge vegetable and fruit gardens to the south of the main building, Paul demonstrated his knowlege of even the lesser-known herbs, which prompted further questions from the canon. As they were walking past the chicken sheds towards the large fishpond, he asked Paul where he was staying and what he knew of Titchfield. Listening to the details of his late afternoon walk of the previous day, when he mentioned the 'beautiful church', the canon immediately interrupted, telling him how proud they were of St Peter's.

'St Peter's, you say, Canon,' Paul commented, looking questioningly at him. 'How curious! I met a monk inside and he said his name was Brother Peter!'

The canon's eyes twinkled slightly as he looked at Paul and told him that he couldn't think of a better person to watch over the workmen building the monk's private chapel than Brother Peter. Then he asked if Paul would like to stay in Titchfield and take over the job of the reeve for the abbey's estates.

Paul looked at the canon thunderstruck. 'What, me?' he stammered. 'Reeve of the whole estate?' He was unable to believe that he really meant it, until the canon put his hand on his shoulder and explained that the previous reeve had died some weeks earlier, and the abbey had been looking for a suitable replacement since then.

'You are very young, I know, Mr Rollesby, but everything I see and hear tells me you are the man for the job. There is a great deal to be done, because as I told you earlier, our yields have been declining steadily for the last few years, the wool quality is not as good as it could be, and the accounting systems have been sadly neglected for some considerable time. Mr Thatcher, a good man but stubborn as a mule, was very old and in his later years became more and more out of touch. If you accept, please stay with us until vespers so that I can introduce you to all our brothers. Can you decide now or do you need more time?'

'I accept, canon. Thank you for giving me the chance of a lifetime. You will not be disappointed in me, I promise you,' Paul immediately replied, hardly daring to believe his good fortune.

'Excellent, Mr Rollesby. May God our Father be praised!' And the canon led him by the arm back inside the abbey to his private rooms to discuss further details, including where he could live and what his payment should be. He explained that they were not poor but also not rich like their neighbours in Winchester, who made life a little difficult for them sometimes, particularly when it came to the sale of the abbey's wool!

Later that evening, as Paul led Blackie out of the main gate and rode back to the Bugle Inn, he was lost in thought as to how he should begin the immense task that lay before him. There was so much to be done and it was already close to harvest time. But at least he had a couple of days to get himself established in a new house the monks would make ready for him the following day in the lower end of South Street, and he would find time to organise himself and get his plans in order. Content in a way he had never been before, he let Blackie pick the way carefully back along the track to Titchfield.

17

A New Life

During the long illness of the old reeve Mr Thatcher, the canon had given one of the monks, Brother Simon, the responsibility for managing the affairs of the demesne, and as soon as Paul began his new job, he had asked the monk to show him what exactly belonged to the manor and all its boundaries.

It was a beautiful day in late September when Brother Simon began by taking him to the large abbey storehouses in the village of Titchfield, more or less alongside the house that had been made available for Paul in South Street. The storehouses were virtually empty but in a few days would be almost bursting with sacks of corn, barley and rye when the harvest was completed. They rode down to the harbour and the monk pointed out the salt-pans on the far side of the estuary that belonged to the monastery. Then they followed the river back up the eastern side of the village to the mill also owned by the abbey, and a good source of income, Paul learned, because all the tenant farmers in the neighbourhood were obliged to use it.

Crossing the bridge nearby, they headed eastwards looking around the farmlands surrounding Farham, another small community of the demesne, where Paul looked carefully at the wheat, grinding the seeds in his hand and saw they were almost ready for harvesting, but the yield looked poor. He examined the soil carefully under the watchful eye of Brother Simon, who had slowly begun to realise that although a young man, his companion knew exactly what to look for; and Paul commented that there was indeed a lot to be done here. The soil badly needed more fertiliser.

Two or three hours later they came across a large flock of sheep grazing on the common pasture land of Portsdown. They covered the top of the hill close to the fringe of Beare Forest as Paul learnt it was called, an area used by all the neighbouring villages. He immediately felt at home as they met one of the shepherds and began to talk the only language shepherds understood: sheep! This time the monk was astonished at Paul's knowledge and the ease with which he could assess the type and various qualities of the fells even though they were far from fully grown. Brother Simon introduced him as the newly appointed reeve of the abbey and noticed that the shepherd had accepted him immediately, in spite of his youth. He had recognised that Paul was an expert who handled it all in a businesslike but friendly way, without any trace of arrogance.

A good half-hour later they made their way slowly down the side of three enormous field areas leading down to the demesne farm of Wicor, close to the sea. The monk explained that the ownership of the three fields – called north, middle and south – was extremely complex, in that one third was owned by the Crown and managed by the constable of Portchester Castle, and the rest belonged to the abbey. Pointing to the battlemented tower of the castle they could just see about two miles away at the far end of Southfield, Brother Simon added that the castle property was in fact scattered across the three fields in varying strip sizes, and there were also a few village landowners who owned a little land within it all! Seeing Paul's look of confusion and dismay, he grinned, patted him on the arm and said he had no doubt he would soon understand who owned what, and at least virtually all of Northfield belonged to the abbey, and there was a large barn alongside it and that definitely belonged to the monastery!

Paul looked a bit more relieved, smiled at the monk and then asked if he would be prepared to work closely with him, since he could not handle everything on his own, particularly at this early stage. Brother Simon, although somewhat suspicious and mistrustful at the beginning of the day, had gradually come to like and respect Paul He held out his hand and placed it on Paul's saying: 'If Canon Matthew agrees, Mr Rollesby, it would be a great pleasure and honour to work for you. Thank you for your trust!' And a bargain and long lasting friendship was thus sealed.

Before they returned to the abbey, at Paul's request, they rode down for a closer look at the marshlands to the west of Wicor. It was clearly a paradise for ducks and other wildfowl, but Paul saw a great opportunity to reclaim a large tract of land for conversion to badly needed pastureland or hay meadows. They walked slowly over the land, carefully picking their way through the swampy ground until they reached the sandy shore, which was covered in places with piles of seaweed washed up by the daily tides. Paul pointed this out to Brother Simon, telling him that it would all help to fertilise the soil, with some sand and ground shells and other marl. But that would have to wait for the autumn. In the meantime, there were many other priorities!

Satisfied that he had seen enough to begin to make his plans, he asked Brother Simon if they could return to the abbey and talk first with the canon before doing anything else. During the relatively long ride back, all the events and conclusions of the day were thoroughly discussed, and by the time they had reached Titchfield, Paul had already prepared the general approach he planned. Once the horses were tethered and had been given their feed, they washed and went to join the canon at vespers.

It was not quite as easy to convince Canon Matthew as he had thought. He was not negative to the overall approach of upgrading the standards of the sheep, and increasing the extent of the pasturelands by land reclamation, but became a little nervous about any reductions of arable land, since corn was such an important money crop. Paul explained that by increasing the yield per acre by only a quarter, that would more than compensate for the arable land reductions he had in mind. He estimated with what he had seen that currently they were only getting around five to six bushels of corn per acre and though he personally believed that ten or more were at least possible, he only mentioned an increase of at least two bushels per acre in his plan to the canon.

Seeing the concern of Canon Matthew, Paul then suggested the compromise of first beginning with the wheat fields close to the abbey so he could show within a year the increases he had in mind, only then developing further across the demesne. The land reclamation should begin immediately after the harvest, he continued, and he would also begin to systematically improve the quality of the sheep. Paul stopped, waiting for the reaction of the canon who had glanced at Brother Simon for some reassurance and seeing the slight nod, quickly agreed for him to go ahead.

At the end of the meal, Paul thanked the canon and then requested that Brother Simon should work closely with him, pointing out the advantages for the abbey to have 'inside' knowledge on everything that was going on, and added that Brother Simon was also essential to the total success of the whole plan.

Canon Matthew burst out laughing at Paul's guile and replied good humouredly: 'I sense a conspiracy here, young man, but I agree nevertheless! I assume you have no objections, Brother Simon?' Seeing the obvious delight on the face of the monk, he turned to Paul and added: 'So that's agreed. May God help you to be successful, Mr Rollesby! I suggest you spend the night here now since it's so late. And you'll need to make an early start tomorrow,' he concluded, to the amusement of the rest of the monks sitting at the long table.

While Paul was being led by a servant to one of the monastery's guest rooms, his brother Tom had just sat down by the fireside with a mug of ale, waiting for Margaret to join him. She had led the young Eric off to bed protesting – he always wanted to stay up late and talk with his parents – and would tell him part of one of the many troubadour tales she knew from her own childhood until he fell asleep.

My God, Tom thought, how he loved that woman! She not only ran the household with a precision that made Tom wonder, but also with a warmth and personal touch that was unique. She could sense his every mood, and when he returned from France she knew immediately that he had suffered inside and was a different man in some respects from the man who had gone off with Paul and a troop of soldiers. But Tom would never forget how she had looked at those French dresses and other clothes he brought back for her, hardly able to wait to try them on. There was that red silk dress, he reminisced, which quickly became her favourite. It hugged her figure, accentuating the lines of her shapely body, and with her long, black hair it made her the most beautiful woman in the world, he had told her. And how she had hugged him. She was so happy. He had then remembered the ring the Earl of Warwick had given him from the Black Prince, set with a large emerald, Searching in his doublet, he had told Margaret to close her eyes and hold out her hand. As soon as he had pressed it into her hand, closing her fingers around it she opened her eyes and began to weep with tears of joy as she looked at the beautiful ring she was holding. The green of the stone matched her eyes perfectly, and as it flashed and sparkled in the light she had whirled around as if wanting to celebrate with some sort of a dance, almost overcome with emotion.

'Oh, Tom,' she had murmured, 'it's truly the most wonderful ring I've ever seen in my life! Thank you, thank you so much!'

A little later, she had wanted to know how he had come to possess such a ring and was both proud and astonished to hear that the king's son had given it to him. Tom told her that he had given the young prince some help during a battle, without going into any details, and it had been presented to him as a token of gratitude. He had then told her that should anything ever happen to him and she needed help, the household of the Black Prince would always take care of her and the children. Margaret had then put her arms around his neck, her eyes filled with tears, and had sobbed that she didn't know how she would be able to live without him.

The following day, when Sir William had returned from a hunting trip, Tom got the manor servants to unload the cartful of booty he had brought back for the lord. Tom had no idea of the value of it all, but knew there was more than 1,000 pounds worth of gold coins, and with all the other jewels, gold and silver plate, carved ornaments, silk and velvet clothes for both Sir William and Lady Mortimer, plus a suit of the finest German armour and a magnificent sword, it was almost a king's ransom!

It had been easy for him to explain Paul's absence and he immediately received the charter of manumission that gave complete freedom to his brother. The arrangements with John Dexter had also worked out extremely well, and Sir William was very satisfied with the performance of the new man destined to be the new reeve. The fact that most of the soldiers also returned to the manor – three had been killed at Crécy, one on the way to Calais – and two thirds of the levied archers and pikemen returned to their villages a week later, was not lost on Sir William, who had realised some time earlier that his guard captain was indeed a most unique man!

Tom had only been back in Castor a few days when he discovered that in the absence of his troops and a large part of the village militia, the incidence of sheep theft had increased dramatically across the demesne. There had been the odd case of a few sheep here and there disappearing in previous winters, but never in summer and nothing on the scale of what had happened in the last two months. Although unaware of the involvement of the Count de Kessinger, he suspected that some powerful hand or other was behind it all.

While he was pondering how best to go about catching the thieves, Margaret came back from the room which served as a bedroom for all three of their children, poured herself a goblet of wine from a pitcher on the table and sat down facing Tom by the fire. It was beginning to smoke a little and since the evening had turned a little chilly, she stirred the embers and threw another log on to it, pulled a lambskin shawl around her shoulders, took a sip of wine and then asked him what he was thinking about, and if something was wrong since he seemed so preoccupied.

He explained his concern about the number of sheep that had been stolen and that he had been wondering how best to go about finding the culprits. Other than that, he said, smiling at her, everything was in order! Margaret relaxed and they discussed the day's events, thinking of Paul and hoping that he was safe. She looked at Tom in surprise when he said: 'Oh don't worry about him, Margaret. Everything is fine and he is happy. I'm sure we shall be hearing from him shortly!'

'And how would you know that, Mr Thomas Rollesby?' she asked him.

Suddenly realising what he had said, he more or less stammered out: 'Well, it just sort of slipped out. I'm not sure how I know, but I know. It was almost as if he was here and had told me himself.'

Margaret looked at him knowingly and remembered what he had once before told her about how the brothers seemed to be able to communicate with each other at times, even when far apart. She nodded, adding that she hoped he was right, and changed the subject.

Now that there were three children and particularly since Eric and Margaret were growing so quickly, she added, she wondered if perhaps they could consider moving somewhere outside the manor house grounds to something a little larger than their quarters. As much as she had enjoyed the first few years, she explained, there was always a danger with the mounted soldiers galloping here and there that the children could be injured. Tom listened carefully, and realising she was right, promised he would discuss it with Sir William and was certain they would find something suitable and safe nearby in the village.

While they were talking by the fireside, watching the glowing embers gradually falling into ash, yawning periodically and thinking it was perhaps time to go to bed as the children were sleeping peacefully, a band of five heavily-armed thieves, hired by a man in the pay of the Count de Kessinger, were settling down for the night in a wood just south of Acle, intending at dawn to fall on a hamlet close to Stokesby and steal a small flock of sheep from the fields nearby. The monks at Titchfield were filing into the Abbey chapel for midnight Mass and Paul had finally fallen into a deep sleep, impatient to start work on the immense task he had set himself. They were all totally unaware of the terrible threat to their lives far to the east, that was gradually gathering momentum and slowly but surely approaching them. An anonymous Flemish cleric informed by a friend who worked in the papal curia at Avignon, was busily writing the following for posterity:

In the East, hard by Greater India, in a certain province, horrors and unheard of tempests overwhelmed the whole province for the space of three days. On the first day there was a rain of frogs, serpents, lizards, scorpions, and many venomous beasts of that sort. On the second, thunder was heard, and lightning and sheets of fire fell upon the earth, mingled with hail stones of marvellous size; which slew almost all, from the greatest even to the least. On the third day there fell fire from heaven and stinking smoke, which slew all that were left of men and beasts, and burned up all the cities and towns in those parts. By these tempests the whole province was infected; and it is conjectured that, through the foul blast of wind that came from the South, the whole seashore and surrounding land were infected, and are waxing more and more poisonous from day to day.*

The plague had begun its fearful course!

---

* De Smet, 'Breve Chronicon clerici anonymi', *Recueil des Chroniques de Flandres*, Vol. III, p. 14.

18

The Manor of Portchester and a Trip to Winchester

In spite of low yields per acre the harvest of 1346 was a good one in the manor of Portchester, at least by comparison with the previous two to three years. Although Paul refused to take any credit – he insisted that it was due to the weather being kind to them – Canon Matthew was delighted with the start he had made, recognising the smooth organisation that his young protégé had installed and the respect that all the estate workers had for 'Mr Paul'. The flour, corn seed and barley filled the demesne barns, and Paul immediately had other, simple barns quickly constructed to store hay for the winter months.

As soon as the wheat fields were cleared, Paul insisted the sheep flocks were moved systematically on them for a few days to begin the manuring process he had planned, and took the opportunity to complete the stock records at the same time. The canon agreed to 'lend' him four additional monks to help him and Brother Simon with the counting procedures, as he himself wanted to check carefully the quality of each of the flocks.

Once this was completed to his satisfaction, Paul organised the collection and storing of seaweed, sand, shells and other marl for the further fertilisation and soil treatment of the fields close to the abbey and the land reclamation project at Wicor. At the feast of St Michael he had explained to the villagers at Titchfield and then later the same day, the estate workers living around Wicor, what had to be done and why, adding that once everything was stored, he would show them how best to use it. When they had understood the advantages of this additional work, they all agreed that within two weeks everything would be in storage and ready for him to begin.

The weeks simply flew by and although he had wanted to visit Tom and his family to let them know all was well and play with the children he loved, Paul simply had no time to spare, particularly with winter so close. Before the long, dark nights began, he knew he must buy-in supplies of candles, ruddle, pitch and a large quantity of lime for his soil improvement plan. He also had to look for some top quality corn seed, and so decided to visit the markets of the city of Winchester, which Brother Simon had repeatedly recommended. The abbey sold most of its flour there – it was an important wool 'staple' city and the see of the wealthiest bishop in England! In almost hushed tones, Brother Simon had also told him that there were at least 30,000 sheep on the bishop's estates and that the Priory of St Swithun's – the Minster of Winchester was the monastery church – had at least 20,000! Paul had politely looked impressed, but kept his thoughts to himself, having heard many stories about their dubious business methods!

Paul and Brother Simon, with three village militia as an escort, and a total of five carts with drivers, left Titchfield in early November, destined for Winchester. Canon Matthew had given them a letter of introduction for the prior of St Swithun's, to ensure they were well received and that the horses and equipment would be taken care of during their visit. They all set off in good spirits for the two-day journey.

Brother Simon had been two or three times before to Winchester and enjoyed leading the group. But it was not at all difficult to find the way. After leaving Titchfield, they headed west towards Southampton for a couple of hours until they reached the River Itching and then followed the river northwards along a roadway that led directly to the city. It was in fact a very busy route and, in daylight, safe from outlaws. They saw groups of soldiers going towards Winchester and others on their way to Southampton, probably to embark for France. There were also packhorses laden with corn, animal hides, dyes, spices and a host of other commodities bound for the markets, workshops, mercers and other traders of Winchester. Paul had also never seen before so many clerics travelling in both directions – monks and friars particularly, in both black and grey robes. Dominican and Franciscan, as Brother Simon explained to him. These contrasted dramatically with other ecclesiastical dignitaries who were mounted on fine horses. They had long, magnificent cloaks, green and red boots, their fingers were covered with expensive rings and they were accompanied by many retainers and escorted usually by several soldiers. Brother Simon merely shrugged his shoulders and sighed when Paul commented on this, clearly embarassed by this unseemly display of wealth by some of the clergy.

Since the waggons were almost empty and the various inns and hostelries they passed were packed with travellers, Paul suggested they should join up with a group of merchants that had decided to camp for the night in a field close to the river. A fire was already blazing when they arrived and they were made to feel very welcome by the others, happy to have their numbers strengthened. Provisions were shared and before long a hot broth was ready, followed by cheese and rye bread washed down by a good ale or wine for those wanting it.

After the broth Paul enjoyed a conversation with one of the merchants who dealt in cloth dyes, and was returning from Flanders. He had been to the famous fair in Bruges. He talked in some detail about the dye called woad, which originated from a plant grown close to Amiens, which when milled, produced the most beautiful blue you have ever seen, he assured Paul. But red was also an interesting colour as far as its production was concerned, he continued. Most of it came from countries in the south, he added, mostly from the root of the 'madder' plant, but the most expensive sort was called 'grain' consisting of the dried bodies of small insects called 'kermes'.

He explained that the cloth industry in and around Winchester was becoming extremely important, and was sure that one day it would be even more important than the wool trade. He described in some detail the various steps of clothmaking, and although Paul was familiar with the washing, sorting, carding and spinning processes, he was fascinated to learn more about the rest. He learnt which cloths were 'dyed in the wool', or in other words, the yarn was dyed before weaving, rather than the finished cloth. After weaving, came the fulling treatment, and although Paul had seen a little of this in Norwiche the merchant described how the material was further soaked and washed before being pounded to consolidate the weave and thicken the cloth, and then how 'fuller's earth' was used to rinse out the fulling agents. Finally came the tentering and finishing processes, and after inspection by official agents, the cloth was finally ready for the market!

'My goodness,' Paul exclaimed, 'I had no idea it was such a complicated business! But it's truly fascinating! Thank you for telling me so much.'

The merchant smiled and nodded in appreciation, and then went on to tell him that after spending some time in Winchester, he planned to visit Salesburye which was also beginning to develop a cloth industry, and from what he had heard, could one day be an even more important centre than Winchester! 'But,' he added, 'we shall see! First things first, I always say!'

Paul had no idea where Salesburye was, but decided to ask Brother Simon some other time, and since he was feeling tired, excused himself, bade the merchant a goodnight, and returned to the waggons. However, before settling down for the night, he arranged a guard system with the three village militia, telling the drivers to keep their daggers and longbows readily available in case of an outlaw raid. A couple of them were about to complain, but seeing the look on Paul's face changed their minds and grumblingly agreed. Brother Simon witnessed the scene and realised that he still had a great deal to learn about the new reeve, his friend Paul, as he made himself comfortable in one of the empty waggons, quickly losing himself in a deep sleep.

It was an uneventful night, and although decidedly chilly, the early morning sun promised a glorious day. Following a simple breakfast prepared by Brother Simon, the group quickly harnessed the horses and moved onto the roadway shortly after daybreak and headed for Winchester.

Since it hadn't rained for more than a week, the ground was dry and they made good progress, in spite of the ever-increasing number of people that were on the road as they got closer to the city. They were mainly peasants taking fresh fruit, vegetables, milk and cheese to the various city markets, and occasionally even driving sheep and cattle along the badly rutted road. Paul particularly enjoyed the company of assorted musicians that tagged along with them from time to time, but was always saddened when they passed groups of wounded soldiers limping their way to the city, or badly deformed beggars in rags, usually barefoot, or even a solitary leper with emaciated features and limbs. Brother Simon told Paul that there was a hospital for lepers just a little east of the city and supposed that the poor soul was on his way to it.

As they drew near to Winchester in the early afternoon, Paul saw a large, almost perfectly circular hill to the east, and what looked like some ancient, ruined fortifications on the top of it, and was delighted when the monk suggested they should ride ahead and climb the hill to get a good view of the city. Following a track carefully that wound its way gradually up to the old ruined fortress, Brother Simon explained that the hill, called St Kathren's, had been in ancient times an important site but nobody really knew much about its history. However, from the top one had a wonderful view of the whole city of Winchester, he continued, and Paul impatiently asked him to hurry up, before it got too late!

It was breathtaking! Taking in the panorama before him, Paul noted how the city was more or less set between hills rising up both to the east and west before them, lying on a broad, green valley floor, with the River Itching flowing outside the city walls and disappearing out of sight in the direction of the sea. He saw one or two small boats on the river, and Brother Simon told him they could well be loaded with wool bales or perhaps cloth on the way to Southampton. He observed that water courses from the river led into the city and it appeared as if they were flowing right through from north to south, even though there were walls and massive earthwork defences all around it.

Brother Simon then pointed out the cathedral or minster as he called it, alongside the priory where they would stay for the following few days, not far from from the bishop's palace of Wolsey just to the right. Shading their eyes from the sun slowly moving towards the western horizon, they could also just make out the walls and turreted round towers of the castle at the far side of the city. Stretching away from it as far as the eye could see northwards, were lines of houses, buildings and gardens, trees and some strips of water, with what appeared to be the the towers of at least twenty churches scattered throughout.

Making their way down to the roadway, they had to gallop for a few minutes before they caught up with their group, and within another hour or so they entered the city by the south gate. A few minutes later, after reaching the priory gate, Brother Simon's letter of introduction ensured immediate attention to their needs. The horses were led off by servants to the priory stables and the waggons taken to separate sheds nearby, where their weapons were also stored. The priory cellarer had appeared by this time, greeted Brother Simon familiarly, and conducted them to rooms reserved for visitors close to the prior's own house. Looking at the militia and the drivers, he informed them directly but politely that they were all in a consecrated area and that their personal conduct at all times must recognise this! Then he turned to Simon, adding smilingly that he was sure Brother Simon would guarantee this, informed them that an evening meal would be served in the guests' hall in two hours and then departed.

While the group of drivers and the three militia men were organising themselves in the dormitory, Simon took Paul to one side and explained that he must see the prior and pay his respects and he then expected to spend the rest of the evening with the monks. He added that he would wake Paul early the following morning and show him the city and the location of the various markets, but he wondered if in the meantime he could keep an eye on the others to make sure there would not be any difficulties.

Paul assured the rather concerned monk that after they had eaten he would personally guarantee that they settled down peacefully for the night, without gambling or any other noisy activity.

But in the morning, before anybody left the priory, they must clarify what had to be done in the following two days, and perhaps the prior would have a point of view in the matter! Obviously relieved, Simon agreed to discuss it with the prior and then left the dormitory.

It had been a long day by the time they had all finished the evening meal, and they were all tired. Once back in the dormitory Paul confirmed that after breakfast he would inform them what had to be done before they left the priory, reminding them what the cellarer had said earlier in a tone that left no doubt about his position. Even though Paul was in many respects very different from his brother, he nevertheless had a certain authority that they all respected, and not only that, he had already demonstrated he was an excellent reeve and they liked how he got things done. And so, apart from the sound of tired men snoring, it was a peaceful and uneventful night!

19

The City of Winchester and Palpitations

The prior had made an excellent suggestion. Once informed by Brother Simon in detail of the supplies they needed, he had recommended that they collect the lime required from kilns to the east of the city, beyond the leper hospital of St Mary Magdalen, and a mile or two on the other side of the Hill of St Giles. Since it was very hilly countryside in that area, he added, the men may need two days for the round trip, and they could always spend the night in a small priory which was also part of the bishop's diocese and was close to the quarry. He had written a short note of introduction, which Simon had passed on to Paul, as he explained the total plan to the reeve early that morning.

Paul accepted the suggestion immediately and briefed the men accordingly, giving one of the more responsible militia men sufficient money for three waggon-loads of lime and a little extra for additional food and drink, instructing him to be back in Winchester by the Thursday evening, so they could leave for Titchfield on either the Friday or Saturday morning. For safety reasons, Paul also insisted that the whole group should participate in the trip, keeping their weapons with them at all times, and promised that if everything went to plan and they returned with good quality lime as required (and above all, he emphasised, it had to be kept dry) they could all have a day free to spend in the city. This was naturally well received by the men and they worked quickly to get ready to leave the priory.

Once the waggons were on their way to the east gate of the city, Paul and Simon decided to make for the cornmarket first before seeking out the pitch, ruddle and candles they needed. They walked to the west side of the minster and Simon promised to show Paul around the magnificent building when they had more time. They passed through the large cemetry area and gardens, opened a gate and made their way past what appeared to be a cluster of small chapels and churches towards the fine church of St Thomas's. The monk seemed to use the churches as landmarks to find his way, which was not surprising Paul thought, because there were so many of them!

Before reaching St Thomas's they were confronted with the massive earthworks and walls of the castle on the other side of a large field (frequently used for hangings and other forms of punishment, Brother Simon whispered in Paul's ear) and Paul noticed the royal flag fluttering on a pole above the soaring stone tower, and shuddered, momentarily reminded of the campaign in France. The movement was not lost on Simon who decided wisely to ignore it. Once at the church, they turned up in the direction of the far west end of the high street and within minutes walked straight into the cornmarket.

This was a new experience for Paul. Everything was geared to the buying and selling of just corn and flour. As well as a host of stalls, most of which were surrounded by seemingly excited and noisy people of all types anxious to get the very best price possible, almost all of the small shops were also dealing with the same products. Paul noticed that there was a 'corn exchange' building at the end of the market close to the high street, which regulated flour prices, checked grain qualities, the market dealers' weights and measures, and supervised the bakers there and in other parts of the city. There were so many people that Paul automatically felt for his purse and dagger, both secured to his belt over a close-fitting doublet and all covered by a light grey cloak, alert for pickpockets and other scoundrels that were undoubtably to be found somewhere or other in the city. The unusual white monk's habit that Brother Simon wore appeared to attract attention from time to time, Paul noticed, making him even more wary.

They made their way slowly through the jostling crowd, looking especially at the corn displayed in open sacks in most of the stalls. Sometimes Paul dipped his hand into one of them, examining the seed critically and asked the stallholder a question or two before moving on to others and repeating the process. Simon followed him patiently but after a couple of hours began to wonder if Paul would ever find what he was looking for, and eventually posed him the question. Paul grinned at him.

'We had a good summer this year and the quality is very good here, I must say. I think I've already found what I want to buy, but just want to make sure there's nothing better for sale. Be patient with me for a few more minutes and the ordeal will be over, I promise!' Laughing aloud at the look of relief on Simon's face, Paul slapped him affectionately on the shoulder and moved on to the next stall. True to his word, shortly afterwards, he retraced his steps to one particular dealer and after a very detailed and skilful negotiation the deal was closed. Twenty sacks were ordered to be delivered the following morning to the priory, with payment on delivery.

Before looking for the other items, Paul suggested that maybe they should eat a little something if Simon knew of a good tavern, and finish all the purchases in the afternoon. They were very close to the high street and Simon replied, clearly delighted by the suggestion, that he had once been taken into an excellent tavern in Staple Gardens which was nearby. Crossing over the cobbled high street, Simon led Paul past some large, wood-framed houses belonging to wealthy merchants, spaced between a variety of trees in all their autumnal splendour set in delightful gardens around each house. They stopped to admire the yellow-gold blaze of colour of the leaves of hazel, oak, beech, lime and sycamore that would eventually turn brown, shrivel and fall to the ground in early winter, prompting Simon to draw a parallel with the life cycle of man. Paul's thoughts at that moment were more in the direction of how nice it would be to own such a house one day!

Further along they passed the guild house of the wool merchants in an equally beautiful setting and then Paul saw a small, discrete tavern on the left side of the road, in an attractive but not so grand garden as the others. It was called The George and, as Simon explained before they went inside, specialised in fine wines and simple but excellent food. The inn was usually frequented by the more wealthy traders and merchants of the city.

It was still a little early for the regular clients and they sat alone in a corner of a light, attractive room, with wood-panelled walls and large oak beams supporting the ceiling. The windows were of plain diamond-shape leaded glass set in a series of arched window frames, in a similar style to some churches Paul had seen. A small pile of logs was neatly stacked alongside an open fireplace, ready for use later in the day, and the coarse stone floor, polished tabletops and chairs were all spotlessly clean. Everything inside the room gave the impression of an extremely well-kept, exclusive establishment, and while they waited to be served, Paul hoped he had sufficient money with him. However, he noted Brother Simon appeared to be perfectly relaxed, so he kept his concerns to himself.

Within a few minutes, a pleasantly smiling server appeared and they ordered a flask of claret and a speciality of the tavern, chestnut and chicken pie, which they later found to be delicious. While they were eating Paul asked Simon questions about the location of the other markets, what else was of note in the city, and then suddenly remembered the dye-trader's reference to Salesburye, and briefly referred to his earlier conversation. The monk told him that although he had not been there himself, he understood it was not much more than twenty miles west of Winchester, and remembered Canon Matthew once telling him that one of the most beautiful churches in Christendom was to be found in that city.

The tavern had steadily been filling up with local traders during their meal, and Paul looked up when all the conversation around them suddenly stopped, wondering what had happened. He had been about to push the last remaining piece of pie into his mouth when he saw her. She had just stepped into the room, escorted by a man and woman whom he assumed were her parents, and was standing and looking around for a vacant table, when their eyes met. He noticed a twinkle of amusement in her eyes and realised he was still holding the knife with the pie on it close to his mouth, and put it back on to his platter immediately, somewhat confused. When he looked up again, they were being led by another serving girl to the one remaining available table in the opposite corner of the room. She was the most beautiful young woman he had ever seen in his life! For a moment it was if the world had stood still. His mouth was dry and he took a swig of wine, ate the piece of pie, assured Simon that he was perfectly all right in answer to the monk's concern that he was perhaps unwell, having noticed the sudden change in his companion.

He tried to react normally and in spite of his determination to continue a normal conversation with Simon, periodically stole a glance in the direction of her table, hoping to catch her eye again. He couldn't hear what she was saying, but she was talking in an animated way with her parents, and from what he could see they were not too happy with her comments. Suddenly, she looked over her mother's shoulder and her light-blue eyes settled on him in what he felt was an appraising way, and he held her stare in an almost challenging way until she looked away and continued her conversation.

Had he imagined a slight blush or was it just wishful thinking? Trying to push away thoughts that wouldn't get him anywhere – she obviously came from a sector of society which was totally foreign to him – Paul asked the serving girl for the bill and was happy to learn that it was not as expensive as he had initially supposed. He and Brother Simon agreed it was time to complete the day's purchases, and standing up, made their way out of the tavern.

Unable to resist one last look, as they neared the door, Paul turned in time to see her eyes following them out, and winking mischieviously he followed Simon outside, albeit somewhat reluctantly! A small but elegant carriage drawn by two horses was standing in the road outside, with a liveried coachman sitting, patiently waiting for his master, and Paul wondered if it could possibly belong to her family. Then, shrugging his shoulders imperceptibly, he caught up with Simon who had already started a brisk pace towards the high street.

Once back in the area of the markets just south of the high street, Paul's thoughts came back to the job in hand. He looked critically at some of the sheep in a paddock as they were passing through the animal market and confided to the monk that he was not particularly impressed at the quality.

'Ah, Paul,' he replied, 'if you come here in springtime to the Fair of St Giles, that's the hillside area just outside the east gate, you will find the very best of everything, believe you me! Buyers come from all over, including many foreigners. It lasts at least two weeks and the canon told me that all the fair taxes go into the coffers of the Bishop of Winchester ... and they're worth a fortune!'

'So, so,' Paul answered, 'I don't think that one is going to die in poverty, do you?'

'Shush!' Simon warned him. 'His excellence is an extremely powerful man and you never know who may be listening to us. You must be more careful what you say, Paul. I've told you before!'

Paul was about to reply (he enjoyed teasing his sometimes very earnest friend) when he spotted a stall laden with candles, and pointing it out to Simon, walked over to take a look. They were just what he wanted and the price was right, and in less than an hour he had also found and ordered for delivery to the priory on the following day his requirements of pitch and ruddle.

Since they had at least another two hours of daylight, Simon suggested they take a look inside the minster before returning to the priory and Paul readily agreed. That would give them both most of the the next day to spend how they wanted. The monk had hoped to find time to study some ancient manuscripts in the priory library and Paul wished to explore more of the city, returning in time to meet the men he had sent to buy the large quantity of lime. What he didn't admit was that he also hoped to catch a glimpse of 'her' again, and try to find out who she was and where she lived.

On the way to the minster, Paul asked Simon if he had noticed the unusually large number of rats in and around some of the market-places. One could expect to see the odd one from time to time, he added, but he couldn't remember ever having seen so many in one day. The monk believed that it must have to do with the many water courses in the city and the fact that there appeared to be a lot of rotten vegetables and offal lying about certainly would encourage them. The sight of the majestic minster tower took their minds off the subject of rats, and Simon began to describe some important aspects of the impressive church.

The building of the original 'old minster' had begun in the seventh century and after about four hundred years of further extensions, work on the 'new minster' had begun in 1079. The new minister, supervised by a Norman bishop Walkelin, was to replace the old one, and they still had not yet finished. The monk told Paul about some of the miracles of the patron saint of Winchester, St Swithun, and once inside the minster showed him his tomb. Paul did find the series of stained-glass windows that ran along the outer northern and southern walls to be very beautiful, but his thoughts started to wander again and he wasn't really listening to all the detail concerning the many tombs, statues, small chapels, and the special uses of Purbeck marble. However he would never forget the 'Winchester Bible'. It was displayed in the library, bound in two great volumes which the monk said had taken the skins of at least 250 calves to create. As Simon carefully, and under close supervision of the librarian, turned the pages, Paul could only wonder at the beauty of the gold leaf and deep blue lapis lazuli of the pages and lettering!

Before returning to the dormitory, while Simon went to Mass in the priory chapel, Paul walked round to the stables to make sure all was well with Blackie. The stallion as always was pleased to see him, but Paul, still unsettled, soon left him and returned to the dormitory to complete the accounts for the day's purchases and prepare his affairs for the following day.

But he was still restless, unable to put the face of the young lady out of his mind. God, she was so beautiful, he thought, and obviously has spirit and humour! But could she possibly be interested in him? Did she really blush when he stared at her or was it only his imagination? What sort of chance could he have, though, he questioned himself, since she obviously came from a wealthy family? I mean, he reasoned, who was he, other than a young man from a very poor family, who had received a little education from the chaplain in Castor, had fought in a campaign in France like thousands of others, and now was just starting out as an inexperienced reeve? Yes, he had already saved a little money, but that was 'blood money' if he was honest with himself, and besides it would be no way near enough to keep a lady like that in a lifestyle to which she must be accustomed. No, he must try to forget her! But he couldn't! Her image continuously flooded his thoughts. He had to see her again, somehow! But how?

Feeling rather depressed and listless, and since he was not at all hungry, he decided to have an early night and make a really early start the next day to explore the whole city and then perhaps, who knows, maybe a miracle would happen. Smiling in spite of himself at the absurdity of it all, he undressed, slipped under the sheepskin bed cover and tried to lose himself in sleep.

20

The Miracle!

Paul slept badly that night. It seemed as if one dream followed another and he always only just managed to catch a glimpse of the face he sought so badly before it moved out of reach and sight. But he didn't give up and each time he got closer he felt somehow as if somebody was holding him back, preventing him from touching her, and when he got really angry at his frustrated efforts, he woke up with a start. Finally, after several similar experiences, he lay awake for some minutes, stretching and yawning and decided to get up, even though it was barely dawn.

By the time he had washed and eaten a light breakfast he was wide awake and impatiently prepared himself for a full day out in the streets of Winchester. He collected his dagger and sword from the store sheds, glanced at his reflection in one of the windows and, satisfied that he looked presentable, started out on his exploratory trip.

He headed first for the east gate where his men had left the city to fetch the lime and followed the city walls up to the northern extremity, crossing over several watercourses that flowed south, joining up with the River Itching outside on its way to the coastal waters of Southampton. Climbing some steps by a round turreted tower, he was able to look outside over the countryside to the north and saw rows of houses just outside the walls, and beyond them rolling hills, lanes and tracks lined with trees, and fields with the odd, large house scattered among them. Looking down he watched the river gurgling under the wall and followed it back with his eyes past a watermill until it disappeared in the hills to the north. Turning towards the city he had a good view of the streets and lanes immediately in front of him which appeared to be largely workshop areas with small, simple cottages and other stone buildings alongside or behind the many business premises, and he decided to take a closer look.

Watercourses ran through most of the streets in this quarter and after walking past Tanner Street he strolled down a very busy and noisy one which comprised mainly of fullers' and dyers' workshops.

It was still very early morning but the street was packed with men and women carrying baskets laden with cloth, or pushing barrels, or leading horses drawing carts full of sacks or bales of cloth yet to be treated by the fullers. Refuse was lying about everywhere, and the smell of horse manure and urine was almost overpowering. The watercourse in the middle of the street was coloured by the dyes used in neighbouring premises and particles of rotten fruit and sewage were also floating slowly past. Occasionally there was a flash of movement as a rat scurried out of the way to disappear in a hole or cranny in the stone-lined watercourse or under one of the narrow crossings. Paul shuddered, resolved to leave the quarter and quickly made his way from Lower to Upper Brook Street, passing large tentering yards with long strips of drying cloth stretched out on the wooden racks, and other workshops all bustling with activity and emitting, for the most, far from pleasant smells.

He then spent the rest of the morning exploring all the other shops and small workshops in the maze of narrow streets and lanes that led down to the high street, gradually working his way towards the west end of the city. He watched potters at work turning moist clay on wooden wheels that were rotated by a foot pedal attached to a rope and a system of pulleys, fascinated by the apparent ease with which they produced jugs, vases and other items. He passed jewellers, bookbinders, saddlers, carpenters and a host of other tradesmen until he eventually found himself in Staple Gardens.

He was now feeling hungry and made for The George, hoping against hope that he might catch another glimpse of the young lady who plagued his thoughts. She was not there and he sat disconsolately in the same corner seat as before, where he could at least keep an eye on the door. The same server approached him, asked if his 'monk' friend was coming, and took his order when she learnt that Paul was alone and not expecting company.

There were very few other customers in the tavern and when the server brought the wine and chicken pie Paul had ordered, sensing that he felt lonely, she asked him if he was planning to stay in the city or if it was merely a short visit that had brought him to Winchester. Paul looked at her, a little surprised initially, but seeing the genuine, open, friendly expression on her face, relaxed, answering that unfortunately it was only a short visit and that he had to return to Titchfield – he was the reeve there, he explained – early on the Saturday morning at the very latest! On impulse, he then reminded her of his visit the previous day, and trying to appear casually curious, wondered if she could remember the family of three people that had arrived shortly before he had left with the monk? He assumed it was probably a local, well-to-do family with a rather spoilt daughter, he added nonchalantly, hoping she wouldn't guess his real interest!

'Oh, you must mean the Polton family and Miss Elizabeth,' she replied immediately. 'They come here once or twice a week. I believe they live a few miles outside the city. Mr Polton has something to do with the cloth trade here, I know, but I don't know exactly what. But Miss Elizabeth is a lovely person. A little spirited perhaps, but a real catch for some lucky man one of these days,' she concluded, looking mischieviously at Paul, with the slightest trace of a smile on her face. 'Now that you remind me, just before they left yesterday, as I was seeing them out, she went back to the table to pick up her gloves and asked me if I knew anything about you, sir!'

He coloured immediately and stammered, 'Really? You're sure she meant me? I mean, there were a lot of other people here also!'

'There's no doubt about it, sir,' the server replied, enjoying every minute. 'She meant you all right. If I may say so, I think you must have made an impression on her, sir,' she added saucily, slightly emphasising the word 'her'. 'Should I give her a message or anything the next time I see her, sir?'

Realising his bluff had been called, Paul looked her in the eyes, and replied, 'Yes, please! Tell her my name is Paul Rollesby. I live in Titchfield village, close to the abbey, and I shall return as soon as I can!' He then stood up, paid her handsomely for his meal, and left the tavern.

Walking aimlessly, only able to think about the fact that she had asked after him, after him ... he found himself suddenly at the west gate and decided to walk down towards the castle before returning to the priory to see if the men had returned with the lime. In this quarter he met several groups of soldiers, mostly undisciplined, lurching from tavern to tavern, frequently bothering passers-by with lewd comments or gestures, which soon brought Paul back to reality, particularly when one of them stumbled into him after being pushed by an equally drunk companion. Seeing the two were harmless, he ignored them and decided to avoid possible trouble by turning away, heading directly towards the minster. He skirted a large field which looked as if it was periodically used for archery practice, passed by the church of St Thomas, and was soon back in the area of the priory stables.

He had just walked out of Blackie's stable when he heard the sound of waggon wheels on cobblestones and the steady clatter of horses' hooves. His men were returning. The three large carts were all fully stacked with sacks covered with animal hides and leafy branches to keep them dry. He checked a sack in each cart and, delighted with the lime quality, shouted his thanks to the men, asking them to store the carts under cover in the sheds and see to the horses. Tomorrow would be a free day for them! Satisfied that everything was in good order for an early Saturday morning start, he told them all to make sure they were on time, and hoped they enjoyed the night out in the city, since he was sure they had already made some plans!

But what about my plans, he thought, what am I going to do this evening and tomorrow? Bells ringing for the vespers service disturbed his thoughts for a moment and Brother Simon, hurrying from the library to the priory chapel, called out to him that they should meet for supper in an hour, and then scuttled off behind several other monks.

At supper, Simon chatted away about his day in the library, but quickly realised that Paul was hardly paying any attention. He stopped and asked directly what was disturbing him. Feeling the need to unbottle his emotions with somebody he could trust, Paul explained the cause and finally added that he believed he must be in love. He couldn't think of anything else except that beautiful girl, as much as he tried! He just had to find a way to meet her again and get to know her better. But how and when?

Simon looked affectionately at his friend and told him that if it really was love that he felt for her, the good Lord would find a way for them to meet. Paul did not appear to be at all convinced, and was about to reply when Simon stopped him, suggesting that perhaps they could take a stroll before it got too dark and continue their conversation outside, since he felt they might distract the others sitting nearby. Paul immediately agreed, but insisted in collecting his sword and dagger first from the store sheds in spite of the monk's protests, adding that the streets were dangerous enough in broad daylight, never mind at dusk!

They had been walking for more than half an hour, first in the gardens surrounding the minster and then outside in the general direction of the castle, so engrossed in their discussion that they hadn't really noticed exactly where they were, when suddenly they heard a scream. They both stopped, peering ahead wondering where the sound came from, and Paul's hand immediately closed over the pommel of his sword. There were now no houses close by, and although darkness had not completely fallen, it was difficult to see more than about fifty paces or so ahead. They were still on a cobbled roadway or rather a narrow lane which seemed to curve around to the right running alongside a large field, which Paul supposed eventually led to the castle walls. Listening carefully, they heard some raucous laughter ahead and slightly to the left of them, followed by a tearing sound and what could have been a woman's voice. There was a moment's silence followed by the noise of a slap on naked flesh and then a muffled sobbing.

Drawing his sword, Paul put his left hand to his lips as a warning to Simon to say nothing, signalled that he should stay behind him, pulled out his dagger and moved silently ahead. Simon followed, terrified of what possibly lay ahead, with his white robe fluttering behind him as he tried unsuccessfully to keep up with Paul who had begun to sprint quietly in front of him. A track loomed up at the curve of the roadway and between some trees about a hundred paces away they could make out a carriage with both side doors open. Paul had stopped running now and had begun to move cautiously along the track, straining his eyes to make sure he didn't tread on any dry twigs. There was a body sprawled on the ground a good twenty paces from the carriage – a man lying motionless on his stomach. Turning the body over carefully, Paul saw that it was a coachman, with a bump the size of an apple on the back of his head, and blood oozing slowly onto his coat collar. He motioned to Simon to stay by the apparently badly injured coachman, and hearing several men's voices and the sound of a woman whimpering not far away, crept further forward to see what was happening.

He heard a relatively young woman's voice saying loudly: 'You are a filthy swine! A coward, an apology of a man!'

Then a man laughed, replying: 'Well at least you've got some spirit, my girl! Not like that whimpering old bag over there. Now for the last time, tell me where you're hiding your money or I'll have to look for it, and you'll like it even less than this!'

Paul circled round in the shadows to get a better look and froze as he saw, in the dim light from a lantern hanging by the coachman's seat, the face of the girl he wanted so desperately to meet, her long blond hair dishevelled, looking defiantly at two other men holding an older woman – her mother, in fact. The third man, wearing a filthy uniform, held Elizabeth's right arm twisted up her back so she could not move and had already ripped part of her dress away at one shoulder and was holding her right breast in one hand.

They still hadn't seen him, but he knew with three of them he had to move like lightning and pitilessly. He was slightly to one side of the ruffian holding Elizabeth and he covered the ten to fifteen paces in a flash of movement. His dagger was at the soldier's throat before he realised what had happened, and prodding it into the skin drawing blood, he hissed into his ear, 'Let her go or you're a dead man.' The tone and the sudden pain convinced the soldier to obey without hesitation, and Paul pulled Elizabeth free and to one side, telling her to move away behind him. He then pointed his sword at the two other ruffians and said in a voice that made Elizabeth's blood run cold, 'I'm only going to say it once. One false movement and your friend here is dead. Release that woman now and sit down just there.' He pointed to a spot within easy reach of his sword. 'Madame,' he commanded, 'move around here to your daughter!' Although still in shock and terrified, she moved obediently to Elizabeth's side.

The situation for Paul was still extremely dangerous even though he held the upper hand and they all knew it. There were three of them and they were looking for the slightest opportunity to reverse the tables. He then shouted out for Simon to come out of hiding and as the monk appeared with his white habit, with the exception of Paul, they all wondered at first if they were seeing a ghost! Before the shock wore off, Paul told him to come round to him carefully and undo a leather belt the soldier was wearing and to take the dagger.

Once that was done, he instructed him to go behind the two ruffians and bind the hands of one of them behind his back as he was sitting, and asked Elizabeth if she could hold the dagger to the throat of the other, guessing that she had the courage and spirit to do so. Holding her dress in place with one hand, she took the dagger from the monk and standing to one side of the ruffian in question, dared him to move. Looking at the sword tip close to his face and the look on Paul's face, he wisely sat stock still. At that moment, the injured coachman appeared and quickly understanding the situation, took the belt off the second man and tied his hands likewise, but considerably harder, before relieving his mistress of the dagger and stepping behind the two sitting ruffians to await Paul's next order.

Calling Simon over to him, Paul asked for the cord that was tied around his habit and told him to bind the soldier's hands tightly behind his back with one end of the cord, which he did. Paul then sheathed his sword and tied a noose with the other end of the cord and slipped it over the soldier's head, tightening it around his throat, warning him again to keep very still until he was finished. Satisfied that the situation was now under total control, he asked the monk to take care of the ladies and to lead them to the coach nearby where they could sit down inside. Elizabeth's mother was shivering and Simon carefully wrapped a large shawl lying on the seat around the older woman's shoulders, trying not to notice Elizabeth's torn dress and the body inside it as she omforted her mother.

Paul had in the meantime led the three ruffians at sword and dagger point to the back of the coach and with the help of the coachman was tying them together, one behind the other in a line, with a length of rope kept under the driving seat. The women inside the coach heard Paul warning them not to try to escape or he would personally take justice into his own hands, and looked at him with some apprehension as he climbed in to join them.

Elizabeth had been studying him carefully outside immediately after he had rescued her, already recognising him as the young man in the tavern, and had been even more reassured when the monk appeared. She examined him now more closely as he addressed her mother, gently asking if she felt better now, also noticing how the monk looked at him when he spoke. He was good-looking, and although probably not rich, she thought, he was not uneducated and certainly had courage. As he spoke, he felt her searching gaze and caught her eyes for a second before turning again to the older woman.

If she had not been sure before, Elizabeth now knew exactly why she had gone back into the tavern under the pretext of forgetting her gloves to try to find out who the young man was with the mischievous twinkle in his eyes! Why, she had suddenly felt a little weak at the knees when she first saw him, and had wondered at the warmth she had felt in her loins! Up to this moment, she had always kept her many admirers at arm's length, not giving any encouragement to one of them. But now! Her own emotions surprised her.

The coach started to move forward at a walking pace and Paul looked out of the window briefly to see if the prisoners were in order behind, then began to speak to Elizabeth's mother.

'Madame, my name is Paul Rollesby. I come from Titchfield, where I work as the abbey reeve, and this gentleman is Brother Simon, who works with me. We came by chance along the road this evening and saw what was happening. Please forgive me for the tone I used earlier with you, but I had to react immediately. I had no time for explanations. I have instructed your coachman to take us first to the castle so we can rid ourselves of these ruffians, and with your permission, we shall be happy to escort you back to your home or wherever you are staying this evening.'

Elizabeth looked at her mother intently as she replied, hoping she would agree, and rejoiced inwardly as she spoke.

'Sir,' she began, 'you have saved us both from a probable terrible death at the hands of those criminals, and the Polton family is truly indebted to you and your companion. I, we, cannot thank you enough for your courage this evening, and we would very much appreciate your company to our home.' She stopped momentarily, frowning slightly at Elizabeth, and signalled discreetly for her to adjust her dress, since it had slipped a little and was displaying too much of her daughter's shapeliness to the strangers. Paul, smiling inwardly, pretended not to notice and politely waited for her to continue, happy to feel the reassuring pressure and warmth of the body next to him.

Before they reached the castle, Mrs Polton explained in detail that they had been to a Mass in the minster, at the special request of her daughter, who had surprisingly confided this special wish to her earlier in the day. On the way back to the west gate, in a dark stretch of roadway, the three ruffians had suddenly appeared, overpowered the coachman, and had driven the coach to where Paul had found them.

Paul wanted to ask some further questions, but the coach came to a sudden halt at the main gate of the castle, and excusing himself, he jumped out quickly, calling for the guard. Within a few minutes, the prisoners were taken into custody to await the sheriff's judgement the following day, after Mrs Polton had imperiously described the nature of the crime to the guard captain, emphasising the brutality of the assault and how she and her daughter had been rescued by Paul and the monk.

The Poltons lived a good two miles to the west of the city, in a large country mansion, set back at least two hundred paces from the road and reached by a gravel and stone driveway. It was very dark when they arrived at the house, too dark to be able to see anything of the land around, other than the outhouses to one side of the house. The coach had hardly drawn to a halt when several people appeared with torches, the front door was opened and an elegantly dressed middle-aged man strode out quickly. It was Mr Polton and as he pulled the coach door open, Paul could see the look of anxiety on his face, which softened as he saw that his wife and daughter were inside.

While he was helping his wife out, she quickly told him that in spite of their appearance, she and Elizabeth were not injured, thanks to the help of the two gentlemen, she added, indicating the other passengers, and that she would explain everything once they were inside. Simon looked on with some amusement as he watched how Paul held Elizabeth when she stepped down from the coach and how he released her hand with apparent reluctance. Their exchange of looks also did not go unnoticed by the monk as he followed them into the house.

Mr Polton took charge of the situation immediately. An elderly servant took Elizabeth off somewhere to change her clothes, Paul and Simon were led into a large room with a blazing log fire where they were served with glasses of steaming punch, while Mr Polton took his wife to another room to hear what had happened to them all and why they had returned home so late.

A few minutes later, Mr Polton strode into the large room alone, thanked them both profusely for the services they had rendered so bravely to his family and before they could say a word, told them that he trusted they would stay for an evening meal and naturally spend the night in his house since it was far too late to return to the city. Paul needed no persuasion and Simon replied that he too would be delighted to accept the kind invitation but must return to the priory at first light the following day.

An hour or so later, Elizabeth returned with her mother. Both women had fully recovered from the ordeal and had obviously gone to considerable pains to look their best. Paul had been talking with Mr Polton, telling him a little bit about his work on the demesne, and how he came to leave Castor. He had briefly mentioned the campaign in France leading up to Crécy, without going into too many details, even though his host had demonstrated great interest in it, asking many questions. Seeing Elizabeth enter, Paul stopped in mid-sentence, staring at her beauty with such an intensity that she blushed slightly and looked down.

'Ah, here are the ladies at last!' exclaimed Mr Polton. 'Come and join us. We are having an extremely interesting conversation. You didn't tell me, Mathilda, that you had both been saved by a young man that fought at Crécy!'

Before Paul could protest that he had only played a very small role and wanted nothing more to do with it all, a servant announced that the evening meal was ready if they wished to eat.

'A splendid idea! I'm sure we're all hungry now,' Mr Polton continued, looking questioningly at his wife who inclined her head slightly in agreement. 'Good! Allow me to lead the way.' With which he steered the group to a long table at one end of the room, which servants had carefully prepared. He arranged the seating so that he sat at one end, placing Paul and Simon to each side of him, with his wife alongside Simon, and Elizabeth opposite her mother and at the side of Paul, to the latter's great delight!

Paul had not known what to think about Mr Polton initially, but later in the evening he realised that behind the deceptively 'hale and hearty' manner was an extremely pleasant person and astute business brain. He had outlined to Paul how he had started in the cloth business and how over the years he had developed his operation into one of the largest in Winchester. He talked knowingly about the political developments in England and explained why he had been particularly interested to hear Paul's account of the campaign in France, commenting on so many other expensive campaigns that always required yet more taxes to finance them and which seemed to lead to little else than the misery and suffering of the English soldiers and the inhabitants of France. Long-term, he continued, he was sure that we would all look back and judge it to have been a complete waste.

Simon agreed, more due to his own religious beliefs than to any specific economic or social grounds, and he like all the others listened spellbound to Paul's description of the terrible slaughter that occurred at Crécy and some of the small French towns and villages, which he used to demonstrate his views on the subject. There were moments when he spoke with a catch in his throat, or tried to conceal the trace of a tear that slowly welled in his eye when he recalled the wanton destruction and the brutality of it all. Although he went out of his way to explain that while his brother was a professional soldier – a hero rewarded personally for his bravery by the Black Prince himself – he had merely been there, but they all understood that it had been much more than that!

Paul spoke with such eloquence that even the monk marvelled at this, up till now for him, unknown aspect of his friend's ability. Mrs Polton, like her husband, had already been impressed by the quiet, self-confident way he had handled himself, particularly after having learnt more about his origins. She had also recognised that within him was a toughness and determination to succeed, in spite of his apparent calmness and sensitivity. She remembered how he had handled the ruffians a few hours earlier. It was almost as if a devil had spoken when he hissed that message to the brute who was mistreating Elizabeth, and then, suddenly, as she looked at her daughter, she understood. She had never seen her daughter look at a man before the way she was looking at Paul now. Quite the opposite in fact. She chased them all away, but now she was absolutely radiant, she observed! And she remembered the one or two glances she had intercepted that Paul had cast at Elizabeth during the evening. He was in love with her and she with him. It must be that, she concluded, yet Elizabeth had been acting differently for the last day or so. But they had only just met – or had they met before?

The answer to her silent question came from a quite different quarter. The monk had been talking about his impressions of the city and at one stage made a reference to The George, and how much he and Paul had liked it the day before, when they had eaten there at midday. Mrs Polton noticed immediately the annoyed glance from Paul and smiled inwardly. So that was it, she reasoned. That's where they first saw each other. That's why my scheming daughter went back for her gloves – she had never forgotten them before!

It was her husband who interrupted her thoughts by commenting that they too found The George to be excellent and went there frequently, adding that incredible as it may seem, they had also been there on the same day. Mrs Polton almost burst out laughing at the expression on her daughter's face, and quickly changing the subject, suggested that since Brother Simon would have to rise so early in the morning, perhaps they should all retire to bed soon, particularly after such a hectic day.

While Mrs Polton was busy organising where the guests should sleep, taking Elizabeth with her, Mr Polton offered the two men a glass of wine before retiring to bed. Simon excused himself politely saying he was almost asleep on his feet, thanked his host for his hospitality and went off in the direction taken by the two women. Paul sat down close to the fireplace waiting for Mr Polton to join him.

Within a few minutes his host came to the point and asked him if he had ever considered working in the cloth business, since he believed that the experience Paul already had as a reeve, particularly in the wool trade, made for an excellent background. Furthermore, he added, he would be delighted to help him get established if he were interested.

Looking the merchant firmly in the eyes, Paul thanked him for the kind offer, saying that nothing would please him more, but he had a commitment at the abbey which required his services for at least another one to two years. The canon at Titchfield, he added, had given him a wonderful chance to prove his theories and put the demesne in order, and he had promised he would. Not only that, he continued, this gave him the chance to prove that he could do it himself, with his own efforts, and that for him was important. But, perhaps – he struggled to express it tactfully – he could maintain contact with Mr Polton and periodically pay a visit when he was in the area, and then maybe, one day if he, Mr Polton, hadn't changed his mind . . . As he was searching for a way out, the merchant interrupted, smiling broadly, assuring him that he would look forward to that, and they shook hands on the agreement.

While Paul was tossing and turning in his bed in one of the comfortable guest rooms, unable to sleep, thinking first about Elizabeth and then her father's offer, Mrs Polton was cross-questioning her husband about his views concerning their guests, and particularly the 'young Mr Rollesby'. He told her that he found him to be an extremely talented and interesting young man and then explained the offer he had made and how Paul had reacted to it, and was somewhat surprised when his wife burst out laughing.

'You men,' she said, 'you don't notice anything! They're in love, those two, believe me! No wonder he asked if he could visit us from time to time. Your daughter would be broken-hearted if he didn't. But we must keep an eye on them, nevertheless. If they are to marry one day, I would prefer they have children *after* the marriage.' She looked knowingly at her husband. 'There's still a long way to go before that, anyway. Who knows what could happen in the meantime! Now, blow out the candle, my love, and come here and keep me warm!'

Elizabeth, whose bedroom was next door to that of her parents, had also been unable to sleep. She had never met a man like Paul before, and decided that come what may, she would marry him one day. She had not deliberately eavesdropped, but became instantly alert hearing her father mention Paul's name, and realising her parents knew and more or less approved, she turned over and fell contentedly asleep.

21

Growing Prosperity

The journey back to Titchfield had been uneventful. Before leaving Elizabeth, Paul had summoned up his courage to declare his love for her, and the thought of her reaction remained with him as he rode home. She had flown into his arms and as he held her close to him, gently stroking her long hair, he could smell the sweet perfume of her body, a wonderful odour he would never forget! It had not been easy to leave her, but he promised to return in the spring at the latest, when he attended the great fair of St Giles.

The winter preparations for the sheep were made, the reclamation of the land at Wicor was well in hand, and Paul had carefully supervised the special fertilisation of the arable land close to the abbey with which he hoped to increase the yield. Satisfied that the affairs of Portchester Manor were in good order and could do without him for two weeks or so, he decided to visit Tom and his family at Castor for the Christmas celebrations. Canon Matthew gave him his blessing, and with gifts for the children and a flask of perfume for Margaret that he had brought back from France, Paul set off with Blackie early morning on a cold but fine day in mid-December.

On the advice of Brother Simon, he rode to Southampton, looking for a merchant ship with a cargo bound for the south-east coast. He arrived in time to board a coastal barge laden with iron-ore that was about to sail for Colchester, the captain being delighted to earn a little extra from a paying passenger. Getting Blackie on board proved to be a challenge, but eventually he was settled in a relatively comfortable stall, alongside two other very placid but huge horses, used for hauling heavy waggons.

The winds were favourable, but it was a cold and damp journey. The barge more or less hugged the coast, rarely sailing out of sight of land and after two days and nights, rounded the coastline of Kent, with its numerous creeks and havens, and tacked towards the ancient city of Colchester. A few hours later, the barge skirted Marsey Island and entered the mouth of the River Colne, reaching the quayside at Colchester by early afternoon.

The captain, when not at the tiller, was happy to be able to talk with Paul, telling him on one occasion on his return journey he would always find something sailing to Southampton. On hearing his destination, the captain suggested it would be better to take a boat down from Yermouth on his way back to Southampton and it might even go directly to Titchfield if he was lucky, he added.

Once he and Blackie were on shore, Paul knew he only had another two to three hours of daylight, and needed to leave the city immediately, making as much ground as possible before the night set in. He had been told by the captain first to head northwards before eventually veering round to the east and the sea, and decided to accompany a long train of merchants and their packhorses he caught up with on the road. Most of them appeared to be making for the Burye St Edmunds area, he soon discovered, and were carrying mainly expensive cloth and silks imported from Flanders and Italy, most of which was destined for the monastery there. 'The monastery?' Paul looked quizzically at the merchant who told him. 'They can afford to buy all that?'

'And a lot more,' he replied. 'They own almost everything around here, and with their tithes and the wool they sell, they're richer by far than the king of England, believe me! They're also very hard businessmen. So long as you work with them, they're fine, but watch out if you don't cooperate!'

Remembering what he had once heard in Norwiche from the landlord of The Mitre, David Cook, Paul merely nodded understandingly, not saying a word more on the subject, since they were just passing a group of monks that had stopped to eat by the roadside.

Close to Sudbury, the friendly merchant, who was also about the same age as Paul, told him that he and the others would stop there for the night, but if he wanted to go a little further, he would come across a sprawling village called Melforde, and recommended he look for The Bull, which was an excellent inn. Thanking him for the tip, before spurring Blackie on, he told him his name was Paul Rollesby, originally from Castor but now at Titchfield, and hoped they might meet again one day. The young merchant smiled, held out his hand to shake Paul's, and said, 'I would enjoy that. My name is William Outlawe, from Wulpet. May you have a good journey, Paul!'

All the way to Melforde, Paul was trying to remember where he had heard that name before and its association with Wulpet, and just as he caught sight of The Bull it came to him. Of course, he thought, he must be a relative of that old woman David Cook told poor Federico and myself about: Alice Kyteler! I hope that's a good omen!

The inn was very good and Paul really enjoyed his evening meal there. The people were mainly friendly, but as usual there were one or two travellers Paul felt would cut your throat for a shilling, given the chance, and so he took the precaution of moving the large chest in his room up against the door before he slipped into the inviting bed.

There had been a heavy frost during the night which made the roadway very slippery, and for the first hour in the early morning, he led Blackie by the bridle. A large church dominated the hillside in front of him, and as he walked along the main village street towards it, he saw that the roadway was lined mainly with inns and clothing shops of every description. The side streets on both sides were filled with workshops and small, neat cottages and he could hear the sound of a water-wheel creaking as it turned in the river nearby. Close to the church along a lane sloping down on the left side of a huge village green were several large, stone and timber-framed houses which Paul assumed belonged to some of the wealthier merchants. It was a very picturesque village and as he continued climbing the hill, taking the route to Burye the inn-keeper had described to him, he passed large gateways on his right-hand side leading to two or three especially grandiose properties.

Once clear of Melforde, he mounted Blackie but kept a slow pace until the frost had disappeared from the main track. It was beautiful countryside, and he resolved one day to return and spend more time exploring the whole area. Even though he had to cross several streams he reached the outskirts of Burye by midday and followed the track that led around the monastery outer walls before branching off towards Diss as he had been told. He lost his way twice but fortunately was able to find somebody each time that knew the way, but saw that he certainly couldn't reach Castor before nightfall, and once in Diss looked for an inn.

He found a small, simple tavern in the village centre, close to the duckpond which had three rooms for visitors. It was nothing special but at least was clean and warm. In fact, Paul grinned when he saw the stable behind the rickety building, which looked every bit as comfortable as his room! But it was better than spending the night outside, he thought. After a meal of roast duck – which was excellent – washed down with a jug of ale, he was soon fast asleep in his tiny room.

The next day a young boy at the stables told him to follow the river, the Waveney he later learned, which would lead him up to

Yermouth, but it was a good day's ride. There were no other travellers on the road when he set off, but he enjoyed the sight of the marshy valleys and pastureland he had earlier got to know so well, and waved friendly greetings to the shepherds and labourers he saw from time to time. He also passed countless water-mills and periodically disturbed flocks of wild ducks and other wildfowl on the lakes and water courses around him, that shrieked and screamed as they rose reluctantly in the air with an urgent fluttering of their wings. It was good to be back, he thought, and rode on quickly towards Yermouth, rejoicing when he saw the first seagull circling high above him.

As he realised he was now very hungry, he began to think of his time in the manor house kitchen with Mrs Galston and smiled when he thought about the little escapade with Nellie, wondering how they all were. But above all, he was looking forward to being with Tom and Margaret and seeing the children again. Fording the River Yerus close to where it joined the Waveney, he knew that that he only had to cross the Burre a mile or two ahead of him and he would be in Castor within two to three hours. He spurred on Blackie impatiently, who also seemed to 'smell the stable door' even though the stallion was not at all from the area!

It was late afternoon when Paul first saw the manor house in the distance, arriving with a clatter of hooves twenty minutes later in the courtyard between the small round tower and the manor house kitchen. As he tied Blackie to a nearby rail, Mrs Galston ran out to him like an excited young girl, calling out, 'Master Paul, it's you after such a long time! How have you been? You look as if you haven't eaten for days. My goodness, you really have grown into a fine man!'

He hugged her close to him and as she took a step back to take another look at him, he saw how she hurriedly wiped a tear away from the corner of one eye. She began to scold him for not letting her know how he was keeping. Paul smiled good-naturedly at the elderly lady who had almost been like a mother to him, explaining he was planning to stay for a week or so for the Christmas celebrations, promising to tell her everything a little later, but he was in good health and happy to see her again. However, he added, he must go and see his sister-in-law immediately or she would never forgive him!

Margaret had heard the sound of a horse galloping into the courtyard, and thinking that maybe Tom was returning home earlier than usual, was already standing at the door when Paul appeared, with saddlebags slung over one shoulder and carrying his sword in his free hand.

'Paul! How wonderful to see you,' she flustered. 'Tom and the children will be so happy. Come in, my love, and tell me all the news!' She led him into their main room, told him to put his things in the corner for now, and before he could say a word, hugged him and kissed his cheek. 'That's for my favourite brother-in-law,' she said, laughing. 'Just wait a minute, and I'll go and collect Eric and Margaret from the manor house. Alice is sleeping. You can perhaps take your horse to the stables just round the back here, and I'll leave word for Tom to come home earlier if he can.' And then she went out, hurrying towards the manor house.

It was a joyful reunion. The two children were beside themselves with excitement at seeing their Uncle Paul again after such a long time – they loved to hear his stories and he enjoyed frolicking with them and seeing their honest and innocent pleasure – while Margaret watched lovingly over them all. Tom arrived home late after all, since he had been patrolling the far side of the demesne, to ensure that the sheep-stealing countermeasures he had put into place were working, now that he believed he had finally put a stop to it all.

His face lit up when he saw his younger brother sitting by the fire, with his daughter Margaret sitting on his knee and the young Eric squatting on the rush-covered stone floor between him and his wife, all listening spellbound to one of Paul's stories. 'By God, Paul,' he exclaimed delightedly, 'what a wonderful surprise!' He hurried over to him and the two brothers embraced.

Before either of them could say another word, Margaret said excitedly, 'You won't believe it, Tom, but Paul has found himself a young lady at last! There was nobody good enough for him round here,' she added teasingly, 'so his *lordship* had to go to Winchester of all places to find the right one!' And they all burst out laughing, while Eric looked at the adults wondering what was so funny, thinking he would never understand them!

The children had already eaten, but Margaret had promised they could stay up until their father came home, but now it was time to go to bed, in spite of all the usual protests. While she and Paul were taking them to their bedroom, Tom, after kissing his children, went outside to wash himself before the evening meal.

They discussed Paul's situation in Titchfield first. He explained his work with the abbey and described the layout of Portchester manor, how everything was organised, what he was planning for the future, until Margaret impatiently asked him to talk more about Elizabeth, how he met her and when would they marry. She would have asked a lot more if Tom and Paul had not protested, albeit in good humour!

Paul immediately began by saying that it was far too early to talk about marriage since he had only met Elizabeth a few weeks previously, and he explained how he had first seen her in The George with her parents, and Margaret immediately insisted that he descibe her in detail, which he did with obvious pleasure. He continued by saying that fortunately, he and Brother Simon had arrived in the nick of time to prevent Elizabeth and her mother from being brutally assaulted and perhaps even worse, one evening in Winchester, and how they had subsequently escorted them home. He told them what a beautiful house the Poltons owned outside the city and that he had been more or less invited to visit them regularly by Mr Polton. He sighed as he said that unfortunately the next trip would not be before the spring fair of St Giles.

Tom asked him about the ruffians, and what he did with them, and nodded as Paul described how he tied and pulled them behind the carriage along to the guard at the nearby castle.

'I'm afraid the violence and brutality don't get any better,' Tom commented. 'The countryside seems to be full of outlaws. Half of them are soldiers returning from the wars in France, brutalised by their experiences, or wounded or disillusioned at having been cheated by clerks or other officials out of the wages they'd been promised. Most of the rest, with very few exceptions, appear to be the dregs of humanity that haven't done an honest day's work in their lives.'

He then went on to describe the extent of the sheep theft of the previous summer. 'You won't believe it, Paul, but we eventually caught one of those bastards in the act, and he admitted after a bit of persuasion before we hung him that he was in the pay of some "count" or other!'

'Count, you say, Tom? It wasn't the Count de Kessinger by any chance, was it?' Paul immediately asked.

'Yes, it was,' Tom replied. 'Now that you mention it. But how would you know that?'

Paul then went on to tell his brother what he had heard about the man during his fateful trip to Norwiche, including his high connections with royalty and that he had also once seen him with Sir William's visitor at that time, the Earl of Dunghall.

Tom nodded his head, explaining that he had taken a distinct dislike to that particular relative of his lord, from the very first moment he saw him.

'You know, Paul,' he continued, 'I reported all this to Sir William. Told him that this count was up to his neck in dishonest business, including stealing our sheep, and you won't believe what happened! Our lord tried to bring a law case against that so-called count, but it was blocked by some very powerful force up top there. It's incredible what the privileged classes can get away with these days. There was nothing we could do about it *officially*.'

'And unofficially?' Paul looked inquiringly at his brother.

'Well, that's another matter,' he replied, grinning. 'We, er, persuaded the outlaw we captured to give us the names of his companions also, before he was hung. And I and a couple of my men eventually caught up with them and by the time we had finished our "discussion", they agreed never again to return to Castor! It seems to have worked quite well so far. Nothing has been reported stolen in the demesne since the summer, but I've also tightened up the security in all the villages to be quite sure.'

Paul warned his brother to be careful of the count and his influence, because he was certainly a dangerous man to be crossed, like most of his sort, and then asked how things were with Sir William and the manor house in general. He learned that the lord of Castor was currently in France with some of his men, participating in the siege of Calais which seemed to go on for ever, he had added with feeling. The manor was doing very well out of the situation, however, since they were continuously sending over large quantities of salted meat and as many longbows and arrows as the bowyers and fletchers could produce. The new reeve, John Dexter, had taken over from Stanley Pettit, who had died three months previously, and was doing well. That was at least one outlaw, that with a bit of luck ('and a good wife' Margaret had been quick to point out) had finally settled down to an honest living, Tom concluded, wondering what he may have forgotten.

Margaret, looking for an opportunity to participate in the conversation, then told Paul that Lady Mortimer had taken over the household accounts in the absence of her husband who was rarely at home, when the old steward, Mr S. died peacefully in his sleep shortly after he and Tom had left for France together. The lord's wife also encouraged young Eric and Margaret to visit her most days in the manor house and took an active part in their education. Margaret added that the mistress loved children but did not seem able to have any of her own, and since Lady Mortimer had always been so kind and helpful to their family, she saw no reason to discourage her attachment to their children.

The subject of education reminded Paul about the chaplain, and he looked hard at them both when they burst out laughing at his question. 'Take a look at young Nellie, the next time you go in the kitchen,' Margaret confided, 'and you'll soon see that the chaplain continues to be very active! But don't tell anyone I said that. I promised Mrs Galston not to tell a soul!'

So, so, Paul thought, some things never change!

By midnight, Paul felt he had more or less caught up with all the main developments in Castor, and feeling the effects of his long journey, a warm room and some good wine, decided he had to sleep as he could hardly keep his eyes open. Margaret quickly prepared a bed for him and before he knew it he was fast asleep, wrapped in a sheep-fleece coverlet, in an alcove in the far corner of the room.

Paul spent the next few days visiting friends and acquaintances all over the demesne, heading first for Mautbye to look out for Ned Giles, the shepherd who had taught him so much. As a favour to the new reeve, John Dexter, he delivered a bundle of candles to Ned and spent the rest of the day talking about earlier times and also what he was now doing in Titchfield. He learnt that the new reeve was well-accepted, and that the estate affairs were gradually improving. The last harvest had been good, the sheep were in good condition and Ned was expecting an excellent lambing season.

'Things are almost too good, Master Paul. I wonder what's awaiting us next year, or the year after,' the old shepherd said, looking towards the distant horizon as if he were expecting something evil to apear at any moment.

Paul hadn't particularly looked forward to it, but was more or less obliged to pay a courtesy visit on his earlier teacher and mentor, the chaplain, Father Ignatius. He was looking considerably older – must be the wayward life he leads, Paul thought to himself – but was now dressing much more extravagantly. He had abandoned his long, black gown and cowl, the insignia of the Benedictine order from which he had originated, and taken to wearing a very short, tight-fitting outer habit, bound around the waist with a belt studded with decorative, and probably expensive, jewellery. He also wore a fancy pair of red and green leather boots. He had lost none of his previous hypocritical piety, and had developed into an even more vain and ridiculous personality. He was, however, interested to hear about Winchester and was impressed to learn that Paul had stayed in the priory. Paul omitted to mention anything about Elizabeth, since the chaplain was the last person he would confide in. As he took leave of him, Father Ignatius asked solicitously after his brother, and 'of course, his charming and beautiful lady wife!' Paul promised to pass his greetings on to them, shuddering inwardly, and once astride Blackie, rode him quickly back to the stables, inhaling deeply the clean, fresh air.

He enjoyed immensely walking with the young Eric and Margaret in the gardens around the manor house, and was frequently joined by the reeve's adopted son Robert, who had turned out to be a credit to John and Annie Dexter. He was also very bright and eager to learn, in many ways similar to Eric, but an even stronger personality. Paul wasn't absolutely sure, but felt that Robert seemed to enjoy particularly the company of the much younger Margaret. Not so surprising, he surmised inwardly, she's a beautiful child, and will probably be an even more intelligent version of her mother. Paul also noticed how Robert defended her from the occasional taunts and teasing of her elder brother, admiring the extremely sensitive and mature way he handled it.

Two days before Christmas Sir William returned unexpectedly from Calais with his troops as escort. He explained later to Tom and Paul during a special banquet in his honour which Lady Mortimer had quickly arranged, that he had seen little point in staying on at the siege, since it was clearly going to take a long time and there was nothing more he could do. The city could probably hold out for at least another six months, he added, and rather than sit around the winter quarters that had been built for the English army close by, listening to the roar of cannon continuously firing their missiles into Calais, he had preferred to return to Castor. He would go back to France later in the following year, he concluded, but in the meantime looked forward to some good hunting in the local forests and maybe a bit of jousting in Burye or wherever.

Following the banquet in the manor house, Paul returned with Tom and Margaret to their quarters, and spent the rest of the Christmas celebrations with the children. Presents were distributed, everybody ate and drank a little too much, and the time for Paul to leave for Titchfield arrived all too soon. After tearful farewells, especially from Mrs Galston and Margaret, Tom told Paul to come again whenever he could, adding that they might well move out into a larger house in the village early next year, but would be easily found! He handed Paul the charter of manumission that Sir William had signed on his behalf, told him to keep it safe, embraced him, wished him a safe journey and then suddenly, in spite of his brother's protests, had Lightning saddled and accompanied him to Yermouth.

On the way to the coast, Tom told Paul that sooner or later he could expect to be summoned to fight again in the king's army in France, and that should anything happen to him, he wanted Paul to make sure his family was well-cared for, and, like their own father had done, he would hide some money in the garden. The new house wasn't ready yet, he explained, but there was one large oak tree twenty paces from the stables at the back, and he would bury a small wooden chest five paces due south of that tree. He would of course tell Margaret; however, it was better that Paul also knew about it. He then turned in the saddle to look his brother firmly in the eyes and uttered words that Paul would never forget.

'Paul, we have rarely talked about the gift you and I have. People like the chaplain would call it witchcraft if they knew – and they must never know! I don't understand it, but like you, I sometimes feel we are talking with each other even though we are many miles apart.'

Paul nodded understandingly, and waited for his brother to continue.

'My duties from time to time are not so pleasant. I have to do with criminals, evil people of all types. I've killed a few in self-defence, never in cold blood, but usually I bring them to the gallows after the lord or another sheriff has sentenced them. I have always managed in the past to put it all out of my mind, although to be honest, what we experienced in France together this summer can never be forgotten, but that was somehow different. Just recently, I've started to have some terrible dreams. I wake up in the morning covered in perspiration and try to remember what it was that frightened me, and you know that I don't frighten easily! Its not the same dream and yet in a way it is, or at least there's a similarity.' He paused, seeking the words to convey the horror of his dreams, and Paul was already feeling very disturbed, only too conscious of his brother's unusual flash of emotion.

'There's always some kind of monster . . . a beast of indescribable ugliness and it is pitiless as it kills and consumes all who stand before it. This creature emerges from a dark lair, deep in the bowels of the earth, is covered in long, black hair and slides or slithers slowly forward, hungry for victims. I stand there, pushing my family behind me and face this beast with sword and lance, can smell its fetid breath, but in spite of my furious defence, it keeps coming on and on. And then I wake up!' Tom's face for a moment showed the horror of this vision, but he then smiled. 'Perhaps I should eat less cheese or drink less wine, or who knows, maybe I'm just getting a little doddery in my old age. It's probably nothing at all, Paul. Let's forget it and talk about something else.' No matter how much his brother tried to probe further, Tom refused to discuss it any more, and scenting salty sea air, changed the subject to Paul's return journey.

As the sea captain had predicted, it was comparatively easy to find a ship at Yermouth destined for the south coast, and Paul arrived safely with Blackie three days later in Southampton, both very happy to leave the cramped quarters of the brigantine that was heavily laden with peat and logs, and set foot on dry land.

The year of 1347 seemed to race by and was an excellent one for both sides of the Rollesby family. Tom and his family moved out of their quarters alongside the manor house into a large, stone house that Lady Mortimer insisted Sir William had built close to the gardens and the canal, so that she could easily visit Margaret and the children, and of course Tom was easily accessible for his many responsibilities. Shortly after the move, Sir William returned to Calais and stayed there until the city was eventually taken in August of that year, fully confident that his wife and the demesne properties were well-protected by his loyal captain, to whom he gave total authority in his absence. Lady Mortimer busied herself even more with the education of Eric and Margaret, while Tom's wife, in addition to looking after Alice, who although only a little over a year old was already beginning to assert her strong personality, had to grapple with all the problems of a new house and garden. It was all very hectic, but extremely satisfying for them all.

Paul for his part did not have a free minute. After the lambing season had ended, the sowing was completed and he had travelled to the fair of St Giles to buy and sell sheep, talk to prospective wool buyers, and of course visit the Poltons, he had to supervise the sheep-shearing and all that was involved. Also, in addition to the normal duties of a reeve, he had to ensure that his various projects across the demesne were developing satisfactorily in line with the agreement made with Canon Matthew.

Each season of the year brought its own special tasks, and Paul wanted desperately to be able to demonstrate a successful and profitable year in order to justify the faith the canon had placed in him, as well as satisfying his own high standards and ambition. As the year progressed he was pleased to see that by and large most things were running smoothly and the demesne's financial position was steadily improving. When he could slip away for a few days to Winchester to be with Elizabeth, that seemed to make all his hard work even more worthwhile, and she was also genuinely interested in what he was doing. His relationship with Mr Polton continued to improve to the extent that Paul began to sense some, perhaps cautious, affection! But, try as he could, he was never completely sure about Elizabeth's mother. She was always polite and to a degree solicitous as far as his well-being was concerned, but somehow he had the impression that she had never really accepted him as being good enough for her only daughter.

Paul thought that possibly with time the relationship might improve, and besides, it was her daughter he wanted to marry and she herself did not give him any doubts! Quite the reverse in fact. Whenever they were able to escape the scrutiny of Mrs Polton for a few minutes and find some privacy, he felt he was standing close to a volcano about to erupt, as she explored him hungrily with lips and hands, and unashamedly encouraged him to do likewise. How he longed for her and the day when they would be free to do whatever they chose whenever they wanted. He had to struggle with himself as he gently moved back from her passionate embrace, telling her softly he loved her more than mere words could express, but they should wait a year or so, until he could marry her. She always reluctantly agreed, but they both knew the time would come when there would be no withdrawal and nature would simply take its course.

At the end of that year it was perfectly natural for the Poltons to invite Paul to their home for the Christmas festivities and he accepted willingly. Brother Simon suggested Paul send a letter to his brother and family in Castor, since he had been without any contact with them for a year, and arranged it all through the monastery's special courier system. Paul knew that Tom could only read falteringly, but was sure the young Eric could help out if necessary, and so briefly described the events of the year, wished them all health and happiness for the future, and promised to visit them in the year ahead if possible.

Mr Polton had been extremely interested to hear from Paul how the affairs of Titchfield Abbey were improving quite dramatically, and complimented him on the progress. He underlined much more concretely his earlier offer, and was not at all surprised when Paul told him that, providing the first half of the following year continue sucessfully, he would be delighted to accept. He explained that Brother Simon could certainly take over from him until a more experienced reeve could be found, and then, looking at both Elizabeth's parents across the table, announced that he had saved sufficient money to get married and requested officially the hand of their daughter. He added slowly, with carefully chosen words, that he wanted their blessing above all, but should they refuse him as a son-in-law, he would take Elizabeth with him to Titchfield and marry her there, nevertheless.

There was a moment of silence as the two parents looked first at each other and then at their daughter, who had already taken hold of Paul's hand and moved visibly closer to him. It was Mrs Polton who spoke first.

'You don't seem to give us much choice, Paul, do you? I must say from what you have told us about your brother and what we have seen and experienced with you, the Rollesby family seem to be a very determined and special family.' As she said the word 'special', she smiled and quickly added, 'I had my doubts initially, to be honest, but I know that I can also speak for my husband when I say it would be an honour for us. May God bless you both!'

Needless to say, that Christmas dinner was a time of very particular celebration. During the following feast days, Paul agreed with Mr and Mrs Polton that the wedding would be in Winchester, sometime in the late summer, and they could confirm more details a little later on. As Paul rode back to Titchfield in early January, he couldn't remember ever being happier, and he felt the touch of Elizabeth's lips on his own right up to the time that he led Blackie into his stable, impatient for the next six months to pass.

The same night in Castor, lying closely together, Margaret took Tom's hand and placed it on her stomach that was already beginning to swell, and whispered to her husband: 'I'm sure it's going to be a boy, my love. I can hardly wait!'

22

The Black Death

Paul waited for the right moment to talk to Canon Matthew concerning his future plans. He had already told him a little about Elizabeth as an explanation for his trips to Winchester, and confided more detail to Brother Simon whom he wanted, initially at least, to take over the responsibility of the demesne when he left. Simon had been sad to learn that his friend planned to leave within a few months but had willingly accepted Paul's suggestion, pointing out, however, that the canon should be informed immediately.

It had been easier than Paul had imagined. He had begun with a discussion on the status of the various projects, and the canon had been delighted to learn that the arable lands around the abbey had produced a yield of slightly more than ten bushels per acre, which was double that of the rest of the demesne! As Paul falteringly began to talk about further activities later in the year, the canon smiled and interrupted him with a question concerning his plans with Elizabeth, adding that he assumed he would want to marry her in the not too distant future.

Listening carefully to Paul, he nodded, sighed and gave him his blessings for the future, saying that he would be sorry to lose him, but had guessed at the outset that he would leave one day. However, he continued, it would be necessary to work even more intensively with Brother Simon to ensure that he could carry on the good work until a suitable replacement for Paul could be found. The canon then raised the subject of the advisability of perhaps signing a contract with the demesne of Winchester concerning the future sale of Portchester's wool. A monk from St Swithun's had recently discussed this with him and it seemed like a good idea. They would after all get their money immediately and it was a guaranteed sale for it all.

Paul was horrified and immediately pointed out that the Bishop of Winchester was renowned for practices like that, adding that they would only pay a low price per sack and then also insist on a discount in kind, in that when they came to collect the wool, they would claim an additional two or three sacks free. He had heard about this in several other areas and although of course the decision must be taken by the canon, he personally suggested that he should not do it! Clearly, Canon Matthew had not heard about the practice and thanked Paul for the information.

And so in the following months, interrupted only by the occasional visit to Winchester and the Poltons, Paul diligently briefed Simon for his future responsibilities, giving him the best possible advice he could on all aspects of running the demesne's affairs, applying the learning of the previous year or so. Simon was a willing pupil and enjoyed working closely with Paul, becoming almost a 'confidant' as his friend discussed his future plans with Elizabeth and the difficulties he could expect in attempting to be accepted within the Polton family circle. Simon had told him that he believed it would only be a question of patience and a little time. Once they saw and understood his qualities, he maintained, it should not be a problem at all. Time solved many of life's issues, he counselled.

One evening in July, they were sitting on the wall running along one side of Titchfield harbour, enjoying the cooling sea breeze, watching the seagulls wheeling overhead and discussing the day's events. Brother Peter had joined them, participating willingly in the conversation. Through Simon, Paul had gradually got to know the shy but efficient guardian of St Peter's church in the village, who always spent the first few minutes updating them on the progress of the private chapel being built there and how he had to keep a watchful eye on the workmen.

It was Paul who first noticed a galley some way out at sea. It seemed to be rolling almost drunkenly in the slightly choppy waves, with its large lanteen sail flapping in the wind. Shielding his eyes from the setting sun with one hand, he tried to make out more detail. The oars were not being used and it gave the impression of drifting rather than being steered. He pointed it out to the others and after watching it for a few minutes, they all agreed that something must be wrong. Their opinion was shortly confirmed by one of the village fishermen sitting nearby, repairing his nets in readiness for the following morning. Pressed by the monks to do something about it, he reluctantly agreed to collect some others and take a boat out, and half an hour later a small group of fishermen rowed out of the harbour to investigate.

Watching every movement, Paul and his friends saw two fishermen board the galley, and some moments later the sail was lowered. A line was slung between the two boats, one of the fishermen climbed back down into the fishing boat to join the others and then, rowing steadily and helped by the incoming tide, they towed the galley slowly into the harbour. They steered it alongside the jetty wall, making it fast to two iron rings, and one of them ran over to the sitting group. Breathlessly, he called out that something terrible must have happened on board the galley. As far as he could see, he gasped, they were all dead and the sight of them was too horrible to describe. Paul did his best to calm the man down and then he and the two monks followed the excited fisherman to the galley.

In spite of the sea breeze the smell on board was unbearable. It was not only that of dead bodies and vomit, but also some other indescribable stench. Four men were lying on deck, sprawled out with their bodies twisted and features contorted by their death-throes. What could be seen of their arms and faces was covered with black suppurating sores of varying sizes. Brother Peter leant over the rail and vomited while his two companions looked at each other in dismay. None of them had ever seen anything so appalling in their lives. It was a picture of such inexplicable horror that Paul was suddenly reminded of his brother Tom's recurring nightmare. With a shudder he volunteered to go below deck to see what he could find while Simon was examining the bodies in more detail.

It was even worse! The smell was overpowering in the cramped rowing quarters. Peering into the gloomy darkness he could just make out the forms of other bodies lying on the bench seats or stretched out on the planks underneath and the centre section between them. From what he could see there were about fifteen or sixteen dead, and he called out to see if anybody was still alive, almost relieved that there was no reply, although he was sure he had heard the rustle and squeaking of rats racing for cover. Stepping over a body lying at the foot of the steps leading up to the helm, he looked more closely at the man's face and recoiled in horror when he saw that the flesh had been torn away by the rats. He dashed up on deck to join his companions.

'There are at least another fifteen dead down there,' he called out to the two monks and the fisherman who was standing by them, looking as if he had just seen a ghost or the Devil in person. 'I'm not going down there again. They're in an even worse state than these four. And the smell!' Paul's grimace and the thought of what he had said was enough to send Brother Peter to the rails again, his body shaking and shuddering with the painful exertions of draining an almost empty stomach.

Brother Simon showed Paul a chart he had found in the

captain's cabin and explained that the galley had sailed from Genoa in Italy and called at Marseilles in France on its way to England. 'These poor men must all be Italians,' he continued. 'May God rest their souls in peace! There's nothing more we can do now other than pray for them and give them a Christian burial!'

'A burial, Simon, did you say? We should tow it back out to sea and set fire to it,' Paul replied explosively. 'I don't know what has killed these men, but whatever it was, we shouldn't bring it on land. And we should get off this boat right away,' he concluded prophetically.

The fisherman had already begun to climb back onto the jetty, and as Paul more or less pushed the two monks to follow, Simon turned to Paul and added that no matter what had led to their death, they would be buried in consecrated ground, even if he had to carry the bodies to the churchyard himself! Paul started to protest but a look from the monk made him realise he was wasting his time arguing, and shrugging his shoulders reluctantly he let the matter drop.

Once on the jetty, Brother Simon instructed the fishermen to make sure nobody else went on board that evening, telling them he would return in the morning to make arrangements for the removal of the bodies. The fear in the eyes of the group of fishermen was enough to guarantee that his instructions would be followed to the letter, Paul noted.

Brother Peter returned to the village church and said he would organise some carts the following morning and make the necessary arrangement for a mass grave to be dug in one corner of the churchyard. Simon and Paul then hurried to the abbey to advise the canon of the tragedy and see what other instructions he might have. Passing through the village, it was clear that word had already spread concerning the Italian galley, as they saw several groups of people clustering together, talking nervously about the great mystery, each person having a special theory about its origin and the possible explanations of the meaning of it all.

Surprisingly, Canon Matthew accepted the terrible news almost as if he had been expecting it. He looked upwards, crossed himself and initially only said, 'May His will be done! Have mercy on our souls!' The canon then led Brother Simon away, leaving Paul in the parlour after having asked him to wait for a few minutes.

Paul waited impatiently for Simon to return, wondering why the canon had reacted in such a strange way, feeling that he would never be able to understand the workings of the clerical mind! About half an hour later, Simon returned alone looking paler than before and even more worried. He explained that the canon had left it to him to decide whether Paul should be informed or not, and then described what he had just been told. Apparently, the canon had received a letter from the Bishop of Winchester, who had recently been visited by some officials from the Papal Curia in Avignon, in which he had quoted some details from a secret report written by Pope Clement VI himself.

Paul listened intently to the tale of horror that Simon recounted. He described an unknown pestilence that had struck Avignon and killed half of the population. One clergyman had estimated that about 11,000 corpses were buried in six weeks in a single city graveyard, and it was also reported that at least 7,000 houses were deserted and shut up. The pestilence had been raging for more than three months at the time the report had been written. Simon looked his friend squarely in the eyes adding, 'Paul, I have every reason to believe that the men in the galley died from this pestilence. When I descibed the condition of the men we found to Canon Matthew, he showed me an almost identical description in the Holy Father's own report. We may ourselves already be condemned!'

Paul, though shocked, asked him what else was known about it, hoping against hope that there must be some mistake. Simon recounted that the pestilence was believed to have originated from the East and was now sweeping across Italy and France, decimating the population in each country, and it appeared, he added, to have finally reached England. He then went on to describe the symptoms as being at first a swelling of body glands known as the bubo. These swellings, found initially in the armpit or between the legs, he continued, could grow to the size of an apple, and then in a few days black spots began to develop and spread over the body, quickly leading to a horrible and painful death. There were some cases whereby people spat blood and other discharges, appearing to choke to death, he added, and nobody knew how to cure it. 'It is the will of God,' he concluded. 'We are being punished for our sins!'

Paul decided not to challenge the monk on this latter point, absolutely sure that there had to be some other explanation for this calamity, and came back to the subject of the planned burial of the dead Italian seamen. He learned that the canon had decided to lead the funeral service himself in the late afternoon of the following day and had given Brother Simon some money to pay the villagers to transport the bodies to the graveyard, with the instructions that the galley had to be left where it was, since it did not belong to them. Simon added that he had been forbidden to have it moved or destroyed and there was nothing more he could do about it. He looked meaningfully at Paul.

His companion was not so sure but made no comment, already thinking over a plan of his own. One thing was absolutely necessary, they both agreed, and that was not to discuss the Pope's report with anybody to avoid any possible panic among the villagers. Once the funeral service was over it would be essential to carry on as normal and trust that whatever it was that had killed the Italians would perhaps pass them by. Maybe it was something else other than the pestilence from the East! At the moment there was nothing else to be done other than pray, Simon pointedly observed.

While eating an evening meal at The Bugle, which Paul usually did two to three times a week, the proprietor, Bob Thatcher whom he had got to know very well since moving into Titchfield, came and sat down at the table and asked Paul quietly what he thought about the 'trouble', as he called it, nodding his head in the general direction of the harbour. There was no other subject of discussion in the village, he commented. According to some, it must be a type of witchcraft, and others believed the men must have drunk poisoned water or perhaps it had been passed on by a leper. Bob knew that Paul had been on board the galley and had come to like the young reeve as well as respecting his opinion. If anybody would know, then it would probably be him, he had thought, and looked inquiringly at Paul waiting for his reply.

It was not an easy question to answer and Paul knew that whatever he did, he could not discuss the Pope's report and must do everything possible to project an air of calmness to help prevent any acts of stupidity on the part of the villagers. Looking confidentially at the innkeeper, and speaking just loud enough for at least one or two other customers to hear, he replied with a conspiratorial air, 'Well, Bob, I talked it over with some of the monks at the abbey who have a much better idea about these sorts of things than you or I will ever have. Nobody knows for sure, but it's got absolutely nothing to do with witchcraft or leprosy, that's quite certain! It may have been something they ate or drank while at sea. One of the monks believes it is a punishment from God for their sins, which I personally don't believe, but I can't say I know either. One thing is clear, however—' and he paused to make sure he had the attention of the two spectators without giving the impression it was for their benefit, '—we need to get on with our work as usual, and mark my words, within a few days, life will soon get back to normal. I'm feeling a bit tired now, Bob, to tell you the truth. It's been a long day, so tell me how much I owe you and then I'm off to bed.'

Before he left, Paul noted with satisfaction that his words appeared to have had a positive effect, sensing a much less strained atmosphere in the inn, and Bob Thatcher also gave the impression of being more relaxed. Inwardly, Paul desperately hoped his optimism was justified, but was nevertheless unable to discard a feeling of doubt and the ominous presence of an unknown danger. He signalled to Bob to come with him outside where he quickly informed him of his plans for the galley and reasons why, asking him to send three fishermen he could trust to his house at nightfall the following day. Reassured by Paul's explanation, he nodded understandingly and agreed to the need for complete secrecy.

It took Paul a long time to fall asleeep. He tossed and turned, unable to put the day's events and the horror of what he had seen out of his mind. Could it really be the onset of the pestilence Simon had described? If so, how could such a thing happen? How could it move from country to country? Would it kill them all if it really came? With a shudder he suddenly thought about Elizabeth, Tom and his family and all the friends he had made in the last few years, and couldn't bring himself to believe that there could be anything so deadly that could possibly threaten them all, or could there? He moved first onto one side, then a few minutes later turned onto the other, tormented by his anguished thoughts. And his plan for the galley? In spite of Canon Matthew's order, he intended to have it taken out to sea, and set fire to it far from the shore, convinced that the evil or whatever it was, lay within that boat. He just had to disobey the canon, certain that he was right, and that maybe this action would put an end to the danger. His eyes, heavy with fatigue, gradually closed and he drifted slowly away into a troubled sleep, dreaming of terrors he could not understand.

More as a token of solidarity than through conviction, Paul attended the burial service at St Peter's the following afternoon. He was surprised to see that it was almost filled with villagers, hoping no doubt to learn more about the mysterious deaths. But in that, they were disappointed. Other than hearing from the canon that God sometimes moved in ways incomprehensible to man, and that perhaps these deaths were a sign to them all to abandon their sinful ways and follow more closely the teachings of His son Jesus, they heard nothing new. A group of monks supervised the actual burial of the twenty corpses, fortunately wrapped in shrouds so that nobody could see the state of the bodies.

Afterwards Paul paid his respects to Canon Matthew and then using the excuse of work that needed to be done, made his way down South Street to his house, changed into his working clothes and prepared everything he would need for that night before he rode off to Wicor. There was in fact nothing essential that had to be done that afternoon, but he wanted to get away from Titchfield for a few hours to be alone.

Tethering Blackie in the shade of a large beech tree, he walked barefoot for two or three miles along the sandy beach, enjoying the cooling effect of the seawater as the incoming tide lapped over his feet and swirled around his ankles. He looked at the stretch of land that was in the process of being reclaimed, eventually to be used for additional pasturage, feeling proud at what had been achieved already in such a short time on the demesne. Surely this can't all be for nothing, he thought! No matter what may come, life somehow would continue as it always had. It can't all be destroyed, he mused, and maybe it's a false alarm anyway. But something inside continued to make him uneasy as he thought back on what Simon had said concerning the Papal report. There was no mention of any cure! It appeared that this pestilence was fatal to all who contracted it, however that happened. Did it come in the wind, he wondered? No, surely that cannot be, he reasoned, as he deeply inhaled the invigorating salty air. It smells so clean, not like that awful stench he smelled on board the galley, and he shuddered at the thought.

The scream-like cries of two seagulls swooping over the water disturbed his thoughts and following their acrobatic flight until they disappeared in the distance, he somehow felt more reassured for the future, and walking towards Blackie began to go over his plans for the destruction of the galley. By the time he reached Titchfield and had stabled his horse it was beginning to get dark, and hurrying back into the house he lit a lantern to prepare himself for the arrival of the fishermen.

Bob Thatcher had decided to bring the fishermen himself to Paul's house, and it was about an hour before midnight when he knocked discreetly at the door. He was accompanied by three men he knew were reliable, could be trusted to keep their mouths shut, and would be happy to earn a little extra money. Paul knew them by sight since he had frequently seen them in the The Bugle, and Bob quickly introduced them as John, Tim and David.

Over a glass of mead he explained carefully why it was necessary, in his opinion, to get rid of the galley, feeling sure that the cause of the malady or whatever was to be found on board. He made it clear that he would take responsibility for everything, but if possible, did not want anybody else to know about it. He admitted that it was against the canon's wishes and should it be absolutely necessary, he would tell him personally why he had gone against them. The men all agreed that it should be done and then Paul went over his plan in detail. Shortly after midnight, carrying a bale of straw, a large jug of pitch, candles and a coil of rope, the five men silently left Paul's house and cautiously made their way down to the harbour.

There was a half moon which enabled them to see a little and walk without tripping over the uneven cobblestones. As anticipated, there was not a soul to witness their arrival at the harbour. Apart from a stiff breeze, the sound of water lapping at the jetty wall and the creaking of the galley timbers, they could hear no other unusual noise. Once they had carefully unloaded the straw and other material on board, the lines holding the galley to the jetty were untied, the lantern sail was partially raised, David took over the tiller and the other two with Bob Thatcher jumped back onto the jetty, pushing the boat clear. They then hurried to a small rowing boat that had earlier been anchored conveniently near the harbour mouth, while the ebb-tide, helped by the sail, took the galley with Paul and the helmsman David on board, slowly away from the jetty towards the open sea.

Paul dragged the straw bale to the steps leading down to the lower deck and pushed it down into the dark void, carefully stowing a handful of dry straw for tinder, the candles and pitch in shelter but easily accessible. The galley had just reached the harbour mouth when he felt a slight bump as the fishermen's rowing boat came alongside, and made fast to it. He heard the oars being shipped and the whispers of the three men waiting impatiently in it. Leaning over the galley rail, Paul waved acknowledgement and then went to check progress with David, who quietly informed him they could leave the galley in about five minutes since they were now making good progress. Stepping down somewhat apprehensively to the lower deck, he ignited the tinder with a flint-stone, lit a candle and spread out the straw from the bale across and under some of the bench seats. Even though all the bodies had been removed it still smelled awful below deck and Paul hurried to complete his preparations. He poured the pitch on the seats, splashing it on timbers and along the deck floor, set candles in the straw, lit them and went up on deck to David. They lashed the tiller in position to keep the galley on course, hauled up the lantern sail higher and then scrambled down to the others in the rowing boat.

After freeing the line from the galley, they watched it move steadily away to the open sea, helped by wind, sail and tide, before beginning to row strongly back to land. The current was strong and it took them a good half-hour to reach the harbour and moments before they were about to enter it, Paul was happy to see a flame suddenly appear on the horizon behind them as the galley began to burn.

Paul paid his helpers and they all returned home unseen by any human eye.

23

An Illusory Tranquility

Titchfield was buzzing with gossip concerning the missing galley. Paul had deliberately left home at daybreak and ridden over towards Portchester to avoid discussing the subject and perhaps having to lie, busying himself the whole day with harvest preparations, checking the condition of the various barns and other equipment.

On returning to the village he looked appropriately surprised when Brother Simon stopped him in the high street to tell him the news. He suggested that perhaps some of the soldiers in the vicinity had stolen it to start a new life somewhere else or to sell whatever was on board. In any case, he added, he believed it to be a blessing in disguise that it had gone, since he had always felt uneasy about it being there, as Simon knew only too well. The monk appeared satisfied with the reply and changed the subject.

There was also no other subject of discussion in The Bugle that evening, and when asked Paul looked knowingly at Bob Thatcher as he floated the same theory he had shared with Simon. He expressed it as a thought, but with such conviction that it soon became accepted by them all as the most likely explanation, and within a day or two, the galley subject was replaced by the supposedly licentious conduct of the miller's wife and the furious reaction of her husband when he discovered what had been going on behind his back!

In fact a feeling almost of euphoria pervaded Titchfield. Both Simon and Paul agreed that it must be due to the villagers' relief that whatever evil thing had struck the Italian sailors had gone, and the slightest excuse for celebration was used by them as an opportunity to carouse and revel until darkness fell. But the hectic time of harvesting was quickly approaching and Paul had to use his authority on more than one occasion to get some of the labourers to work the way he wanted. A week went by, and then another, and even Paul began to relax, believing that the danger had passed by as village life gradually returned to normality.

He had got to know the village barber one evening in The Bugle, and learned that he also practised some types of simple surgery which included the removal of bad teeth. The barber had laughed loudly when Paul confided that he shouldn't take it seriously, but he hoped he personally would never require his services, particularly as far as his teeth were concerned! The barber was a very practical person who did not overestimate his knowledge or give the impression that he knew everything, and Paul came to like him. Whenever they met, they had long conversations on many subjects. Paul also learned that William, the barber, shared many of his views concerning the Church, particularly a dislike of the abuse of power demonstrated by some of its leaders. Canon Matthew and the other monks at the abbey were excluded from most of the criticism, but the barber nevertheless had strong views on the Church's control over medical subjects. Any sort of anatomy work or other similar study was completely taboo, he maintained. Furthermore, when people were really ill, the priest either kept the doctor or physician away or only allowed them to see the patient when it was too late to do anything.

Paul told William openly that to be honest, he was also somewhat sceptical concerning several apparently preferred practices of the medical profession, particulaly that of using leeches to draw blood, and surprisingly the barber agreed with him. But many of the problems that medical men have, he pointed out, were due to the fact that the Church forbade them to experiment, making it virtually impossible for them to progress their current learning. He admitted that most of his knowledge on the use of herbs and other plants he had picked up from his mother, and as a boy had seen how his father had once used splints on a farm labourer's broken arm and it had worked. He had subsequently performed one or two similar operations and they had been successful, but he had to be extremely careful to avoid some malicious tongue accusing him of witchcraft, and made Paul promise not to repeat to anyone what he had just told him.

It wasn't long before the question of the dead sailors arose and William added that in such cases, in spite of possible danger, one should examine a corpse internally to see what one could learn for the future. Their conversation on this subject covered many possible aspects but Paul did not disclose what he had heard from Brother Simon, having given his word not to discuss the Pope's report with anyone else.

While the two of them were busily engaged in examining the advantages of more anatomical knowledge for the benefit of future generations, Mrs Galston came out of Margaret's and Tom's bedroom in Castor, carrying a baby in her arms to show Tom his newly-born son. As always, she helped Margaret at the time of birth, and she looked so pleased and proud at that moment that one could have almost believed it was her own child!

'Here he is at last, Master Rollesby,' she excitedly exclaimed, 'and it looks as if he is going to be as large as his famous father!'

Tom hardly heard what she said, gazing fondly at his son, but asked immediately if all was well with Margaret. She told him that she was sleeping now and needed some rest since the birth had been a little difficult on account of the baby's size, but he could go in and take a look. However, he must not wake her!

Even though Tom stepped quietly up to the bed, Margaret opened her eyes briefly and smiled at her husband, taking hold of his hand. He looked at her with concern, asked her how she felt and told her that he loved her more than anything else in the world.

She gently squeezed his hand and softly replied, 'I'm fine, Tom, my dearest. But I'm so tired. Please ask Mrs Galston to stay tonight and I'll take care of the little one tomorrow.' She paused a second and then added, 'But he's not so little, may even be as big as his father one day.' She smiled again, closed her eyes and fell into a deep sleep. Tom gently moved her long, jet-black hair from her face, his fingers barely touching her moist skin, stood a moment looking at her and then turned away, quietly closing the door behind him.

Mrs Galston was rocking the baby in her arms at the fireside and seeing Tom, without him saying a word, advised him that she would stay the night with the baby, and get one of the lord's servants to help on the following morning.

Tom thanked her profusely, led her to the specially prepared small bedroom that had been the last addition to the new house Sir William had had built for them close to the manor house gardens, and sat down in front of the fire. Mrs Galston had insisted on having a large fire earlier for heating a cauldron of water, and Tom watched the last embers glowing, thinking how fortunate he had been to meet Margaret, and that in spite of all the difficulties of his youth, how good life had been to him and his family. It was almost unbelievable, he mused, the lifestyle he now led. He was the owner of a beautiful house, had four children and a wife he adored, was not only the captain of the lord's guard, but had been endowed with special power in the demesne to represent Sir William when absent. He would talk with his lord in the morning to let him know the good news about his son, and began to think about a suitable name. Margaret must decide, he concluded, but if she was in agreement, he would call him John.

The lord of Castor and Lady Mortimer were delighted with the news the following day and that all was well with Margaret. To Tom's complete surprise they gave him a small, local farm as a gift for the occasion. The farm was very close to their new house, and would not only provide a rent of ten pounds a year, Sir William pointed out, but would also give them a good supply of fresh fruit and vegetables. Lady Mortimer also made further arrangements for servants to help Margaret until she was on her feet, and told Tom she would visit her later in the day.

It was then that Sir William informed him he would shortly be leaving again for Calais, since now that the city had been taken over by the English there was important work and garrison duties that required his services. They spent most of that day checking the various arrangements to be made for the trip and other items concerning demesne administration.

Three days later as Sir William was boarding a ship at Yermouth, Mr Polton was taking leave of his wife on his way to Southampton. He usually went every summer for three weeks to the annual fair at Bruges to sell cloth and buy certain special dyes, travelling with a group of other merchants from Winchester accompanied by a very large number of packhorses, servants and an escort of ten soldiers from the castle garrison. He embraced his wife and then Elizabeth and reassured them both that he would be back in no time at all. He told them to take good care of themselves, and that he would bring them each a silk dress back from Bruges. He mounted his horse and joined the rest of the group impatient to get started for the coast, little knowing what would await them on their return.

Bands of gypsies had also been gathering in various parts of England at this time, setting up camps close to manors that they knew from experience would need additional workers to help at harvest time. Many of them were decent folk wanting merely to enjoy the freedom of travel and working where necessary to earn the cash to buy utensils, clothes, or horses, for which their expertise was renowned. Some, however, were more inclined to steal what they needed, and most villagers tended not to trust gypsies at all, keeping a careful watch when they were in the neighbourhood and warning their children to keep well clear of them, since it was rumoured that they were sometimes kidnapped, never to be seen again! There had been the odd bloody reprisal from angry villagers at different times when a child had disappeared, resulting in the slaughter of many innocent gypsies in the neighbourhood, so they also had to keep alert and be prepared to defend themselves.

Meanwhile, a messenger from the Spanish Prince Don Pedro, heir to the throne of Castile, was on his way to to meet the Prince of Wales at the palace on his manor of Kennington, carrying an offer of marriage to the Black Prince's sister, Joanna.

Marco Paulini, the Genoese crossbowman working for the Earl of Dunghall, had completed his master's business with the smuggled wool and for months had been establishing relationships and contacts for dealings in the future with a much larger group of Italian buyers. At the time that Boccaccio was describing the terrible effects of the pestilence in Florence, Marco was supervising the burial of his parents and most of his relatives in Genoa, all victims of the Black Death that was sweeping through all of southern Europe. He hoped to survive by taking refuge afterwards in a deserted country house in the hills, isolated from the rest of the community, and when all was clear to take a boat back to Ireland.

Only the higher echelons of the Church in England were aware of most of these developments outside, and apart from the monks at Titchfield and Paul Rollesby, nobody had any indication that the Black Death could possibly break out in Portchester manor at any moment.

The harvesting had just begun. It was a beautiful day. A group of labourers were sitting under the shade of a clump of beech trees at the edge of a large field between the village and the abbey, enjoying a midday break. They had already eaten and were quenching their considerable thirst when one of the older men, Ted Smythe, suddenly felt uneasy. He stopped talking and wondered what was the matter. He felt his face was burning, his stomach was turning and strength seemed to leave his legs. One of his companions asked him if he was ill because he looked so flushed, and he replied he must have got a touch of the sun and just had to lie down for a while. The others looked at him, agreeing it was the best thing to do, and putting away their mugs, left their belongings by him and walked back to the far end of the field to resume work.

Ted fell asleep, moving restlessly from one side to another, dreaming a series of dreams the likes of which he had never before experienced. When he awoke with a start he could only remember that he had somehow been terrified. He tried to get up but didn't have the energy to push himself off the ground and fell back, exhausted, with a terrible pain in his stomach. When the others returned at the end of the day he was lying on his back with his legs drawn up, holding his stomach and moaning in pain. His breeches and smock were soaked in perspiration and his eyes seemed to be almost starting out of his head.

His brother John and a friend picked him up carefully and carried him home, very much concerned. John was a good ten years younger than his brother, who to the best of his memory had always been fit and healthy. Ted's wife had died many years ago at the birth of their first child, which had also died within a few hours of being born, and he had not remarried. He had simply moved in with his old mother whom he supported, deciding to stay single at least until she died and then he would decide what he would do. They lived in a small, simple wattle and clay cottage with a thatched roof in a lane off East Street, very close to the river, and his mother stood at the door wringing her hands when she saw her eldest son being carried inside. They laid him gently onto a sheepskin in the one and only bedroom (his mother slept in the main living room close to the fire), covering him with another skin which the old lady handed to them, and then left, saying he probably had a bad attack of sunstroke and they would call by in the morning to see how he was.

Some hours later the fever got even worse. Ted had a roaring in his ears and a headache that almost drove him mad. His mouth was dry and through parched lips he called for water which his mother immediately brought to him. He continued to toss and turn, and pushed the sheepskin off since he was so hot and sticky, eventually dropping off into a troubled sleep.

He awoke early the next morning. His skin felt as if it was burning and he could feel that he had a painful lump under each armpit and on one side of his neck. His mother took one look at him and left the cottage, making her way as quickly as she could to the barber's house in the village square. He went immediately to see if there was anything he could do for Ted, intrigued with what the old lady described to him, and for political reasons he suggested that she should go to St Peter's and inform one of the monks there before returning home.

William pushed open the cottage door and walked directly into the bedroom, announcing himself to Ted who was sleeping fitfully. In the short time since his mother had left his condition had further deteriorated. He felt his whole body was burning, and some dark-coloured spots had already begun to appear on his face and body. Barely able to speak, he asked the barber to get him some water, and William held the wooden goblet for him as Ted greedily quenched his thirst, wiping his mouth and chin dry with the back of his right hand.

It was clear to the barber that Ted was being ravaged by a fever of a sort that was new to him, for although he had occasionally seen the effects of different types of pox, particularly on children, he had never seen these dark spots before nor the swellings at the neck and under the armpits.

'What is it, William?' the labourer gasped out, in obvious pain. 'I've never had the likes before, and these swellings hurt so!'

The barber looked at him, slowly shook his head and said that he really didn't know. He asked Ted if he had perhaps eaten something suspect, or had he been bitten by a dog or some other animal?

Ted looked up at William, perspiration dripping from his forehead, his eyes protruding and his face contorted with pain, and whispered, 'No, nothing like that . . . nothing I can think of. What can it be?' Then, suddenly to the barber's surprise, he asked for a mirror and when he saw his own reflection, he gasped, and blurted out, 'Just like those sailors a couple of weeks ago. I look just like they did. Oh, my God . . . I shall die, I know it!'

As the barber was trying to reassure the labourer that he shouldn't think of such a thing, that a strong man like him had to survive, Ted's mother arrived with the monk Peter from the village church, who more or less propelled William out of the bedroom, and angrily told him not to interfere in the affairs of the Almighty. He, Peter, he added, would let him know later if his dubious services would be required, and in the meantime he should leave them in peace.

In order not to upset Ted's mother further, the barber took leave of her and returned home, fuming with anger and at the same time wondering about what the labourer had told him. The only way he could have seen the faces of the Italian sailors, he reasoned, was if he had been on board that galley, and that meant he must have been one of the villagers that helped take off the bodies and transport them to the graveyard.

While William was pondering this and other related subjects, unknown to everybody else, one of the fishermen that had helped Paul secretly remove the galley from the harbour had fallen unconscious, alone in his small boat, with similar symptoms to the labourer. The boat began to drift further out to sea at the time the monk Peter was giving absolution to Ted, who was getting weaker and weaker, to the desperation of his old mother.

In The Bugle that evening, Paul was about to start his evening meal when the barber hurried to his table, sat down next to him and in a lowered voice told him about the events of the morning, including the clash with Brother Peter. The barber did not have the backgound knowledge of the pestilence that Paul had, but when he described the state of Ted and the swollen buboes, he knew that the Black Death had finally reached Titchfield, and shuddered at the thought. Before they could discuss more, one of the fishermen that had helped Paul dispose of the galley came over to them and said that David and his boat seemed to have disappeared. He should have been back in the harbour in the late afternoon, he continued, but nobody had seen a trace of him since early morning.

Paul asked him if David had been in good health the last time he saw him, and the fisherman paused and then said that he believed he had complained about a headache and felt a little off-colour earlier that morning, but otherwise appeared to be quite normal. Ted and Paul exchanged looks but made no comment, and tried to reassure him that David would surely turn up shortly. He had perhaps lost an oar and would arrive later, Paul said, anxious not to cause any undue alarm, and the fisherman agreed that it was a possibility before leaving them to talk to some of his friends sitting nearby.

Later that evening, Bob Thatcher joined them, bringing a jug of wine and three goblets with him, clearly wanting to hear Paul's opinion on Ted's illness, which was now common knowledge in the village, wondering if it could have anything to do with the Italian galley. He looked knowingly at Paul and although sworn to silence on its disappearance, was nevertheless concerned since he had also been on board.

'Well, Bob,' Paul blustered, 'as you know I went on board with the monk Simon when it first docked, and I feel fine, so I don't think it can be that.' He hoped he sounded convincing, and slapped Bob on the back as a friendly gesture. Bob took a long draught of wine, appeared to be a little relieved, and, visibly relaxing, changed the subject.

Before leaving The Bugle, Paul and the barber agreed to visit Ted early the following morning to see how he was. Neither of them, however, without admitting it openly, felt too confident about what they might find!

Their fears were not unfounded. As they pushed the cottage door open, the vile smell Paul could never forget hit them. Ted lay twisted on his bed, eyes open and staring unseeing up at the roof, with vomit on his lips, chin and lifeless body, and a black liquid oozing from sores all over him. The barber, his face wrinkled as a reaction to the stench, closed the labourer's eyes and touching the now cold forehead, confirmed that he must have been dead for some hours. His old mother disturbed them as they were standing at the bed, stumbling heavily into the cottage carrying a pitcher of water, spilling most of it on the rush floor. She stood there, swaying on her feet, her eyes swollen from weeping. The barber gently led her to a stool so she could sit, taking the pitcher from her and placing it carefully on the small table under the window in the living room.

'He passed away in the middle of the night,' she sobbed. 'He was in terrible agony. May his soul rest in peace, my poor Ted!'

They both tried to console her to no avail. She had not only lost her eldest son but wondered how she would manage alone. Her youngest son had his own large family to support, and on top of that she also believed she was infected with whatever it was that had killed Ted.

She was still sitting on her stool, holding her head in her hands sobbing, when they left the cottage to look for Brother Peter to inform him that Ted was now dead, and that it looked as if the pestilence had arrived in the village. They found him at the church kneeling before the high altar and praying. Hearing approaching steps, the monk turned his head towards them and Paul realised with a start that Peter was also infected. Seeing Paul's shock, he stood up with some difficulty, nodded with understanding, and said softly, 'It began early this morning. I shall soon be joining our Father. May he give me the strength to withstand the pain! Take this letter to the canon, please, Paul, and leave me now. He will know what to do and send a replacement for me.' Then, handing the letter to the reeve, he signalled with both arms that they should go immediately.

The day had hardly begun and there was already at least one person dead and two others infected! The barber returned to his house and promised that he would say nothing and keep a lookout for any others in the village, informing Paul that evening at home of any new developments. Canon Matthew read the letter carefully that his reeve handed to him half an hour later, asked him to join the rest of the monks in the refectory until he returned, and hurried off to his private rooms to write a short report for the Bishop of Winchester.

In the meantime, Paul had recounted to Brother Simon what had happened and that they must now prepare themselves for the worst. At the end of the mid-morning meal, the canon reappeared and with an appropriate degree of solemnity, informed them of the calamity that had arrived in Titchfield, believing it to be a punishment from God for all their sins. He appointed a successor for Brother Peter and made arrangements to care for the stricken monk and other preparations to handle many more victims of the pestilence. He bade Paul to continue with his duties as best he could, blessed him and then left the stunned assembly.

While Paul was riding out across the demesne to supervise the harvest work that was now in full swing, tragic scenes were being enacted in several other village cottages. Three other labourers were unable to rise from their beds in the early throes of the fearful plague, two young babies had died during the night, and the fisherman Tim's wife was struggling unsuccessfully to pull herself up from the floor where she had fallen in a daze some minutes previously, moaning in pain on the rushes by the fireside.

It was no longer a question of keeping quiet about the pestilence – there was no other topic of conversation across the entire manor – but more of who would be the next victim and who was responsible! Listening to the men at work in the fields, Paul heard that there were clearly already three or four deaths in Titchfield, several others were almost certainly infected and at least ten harvesters had not turned up for whatever reason.

The barber also confirmed a similar picture that evening at Paul's house and told him that David's rowing boat had been found empty in the afternoon, washed up on the beach at Wicor. It was all like a nightmare. The evil thing continued to develop around them and they were powerless to stop it. Panic could break out at any time now, they both agreed, with possibly terrible consequences. The only sensible thing to do, in spite of everything, was to remain calm, try to persuade others to do the same, and organise the removal and burial of the bodies with Canon Matthew and the rest of the monks at the abbey.

The following six to eight weeks were the worst in Paul's life. It seemed a miracle that neither he nor the barber were infected. The pestilence struck most families in Titchfield, particularly the very young and the old. Normal village life was paralysed during this time, and there was only one case of violence, which unfortunately cost three innocent lives. A gypsy family camping near the river was attacked by some angry villagers, convinced that they had poisoned the water and were responsible for their misfortunes. By the time Paul and Brother Simon arrived, three bodies lay by the embers of a fire, sprawled out between cooking utensils and a few other personal possessions. Both the man's and woman's bodies were fearfully mutilated and the child's skull had been smashed with a large stone. Canon Matthew himself conducted the burial service at St Peter's and lambasted the congregation for their intolerance, cruelty and stupidity in blaming innocent people for a punishment that surely came from God! The fact that the Black Death continued for some weeks after that tragedy convinced them all – more perhaps than the sermon of the canon – that innocent people had been killed, and nothing similar happened again in Titchfield.

Towards the end of September, the number of reported deaths declined to a trickle, and by the middle of October, the pestilence had run its course in the demesne, continuing to advance to the north and west. Ships from France, Spain and Italy, docking in other ports, carrying soldiers from the various campaigns; clergymen returning from pilgrimages in Avignon; merchants with wine, cloth, dyes and other goods; and simple travellers all helped to ensure that most other regions of England were not spared.

24

Social Upheaval and Family Tragedy

The villagers of Titchfield could hardly believe that it was over. The pain and suffering had been unbearable. At least a hundred people had died in and around the village as a result of the pestilence and from what Paul and Brother Simon could see, it had claimed about one third of the population of the total manor of Portchester, including fifteen monks at the abbey. The church graveyards were almost filled and in some instances new ground had to be consecrated. What had been a prosperous demesne had within three months been so badly mauled that many families wondered how they would survive the coming winter. The harvest had been a catastrophe in spite of good weather and excellent crops – there were simply not enough workers to complete the work and at least half of the wheat and barley was left to rot in the fields. Many survivors were so shocked and morale was such that they lost interest in the affairs of the demesne and several just left their homes to start again in another manor, unable to believe that it could possibly be worse elsewhere.

Discussing the situation with the canon, Paul pointed out that they could expect minimum rents and tithes from the freeholders, and that since they were so chronically short of labour, they must try to persuade more outsiders to settle in the demesne and allocate land generously to the surviving freeholders to encourage them to do the work of at least two people. The abbey had nevertheless received considerable sums of money in death duties and heriots, often in the form of cattle, which short-term at least provided cash and goods in kind, and the reeve argued that they must invest more than usual for the well-being of the villagers or the demesne would degenerate into wasteland. Furthermore, he continued, wool would provide adequate funds for the following years to maintain the standards of the abbey and help the poor and needy. It would not be easy, but with goodwill and understanding, the demesne could recover its former position within a few years.

Both Canon Matthew and Paul understood perfectly well that if they didn't move quickly, many people would take the law into their own hands and there would be complete anarchy. It was already apparent that the moral fibre of the demesne inhabitants had weakened dramatically, as the canon knew from his experiences in the confessional and from what he had himself observed. The ties of marriage had come to mean very little, and both men and women, happy to be alive today and far from sure about the future, were indulging in frequently outrageous and licentious lifestyles.

Following a series of meetings with the surviving village elders throughout the demesne, the abbey was able to establish a catalogue of the status and needs of each village and berewick, and began to put into motion the basic plans that Paul and the canon had forged together. The drifting stopped, and gradually a form of order slowly came to bear in the manor of Portchester, although it was never to take on fully the pattern of earlier days.

Paul had agreed to stay a little longer to help supervise some of the many changes necessary in land ownership and also village defences – marauders were appearing from all directions – but in mid-November, with the blessing of Canon Matthew, rode off to Winchester for a few days, anxious to see if all was well with Elizabeth and her family.

Drawing closer to Winchester he was astonished to see hordes of people streaming out of the city in all directions. Some were on foot, but most were on horseback or sitting in carts and other waggons loaded with personal belongings and provisions, giving the impression that the Devil himself was behind them, judging by their haste. It was a panic exodus because, as one man quickly explained to Paul before he galloped away at full speed, the pestilence had broken out in the city and those that could were seeking shelter or a safer place outside.

Spurring Blackie on, he entered the south gate which surprisingly was unmanned, and skirted round the castle up towards the west gate, keeping a watch out for any ruffians prepared to waylay the unwary traveller. However, the criminal element was too busy looting empty shops or houses to take particular interest in Paul and he was shortly out of the city and twenty minutes later entered the driveway of the Polton's mansion. Vaulting down from his horse, he impatiently hammered on the door which was opened with an apparent reluctance by a servant a few moments later. As he stepped inside Paul noticed that two servants with drawn swords were standing nervously in the hallway, barring the way for any unwelcome intruder. He then heard Elizabeth's voice telling them to sheath their swords, and seconds later she almost crushed him with a passionate embrace, murmuring, 'At last, at last my love, you are here! Thank God you are safe!'

Leading him by the hand into their large reception room, she closed the door behind them, took him over to the fire and caressed his cheeks gently. She looked deeply into his eyes and then kissed him tenderly, drawing his hands around her back, pulling him as close as possible to her. For a moment the world seemed to stand still. Then, drawing themselves slowly apart, they both began to speak at once. Smilingly Paul excused himself, asking her to continue.

He learnt that the plague had first appeared in Winchester two or three weeks previously, and Elizabeth described the scenes he knew only too well as the pestilence began to spread. Apparently, in some of the crowded city quarters, the casualties were horrific, particularly among the poorer families. Corpses littered the streets, eventually to be loaded onto carts organised by the authorities and buried in their hundreds in pits outside the city walls. Only the more wealthy people were buried in the churchyards within the city, she continued. She had heard that scores of houses belonging to the well-to-do had been abandoned by their owners, either killed by the pestilence or, in most cases, fleeing with their families to more secluded areas.

Paul was suddenly aware of an aromatic smell in the room and in answer to his question, Elizabeth told him that they were burning juniper and rosemary in all the house fires, on the orders of the house physician. From time to time they also threw a powder on the fires which her father had brought back from Bruges on his last trip. Apparently an Italian merchant had sold it to him at the trade fair, and she understood it contained sulphur, arsenic and antimony, which supposedly cleansed the air and kept the pestilence away. Nobody, however, she exclaimed almost in desperation, had any idea what it was, where it came from or what cured it.

'The local priest says we are being punished for our sinful ways. Last week he read out a letter from Bishop Erdington which instructed him, would you believe, to inform us we should not only attend the sacrament of penance on Sundays, Wednesdays and Fridays, but also should walk barefoot in processions around the market-place or through the churchyards, reciting litanies! When my father heard that,' she concluded, 'he almost exploded in anger, and told us in no circumstances would he permit that, and that we should stay at home and keep away from the city and crowds of people!'

Paul smiled on hearing about her father's angry outburst, wondering how Simon would have reacted to such a comment, and then asked where her parents were, since he had seen no sign of them. Her mother, he learnt, was staying a few days with a sister in Sombourne and Mr Polton was out for the day on business. As a result of the pestilence, normal trading had virtually stopped and special precautions had to be taken to prevent looters and other ruffians breaking into warehouses to help themselves. That was why the servants were armed, she added, and for the first time in years, her father was home every night.

Paul then told her about what had happened in Titchfield and she listened in horror to his description of what they had found on the galley and the subsequent trail of death and suffering. She understood why he had agreed with Canon Matthew to stay on a little longer as reeve, and they spent the rest of the day discussing their future plans, agreeing that come what may, they would marry in the following spring.

In the late afternoon of the same day, Paul's brother Tom was riding back to the manor with a small patrol, returning from a trip around the demesne. Castor, like almost every other manor in the country, had not been spared from the relentless advance of the plague, and they like everybody else were powerless against it. It had first broken out two weeks previously and was now raging throughout most of the villages. There had not been any cases of looting but one or two innocent people had been accused by groups of villagers in some of the more isolated communities of poisoning the wells. He and his men had managed to save one of them, arriving just as one group were about to take justice into their own hands and hang the poor unfortunate. At another small village, they found the mutilated corpse of an old woman that he later discovered had supposedly been a witch who had used an evil potion that resulted in the death of several villagers. They had clearly had the pestilence and Tom told the village elder that should such a crime occur again, he would personally hang him.

Tom and his men were all feeling somewhat depressed. The good work of the last few years was suffering badly with increasing lawlessness and a rapid breakdown of discipline and morale in most of the communities. They had at least managed to bring in the harvest safely before the Black Death had arrived, but the reeve had informed Tom he was having great difficulty getting the villeins to do any further work, and surprisingly, even the freeholders seemed to have lost interest. The people gave the impression of having given up hope for the future and were merely living for the present, day by day, as long as they were alive. He had also heard that most of the priests in the village churches, at least those that remained (several had left immediately it became known that the pestilence was rife in their village) used it as a means to give them more power over simple folk, extorting even more money from them in order to save their souls from perdition! This infuriated him most of all in that, just like the plague, he was powerless to stop it. He never ceased to wonder how some people could be so easily persuaded to donate so much of their meagre savings to such a wealthy institution that all too frequently gave so little in return.

Burdened with these and other thoughts, he led his men back to the manor and once he had clarified the duties of the following day to his newly-appointed lieutenant, the longest-serving Genoese, Carlo, and got the stableboy to take care of Lightning, his spirits brightened as he walked the short distance to his house, looking forward to seeing Margaret and playing with the children. It had been a long, depressing day, but hopefully, he thought, the pestilence would pass by, and things could get back to normal.

Pushing open the back door to the kitchen quietly – he wanted to surprise his wife with a kiss – he stepped carefully inside but she was not there. He called out to announce himself and Eric and young Margaret came running through from the living room to greet him. His daughter clasped him around the neck as he scooped her up in his arms for her usual hug while Eric stood by a little awkwardly and told him that 'Mummy is not feeling very well and she's lying down to rest.' Tom immediately put his daughter down and walked quickly to the bedroom to see how she was. He moved Alice gently away from the bed, placing her on a chair next to the cot where young John was sleeping peacefully, and sat down by his sleeping wife.

Feeling the movement on the bed, Margaret opened her eyes and seeing her husband, smiled with pleasure and greeted him with an unusually weak voice. Tom stroked her long, black hair, moving it away from her eyes and as he touched her forehead he could feel the fever in her body. Alarmed, he asked how she was feeling and his wife tried to reassure him that it was nothing to worry about; she was sure it would quickly pass by and she would get up and prepare his supper. The children had all been fed, she assured him, so that was taken care of, and young John would sleep for at least another three or four hours. Even those few words seemed to be almost too much for her, and she turned her head slightly, closed her eyes, and slipped back into an albeit troubled sleep.

Tom led the three other children out of the bedroom, closed the door quietly and took them to the living room. It was quite clear that Margaret was extremely ill, and he hoped against hope that it wasn't what he feared it might be. Not wanting to frighten the children he told them that their mother needed absolute quiet and instructed Eric to watch over his sisters while he slipped out for a few minutes to talk with Mrs Galston and arrange for some help.

He returned shortly afterwards with one of the manor house servants and Mrs Galston who quickly put together a meal for Tom and helped put the children to bed. The cook had sent a message to Lady Mortimer before leaving the kitchen, and she also appeared with a servant later that evening, enabling the cook to return to the manor house. While the servant was clearing the food away and cleaning up in the kitchen, Lady Mortimer sat with Tom for a while discussing Margaret's illness. She had already seen several victims of the pestilence and tried to prepare Tom for the worst of all scenarios, trying nevertheless to give him some hope by adding that she had heard that sometimes the stricken person had recovered. She promised to return early the following morning and should his wife not show any signs of improvement, they would need to make arrangements for the children. Reluctantly, he agreed and she then left with the servant, leaving him shaking his head in disbelief at this sudden turn of fate.

He sat up the whole night, periodically looking in on Margaret, hoping to see some sign of improvement in her condition, noting with concern, however, that he saw only the opposite. She called for water in the early hours, and as he held her tenderly so she could drink he felt a small tear trickling down one side of his cheek. His beloved Margaret was burning up with fever and there was nothing he could do to help her. In the morning light he noticed a swelling on her neck and as he helped her drink again, she complained of terrible pains in her stomach and under her armpits which, unknown to them both, came from the formation of additional buboes.

By the time Lady Mortimer appeared it was clear that Margaret was dying from the plague and she led Tom out of the bedroom by the hand, made him sit down on a stool and tried to console him in his grief. She knew only too well the wonderful relationship they had both enjoyed, and had been a little envious. Sir William was a fine man but he was away so often from home, and gave the impression of being more interested in hunting and jousting than in being with her. The fact that they had not been blessed with any children also did not help, and she suspected that he sought consolation elsewhere from time to time, although she had no firm evidence. The man she was comforting was a very different person, she mused, and had to take herself in check as she was holding him around the shoulders, feeling tempted to demonstrate what she was struggling to repress.

Moving decisively a pace backwards, she made him understand that the children could live with her in the manor house, where he could visit them any time he wanted. They would be well cared for and it really was better they left Tom's house as soon as possible. Perhaps he could bring them to her in an hour or so, she added, and she would take the baby John with her immediately, since he needed feeding and to be washed. He nodded in agreement and she busied herself gathering John's things together, and holding him in her arms walked out of the living room and made her way back to the manor house.

It was like a terrible dream. In the space of a few hours Tom's world had changed dramatically. They had always been so happy together and he had come to think that it would continue so, never believing for a moment that fate could be so cruel. And the children? Without the influence of their mother what would become of them? At least they knew Lady Mortimer well and she had already spent considerable time with both Eric and the young Margaret, ensuring that they should have as good an education as was possible in the circumstances. Baby John was too young to realise what had happened, he reflected, but Alice had been so dependent on her mother. That would not be so easy, particularly as she had such a strong personality!

It was Alice that brought him out of his reverie. Impatient as ever, she ran out of the kitchen where her brother and sister were waiting for Tom to call them, pulled herself onto his knee and hugged him, asking when could they go and see their mother. He stood up, holding her under his right arm close to his chest, called the other two and explained that since their mother was so ill, he was taking them to the manor house where they would stay for a few days until she was better, and that he alone would remain in the house with her. He couldn't bring himself to say more, other than they would all go and see her before they left.

Leading them all into the bedroom they stood around Margaret while Tom sat on the bed and gently told her what he had decided with Lady Mortimer. She nodded in understanding and although in great pain, smiled at the children, and, looking particularly at Alice, explained in an extremely weak voice that they must be on their very best behaviour in the manor house, and that when she was better they would all go and visit their Uncle Paul and have a holiday by the sea! Barely able to hold back her tears, she embraced each of her children briefly and then told Tom to return as soon as he could.

Servants were waiting for them at the manor house and within minutes the children were led off to hastily prepared rooms to settle themselves for the night, after Tom had promised to bring all their personal things the following day and kissed them goodnight. Alone with Lady Mortimer, with a catch in his voice, he thanked her for her kindness, took leave of her, saying he must get back home immediately to Margaret who was suffering terribly, turned away to conceal his grief and walked out of the reception room.

He had no sooner returned when Margaret, pointing to the large chest at the end of the bed, asked him to open the hidden drawer inside and give her the ring he had brought back from Crécy – the gift from the Black Prince. She held it up to the light from the oil lamp, admiring for a moment the beautiful emerald reflecting all possible shades of green from its many facets, sighed and handed the heavy gold ring to Tom, pushing it into his hand.

'Give this to Margaret when I pass away, my love,' she whispered. 'Something to remember me by!'

He tried desperately to persuade her that the fever would be gone in a few days and she would soon be up on her feet again, not wanting her to give up at this stage, hoping against hope that by some miracle she would survive. But it was all to no avail. She shook her head, smiling bravely, concealing as best she could the pain that was wracking her entire body, and took hold of his hand, fighting back her tears.

'If only that were possible, Tom! But I know that I have the pestilence. It's eating me up inside, I can feel it. Tom, oh Tom! We've had such a good life and have been so happy together. Remember our good times and take care of our children, and I promise I shall watch over you all. We shall meet again one day, I am sure and all be together again. Promise me you will take another wife to help you, please!'

He looked at her and in spite of himself had to wipe away a tear. He told her that she should not worry about the children, and that he would do anything she asked him except he could not promise to remarry. He would never find a replacement for her and he put his fingertips lightly on her lips as a sign not to protest, watching her intently as her face relaxed for a moment before she slowly nodded in understanding, closed her eyes and slipped away into a troubled sleep. Standing up, he quietly left the bedroom, closing the door noiselessly, walked outside the house into the garden and burst into tears for the first time since his childhood.

Some twenty minutes later, looking up at the starry sky and shivering slightly as small, but very high cloud formations scudded by overhead, driven by a cold wind from the east, he murmured, 'If you really exist, please don't let her suffer any more. Let her end come quickly now, please God!' He took the emerald ring out of his doublet pocket and held it firmly in the palm of his right hand. He stood stock-still for a moment in deep concentration, as if he were silently communing with the Almighty himself, and then walked purposefully back into the house.

His brother Paul awoke with a start, feeling sure he had heard a familiar voice calling him, and remained awake for the rest of the night wondering if he had imagined it or something fearful had happened. Tom, in the meantime, poked some life into the fire in the living room, threw on two logs, and settling into his chair, spent the rest of the night in a silent watch, visiting Margaret periodically to see if she needed anything.

She died at dawn as he stood watching her during one of his visits. She sighed, opened her eyes for a moment, looked at him intently as if wanting to fix his image in her mind, turned her head slowly to one side and stopped breathing. It was over! Tom closed her eyes and left the room grief-stricken.

Lady Mortimer came to the house not long afterwards with a servant and one look at Tom was enough for her to understand. While the servant was busying herself with collecting the children's clothes together, she stood alongside him, patted him affectionately on the back and tried to comfort him. She realised that he had to be kept busy somehow and more or less pulled him to his feet, telling him to make sure the servant did not forget something important, and to help carry the children's clothes to the manor house. While he was doing this, she hurried back to find the chaplain to inform him of Margaret's death and to begin to make the many other necessary arrangements.

Meanwhile Paul Rollesby was sitting next to Elizabeth having breakfast with her and her parents. Her mother had returned earlier than expected from her sister and Mr Polton had decided to spend the day at home. He and Paul were discussing the pestilence and Paul learnt that it was raging across the entire country. Mr Polton had talked with several foreign merchants during his trip to Bruges who had informed him about how it had mercilessly ravaged other European countries, striking particularly the poor and undernourished, but also claiming tribute from the wealthier classes. Nobody was immune and even the clergy had to take a share of the fatalities, he noted! Mrs Polton then confirmed that the Bishop of Winchester's diocese was apparently very badly stricken. She had heard that half the churches were without priests and for that reason large numbers of corpses were lying around in some streets, awaiting eventual burial. Mr Polton cynically commented that it was more likely that the priests had run off somewhere in the country to save their own skins rather than staying in the city to succour the needy, and his wife scoldingly silenced him. Fortunately she did not notice the fleeting look of understanding that passed between Paul and her husband or she would certainly have said more on the subject, since she was much more of a devotee than the rest of her family.

Paul voiced concern for his own family and hoped that Castor might be spared the tragedy, even though he had considerable concerns which he did not discuss, other than the fact that he had had some bad dreams the previous night. He intended to tell Elizabeth one day about how close he was to his brother, to the extent that he sometimes seemed to know what he was thinking, but not yet. Lost in his thoughts, sensing that Tom needed help or something terrible had happened, he was brought back to reality by Mrs Polton asking him if he was unwell since he had suddenly become so quiet. He found them all staring at him, particularly Elizabeth who had concern written all over her face. Forcing a smile he reassured them that all was well and tried to focus his thoughts on something else.

Since he had to return to Titchfield early the following day, they spent an hour or so discussing marriage plans. The Poltons had fully understood Paul's reason for the delay – he sensed that Mathilda Polton may even have been a little relieved – but Elizabeth was their only child and they wanted to ensure that the wedding was a great success and that all their friends and acquaintances were duly impressed! Elizabeth had tried to tell her mother that it was too early to fix firm dates due to the chaos associated with the pestilence, but to keep the peace, she and Paul went along with her wishes. Mr Polton had learnt long ago to keep quiet on these occasions and that day was no exception!

Before Paul reached Titchfield, Margaret Rollesby had been buried in the cemetery of the small parish church of Castor. Almost all the surviving villagers attended the funeral service out of respect for Tom, who was a revered person in the demesne. The soldiers that were not with Sir William in Calais were also present, since they had all known Margaret and had not only been impressed by her great beauty but even more by her kindness, humility and general friendliness to them all.

A messenger from Calais was waiting for Lady Mortimer at the manor house when she returned with Tom and three of his children, and handed her a letter from Sir William. It was merely to inform her that he was in good health and the pestilence had run its course in Calais and the surrounding area so that it was safe to travel. He expected to be home within a week or so and looked forward to seeing her. There were some instructions for Tom to make sure his armour and other equipment was in good order since he planned to take part in a jousting tournament organised by King Edward at Windsor. Tom took leave of Lady Mortimer, embraced his children and went off to organise things for his lord's return.

Three days later, a servant from the manor house breathlessly managed to reach Tom before he left his home for an early morning patrol, with instructions that he should go and see Lady Mortimer immediately. He questioned the servant about the reason for the urgency and understood that it had to do with Alice not being very well. Almost panic-stricken he raced Lightning up the lane leading to the house, handed the reins to another servant waiting at the main door and dashed into the reception room where Lady Mortimer was sitting by a window looking out over the gardens. She stood up at once and he could see that her face was drawn and pale as she walked towards him, and that her eyes were heavy from lack of sleep.

'Oh Thomas,' she exclaimed, 'I've been up with Alice all night. I think she has the pestilence!'

Speechless with shock, she led him quickly to a room where Alice was alone, lying in a small infant's bed covered in perspiration, with her eyes protruding in the way he had seen on so many victims of the plague. He moved closely to her, feeling on her brow the fever that was destroying his youngest daughter, and slipping his hand gently under an armpit found the bubo he had desperately hoped would not be there. He spoke soothing words to her, trying to ease her fears, wishing he could only help her in some way, to at least relieve the pain that was coursing through her body, knowing only too well, however, that he was powerless in this respect. Tom would have willingly given his own life to save her, but it was useless. She was dying.

Once outside the bedroom, he asked after the other children and Lady Mortimer reassured him they were all well, including the young John, and sleeping soundly, but he insisted on seeing them before he left, offering a silent prayer that they might be spared from the pitiless advances of this evil monstrosity, whatever it was. Wanting to be alone, he thanked her for her efforts, saying he would return later, and walked out into the gardens.

Paul had only been back in Titchfield for a day. He had quickly checked over the demesne affairs with his friend Brother Simon, who had coped admirably in his absence, in spite of the manpower problems. Satisfied that things were progressing as planned, Paul went to see Canon Matthew to explain why he needed to travel to Castor. He told the canon that he had not been able to sleep properly for almost a week and was convinced that his brother somehow or other needed his help desperately. He did not go into further details but the Canon saw that it was extremely important for him, and since Paul had already delayed his final departure from the demesne to help them, he gave him his blessing and wished him a safe return.

Paul was lucky to find space for himself and Blackie on a merchant ship sailing from Southampton direct to Yermouth, scheduled to pick up supplies there *en route* to the English garrison in Calais, and on the morning of the third day after leaving Titchfield, found himself about to ford the River Burre only a few hours from Castor. He was pleased that the trip had gone so smoothly but was still not able to shake off an inner feeling of dread that had been bothering him for more than a week. It was almost two years since he had last seen his brother and family when they had spent a joyous Christmas together, and although wanting to meet them all again he was nervous as to what he might find.

These thoughts were still buzzing through his head as he cantered the last half mile or so towards Tom's new house that he had not yet seen, but knew was close to the manor house gardens, and on impulse decided to stop first at the kitchen to see Mrs Galston. She was already at the door just as he had sprung down from Blackie, and turning round, he saw her tear-filled eyes and drawn face as she ran to him and flung her arms around his neck.

'Oh, Master Paul,' she breathed through her tears, 'praise to God you are safe and back with us! It has been terrible here. They're all at the church in the village. Poor little Alice is being buried today. Sir William and Lady Mortimer are also there with Mr Thomas and the family. Hurry now and you'll be in time!'

It was not until Paul had sprung back on his horse, turned its head and begun to gallop away that the cook realised that he probably didn't know about Margaret, either, but he was already out of earshot, intent on getting to the church as fast as he could.

A few minutes earlier, Lady Mortimer, who was sitting at Tom's left side in the front row of the tiny but packed church, had turned to him and whispered that it was a pity that his brother could not be there. She looked at him questioningly when he replied, 'Paul will soon be here, my lady. He is already on his way!'

Before she could say anything else, the door opened at the back, and turning to see who it could be, she was astonished to recognise Paul making his way hurriedly towards them. The children made room for him as the two brothers briefly embraced each other and sat down, Paul wondering where his sister-in-law was but deciding to say nothing. The answer to his growing concern was shortly given by the priest who made reference to the earlier death of the 'poor child's mother also stricken by the pestilence', and he sat there with tears in his eyes, hearing nothing more of the priest's words.

At the graveside he stood by Tom as the villagers offered his brother their condolences and also paid their respects to Sir William and Lady Mortimer who were standing nearby, recognising a few of them from earlier days, including the Dexters, who with their adopted son Robert, remained with them until all the others had gone. Robert, he noted, had moved so that he was close to the young Margaret, and had touchingly taken her hand as the priest was saying his final words. Paul was both surprised and pleased to see the concern and care which Sir William showed in handling his brother at this time, and how he had arranged a tasteful wake at the manor house afterwards for family and close friends. It was almost as if the lord was mourning the death of one of his own family and he had repeatedly assured Tom that even though he had lost a wife and child, he personally and Lady Mortimer would do everything in their power to help him raise his family and overcome the pain of his suffering.

The following day as Paul reminded his brother of Lord Castor's words and asked him how he could best help, his brother led him out of the house to the oak tree he had mentioned during his earlier trip, walked five paces southwards, and pointing downwards, repeated his previous words.

'The fact that you came here, Paul,' he added, 'during my time of need has been a tremendous help to me, and gives me the complete reassurance that you will care for my children should anything happen to me.' He then hugged his brother and continued to discuss the children. He believed that Eric would make his way within the demesne and would probably become the manor reeve or steward, or perhaps even be trained to be a clerk for higher office if his ability continued to develop. Sir William had high hopes for him. Margaret, he felt, would make her way with help from Lady Mortimer. His daughter was beautiful, highly intelligent, but with a temperament even more fiery than her mother. He had also noticed the attention the young Dexter showed her and smiled, adding that it was far too soon to make any plans on that score. As for John, he concluded, pride showing all over his face, 'In spite of his tender age, I'm sure that one will be a warrior and probably a lot smarter than his father!'

Paul once again told Tom not to have such morbid thoughts, but should anything happen he would of course instantly be there to help. The brothers looked at each other knowingly, and Paul noticed that Tom had returned more to his normal self, even though he sensed all too well the inner pain he was concealing. Determined to try to motivate him further, he told him about the forthcoming wedding and insisted that Tom should come to Winchester and participate, and if possible bring the young Eric and Margaret with him.

Tom clasped his brother by the hand and swore: 'By all that's holy, Paul, only the pestilence can prevent me from being at your side on that day. I shall bring them both as you wish if they are fit and well, and shall arrive two days before Easter Sunday and look forward so much to meeting your Elizabeth, the lady that has managed to capture the heart of my only brother!'

It was a touching moment that neither would ever forget and was later to have far-reaching consequences.

25

The Marriage

Paul left his brother two days after Alice's funeral, returning to Titchfield in time for the Christmas celebrations at the abbey. He was sad to leave his brother but had seen that the lord and his wife, the reeve John Dexter and Annie were all helping Tom over this difficult period, and that he was in good hands. The canon was delighted to see him safely back since there was still much to be done before Paul left them for good at the end of March. But first there was time and the need to celebrate!

The following three months raced by and shortly before the end of March 1349 Paul bade the monks, Brother Simon and Canon Matthew farewell, packed his belongings at home into a waggon drawn by two horses he bought from friends in the village, and after taking leave of all his surviving friends including the barber William Green and Bob Thatcher at The Bugle, headed for Winchester with Blackie in tow. In spite of his earlier protests, he was thankful that the canon had insisted on providing him with an escort of four soldiers, because the whole area was infested by marauding bands of deserters and other vagabonds looking for easy pickings from unprepared travellers. Before reaching the city boundaries he noted ample evidence of their activities close to the main tracks, including burnt-out waggons, dead horses and the odd human corpse pierced by arrows or hacked to pieces by swords or axes. It was an extremely dangerous period to be travelling and he hoped that nothing would happen to Tom's children if they should accompany him on the way to the wedding. He need not have worried, however, as events were shortly to demonstrate!

In the meantime, there was frantic activity at the Poltons' house. The wedding was only a week away, as Mathilda Polton had pointedly observed to her husband, and there was still so much to be done. Invitations had long been sent out to all immediate relatives, a large circle of friends and influential business people (the majority from the Winchester area, so accomodation was not required for them) but there were several merchants from Salesburye for whom rooms had been booked in the George, the Blue

Boar, other inns in Winchester and the area to the west of the city. They had several guest rooms in their house, one of which was reserved of course for Paul, but Mrs Polton insisted that as a precaution, suitable tents be erected in the spacious grounds for unexpected guests and some of the perhaps not so important people. Two huge marquees were in the process of being erected close to the house when Paul arrived – to seat the two hundred or so guests for the wedding feast as he later learnt – with servants and other helpers swarming round them, all being directed by Mrs Polton.

Mr Polton warmly welcomed Paul and servants were immediately dispatched to store away his possessions, stable Blackie and take care of the waggon and other two horses. Leading him into the house for refreshment after his journey, he told Paul that Elizabeth would join them shortly, but at the moment the seamstress was with her making final alterations to the wedding dress. His wife was in her, element, he explained, grinning knowingly, and it was probably better they both kept out of the way for the time being!

Paul liked him immensely and knew that the feeling was mutual. Mr Polton had recognised Paul's calibre almost immediately on meeting him, respecting how he had developed as a businessman and cultured person in spite of the lowly birth that seemed to concern his wife, for whom appearances and 'good family' were critical ingredients. He also admired Paul's inner strength and undoubted courage, characteristics that even Mrs Polton recognised, never able to forget how he had rescued her and Elizabeth from the ruffians in Winchester. The fact that his daughter clearly adored Paul was enough for Mr Polton, and she was strong-willed enough to defy her mother if necessary. Mrs Polton knew this and had had to come to terms with the fact that her future son-in-law did not bring a famous family name with him!

While he and Mr Polton were discussing the course of the plague (which fortunately appeared to have abated in southern England at least), the after-effects on labour and prices, the taxation situation that was burdening everybody, the apparently never-ending campaigns in France and the very doubtful value of it all, Elizabeth suddenly appeared, indignant that nobody had told her that Paul had arrived. After a brief explanation, Mr Polton tactfully left them together and went off to busy himself in another part of the house.

Elizabeth's indignation was extremely short-lived. She almost flew into Paul's arms and hungrily kissed and caressed him with a passion that had been smouldering within her during their separation of almost four months. She wanted him desperately and Paul himself needed little persuasion, as her exploring fingertips soon discovered. They both knew that it was not feasible to make love in that room as they could be disturbed at any time, and hearing approaching footsteps, Paul gently un-entwined Elizabeth's arms from around him, sighed deeply and commented that they only had to wait a few more days. He stepped back from her seconds before Mrs Polton entered the room.

Pretending not to notice the flushed faces, she began with, 'Ah, there you are, dear boy,' welcomed him as warmly as she was able and told him his room was now ready, his clothes were unpacked and that dinner would be served in an hour. She looked forward to talking to him then but had no time right now. She then flounced out of the room. When she had gone, they both burst out laughing and Elizabeth confided that her mother had been acting like that for at least ten days and promised she would be more normal when the wedding was over. Paul kissed her once more, excused himself saying he needed to wash and change after his journey, and reluctantly left her to go to his room.

The conversation during dinner was dominated by Mrs Polton and the topic of the forthcoming wedding, to the discomfort of the young couple and the concealed amusement of Mr Polton who had long since stopped taking his wife seriously on this particular subject. She asked Paul on his views as to the proposed banquet she was planning and he politely suggested that he was sure it was better left in her very capable hands since he was extremely inexperienced in such matters. Unexpectedly, immediately afterwards, she asked him if anybody from his family would be coming, and Paul confirmed that his brother Tom had promised to attend and would probably bring his eldest son and daughter. He explained the tragic deaths of Margaret and Alice, that he and his brother were very close and that it meant a great deal to him personally that he should be present.

Elizabeth and her father were genuinely delighted to have the opportunity to meet members of Paul's family at last, but Mrs Polton's first comment was, 'He's a soldier, I seem to remember you telling me once, isn't he Paul? I'm sure he will not object to sleeping in a tent. He must be used to it. How old are the children, by the way, the poor things?'

Slightly irritated by Mrs Polton's insinuation, and in a tone that made Elizabeth look sharply at him, but was totally lost on her mother, he replied, 'Yes, he's a soldier, Mrs Polton, and a very fine one at that. I owe him everything I have. I'm sure you will like him and his children. The boy, Eric, is almost eight and the girl,

Margaret, is six. They are both highly intelligent, well-behaved and Margaret is a beautiful child as you will see. They will not cause you any trouble.'

Fully understanding the sensitivity behind Paul's reply, Mr Polton immediately responded by saying how pleased they would all be to meet them and that they would do everything possible to make them feel welcome and comfortable. He glared firmly at his wife, who wisely nodded and confirmed his sentiments.

The rest of the evening passed without incident and Paul learnt that they were to be married in the church of St Thomas, one of the oldest and most famous churches of Winchester, and that a special carriage was being prepared to take them there on the great day. Mr Polton added that unfortunately, because of the times, it had been necessary to arrange an escort, but he was sure he could understand that they didn't want any unfortunate incident to mar the wedding! Paul nodded in agreement, thinking inwardly how happy he would be when it was all over and he and Elizabeth could begin to lead a normal life without all the fuss and ceremony!

During the next few days, Mr Polton introduced Paul to some of his business friends and colleagues and kept him generally occupied with plans for their future cooperation, while his wife and Elizabeth were working flat out on all the many details of the wedding arrangements. Paul noticed the enormous quantities of food and wine that were being continuously delivered and understood the importance the Polton family and relatives gave to the outward trappings of appearance, doing the 'right thing' and making a good impression. Fortunately Elizabeth was more of a rebel and shared most of his views on the more important values of life.

On the Thursday before Easter Sunday, at the time Paul was beginning to get a little anxious about news from his brother, Mrs Polton proudly showed him the menu she had planned with the cook. He looked at it over Elizabeth's shoulder and his first thought was how could one possibly eat so much! There were three main courses beginning with a beef broth flavoured with almonds, followed by baked mallard, teals and a variety of small birds served with an almond milk. Then came roasted veal and pork, herons and sweatmeats. He glanced quickly at the second and third courses which included pheasant, roast rabbit, wild boar and a roasted peacock, pears in syrup and a host of other items. He smilingly added that nobody could possibly go hungry with such splendid fare and thanked Mrs Polton for all her care and trouble, inwardly feeling a little awkward at his own apparent inadequacy. She beamed at his compliment and was about to make what she considered to be an appropriate comment when they were all interrupted by a servant saying excitedly that there was a royal messenger at the door with a message for the Polton family.

Mrs Polton paled and even Mr Polton lost his confidence for a moment while Paul and Elizabeth merely looked at each other in amazement.

'A royal messenger, you say? Are you sure, man?' Mathilda Polton asked in an imperious tone.

'Yes, quite sure milady. He belongs to the household of Prince Edward of Wales,' the servant stammered nervously, 'and told me he had urgent and important news for you and the master.'

'Bring him in immediately, then,' Mr Polton ordered. 'We mustn't keep him waiting!'

A minute later, the servant ushered the messenger into the main living room, indicating his master and mistress who were standing together looking somewhat nervous. He politely bowed, handed his credentials to Mr Polton – a document with the royal seal identifying the carrier to be a certain John Fry, an honourable yeoman within the household of Prince Edward and to be handled with all due courtesy and respect – and waited until he had read it before saying a word. He acknowledged Paul and Elizabeth with a slight gesture of his head and turning to the Poltons said, 'His royal highness, the Prince of Wales bids me to give you his friendliest greetings and congratulates you on the forthcoming marriage of your only daughter Elizabeth to Mr Paul Rollesby, the brother of his most esteemed subject, Thomas Rollesby.' He paused slightly, seeing the looks of absolute amazement of the whole family, adding, 'That is correct, isn't it, they are to be married on Easter Sunday?'

Mrs Polton stammered a weak 'Yes.' Hiding the most discreet of smiles, the messenger continued. 'His highness holds Mr Thomas Rollesby in such respect, in that he not only saved his life at Crécy and further demonstrated his bravery and leadership throughout that campaign but subsequently last week at Windsor, defeated all the greatest names of the land in a special jousting tournament set up by our good King Edward.' He then looked at Paul before continuing. 'Your brother Thomas was asked by his majesty what honour he could bestow on him, and he respectfully requested that it would be sufficient if perhaps his son and the Earl of Warwick would accompany him to the wedding of his only brother Paul at Winchester and that was of course, willingly granted.' At this stage Mathilda Polton almost fainted and Paul squeezed Elizabeth's arm gently, drawing her closer to him, wondering what was coming next, and they were not disappointed.

'In addition,' John Fry resumed his startling message, 'his majesty has requested that the marriage shall be celebrated in the cathedral church of Winchester and duly carried out by his loyal subject, Bishop Erdington, who once served in his personal household. The celebrations should be held in the grounds of your fine house, and since it is such short notice, waggons are already on the way loaded with tents, food and drink, cooks and helpers and all that is necessary for a great banquet. The soldiers escorting the provisions will serve as a guard of honour from your home to Winchester on Sunday and will of course return here afterwards until the celebrations are over. Most of them will camp outside your property, and will keep discreetly out of the way until required.' The messenger paused for breath, and ended by asking if there were any questions.

To say that the whole group had been taken completely by surprise would be a gross understatement, but Paul at least wanted to know when he could expect to see his brother. The messenger was seemingly prepared and answered immediately.

'Your brother, Mr Thomas Rollesby, sir, is already on his way from Barkhamsted where he has been staying these last few days with his highness, at his country home. He is accompanied by the Earl of Warwick, a squadron of troops and also has his son and daughter with him. I imagine they will be with you tomorrow morning, sir.'

Mrs Polton then enquired about the Black Prince and was informed that he would meet them in the cathedral at noon on Sunday, just before the wedding, as he would have probably attended an early Mass there that morning. Then excusing himself graciously, John Fry said he must return as soon as possible back to the prince, and at the request of Mr Polton agreed to inform the curate at St Thomas' of the change of wedding plans and ask him to re-direct guests unaware of the change of plans to the cathedral.

Watching the messenger ride off towards Winchester, escorted by four hobelars, the family group returned to the main living room, bursting with excitement. Inwardly, Paul felt so proud of his brother and was happy for Elizabeth, who was really going to have a day to remember! Mrs Polton hugged her husband, absolutely enthralled at the prospect of meeting royalty and hardly able to wait to see the expression on the faces of her closest friends when they heard about it all! Mr Polton was also delighted at the honour being shown to his family and was already beginning to think about how they could best inform all the guests about the new venue.

A bottle of the best wine was opened to celebrate, and Mr Polton drank a toast to his daughter and future son-in-law, looking firmly at his wife as he mentioned how he looked forward to meeting Paul's 'Soldier brother and family!' His meaning was not lost on them all, and Paul, grinning at Mathilda Polton, gave her a hug and told her that he was sure she would not be disappointed at being associated with the Rollesby family! Elizabeth was ecstatic. She had always loved Paul and believed in him as a person, in spite of her mother's tacit disapproval, and now her faith had been more than justified in an aspect that even she had not expected. She had also genuinely always looked forward to the prospect of meeting his family, since she had understood long before how important they were to him, and shared Paul's happiness. Her mother, in the meantime, had dashed off to the kitchen to warn the cook about special preparations for the next day.

The activity in the Polton household on Good Friday was even more hectic. Mrs Polton was up at dawn, instructing the servants to prepare rooms for Tom and his children, and the earl of course. Suddenly nothing was too good for them, and several servants received severe tongue lashings for initially not using the best bed linen or making the rooms as comfortable as she thought fit! Outside the kitchen door, preparations were also being made to roast a wild boar, an ox and several game birds to ensure that a splendid meal could be served to their expected guests, and Paul secretly hoped that his brother would play the game that was expected of him so as not to disappoint the family and the many helpers.

He need not have worried. It was at about eleven o'clock in the morning that they heard a fanfare of trumpets in the distance and the noise of what appeared to be an army on the move! They all went out to the main door to see what was happening, including most of the servants and helpers who were peering discreetly around the sides of the house, not wanting to miss any of the excitement. They heard the sound of many hooves drumming on the road leading to the main gate of the Polton property, the creaking of waggon wheels, some shouting and the occasional crack of a whip from drivers urging their horses to keep up with the soldiers ahead, the jingling of spurs and harnesses competing to be heard above all the other noises of an army on the move. Paul was reminded of the approach of the French army at Crécy and shuddered at the memory until he suddenly caught sight of Tom riding between two knights with the green and white colours of the Black Prince and those of the Earl of Warwick fluttering proudly from the tops of their lances, and was almost dazzled by the sun reflecting on their chain-mail and shields. Tom's shield was strapped to one side of Lightning and Paul could just read the motto under the family arms his brother had once shown him: 'Tutor et Ultor'. Behind the three men-at-arms were more than a dozen yeomen followed by what looked like a hundred mounted archers, and the whole column came to a halt in front of the almost overwhelmed Polton family. Before springing down from their mounts, Tom, the Earl of Warwick and accompanying equerry saluted the group by lowering and raising their lances, handed them to squires that appeared from nowhere to take charge of the horses and walked towards the group.

Elizabeth knew instinctively which one of the three was Paul's brother and curtsied automatically as he approached them, slightly ahead of the earl and equerry. Paul was watching his brother's face intently, noting the trace of premature grey hair and the one or two lines close to the eyes, which certainly were the result of his suffering of the last months. But the sparkle was back and as their eyes met Paul recognised both the warmth and the hidden amusement as he took stock of the situation. Towering over Mrs Polton, he gently took her hand (she almost swooned), kissed it, and in an almost reverent tone, greeted her.

'Your faithful servant, my lady. My brother has told me so much about you and your family, but omitted to inform me that the mother of his intended bride was such a beauty.' Before she could say a word, he turned slightly to Mr Polton, shook him warmly by the hand, thanked him for the invitation and then concentrated his attention on Elizabeth, who was blushing slightly at his piercing gaze. 'You must be Elizabeth,' he said. 'I can easily understand why my brother wants to marry you. If he doesn't treat you well, let me know and I'll beat him to a pulp!' He then burst out laughing and clasped his brother close to him, hugging him with obvious affection, until a voice over his shoulder reminded him to introduce them to the group. Within a few minutes all the shyness and nervousness of the family had evaporated, and they began to talk to each other as if they had been friends for years, until Tom suddenly started and said, 'What an oaf I am, I'd almost forgotten my children.' He turned back to the squires and asked one of them to fetch the young Eric and Margaret, who needed little encouragement to run to their father.

They were dressed in their very best clothes and Elizabeth saw the resemblance to Tom in the young Eric, and the girl, she thought, must take after her poor mother. But what a beautiful child! She looked at her long, raven-coloured hair, glistening in the sunlight and then noticed her green eyes, imagining the effect she would have on young men in a few years. Paul had said she was a very spirited girl and she watched him making a fuss of her as she stood close to her father, for a few seconds wistfully thinking about the future and what it might bring them both. Her reverie was soon disturbed by her parents, anxious to take control of the situation and get their guests settled into their rooms with all their baggage and other affairs. The earl asked the equerry to get the soldiers organised in a camp outside the Polton property, ready to be assembled as had been earlier agreed and then followed Mrs Polton, who led him to his quarters.

Before dinner, while they were all enjoying a glass of claret, Tom excused himself and left the room briefly, returning with two large packages under his arm, handing one to Mrs Polton and the other to her husband, remarking that he would be pleased if they would accept them as a small token of his gratitude for their hospitality and the kindness they had shown to his brother.

He had brought magnificent robes for both of them, but the one for Mrs Polton comprised of a tunic, a super-tunic, a cloak with a hood and a furred coverlet, all of russet, as well as a coverlet of rabbit skins. She gasped with surprise when she saw the quality and beauty of her gift, knowing that it would certainly be the envy of all her friends, and her husband, recognising both the value of the gifts and seeing his wife's intense pleasure, thanked Tom for his generosity and thoughtfulness. Mathilda Polton wiped a tear from her eye, placed the clothes carefully on a nearby chair, went over to Tom, reached up to place her arms around his neck, hugged him, kissed his cheek, and said simply, 'Thank you so much, Thomas. It is a wonderful robe!'

From that moment on, Tom could do no wrong in the eyes of Mrs Polton. Her initial scepticism disappeared totally, and she was also astonished at the degree of his eloquence, in spite of the fact that, as she had learnt earlier from Paul, he had had virtually no education. All admired his modesty and it was the Earl of Warwick who had to recount details of Tom's victory as champion at the recent jousting tournament at Windsor.

'He defeated them all, Madame,' the earl said in answer to Mathilda's question. 'The best we have in England as well as those in Flanders. I also had the privilege to see him in action against the French, and pray to God we would never have to fight against such a man! Not only that, he would never tell you himself, but he is probably the finest archer in the kingdom and . . .' He was then interrupted by Tom, who smiling at the earl and Mrs Polton, added that the earl was sometimes prone to exaggerate a little and adroitly changed the subject by asking Mr Polton if he had seen or heard of the 'flagellants'. Seeing the look of bewilderment on all the faces seated at the table, he began to describe what he had seen on his way from Castor to Windsor.

He explained that he was accompanying his lord, Sir William Fastolfe, a frequent participant in the royal tournaments, whom he subsequently represented when he fell ill at Windsor. They had reached London and were staying in an inn close to the fine church of St Paul's, and were about to leave early in the morning and wondered why all the church bells in the area were ringing. They had no sooner mounted their horses and begun to ride towards St Paul's when they saw a long procession of several hundred people silently marching two-by-two in front of them. They rode carefully past the long column, tethered their horses in a side street with a guard and walked closer to St Paul's to get a better view and to watch the proceedings.

They were all wearing drab robes with red crosses on the front and back. Cowls covered their heads and concealed their faces. Some also wore caps with red crosses on front and back. They all walked with eyes fixed to the ground and a heavy scourge with three or four leather thongs tipped with metal studs hanging over one shoulder. The group was led by a master and two lieutenants carrying banners of purple velvet and golden-coloured cloth. As they approached the square by the church they began to sing a hymn, which somebody told them was in Flemish, since the 'Brethren of the Cross', as they were called, apparently came from Flanders. Once they reached the square, he continued, the long column stopped and a large circle was formed. The men stripped to the waist, putting their garments inside the circle, and began rhythmically to beat their naked backs and chests with the scourges.

Tom paused to take a swig of wine, and then added that they were all chanting and beating themselves until blood flowed down their bodies, writhing and twisting in a frenzy of emotion. From time to time they threw themselves on the ground, rising again to continue punishing their torn bodies. The watching townsfolk who had gathered to watch the spectacle gradually became influenced by this outpouring of passion and emotion and started to moan and groan in sympathy and shout encouragement to the fanatical pilgrims who continued to beat themselves and the bodies of other penitents alternately.

'How terrible,' Elizabeth commented. 'Why were they doing it, Thomas? How long did it all go on?'

'You shouldn't interrupt Thomas, my dear,' Mrs Polton quickly said. 'Let him continue this fascinating tale.'

'There really isn't much more to say, Madame Polton,' he interjected. 'We watched them for half an hour or so and then had to continue our journey to Windsor. I gather they do it as a form of penance due to the pestilence, believing, I suppose, that the Almighty will forgive them their sins and perhaps that their punishment will serve as an atonement for the rest of mankind. Something like that, I think, but it is too exaggerated and brutal, in my opinion. Some friends at the tournament told me they are called the 'flagellants' and have made similar processions in other countries. Sometimes, I gather, their processions and demonstrations get out of hand and can be very dangerous.'

They all continued to discuss this phenomenon for a few minutes until Paul steered the group to another subject, knowing that anything concerning the Black Death would disturb his brother at this time. Before the meal was finished, while Tom was putting his two children to bed, Mr and Mrs Polton made a great point of emphasising how happy they were that Paul's brother and family would attend the wedding and that they were more than honoured by his and the earl's presence. Paul smiled inwardly, both he and the earl taking the comments with grace. The moment Tom rejoined them, Mr Polton asked if perhaps on the following morning he would be prepared to demonstrate his skill with the longbow, adding that he had practised a little in his youth and would really like to see an expert handling a bow. He had targets in one of the stables and would have them set up early in the morning if Tom was willing.

Seeing that it would please his host, Tom immediately agreed, but added laughingly, 'I'm sure Paul would also like to join in with us since he's probably a bit out of practice! You still have your longbow, Paul, don't you? It will be like old times, eh?' And then, turning to Mr Polton who was clearly delighted, he told him that their own men would make all the necessary preparations, and after a little demonstration he would arrange target practice for the mounted archers.

Their subsequent conversation covered a broad range of topics and both Mr Polton and Paul were particularly interested to hear the earl's viewpoints on the political front. Although careful not to give the impression that he was critical of the king's decision to campaign almost continuously in France, he wondered what it would all bring long-term to the country, especially since the Black Death had taken such a terrible toll on the entire population and there was so much that needed to be done at home. The shortage of labour on his estates was acute and he was having to pay extremely high wages to get the work done. He felt he was almost being robbed by his labourers and wondered how it would all end. He had raised the subject several times in parliament, he told them, but most of the parliamentarians seemed to be more interested in extracting from the state salaries for themselves that were unaffordable, rather than dealing with the really important national issues. Wherever one looked, he concluded, one found evidence of hypocrisy and corruption in the political scene.

Sensing that they were touching dangerous ground, and since it was getting late, Mr Polton suggested they should all perhaps retire to bed to ensure they were ready for the exertions of the following day, and it was agreed they should meet in the large meadow at the extreme west of his grounds at mid-morning for the archery demonstration.

Both Tom and Paul were up early that morning. Tom was organising the butts with the troop of archers and Paul, after stringing his longbow and carefully testing the tension, picked up a quiver of arrows and made his way to the meadow to check that he hadn't lost his old skill. Since the nightmare of Crécy his longbow had been unused. He had always kept it with him on his various journeys as a precaution, but thankfully never had need to use it. Avoiding the intensive activity in the meadow, he walked around it until he found a more secluded area where he could practise undisturbed and unobserved.

An old oak tree, years previously mortally struck by lightning and almost split into two parts, stood alone at one end of a long, narrow strip of land running alongside a boundary stone wall and made an ideal target. He marked a rough circle with his dagger on what was left of the barkless trunk and initially walked back fifty paces from it and took aim. After firing two arrows, he easily found the target centre with the third and fourth, and successively increased the range up to almost three hundred yards. Half an hour later, satisfied that he wouldn't disgrace himself, he retrieved his arrows and retraced his steps to the meadow.

His brother had not been idle in the meantime. Three targets had been set up for the family demonstration with stakes marking ranges that looked like around fifty, one hundred and two hundred paces, Paul estimated. A large tent, open on the side facing the targets, had been erected on a slope to the left which would not only keep the family clear of any danger but would give them an excellent view of all the targets. It was a wise precaution, particularly as far as the children were concerned! Paul also noted that as well as ample supplies of arrows and spare bows, there was also a refreshment waggon at hand with frantic activity going on around it.

'Ah, there you are, Paul,' Tom greeted his brother. 'Been getting in a bit of practice I see. Looks like I shall have to look to my laurels!' And then laughing, he reassured his brother that it was all meant to be a bit of fun for Mr Polton, and that it was not to be taken too seriously. He added that he intended to encourage Mr Polton to try his hand and that was the reason for the nearest target. After he and Paul had fired a few at the longer range targets, he would give a special prize to the host, and then invite the family to a lunch prepared by the earl's cooks.

One of the earl's squires escorted the Polton family and the two children to the tent that had been set up for them where they were immediately joined by Tom and Paul, who after a warm greeting served each of the adults a goblet of wine. Tom explained what they proposed to do in the following hour, presenting a bow to Mr Polton and then persuasively led him, mildly protesting, to the intense amusement of Elizabeth and her mother, to the firing position in front of the target set at a range of fifty paces.

But Tom had no intention of making him a laughing stock and he showed him the best way to hold the longbow and sight an arrow, making him practise this several times before releasing a single shot. Satisfied that he would probably at least reach the target, he gave the command 'fire', and was delighted to see the first arrow sink into the outside edge of the target.

'You see, it's not so difficult as you thought,' Tom commented encouragingly. 'Let's see how many more you can put into that butt!'

To the surprise of Mr Polton (and his wife), out of a total of a dozen arrows, six landed more or less in the target, and all the spectators, who included the earl's retinue and the troop of archers, applauded enthusiastically. Totally exhausted with the effort of drawing the powerful yew longbow, his arms still trembling with the exertion, but inwardly bubbling with excitement and pleasure at his unexpected success, Mr Polton thanked Tom profusely for his help and encouragement, handed the bow back to him and acknowledged the cheers from Elizabeth and his wife.

'Well, Thomas,' he commented breathlessly, 'it's the turn of the Rollesby family now. Let's see what you two can do!'

'With your permission, sir,' Tom repectfully said, 'my brother and I will see what we can do with the other two targets, since you have left so little space on yours. Perhaps you would like to rejoin your family where you can better see how we fare, and also keep an eye on young Eric and Margaret who both have difficulty in sitting still for more than a few minutes!'

Mr Polton willingly agreed and walked off towards the tent, proud of his achievement and hardly able to wait to share his pleasure with the family. Tom led Paul to the stake marking the firing position for the second target where he had earlier placed twenty arrows, stuck into the ground within easy reach, and once Mr Polton was out of earshot he quickly explained how they were to proceed.

In the meantime, Mr Polton was busy telling his wife how surprised he was that he had managed to hit the target, and wondered how one could possibly hit the other two that were so far away that one could only just see them. To the intense amusement of Elizabeth, Margaret looked solemnly at Mr Polton and exclaimed earnestly and in all innocence, 'Have no fear, sir, I'm not too sure about Uncle Paul, but I've seen my daddy hit targets that were only specks in the distance, even when there was an ill-favoured wind!'

'Shush, Margaret,' her brother Eric interjected, 'Uncle Paul is about to fire and I bet he gets more arrows on the target than Mr Polton.'

The laughter from the tent was so intense that Paul's concentration was affected to the extent that his first arrow flew over the top of the target and thudded into a single pine tree some forty yards behind. Elizabeth held her breath as he carefully took aim a second time and cheered encouragement as the arrow flew into the bull's-eye. In all, Paul fired ten arrows and scored four bull's-eyes and four outers, confirmed by a scorer shouting out the result after each shot. The Poltons were lost in admiration, never dreaming that Paul was such an accomplished archer, and while the arrows were being removed wondered how Tom could possibly improve on such a result.

Tom casually rearranged the arrows in the ground behind him so that he could quickly draw out one after the other without even looking, took aim and released the first arrow which sunk plumb dead-centre in the bull's-eye. The following nine followed so quickly that each one was in the air almost immediately after the previous one had hit the target! Even the watching archers applauded and cheered, few of them having seen their leader in action with the longbow. Paul congratulated his brother, and in spite of his protests, walked over to the Poltons' tent, smilingly saying that at least he wasn't as rusty as he had believed, but wanted to watch himself the final act of the master! The scorer confirmed: ten bull's-eyes!

Elizabeth whispered questioningly to Paul as his brother moved over to the position in front of the target set at three hundred paces distance, if he really had a chance to hit it at such a range. Paul smiled and told her that they had both practised together years earlier at even longer ranges, and his brother had won every contest entered. As the earl had started to say the previous evening, he added, he really was the best archer in the country, even though he himself would never agree with such a statement.

Now there was absolute silence as Tom checked the wind direction and its strength, took careful aim and then released his first arrow. It rose high in the air, moving slightly towards the right, carried by a gentle south-westerly breeze and then dropped right into the centre of the target. Mr Polton shook his head in amazement, understanding only too well the skill and strength required for such a shot, and then with everybody else, applauded enthusiastically. And, with consummate ease, Tom fired the remaining arrows in rapid succession with the spectators breathlessly watching as each arrow competed for the available space in the distant bull. They were so tightly clustered that one of the arrows had even split the first one he had fired into two halves.

Looking a little embarrassed by the cheers and wild applause of all the spectators, he walked over to the tent to join Paul, the Earl of Warwick, the Polton family and his excited children. Margaret ran to her father, calling, 'Daddy, daddy, I knew you would win! I just knew!'

He scooped her up with one arm, carrying the bow over his left shoulder, smiling with pleasure and lovingly holding her close to him. He thanked her for her praise but pointed out that it wasn't a contest, merely a short practice and exhibition shoot. He handed the longbow and a quiver to Mr Polton, saying that he would like him to accept it as a memento of the occasion, adding with a twinkle in his eye not to forget to keep in practice now that he had made such a good start! Lowering Margaret gently to the ground, he playfully ruffled Eric's hair, saying he hoped they had both been on their best behaviour, and before he had a chance to reply, Mrs Polton interceded immediately, commenting that there was no need for concern since they were adorable children and had behaved perfectly in his absence. Even Elizabeth was a little surprised at the spontaneous reply of her mother, wondering how her haughty manner had changed within a few hours of Tom's arrival. She had become a much warmer person, she observed, was genuinely at ease with the children, and for the first time began to demonstrate respect and affection for Paul.

Tom thanked her for her kindness, and then led the group to the specially prepared meal awaiting them on a long trestle table set up behind the tent, more or less surrounded by servers that ensured everything went smoothly. It gave the Polton family an opportunity to relax for an hour or two and seemed to further integrate both families prior to the wedding. The Earl of Warwick also took the opportunity to run through the arrangements that had been made for the following morning: the escorted journey to Winchester and the arrangements within the cathedral where they were to be joined by the Prince of Wales; the banquet after the ceremony; and other details. He then left the group to brief his equerry and rode off shortly afterwards with an escort to meet Bishop Erdington.

It was an occasion that both Paul and Elizabeth would never forget, and for years after it was recalled with respect and affection for Tom who had not only made it all possible, but whose charm, warmth, modesty and generosity had won all their hearts. Elizabeth understood for the first time why Paul had always spoken so highly of his brother, and although she didn't discuss it at the time, she gradually became more aware of how the two brothers sometimes seemed to communicate without speaking.

The earl had no sooner left for Winchester when surprisingly Tom stood up and made a short speech. It was witty, eloquent and thoroughly enjoyed by all the family. As he was close to finishing, he called over a squire who handed him a leather pouch, and opening it carefully he walked over to Elizabeth, took hold of her right hand and dropped the contents of the pouch into it.

'Your wedding present, my dear Elizabeth,' he said. 'May it give you pleasure and happiness for many years!'

She gasped as she looked down and saw the jewels glistening in her hand. It was a magnificent diamond necklace with a huge, beautiful ruby in the middle, set in a cluster of smaller stones. They all knew it was worth a fortune and as Elizabeth tried to find the right words of thanks, Tom handed a document to Paul who sat next to her.

'The property is in your name, Paul. I have all I need at Castor.

Sir William gave it to me some time ago from part of an estate he inherited in Wiltshire. I understand there is a handsome country house there, called "The Willows" with a couple of farms belonging to it, two to three miles to the south-west of the city of Salesburye. I'm not sure of your future plans, Paul, but I suspect it will be ideal for you both for the next few years at least!'

They were all overwhelmed with the extent of his generosity, but Tom merely shrugged his shoulders, smiled and wished them both all possible happiness for the future.

'Margaret would also have wanted it so, I know!' Tom concluded.

The following day proved to be equally momentous. Everything took place as the Earl of Warwick had arranged: the coach Mr Polton had provided for the occasion was escorted by what appeared to be an army of mounted archers, men-at-arms and squires, all led by Tom and the earl's equerry in full regalia; once at the cathedral, they were welcomed with a fanfare of royal trumpeters and greeted personally by the Prince of Wales and the Earl of Warwick; the bishop himself led them from the doorway to their places while a choir of monks chanted a 'Salve Regina'; and after the wedding ceremony, just before they returned to the banquet at the Poltons' home, the happy couple were presented with an assortment of gifts from the Prince and his entourage.

The magnificence of the ceremonial arrangements and pageantry exceeded by far the expectations of Mrs Polton, who positively glowed with pride and pleasure, enjoying every minute, knowing all too well how impressive it was for her friends and relatives. Paul only had eyes for Elizabeth, whose natural beauty was further enhanced by the magnificent wedding dress and of course the necklace she proudly wore. He rejoiced that at last they would be together, able to lead their own lives and make a new start.

Early in the morning following the festivities in the Polton home, Tom took leave of them all, explaining that he must return quickly now to his duties at Castor – he had already been three weeks away from the manor, and after the two children took a tearful farewell of their beloved uncle and new aunt, not forgetting Mr and Mrs Polton either, they all left with an impressive escort for the comparatively long journey home. In spite of leaving Paul, Tom was happy to be returning to his more familiar environment, missing also his youngest son, John, who although little more than a baby, occupied a special position in his father's affections.

26

'The Willows'

For the Polton household, with the exception of Paul and Elizabeth, the days following the wedding were somewhat of an anticlimax. Tents were dismantled and stored with all the other accoutrements that had been required for the festivities; the whole property had to be cleaned up and the refuse left by the soldiers and other guests cleared away; the extra helpers employed were dismissed and gradually life returned to normal. The two newly-weds had willingly helped during the day, and after the family evening meal retired to the room Mrs Polton had set aside for them, possibly with the hope that they would remain in their household. For Paul and Elizabeth these were wonderful days of discovery and passion. They gently and tenderly explored each other's body until their passions exploded, culminating in fervent lovemaking, continuing long into the night, until both finally slipped into the contented sleep of happily satiated lovers.

Paul had originally planned with Mr Polton to join his cloth business, initially living in the household until he had found a suitable house in the area. Tom's gift had changed that, and even Mr Polton agreed that it now made sense for them to settle near Salesburye, which as he repeatedly pointed out to his disappointed wife Mathilda, was not so far away. Paul explained tactfully that he had saved a considerable sum of money since his campaign in Crécy, which was more than enough for them to renovate a house and live on for a couple of years at least, if need be. Besides, he added, it was essential that he and Elizabeth should make their own way in life, promising Mrs Polton that they would nevertheless maintain a close contact with them, perhaps one day even cooperating in building up a really major family clothmaking concern.

It was, therefore, a completely logical step about ten days after the wedding for Paul to saddle up Blackie and make his way to the house and property his brother had given him, accompanied by two trusted servants Mr Polton insisted he should take with him. They would not only afford some protection, he explained, but there was bound to be a whole host of affairs to be set in order at the new house before he and Elizabeth could comfortably move in.

Salesburye lay about forty miles due west of Winchester, and Paul noted with pleasure the large number of sheep they saw grazing in the low chalklands and arable fields all around, seeing ample opportunity to start up as a wool brogger, he thought. After a couple of years, he mused, having built up some capital and establishing the right contacts, he would focus more on the cloth production side and eventually develop more into the activities of a merchant, perhaps even exporting good-quality cloth and importing other merchandise for the Salesburye market. But that was for the future! In the meantime, a lot of other things would have to be done, he concluded. These and other thoughts occupied his mind for most of the journey and it was almost nightfall before they reached the southern outskirts of the city.

Crossing over Harnham Bridge, within minutes of paying the toll they reached the inn that the gateman had recommended, and found comfortable lodgings for the night. The village they were heading for, Longeforde, lay between Wilton to the west and Downton more to the south-west, the innkeeper explained to Paul that evening after supper, and he gave clear directions how to find it.

Early the following morning, Paul and the two servants retraced their steps back over Harnham Bridge and then followed the River Avon up towards the north until they found the Wilton road. After about two miles they came across the old watermill the innkeeper had described and then followed the track on the left-hand side which led to Longeforde. Within twenty minutes they had reached the small village and a local they met outside The Bull inn directed them to The Willows.

The property, Paul discovered, was surrounded by a good stone wall about six feet high, with a large wrought-iron gate, framed by two large willow trees, which opened more or less onto the lane leading to the village centre. The cobbled driveway to the house badly needed weeding, but the initial impression of the grounds was very good, and Paul was bubbling with excitement as they walked the horses over the cobblestones, wondering what sort of house he would find and in what condition.

They rounded a curve flanked on both sides by magnificent rhododendron bushes that had reached the stature of small trees, their purple, red and white blossoms already beginning to bloom, forming a beautiful canopy of blazing colour over the pathway which lead directly to the front door of a very large, and to Paul, wonderful house. It was built, he was later told, of Chilmark stone, which as it had weathered turned to an attractive grey-green colour. He stopped twenty to thirty paces in front of the imposing main doorway, in order to take in all the detail of the initial impression that he would describe to Elizabeth.

The almost dome-shaped door was of massive oak, covered with black-painted metal studs – it looked strong enough to withold a battering ram, he said later to his wife – and was protected from the elements by a cream-coloured porch of carved marble pillars supporting a black-tiled roof. In each corner of the triangular-shaped plastered facade above the porch, a green fleur-de-lys was painted, reminding him of the banners some of the men-at-arms had carried at Crécy, and he wondered if there was a connection of any sort. The house had three floors. The top floor had small, gabled windows set into the slate roof which had one large, stone chimney stack rising a good six feet from the right-hand corner. The ground and first floor had a set of large, leaded windows with small but thick glass panes on each side of the main door and porchway. It looked as if an extension had been built onto the right, front side of the house, and its huge, horseshoe-shaped leaded window suggested it illuminated a large hall on the first floor. A very high stone wall joined this extension, with a locked, small, but clearly strongly-built door leading into a totally enclosed vegetable and fruit garden, set out on the west and south side of the house. A sense of balance to the idyllic setting of this beautiful house was given by a massive chestnut tree on the left side. A broad pathway led round to a set of outhouses Paul could just see, and stables, he supposed, judging from the slight odour wafted by the south-easterly breeze.

If the inside is anything like the outside, he mused, we shall be so lucky; but his thoughts were suddenly disturbed by the sound of the main door slowly creaking open and an old, white-haired man appeared who waited patiently until Paul and the two accompanying servants got closer, before politely greeting them.

After brief introductions, the old man directed the two servants to where they could stable the horses and invited Paul into a parlour to take a glass of wine. He explained that he had been a retainer for an earlier owner, Canon Hetherton, for most of his life, in fact up until the time that he had died of the pestilence a little more than a year previously. The property had been inherited by a relative of the canon, he explained, living far away in Suffolke, who had agreed with the clerk in Salesburye handling the transaction that he and the housekeeper and cook, a Mrs Spinner, could remain in the house until further notice, and that a gardener should also be retained to care for the rather extensive grounds. The total services, food and supplies for the current household cost around ten pounds per year, which was more than covered by the income from two large farms belonging to the property. He then offered to show the household accounts to Paul, who said there would be plenty of time later for such details, and respectfully asked the old man if he would mind showing him around the house.

To Paul, it was a dream come true. There was a fair bit of maintenance required, he observed, but by and large the house was in excellent condition. It was dry, well-aired, the interior stone walls had retained their fresh cream colour, all the ceilings were panelled with beech or pine that over the years had attained a rich, attractive patina, and the staircases were of oak. He lost count of the number of rooms he saw, including those of Mr Laverstock and Mrs Spinner on the top floor, and was delighted to see that as well as a large fireplace in the main hall, most of the bedrooms also had a fireplace connected to the main chimney. The furniture was somewhat spartan and he saw that some rooms were completely empty, but that was an advantage, in a way, he concluded, in that he and Elizabeth would be more easily able to impose their own taste and character on them in due course.

As far as Paul could see, the kitchen at the back of the house was well equipped with utensils and a pantry, with easy access to a well outside the back yard. There was some work to be done on the privy, he noted, wrinkling his nose as they approached the far end of the yard, but all in all, they were extremely lucky to have this house, and he vowed to send a letter of thanks to his brother as soon as he returned to the Poltons.

He found the two servants waiting at the stables and asked Mr Laverstock if he could also show them around the house so they could note items that would need replacement or other things that would have to be immediately transported from Winchester. He, in the meantime, wanted to stroll alone around the grounds to see everything and agreed to join them an hour or so later.

For the rest of the day after a midday meal prepared by Mrs Spinner, who had returned from the village in the meantime, lists were drawn up and Paul gained as much information on the neighbourhood as possible from Mr Laverstock. This included the name and address of the clerk in Salesburye who had handled the family inheritance affairs, who Paul planned to visit and familiarise himself with the city at a later date when there was more time.

Early the next morning, they returned to Winchester and began the preparations to move the possessions of Paul and Elizabeth to the new home.

By mid-May of 1349, in spite of the protests of Mrs Polton concerning their haste to leave, Paul and Elizabeth moved into The Willows at Longeforde to begin a new phase of their lives. Elizabeth was enthralled with the house, believing that her husband had exaggerated earlier when he had described everything in detail, finding that it was even better than she had anticipated, and quickly set about making it a comfortable home. Paul, in the meantime, busied himself finding out how the wool trade was organised in the area, helped by the two tenant farmers whose land he owned, with whom he had established an excellent relationship.

The letter of thanks Paul sent to his brother reached Tom just as he was on the point of leaving Castor with his lord, to celebrate the founding of the 'Order of the Garter' at Windsor. Not included in the élite few – knights of noble family led by King Edward and his son, the Prince of Wales – they were however invited to participate in the jousting tournaments and extravagant feasts arranged for the occasion. It was at this time that Tom learned from his now close friend, the Earl of Warwick, that the petition the latter had made earlier to the king for Tom's knighthood had been rejected as a result of the slanderous lies of the constable of Norwich, the Count de Kessinger, and a kinsman of his own lord, Roderick, Earl of Dunghall, whom he observed laconically died miserably of the plague shortly afterwards! In spite of the disappointment, Tom smiled knowingly, shaking his head and explained briefly how he had come to have such powerful enemies – worthless individuals, born into renowned families, but dishonest scoundrels nevertheless – concluding that there was probably a purpose to it all, but he was still perfectly happy with his own life and was sure his children and those of his brother Paul would bring greater honour to the family one day.

For Paul and Elizabeth, the rest of that year seemed to pass by in a flash, in spite of all the hard work. Elizabeth had quickly established a good working relationship with Mr Laverstock and Mrs Spinner, even though they both had set ideas about how things should be done, and within a few months the house had already begun to change its character, emanating a much greater feeling of comfort and warmth. She had brought some chests, chairs, a bed, table, cupboard and other individual items from the Polton house and a local carpenter had completed some excellent renovation work on the stairs and some of the ceilings. All the woodwork had been polished, the stone floor at ground level repaired and an additional gardener had been hired to weed the driveway and generally bring the grounds back to good order. Wood had been ordered for the winter and was neatly stacked in one of the nearby outhouses. The stable roof had been re-thatched, the stalls cleaned out, and sufficient hay put to one side for the two horses: Blackie and a beautiful mare, Chestnut, that Mr Polton had given to Elizabeth as a wedding present.

Paul had made such a good impression on the tenant farmers with his constructive suggestions concerning soil improvement techniques and new crop planting methods that they had willingly kept him regularly supplied with fresh eggs, milk and butter, as well as some fruit and vegetables from time to time, until he had had a chance to get his own fruit and vegetable garden in order. He also obtained an annual rent of fifteen pounds from each of them, but came to see that without some significant changes, they would have difficulties paying it in the future. On the one side, following the crippling mortality of the Black Death, labour was not only scarce but becoming increasingly expensive. In addition to that, the taxation burden became heavier each year. The king was continuously looking for new ways to finance his never-ending campaigns in France and levied an additional 'poll' tax on top of all the other variations that not only irritated the total population but caused genuine hardship with many of the numerous poor.

Recognising the rising spiral of wage costs, parliament, pressured by the landowners, introduced an ill-fated 'Statute of Labourers' in June of that year, in an effort to prevent any further increases; but this one-sided measure served only to aggravate the situation of the villeins further in the face of increasing state and Church taxes. As Paul travelled around the area, beginning to interest some of the smaller wool producers in selling to him, he quickly realised that the large flocks belonged in the main to both the Bishop of Salesburye and the Bishop of Winchester, or the flock owners were contracted to sell their wool to them. He visited many small homesteads, hamlets and small villages, and was frequently shocked at the poverty and suffering he encountered almost everywhere.

He spent many evenings discussing with Elizabeth what he had seen during the day, wondering how it would all end and feeling a little guilty about their own very comfortable position. He described the condition of the earthen-floored cottages or hovels that many people lived in, usually with several small, dirty children in rags or often naked, running around them, playing the games that all children have played during the ages. In many instances, one or other of the parents had died from the plague. If it had been the mother, the children were often living with relatives, or in the case of the man, a woman alone was trying to bring up a family and earn a little money herself, somehow. A few managed to earn a pittance by spinning wool they had scavenged, on a crude spinning wheel late into the night. Others took in washing, or if they were lucky, found some work in the household of the village priest or the local squire or landlord. Some took to offering their bodies wherever they could earn a penny or two from visiting tradesmen or a lord hunting in the woods and forests around them, or even a not so pious clergyman who happily committed the sin in private that he regularly publicly condemned!

'These poor people,' he stated with considerable emotion one evening to Elizabeth, 'are happy if they can at least get something to eat each day, and from what I've seen they frequently do not! Now with all these extra taxes and tithes to pay! It's even more difficult for them, particularly when they see how people like us can live so well. It was bad enough when I was a child. Life then for Tom and me was far from easy, but we managed and could see that there was a future. Many of the poor today seem to have lost hope, surrounded by suffering and misery, getting further into debt and having to pay more fines because of outstanding debts. Have you seen how many of the remaining men have been crippled or badly wounded in all these wars we are fighting outside of England? Even those that returned home in one piece were often cheated of the wages owed to them, money that some corrupt clerk or official pushed into his own pocket. It's a miracle there hasn't been a revolution here, and I'm sure it can only be a matter of time!'

Elizabeth had seldom seen Paul so angry as on that particular evening, and realised that it also reflected some of his own frustration at his efforts to develop a business. It was far from easy. She knew from what he had described on previous evenings that the large flocks of sheep were more or less firmly in the hands of the powerful nobility or the Church, and Paul had only managed to persuade half a dozen or so small producers to sell their wool to him after more than two months of hard work. But he was determined to continue as he had planned, convinced that he would eventually succeed in building a large network of suppliers. It was only a matter of time and patience he had said repeatedly, and she always encouraged him further. In fact, it was her idea a week or so after his impassioned outburst that he should try the canon at Titchfield Abbey, even though she knew it would mean his absence for a few days. She shared his excitement when he told her that he had succeeded in purchasing a large quantity of woolfells for collection a month later. Furthermore, the canon had agreed that provided the financial side worked out as he had promised, he would make a contract for the following year for all the abbey's wool.

Paul had already employed two men to clean out, repair and slightly extend one of the stone outhouses so he could initially store the wool bales prior to selling them, but now realised that he would require a much larger building for the following year if he was to handle all the wool from Titchfield Abbey, and began to plan its design and the ideal location for it. There was also the question of transport and to what extent he should invest in packhorses himself or use those of somebody else, and a host of other possibilities and questions he had to resolve, which kept him fully occupied for some months.

Shortly before Christmas at the time Paul and Elizabeth were about to leave for Winchester to spend two weeks or so with the Poltons, Sir William, lord of Castor and Tom were summoned to London by special messenger where they were informed that they and a large force of men-at-arms under the leadership of the king and the Black Prince would shortly leave for a special foray in France. After a few days of frantic preparation, still unaware of the details of the raid, Tom, Sir William and the whole force of men, horses, arms and other supplies were transported by a large number of barges and other ships along the Thamesis Flut around to Rochester where a whole fleet was awaiting them. After brief Christmas celebrations and a Mass held in the castle chapel, the king explained to the group that he had discovered a treacherous plan to surrender the fortress at Calais to a certain Geoffroi de Charney, commander of the French garrison at Saint-Omer at midnight on 31 December, which had to be prevented at all costs.

They arrived at the port of Calais during the night of 30 December, entered the castle secretly and remained out of sight for the whole of the next day, spending the time sleeping, and then, after a good meal, running through all aspects of their plans and preparing themselves to ambush the enemy. Tom was given the command of a company of archers around the Boulogne Gate and a small group of pikemen, while the king deployed the larger force of men-at-arms close to the North Gate. As he later described to Paul, apparently a detachment escorting the 20,000 crowns intended as a bribe for the senior officer, one Aimeri of Pavia, who had informed the king of the plot, were immediately captured and thrown into the castle dungeons. King Edward then rushed his men-at-arms around to the Boulogne Gate to meet the main force of the French commander, Charney, who mistakenly believed the gate would be open for him to enter the town.

Once the French contingent of men-at-arms, crossbowmen and foot soldiers finally reached the gate in question, on the command of the Black Prince it was quickly opened, which was the signal for Tom to get his waiting archers to quickly pour volley after volley of arrows onto the completely surprised Frenchmen. This was immediately followed by a mass attack by the English mounted men-at-arms who galloped out to do battle with all survivors. But the massed French troops soon recovered enough to fight back desperately and within minutes there was a fierce battle of close-quarter fighting. At one stage, King Edward himself was almost taken prisoner, but both his son and Tom saw the danger and came to his rescue in the nick of time.

Hearing the noise, the English king's force was soon joined by the balance of the garrison that had not been informed of Edward's plans for fear of betrayal, and this quickly swung the balance in favour of the English, causing the remains of Charney's army to withdraw, leaving hundreds of dead and a large number of captured knights, including Charney himself. Tom never described his own participation in any detail, but merely said that that he was pleased to get back home in one piece, and for him at least the New Year had begun well. He was uninjured, and he had been generously rewarded for his services!

27

Reunion

All the way back home, Paul couldn't get his brother Tom out of his mind. After a long spell of silence Elizabeth, nestling closer to him in the coach her father had given Paul as a wedding present, asked if anything was bothering him. They had had an extremely enjoyable stay at her parents' home, made all the more pleasurable by their both tender and passionate lovemaking. They had been so busy in the months prior to Christmas that they seemed to have had too little time for each other. Paul had often been away travelling, visiting fairs, looking up old contacts, and had even been to Wulpet to find William Outlawe in order to discuss possible future developments for wool export, the best products to import and more efficient ways to get the goods to various important English markets like Norwiche, Winchester, Salesburye and of course, London, which was growing at a faster rate than most other cities. Elizabeth, for her part, had by now transformed their home into what Paul called 'their own special retreat of warmth, beauty and happiness' and had learned all she could about gardens and the care of fruit trees, vegetables and herbs to ensure they would be more self-sufficient in future years.

Shivering slightly and pulling his cloak around them both – it was a very cold, early January afternoon, threatening snow at any time – Paul hugged Elizabeth almost guiltily, realising his thoughts had been elsewhere for some considerable time, and quickly reassured her that all was well with him, apologising for his lack of attention.

'To tell you the truth, my love,' he said, 'I've had Tom on my mind for most of the day. It is difficult to explain but I'm sure he's been in some great danger recently and now is not far away from us. I'll tell your father's servant to hurry since we must be home to greet him as I'm certain he's on his way to our house.'

But Elizabeth was not prepared to just let it go like that. She had often wondered about Tom and her husband and how, as incredible as it appeared to be, they seemed to be able to read each other's thoughts at times, and judged the moment right to discuss it with Paul. Almost reluctantly, at her continuous insistence, he tried to explain what he himself did not fully understand.

She listened spellbound as he described the many instances this had happened, particularly at moments of danger, or sadness or extreme joy, prompting Elizabeth to silently wonder if her brother-in-law could possibly have been aware of the previous hectic night that she still felt in her loins, and blushed slightly at the thought!

Paul believed it was a special sort of gift that they had somehow inherited, but warned Elizabeth not to discuss it with anybody else, since there were so many malicious tongues about looking for any opportunity to point the finger at innocent people, accusing them of witchcraft or sorcery or some other heretical practices.

'And I mean nobody, Elizabeth,' he added with emphasis, 'and that includes priests and any other cleric. They are often the worst of all, particularly if they can see a chance to gain some form of wealth from the poor, unfortunate victim!'

Somewhat shocked by the vehemence of Paul's outburst, she reminded him of Canon Matthew, and how kind he had always been to him, not forgetting his friend, Brother Simon, with whom he still corresponded occasionally, forcing him to amend his view a little. However, he continued by saying that even though he liked and respected these two clerics enormously, he still would not tell them about that particular thing, feeling that even they could possibly draw false conclusions, and made her promise to keep it to herself.

By the time they had finished their discussion, the coach was swinging into the gateway of The Willows, and they were greeted a minute later by Mr Laverstock and Mrs Spinner at the main door. To their delight, a blazing log fire greeted them in the living room, where they were shortly served a hot broth with a hunk of fresh bread and a good ale to wash it down. Elizabeth tried not to look surprised when an hour or so later, after a loud knocking at the door, Mr Laverstock came into the room to announce a 'Mr Thomas Rollesby'.

It did not take Tom long to realise that Elizabeth was now fully aware of the communication gift he and his brother shared, and he too cautioned her to keep it to herself. 'The womenfolk close to us sense it, you know Paul,' he continued. 'Margaret was just the same, and I believe Lady Mortimer has also tumbled to it.' Then, realizing what he had implied, he immediately added, 'She has almost been a mother to the children, especially young John.' He was about to say more, but then suddenly changed the subject to explain how he had come to visit them, after the ship bringing him back to England had been forced by a storm and fierce currents to land at Southampton. After helping the constable of Portchester Castle with the arrangements for the captives on board to be taken to London, he had decided on the spur of the moment to pay them both a surprise visit in their new home. Once in Salesburye he had been directed to Longeford.

'Everybody in the village seems to know where the Rollesby family lives,' he had added, grinning at them both.

He then talked for a while about the skirmish in Calais, as he called it, but as usual played down his role, saying how pleased he was to be back, unscathed and away from it all. Afterwards he began to politely question them about their activities of the last months until Elizabeth began to yawn and suggested that perhaps since it was so late, they should discuss that the next day, and left them to help Mrs Spinner prepare the guest room while the two brothers drank a hot grog and talked about old times.

The following morning after a hearty breakfast, at Elizabeth's suggestion, it was decided that Paul should show Tom around Salesburye, especially since it was a Tuesday, one of the weekly market days.

Once clear of Longeforde and on the Wilton-Salesburye road, even though they rode slowly as Paul was describing the progress of his business and some ideas of how to develop it in the future, in what seemed only to be a few minutes they passed through Fysherton Anger and shortly afterwards trotted along the cobblestoned Fysherton Street on the western outskirts of the city. Tom noted the considerable building activity that seemed to be in progress on both sides of the street and Paul explained how the city was quickly growing and expanding outside the original limits, above all in that particular area. He pointed out it was mainly inns and taverns that were being built for the multitude of visiting merchants and other travellers, and it was there they left their horses in a good, reliable stables he regularly used, only a stone's throw from the River Avon.

Within minutes, in spite of the bustling crowd of people, they were in the city close to St Thomas's Church, and could already hear the lowing of cattle and bleating of sheep from the huge market that extended to the north, east and south side of it.

'Watch your purse, Tom,' Paul warned his brother. 'Unfortunately we are not spared the usual number of pickpockets and other ruffians to be found in all cities, particularly on market days and the times of the major fairs!'

'Have no fear, Paul,' Tom replied laughing. 'I never carry much money on me, and I think the pair of us should be able to handle most situations anyway, don't you?'

Nodding and grinning as Tom demonstratively touched the hilt of his sword and dagger handle, Paul began to show him all that the city had to offer, beginning with the market-place. Rounding the churchyard walls they came immediately to the market cross, the centre for all dealing in foodstuffs and household goods. The whole area was packed with people jostling to find bargains on the rows of stalls offering fruit, vegetables, bread, milk, cheese, nuts, fish, poultry, meat and a host of other food items, as well as ironmongery, shoes and miscellaneous leather articles, bottles, pots and pans, barrels and other wooden utensils. They slowly made their way through the crowds, stopping to sample a piece of cheese or to listen to and enjoy the bargaining and bantering of the market traders with their customers.

As they reached more or less the centre of the market-place they saw a group of people standing around a pillory in which an unfortunate woman was standing fastened, bent forward, firmly secured by the wooden bar over her neck and wrists. Getting closer, they saw hanging from the lower bar was a sign with the bailiff's seal on it, which stated her crime to have been repeated short-weighting of her bread, punished with a fine and twelve hours in the pillory. She was trying to ignore the jeers and jibes of some of the younger children – merely standing there was a sufficient humiliation, never mind the aching back, arms and legs – but she was having to endure much more! She was not unattractive, and an unkempt brute of a man, probably about thirty years old, was standing close behind her, roughly handling her breasts and trying to force one hand under her skirts, between her legs. In spite of her anguished protests, nobody went to help her, afraid to confront the ignorant but powerful lout who was abusing her.

Tom took one look at Paul, muttering, 'My God, how I hate these animals,' and pushed his way quickly around to the other side of the pillory, closely followed by his brother. Seeing his size and the look on his face, the crowd parted and drew back out of the way as Tom seized the man's arms in a vice-like grip, forcing him to release his hold on the woman, turned him round and struck his face once with his open hand with such a force that he went spinning to the ground at the feet of two young men who were apparently friends of his. They helped him back on his feet, then shaking his head and snarling with rage at the affront, not used to being challenged, he drew a dagger and waved it menacingly at Tom. Encouraged by what he believed to be safety in numbers, the ruffian slowly approached with his companions behind him, also similarly armed, wondering why this very large man stood his ground and merely smiled at him.

Tom quietly said to Paul, who had already drawn his sword, that he shouldn't kill anybody, but merely try to keep the riff-raff out of his way until he had dealt with the leader. He then undid his belt, dropped his own sword and dagger to the ground, and in a loud, clear voice said:

'Boy, I could kill you in three seconds if I chose to use my weapons, but you are not worth it. If you leave peacefully now, we can perhaps forget what you have done. But if you try to use that dagger on me I am going to break your arm and give you a beating you'll never forget. You others there, keep out of it or you will be run through by my brother here, who is itching to keep in practice.'

Paul moved to one side of his brother and signalled with his sword to the others to move away, and they, sensing already that they were completely out of their class, needed little encouragement to abandon their so-called leader to his fate, sheathed their weapons and distanced themselves from danger. The leader, however, feeling committed to some kind of action, and not wanting to lose face in front of his companions and the silent crowd of people that had gathered round, drew closer to Tom, making slow circular movements with the dagger, hoping perhaps that he could call his opponent's bluff and that he would back down at the last minute. On this occasion, however, his luck ran out. There was a flash of movement as Tom's massive hand closed on the lout's wrist, the dagger clattered on the ground, followed by a sharp crack and a scream as the arm was jerked and broken, and a second later the man was lifted up high in the air and then flung down to the ground with terrible force. He lay still. Tom dropped a silver coin next to him and pointing to the two friends, told them it was for the surgeon's bill. The crowd, who was slowly regaining courage now that the danger was over, watched in awe, and as Paul sheathed his sword, Tom picked up his belt, buckled it on and walked to a market stall selling hot grog.

The woman at the stall refused to accept any money for the grog, having witnessed what had just happened. She watched Tom intently with more than admiration in her eyes as he walked back to the woman in the pillory and held the beaker carefully as she gratefully drank the hot, refreshing contents. He then took a clean piece of linen from his doublet pocket, wiped her mouth gently, dried the tears from her face and tried to comfort her a little, quietly adding that he would be back later to see that she was not further molested. As he and Paul moved away from the pillory, a gap appeared as if by magic in the throng of people milling around, to make room for the fearsome strangers, and once clear, the whole situation became the topic of the day for most of them, particularly those who had been about to go to the assistance of the unfortunate woman in the pillory!

Deciding that it was the right moment for some refreshment, Paul led his brother to a small but busy inn called the Blue Boar in a narrow side street close to the corn market on the north side of the market square. A table was free in one corner of the room and once seated, Paul ordered two ales and a hunk of chestnut pie from an attentive server who had been standing by the fire warming her hands.

It was far from an elegant establishment, but Paul knew from previous experience that the ale was good and the freshly made pies were always excellent, as he had mentioned to Tom when they sat down. Clearly, Tom's thoughts were still in the market-place as he sat there silently looking around him at the throng of people seated at the other tables or standing at the counter, all appearing to be talking at once. Paul waited patiently for his brother's comment.

'You know, Paul,' he eventually said, 'that woman somehow reminded me of Margaret. She was so helpless and when I saw what that swine was doing to her I could have killed him. Do you think she was really guilty of cheating with false weights? She didn't look the type, in my opinion, and I still don't believe she deserved such a punishment, whatever she did or was supposed to have done!'

Paul looked at his brother closely, smiling inwardly, realising that even if the woman was guilty, Tom would find some excuse or explanation for it. She had certainly made a deep impression on him, and only later in the day was to discover its extent. Before he could reply, the server appeared with two large mugs of ale and the pie. She thankfully pocketed the groat Paul generously slipped to her in payment, before moving away quickly to another table.

'Who knows, Tom?' Paul replied. 'It may well have been a false judgement or the work of a malicious competitor who bribed the bailiff. Unfortunately, one can never be totally sure these days. Corruption seems to be the norm in so many aspects of our society no matter where you look. The values which were so important for us appear to have little worth today.'

Tom nodded in agreement, took a bite out of his pie and a moment or two later began to question his brother on what else was to be seen in Salesburye. He asked if the watercourses they had already seen ran through the whole city, and finally added that they should perhaps buy a little gift for Elizabeth before they eventually returned to Longeforde. In fact, he did everything possible to change the subject!

After their snack, they walked around to the eastern side of the market-place to look at the bishop's guildhall more closely, an impressive two-storeyed, stucco-faced, long building with a series of small shops built against both sides of it. Paul explained that the bishop was not only the main landlord of the city, but also gained considerable revenue from the market tolls, fines levied on traders breaching market rules (like the poor woman in the pillory) and other taxes called 'tallages' that he imposed on all citizens, not forgetting of course the fortune he made from his flocks of sheep. He was, of course, grateful that the bishop had personally officiated at their wedding, but felt nevertheless that it was inappropriate for churchmen to be so wealthy when there was so much poverty and misery around them, particularly, he added, when one considers some of the main tenets of Christianity. But, he concluded, that was enough philosophy for the day since there was still a great deal to be seen in the city!

Walking past several rows of food tradesmen's stalls: Butcher Row, Fish Row, Ox Row, Oatmeal Row, each with its own very distinctive smell and targeted by the city's stray dogs and cats, watching carefully where they trod to avoid not only the abundant traces of animal excrement but also scraps of meat or fish that had either fallen off the stalls or been deliberately thrown on the ground, Paul steered his brother around to the centre of all the wool and cloth trading on the eastern side of the market-place. Like everywhere else it was packed with people either looking for a bargain or traders anxious to sell their remaining stocks of all possible grades of wool or bales of cloth or whole ranges of yarn. There were also some stalls laden with imported dyes mainly from France or Italy as well as ample stocks of saffron from Essex and other products used in the fulling and weaving processes.

Paul described the various steps in clothmaking and crossing over one of the many city watercourses pointed out the rows of workshops and yards behind the yarn market, bustling with people engaged in all these production processes. They watched both men and women working the rough cloth with icy water and fuller's earth, thankful that they themselves did not have to earn a living with such an occupation. Paul told his brother that he was sure one day a much more effective way would be found to pound the cloth that would both speed up the process and eliminate the awful working conditions of the current system, and already had some ideas how it might be done. However, noting that Tom's thoughts appeared to be elsewhere, he changed the subject and suggested they could perhaps explore the area leading to Grencrofte Street and the Winchester Gate, a little further east, where he believed the Epiphany fair was still running, not mentioning they would need to walk along 'Love Street' to get there!

While strolling slowly along Silver Street, stopping from time to time to watch the silver and goldsmiths inside the shops busy at work making jewellery, table ornaments and other fine things, Tom began to talk about his children. Eric continued to make good progress with his studies, so Lady Mortimer had recently told him. He was quickly growing up, and from what Tom could see looked as if he took more after Paul, and would probably be the scholar of the family. He had made sure he could handle a longbow, he added, but although he certainly had talent with the weapon, he did not appear to have any real interest in developing it. He was not exactly a pacifist, he added, grinning at his brother, but he may have more brains than his uncle! Margaret was now living with the Dexters, where John and Annie kept a good eye on her, and Lady Mortimer visited her regularly to make sure her studies were not neglected. But, Paul learned, Margaret was not an easy child at the moment. She had the temperament of a wild stallion, he added, and had she been a man would undoubtedly have become a famous warrior. Yet she had nevertheless inherited the warmth and gentleness of her mother, and might well grow up to become even more beautiful. Perhaps her rebelliousness was just a phase, he sighed, which hopefully would soon pass. Even though Margaret frequently appeared to handle the young Dexter boy terribly, he said, Robert seemed to accept her tantrums patiently and was always there if she needed help. John, the baby of the family, apart from being spoiled by Mrs Galston and the manor house servants, was making fine progress. He was extremely robust, very large for his age – looking more like a four-year-old than eighteen months – and Lady Mortimer treated him almost as if he were her own child. He was the spitting image of his father, Tom added proudly, and he really looked forward to the time when he could teach him all the things a young man needed to know.

Then, to Paul's concern, almost as if he had had a premonition,

Tom suddenly seized his arm and made him swear to take good care of his youngest son, if anything should happen to him. Once again, Paul assured him that he should not concern himself about that, and asked him directly if he was suffering from some illness or other that made him so unsure about the future, reminding Tom of their earlier conversation in Castor after Alice's funeral. Putting one arm around his brother's shoulder and squeezing him slightly, Tom smiled and replied, 'I've never been fitter, Paul and maybe I'll even live to be a hundred.' They both laughed good-naturedly. 'But what about you and Elizabeth?' he continued mischieviously. 'When are you going to make me an uncle, eh?'

A little embarrassed, Paul told him not to worry about that, but to just be more patient. It was not for the want of trying, he added, and they both began to chuckle.

By now they were out of Silver Street and Paul judged that by the number of women of doubtful virtue that were standing around in small groups, laughing and flirting with potential customers, they must have reached Love Street. They were soon noticed and then surrounded by a group of them, hoping that at least 'one of the fine-looking gentlemen' would be interested in their charms! But they were out of luck. Neither Paul nor Tom could be tempted, and extricating themselves from the hungry clutches of the street whores, they quickened their pace, making for the Epiphany fair that spread from Grencrofte Street right up to the city boundary leading to the Winchester Gate, drawn by the sound of musicians, the shouting of tumblers and street acrobats demonstrating their various skills, the delicious smell of grilled meat, and what sounded like the occasional roaring of a bear.

Although the fair was almost over – it was scheduled to close on the following Saturday – the whole area was packed with people, many of whom had travelled from abroad either to sell their wares or buy from the huge selection of merchandise, which included agricultural produce, livestock, cloth, wool, and luxuries of all descriptions. Paul explained that there were five such fairs in the year, the others being held in March, Whitsun, September and November. They were all extremely important, particularly for business contacts and the exchange of ideas and new methods.

They saw many beggars and other impoverished people including young children, most of whom, in spite of the weather, were barefoot and scantily clad, either standing and asking passers-by for alms or moving around the food stalls, hoping that they might be able to pick up some of the leftovers. They stopped to eat a slice of roasted ox served on a bread trencher from one of the numerous meat stalls, observing the entertaining hustle and bustle around them, but saddened a little by the number of poor people they saw.

'My God, Paul,' Tom commented, 'even though we have had our share of ups and downs, you and I, we've almost always had enough to eat and a roof over our heads at night. Just look at some of these wretches here! Most of them are as thin as rakes, and will be lucky to survive the winter.'

'I know, Tom,' Paul replied. 'It has also given me a lot to think about and be grateful for our many blessings. It all seems so unnecessary when you think about it. We've got problems to find enough people to do the work that has to be done in all the estates and workshops, and in spite of all the campaigns you and others like you are fighting abroad from time to time, nothing changes for the better. In fact, on the contrary, the living conditions of the vast majority of the people appear to be getting worse each year. I was just talking to Elizabeth about it not so long ago.'

Before his brother could comment, a street urchin not more than six or seven years old who had been gradually sidling closer and closer to the stall, suddenly snatched the remnants of Tom's trencher from the counter top and raced off with it. Not sure what he had stolen, Paul immediately shouted out, 'Hey, stop that thief!' before his brother could stop him. The boy was tripped by an alert merchant and he fell to the ground, rolled and twisted like an eel, sprang to his feet and was about to sprint away when unfortunately for him a passing bailiff on a daily patrol around the fair grabbed hold of his smock and held him fast.

'Now what have you been up to, me lad?' the bailiff bellowed at him, shaking the terrified youngster who was still holding the piece of bread tightly in his right hand, trying hard not to burst into tears. 'What have you been thievin' today, eh?'

Both Tom and Paul by this time had reached the bailiff and Paul, now fully understanding the situation and feeling sorry for the urchin, quickly explained that it was all a misunderstanding; he hadn't realised that his brother had given the boy the bread. Seeing him suddenly running away, he added, he had assumed the boy had stolen something, but that was not the case as one could now see. Then, crouching down to look the young boy in the eyes, he smiled, gently removed the bailiff's hand from the child's smock, smoothed it down, apologised for his mistake, took hold of his free hand and stood up.

'Thank you for your help and attentiveness, bailiff,' he said. 'You are a credit to the city.' Paul slipped a silver groat into the man's hand, and accompanied by Tom who had been watching with a twinkle of amusement in his eyes, admiring the smooth way his brother was handling it all, led the boy by the hand back to the meat stall. While Tom ordered another slice of ox, Paul was reassuring the youngster not to be afraid, and that after he had eaten he would be free to go whenever he wished. Wide-eyed, the urchin nodded silently, wondering if he was dreaming it all when Tom handed him the succulent meat and told him that it was for him and he should eat it slowly.

In spite of Tom's well-meant advice, the meat and bread were consumed with great speed, and after wiping his mouth and chin with a grimy sleeve of his smock, the boy looked up at them both, and asked if he could do anything for them in return, indicating with his head the small wood across the field alongside the city wall. Horrified, the two brothers exchanged glances, understanding only too well what the child had offered, and then Paul immediately replied that they wanted nothing in return and he was free to go home.

'Don't have no home, mister,' the boy retorted. 'I sleep anywhere I *kin* find if it's quiet an' dry!'

'What about your parents?' Paul enquired.

'Don't have no parents,' the boy answered. 'Me mum an' dad are both dead.'

'What's your name, boy?' Tom suddenly asked.

'Marky.'

'Marky who?' Paul asked.

'Don't know, mister!'

'Would you like to come home with us, Marky? We don't live so far away from Salesburye, and if you don't like our house you can leave whenever you want. What do you say?'

Tom, somewhat surprised, looked at his brother questioningly, but said nothing, waiting for the youngster's reply. There was no immediate agreement from Marky. He thought for a moment, asked what would be expected of him and only when satisfied that there appeared to be no hidden catches in the offer, he smiled for the first time, shook Paul's hand and agreed, while Tom, grinning at the youngster's precocity, remained silent.

Since the afternoon was well advanced and Paul wanted to return home before nightfall, he told Marky that they should leave the fair now and go and collect their horses from the stables in Fysherton Street, which was on the other side of the city. As they got closer to the market-place, Tom took Paul totally by surprise by telling him that he would stay the night in Salesburye since he had some unfinished business to attend to, and would return to Longeforde the next day. Seeing Paul's confusion, he quickly reminded him of what happened at the pillory and that somebody needed to help the woman when she was released. Besides, he added with a grin, it was probably better that he was alone when he explained to Elizabeth about the young guest he had brought home with him!

Nodding his head in silent agreement, Paul told him to look out for himself and with the street urchin in tow behind him, slowly made his way around the market-place while Tom walked purposefully towards the pillory.

28

A New Start

There was still at least an hour to go before the woman was to be released, and after satisfying himself that she had not been molested by anybody, Tom walked round in front of her, smiled and spoke a few encouraging words before telling her he would be back when she was released. Her face had lit up when she suddenly saw him standing there, and she moved her head slightly in acknowledgement before he moved away, watching him until he was out of sight. The old woman who had given Tom the glass of grog earlier was also watching him attentively and sighed a little, wishing she were thirty years younger!

Tom returned to the Blue Boar which was much quieter than earlier that day, ordered a hot grog and sat there alone in a corner, mulling over in his mind what he was going to do when the woman was released and what were his true feelings in the matter. If he was honest, he mused, he found her very attractive and he had been without a woman since Margaret's death. He knew people gossiped about him and Lady Mortimer, but his conscience was absolutely clear on that one. He admired and respected her immensely, was grateful for her continuous help and support with the children, and although he had sensed on one or two occasions that she might have wished for more than a platonic relationship with him, his loyalty was such to Sir William that it was absolutely out of the question.

But he didn't know this woman in the pillory at all, he reasoned. Of course he had felt sorry for her and certainly would help her to get safely back home, but he would not take advantage of the situation, and besides, he reflected, perhaps there was somebody there waiting for her, and if she really was a criminal, why should he become further involved? His thoughts were then disturbed by the server asking him if he wished for anything else to drink or something to eat, but not feeling particularly hungry he merely ordered another grog to fill in the time.

Nevertheless, time seemed to drag and not able to sit still any longer Tom drained the mug, paid the server and left the inn to stand nearby where he could see the woman in the pillory, waiting impatiently for her release. Eventually, the main door of the bishop's guildhall opened and a uniformed official strolled out carrying a large key. Walking slowly and pompously to the pillory, he unlocked the padlock at the side, lifted the top arm upwards and said in an officious tone that she was free to go, making absolutely no move to help her extricate her head and arms, even though he fully knew that she was so stiff and numb it was almost impossible for her to stand up straight without assistance. He found her plight quite funny, until he realised an extremely large man was at his side who shouldered him out of the way and without a word gently took hold of her arms and slowly eased her out to a standing position.

The official began to protest until Tom told him savagely to get out of his sight before he forgot himself, and the former, quickly taking the course of discretion rather than valour, walked faster than he had done in the previous ten years back to the safety of the guildhall. The woman was shivering with the cold, and the pains running through her shoulders and arms were almost unbearable for a minute or two until the blood circulation began to normalise. Her back was aching terribly from the unnatural position she had been obliged to keep for most of the day and her bladder was almost bursting! All this Tom gathered in the few minutes it took him to return with her to the Blue Boar.

While she scurried off to the privy, he more or less commandeered a table next to the fireplace, threw on a couple of logs stacked nearby, ordered two hot grogs and two pieces of game pie, since he reckoned she must be hungry and he knew she was cold, and waited impatiently for her to return. The server could not have been more helpful. Recognising the plight of Tom's companion, she had gone off to fetch a jug of warm water and a towel and took them out to the woman so she could also freshen up a little. It must have been at least ten minutes later that Tom looked up and saw her standing in front of him, smiling, her cheeks glowing, her long, black hair brushed and shining, looking even more attractive, her eyes twinkling in amusement as Tom got to his feet awkwardly and invited her to sit down at the one available seat.

'Thank you, kind sir,' she replied, and eased herself down onto the chair with a little difficulty. 'My name is Jessica, by the way,' she added, 'and I cannot thank you enough for your help earlier today.'

'It was the least I could do,' Tom said awkwardly, saved from further embarrassment by the arrival of the server with the hot game pie and grog.

The warm fire and the hot food helped Jessica to recover quickly from her ordeal, and after she had finished eating, she sat silently looking at Tom intently as she sipped her grog. Finally breaking the long silence, she asked him his name and where he lived, listening carefully as he also explained how he came to be in Salesburye with his brother, and that his children were back home in Castor. Since he made no mention of his wife, she asked if she was also staying in Longeforde and was genuinely saddened to learn that she had died of the plague some eighteen months or so earlier, noticing how his manner changed when he talked about Margaret.

'Ah, the pestilence,' she commented, 'that has been responsible for so many tragedies, so much suffering and so much inhumanity!'

Tom looked at her closely when he heard the word 'inhumanity', wondering what lay behind it. Noticing the questioning look, Jessica continued, and described her family background. He learnt that her grandparents had been Jewish, and in common with the majority had left England towards the end of the previous century, at the command of King Edward I. She had been born in Flanders – her mother had been a seamstress, her father a Flemish baker – and that was where she had learnt the art of making bread and a selection of sweetmeats. The family business had prospered, and although her father did not have the Jewish faith, he mixed freely with his wife's friends and the local Jewish community. That was how she had learnt what happened in some other countries where the plague first appeared. Jews were frequently blamed as being responsible for the terrible disease, often encouraged by so-called Christian priests and other members of the clergy, and were brutally murdered by mobs of townsfolk. The same thing happened in Flanders when the Black Death arrived, she continued. Her mother was whipped to death by a group of 'flagellants' led by the local pastor who knew only too well that she was Jewish, but whose real reason was that she had refused his many improper advances! Her father had tried to protect her, but had been beaten to the ground and badly injured. When he recovered, determined to leave Flanders and hopefully to escape the plague and further persecution, they managed at great expense to buy their passage on a ship sailing for Southampton, subsequently making their way to Salesburye and eventually opening a small baker's shop.

Within a short time they were extremely successful, to the extent that some other bakers became envious, continuously looking for ways to discredit them in one way or another. Her father had somehow always managed to keep them at bay, but then the plague came to Salesburye and he was one of the many victims buried in a communal grave outside the city. They left her in peace for a few months as she struggled to keep the bakery going, she explained, and all went well until a clerk from the bishop's guildhall paid her a visit. He made a careful inspection of her little shop, checked the weights she used, examined the business records and then tried his luck with her. She had been able to push him away and that was when he told her either she must pay him a half florin each week or he would make sure she would be accused of using false weights. The whole thing would of course be forgotten, he had concluded, if she became his mistress, but otherwise . . .

Tom had been listening carefully to her story, nodding his head sympathetically from time to time, inwardly delighted that she was innocent of the charge that had brought her to the pillory but furious at the injustice of it all.

'Would you recognise that clerk if you saw him again, Jessica?' he asked.

She glanced at him nervously, sensing his anger and guessing what he had in mind, and said she wasn't certain, and besides, as an employee of the bailiff who worked for the bishop, he was protected by an extremely powerful patron. Without really concrete proof of corruption, a stranger like himself in a situation involving a foreigner like herself – half Jewish at that – would not have a chance, she concluded. Then, touching his arm gently and looking him full in the eyes, she said pleadingly:

'Please, Thomas, I want to forget it all. Thank you for everything. You have been so kind to me. I'm truly grateful but please do not get involved with the city authorities, it's simply not worth it!'

Seeing her genuine concern, he calmed down, took a deep breath and reluctantly agreed to let the matter drop, to her obvious relief. He smiled and asked her if she would like anything else to eat or drink. She politely declined, saying she ought to return home now since she was feeling tired after the hectic events of the day, and while he was paying the server she wondered a little apprehensively how things were going to end. He was a very attractive man, appeared to like her, clearly was kind and generous, but she felt somehow nervous of his strength and the power that she sensed lay within him. On the other hand, she had never met a man like him before, and if he should make the right moves she was not sure how she would react. Certainly not how she had handled the clerk!

All such thoughts were quickly dispelled from her mind when they reached the small bakery shop. The door was not properly closed and as they went inside, in spite of the failing light, it was clear to see that it had not only been plundered, but systematically destroyed, including the oven and all the other equipment in the back room leading out to the yard. The shock was such that she could only stand stock-still and stare blankly at the desolation around her, until overcome by emotion she began to sob disconsolately, sinking slowly to the ground, holding her head with both hands. Tom sat down beside her, put his arm around her shoulders, held her closely to him, gently rocking, and did his best to calm and comfort her for a while. Seeing a narrow staircase in one far corner, he slowly extricated his arm and stood up, saying he would be back in a minute. Quickly, he mounted the stairs. A similar state of devastation was to be found in the two minute bedrooms upstairs. Everything was smashed to pieces – beds, chests, chairs and water jugs. What few clothes had been in a chest were ripped up into small pieces and lying on one of the beds on top of the bedding, which smelled of urine and was covered with human excrement. There was nothing of any value to be seen and so Tom assumed that if there had been anything, the people responsible would have stolen it, so he made his way back down the stairs.

'Well, one thing's for sure, Jessica,' he said. 'You can't stay here for the night. It's even worse upstairs. Nothing has been spared and the swine have even used it as a privy. Let's get the hell out of here!'

He hauled her gently up from the floor, wiped her tear-stained cheeks, smoothed her long black hair from her face, and in spite of her mild protests led her slowly out of the shop to the street outside. Holding her closely to him, he guided her across the market-place towards the high street, guessing that there must be some kind of respectable inn where they could at least overnight. Within a few minutes they had found The George, and Tom soon had two, comfortable single rooms organised. He only left Jessica – promising he would fix everything the next day – when she was more settled after drinking a strong nightcap and he was satisfied she would sleep.

He lay awake for at least an hour, wondering how he could best persuade her to leave Salesburye with him, and when sleep eventually came the problem was still not resolved!

At breakfast the following morning Jessica was unusually silent, and Tom could see that understandably she was still suffering from the previous day's events, no doubt worried about the future since she had yet again lost everything. Determined to clear away the depression, he informed her that the first thing they were going to do was to buy some clothes, and before she could object, he more or less swept her to her feet, paid for the accommodation and led her to the largest drapers he could find in the high street.

'Don't you worry about the cost,' he reassured her, 'it's absolutely no problem at all for me.' He instructed an assistant to help Jessica find two complete outfits. He enjoyed watching her as her mood gradually changed while she tried on various dresses and mantles, looking first in the mirror to check the effect and asking Tom what he thought until eventually the final choice was made. At his suggestion, she changed into one set of the new clothes and while the assistant was folding the rest into a linen bag, he told her how beautiful she looked and then asked her if she would like to stay for a few days with him at his brother's house in Longeforde, to give her a chance to decide what to do. She couldn't possibly return to the bakery, he added, and unless she had close relatives or other friends in Salesburye with whom she would prefer to stay, he was sure that was the best solution.

He waited apprehensively for her reaction and reply. After a moment's thought she confirmed what he had guessed (and hoped for), that she was quite alone in the city, and provided there were no strings attached, she would be glad to accept his offer, and would repay him fully for all the expenses he had so far incurred as soon as possible.

Happy that she was over the first hurdle, as they were walking to the stables in Fysherton Street he talked a great deal about his brother Paul and wife Elizabeth, whom he was sure she would like and would certainly make her feel at home. As they were riding slowly away from the city precincts he was very conscious of her closeness, smelling her perfume from time to time, and her hair as the breeze wafted it intermittently into his face; and she enjoyed, too, his warmth and the feel of his body behind her as he moved rhythmically with the movement of the horse. His down-to-earth comments about what they saw on the short journey made her laugh frequently and forget her troubles, making her happier than she'd been for months.

Seeing a small boy holding out both arms for balance as he made his way precariously along an uneven, stone wall reminded Tom of the young Marky and he recounted the story of how they had got to know him in the fairground, and how Paul had persuaded him to go back to Longeforde with him, only omitting the offer the young urchin had made to them both.

'It won't be so easy with that one,' he added. 'He's been used to the freedom and the harshness of life in the streets, and will certainly have some problems to settle down to a more normal life. I'm sure he's also suffered a lot. In a way, he reminded me a bit of a caged animal, suspicious of everything and everybody, but that boy's got a way with him that makes him somehow more special than most.'

They talked about Marky for a while longer, in fact until they came to Longeforde, and minutes later they were trotting up to the main entrance of The Willows, totally unaware of the drama that had been enacted there the previous evening.

Not surprisingly, as Paul later recounted the story, Elizabeth had not expected him to bring a street urchin home, particularly one that was covered with lice, probably hadn't washed for weeks, had little respect for adults and used language that would make a soldier blush! There had been absolute chaos in the house, especially when she had insisted that before he put on any clean clothes (and apart from a smock there were no other garments small enough for him), he had to be scrubbed from head to foot. Since Paul had brought him home, she insisted he did the washing and besides, Marky wouldn't go near her at first. While Paul was busy trying to do that, Elizabeth began to prepare a meal for them all, far from happy with her husband, Paul had added, grinning wistfully.

Eventually, they all sat down to eat, and since the boy was hungry, he was more or less prepared to follow their wishes at that stage, but only more or less, Paul continued somewhat ruefully! Between mouthfuls of food, Marky had told them a little about his life in Salesburye with a gang of abandoned children and a pickpocket that had taught them how to steal purses and other items from unwary visitors to the city. They had had to learn how to fend for themselves and were beaten by the man if they brought nothing back to him. Sometimes, he said, they had to do other things also. At this point, Elizabeth, reared in a wealthy family, without any personal experience of such a life of misery and poverty, visibly softened in her attitude to Marky and asked him what sort of things he had had to do. She listened horrified as he began to describe falteringly, in a simple and direct language, the bodily abuses he had suffered and some acts he had been forced to perform. Elizabeth had looked at her husband from time to time, hardly able to believe what she was hearing. Marky clearly was not expecting any sympathy, giving the impression that if you were poor it was apparently part of your fate, and certainly gave no signs of being ashamed.

Once the meal was over, the difficulties further developed when Elizabeth led Marky to a small bedroom, explaining that it was bedtime, he should sleep there and they would see him in the morning. He had never slept in such a bed before and appeared to have a fear that he was going to be left in a locked room as a sort of prisoner. It was only by leaving the door wide open that she could persuade him to lie down and sleep, and he had looked at her with large, worried and puzzled eyes as she leant over him, gave him a kiss on his forehead and wished him goodnight.

She and Paul had talked a long time that evening about the young guest, and it was clear to both of them that should Marky stay with them, life was not only going to be very different, but they would have a real challenge on their hands. Whereas Elizabeth had initially been angry with Paul, she had begun to understand his sympathy for the child and felt already a considerable warmth for him, in spite of his wildness. She saw much better than Paul that it would take a long time to heal the wounds Marky bore, and tried to make him realise that it might require some years of patience and understanding.

When Marky first saw Tom the next day his face lit up, recognising immediately the man who had handed him that slice of meat and bread at the fairground. Jessica initially was pretty well ignored by the street urchin as she stood a little awkwardly at Tom's side, wondering how she would be received and whether she was doing the right thing or not. But she need not have worried. Even though Elizabeth had expected Tom, when Paul had explained his brother's absence, she had suspected that he might not be alone, and warmly welcomed Jessica, leading her and Tom into the living room, delighted that her brother-in-law appeared to have at last found a companion.

Paul was also relieved to see his brother, hoping that perhaps he might be able to help him a little with Marky during the first few days of what he judged was going to be an extremely difficult period of rehabilitation. The two women felt comfortable with each other from the first moment of meeting, and what could have been a tense situation was from the outset a very harmonious relationship, in some strange way helped by the problem of young Marky.

The young boy seemed to recognise the hidden strength and inner power of Tom and reacted accordingly with him. Tom for his part, in his unique way, began to lead him towards a more disciplined approach to life, using archery lessons for the first steps. He made him a bow and a dozen arrows and demonstrating infinite patience, within ten days laid the foundations to ensure that, with continuous practice, Marky would become an accomplished archer. It was the first time in his life that anybody, other than his mother when she was alive, had ever taken time to teach him anything and not expected more than respect and recognition of the kindness that was being offered in return.

Jessica had watched Tom handling the boy, marvelling at the combination of gentleness and firmness with which he managed to win Marky over. He was never unfair, but once a position was established, she saw how Marky understood immediately that no other conduct would be tolerated. Paul also began to have some success with the boy whom he came to discover had an incredible curiosity about almost everything, was eager to learn as much as he could, gradually, and very, very slowly, came not only to trust him and Elizabeth, but even signalled the first signs of affection. For Elizabeth it was a wonderful day she would never forget.

On that particular day Marky had slipped on an icy patch – it had snowed slightly in the morning – and cut his right hand. He had not cried like most children even though it must have been painful, but merely stood there with the trace of tears in his eyes, watching the blood course down his fingers and drip onto the snow. Elizabeth had been with him in the garden when it happened and without making a big fuss she led him gently into the house, wiped his hand clean and carefully bound it with a strip of linen as her own mother had taught her years previously. She crouched down on the floor to tie it more easily and had just finished when Marky put his arms around her neck, gave her a hug, thanked her and ran off to find Paul.

During the relatively short period of time that Tom and Jessica stayed with them, the two women developed an excellent relationship with each other. Jessica showed Elizabeth the way to bake bread and prepare good sweetmeats, while Elizabeth taught Jessica a great deal about garden herbs and vegetables, an area in which she had become quite expert. They naturally talked a great deal, and Jessica discussed her uncertainty about the future, explaining that she liked Tom 'more than a little' but was still not sure what he had in mind. He had not imposed himself on her in any way, she explained, wanting her to have sufficient time to decide what she really wanted to do, she supposed, but sometimes one required someone to help the process along a bit, she sighed. Tom had already announced that he must soon return to Castor to his duties there and of course his children, but had not really invited her to join him.

Elizabeth took the opportunity to give Jessica more background on her brother-in-law, telling her about the role he played in her wedding, the respect he clearly had from the nobility which even included the Prince of Wales and the king himself, and other things she had learned from Paul. She should not have concerns about this man, she added, but believed, surprisingly enough, he could be a little shy with women who really interested him, and with a knowing look, she concluded by saying, 'He almost certainly needs a bit of encouragement from you, just to clear the air, I'm sure. But don't wait too long, Jessica!'

Unknown to the two women, a similar conversation had taken place between the two brothers earlier the same day, when Tom had asked Paul what he thought about Jessica, and did he think she would return with him to Castor if he asked her, and a host of other questions. What had bothered him most of all, Paul learned, was that even though Margaret on her deathbed had begged him to take another wife, he had more or less refused to consider the idea. He could never forget her, he added with passion, and as much as he was now attracted to Jessica, it would not be fair to her if the picture and memories of his first wife were to remain so firmly and clearly in his mind!

It had taken Paul some considerable time to convince his brother that nevertheless he should not lose this opportunity to give his children a mother again and to begin to lead a more normal life once more. He may never meet a woman like Jessica again, he continued, pointing out that Margaret had understood his needs only too well, and she herself had wanted him to take another woman. It was not being at all disloyal, he had emphasised, and had concluded by saying, 'Tom, you have no reason to forget Margaret. You loved each other and produced four children, and in spite of the pestilence, three of them survived and look like leading happy and successful lives. This is something to be proud of and thankful for. But life must continue. Memories remain but the future must also be handled. You've told me about your feelings for Jessica, and judging by the way she looks at you, I think she feels the same way. Don't waste this wonderful opportunity. Begin to live again. Appoach her and ask her if she would like to go back with you to Castor. Tell her why you want her to say yes. Tell her today. Tom, Tom, you're my only brother and I want you to be happy. You've done so much for me, also for Elizabeth whom

I adore. Let me help you now. Go to her, go now before it's too late. It's time you made a new start!'

It had been an emotional discussion, and as Tom took his brother in his arms, he thanked him for everything and then walked away to be alone for a while. Paul watched his brother go and then went to look for Marky to see he was not getting up to any mischief, determined to arrange with Elizabeth an opportunity for Tom and Jessica to spend some time together on their own as soon as possible.

In fact, by the time he was able to talk alone with Elizabeth, it had already been arranged, to his great surprise! She told him that since Marky had so few clothes, she had arranged to visit the seamstress in the village the next morning and she wanted Paul to go with them both. Jessica had agreed to bake some bread then and this would also give Paul's brother some time to get his affairs arranged before he left them. Elizabeth had expected more resistance from Paul since she knew he hated spending time buying clothes, but took his immediate agreement as recognition that he also had a responsibility towards the young Marky.

The next day they returned home well into the afternoon – Elizabeth had ensured that it would take several hours to agree on all the materials, the types of clothes and the cost – and she and Paul pretended not to notice the distinct change of atmosphere between Tom and Jessica, waiting for one or the other to say something. Whether Jessica was flushed from the heat of baking bread or something else was not totally clear, but they both seemed to want to be closer to each other! Even Marky noticed that his 'Uncle Tom' had little time for him when he first scampered into the house.

They did not have to wait long before Tom began falteringly to explain that he had decided to leave for Castor as soon as he had bought another horse – for Jessica – because she was going to leave with him. He added in a rush, that she had agreed to marry him when they got home. The tension was broken by young Marky asking Jessica if she would then be his auntie, and if so, he would like that! After the usual back-slapping but genuine expressions of delight and congratulation, Paul brought out his best wine for them to celebrate, wishing them both all possible happiness for the future.

It was a momentous occasion that marked for both brothers and their families the beginning of a truly new phase in each of their lives, and even though Tom and Paul did not know it, when they embraced the following day before Tom and Jessica left The Willows, it was to be the last time they would see each other.

29

'Marky'

The sudden departure of Tom and Jessica was truly mourned by the young Marky, who had hero-worshipped Tom, and frequently had to be consoled by Paul and Elizabeth in the following days. Paul delayed some planned trips to business contacts so that he could spend more time with the boy and Elizabeth kept an ever-watchful eye on him, trying desperately to win completely his trust and love, but it was not easy. Due to his life in the streets he had built a defensive shell around himself to protect his inner feelings, and although he had begun to open up to Elizabeth in particular, he seemed almost afraid to take it further as if terrified of even more disappointment or pain, in spite of the kindness and affection both she and Paul tried to show him. It was a source of great frustration for her, sometimes leading to a tearful episode when she talked with Paul on the subject, not at all helped by her burning desire and lack of success to have her own child, which led her to feel that she had somehow failed her husband. For whatever reason, she not only was unable to become pregnant but felt now almost rejected by Marky, to whom she tried to transfer her frustrated love. It was an extremely difficult time for all three of them.

The breakthrough first came in spring that year. Marky had been helping Elizabeth to muck-out the stables and feed the two horses, Blackie and Chestnut, both restless for exercise and fresh grass now that the ground was free of any snow or frost. Marky liked horses and willingly helped with those chores, and Paul had promised to teach him to ride that year. Blackie, always difficult with strangers, had got used to Marky and stood patiently in his now clean stall while the youngster, on tiptoes, brushed him. Elizabeth, having finished grooming Chestnut, went to see how he was getting on and startled Blackie as she pushed the door open. He backed suddenly, tossing up his head and accidentally hit Elizabeth with his rump, knocking her out of the stall up against the stone wall on the other side of the stable. Totally unprepared and winded, she took most of the initial impact on her buttocks and back, but as her head snapped back she received a hard blow on the back of her head, and sank unconscious to the ground. Marky pushed the horse back into the stall, fastened the door and ran fearfully over to Elizabeth, who lay crumpled over on one side, with a trickle of blood oozing out of a gash on her head onto a straw bale alongside her.

He was horrified. What if she were dead, he thought! 'It can't be, it can't be,' he had wailed, 'not again,' seeing once more the anguished face of his mother in her death-throes, an image he had managed to put out of his mind after months of trauma a year or so ago. He looked at the blood, remembering how Elizabeth had once bound his hand, and tore a strip of linen off his tunic, tying it around her head to cover the gash. He tried to move her slightly to make her more comfortable but she was too heavy for him, and with his heart pounding in apprehension, he raced back to the house to fetch Mrs Spinner and Mr Laverstock.

Hearing his shouts they were already at the door and when he breathlessly tried to explain what had happened they took one look at each other and then hurried to the stables, fearful of what they might find, with the elderly Mr Laverstock doing his best to keep up with Marky and the housekeeper.

'Well, at least she's breathing,' Mrs Spinner panted, pulling Elizabeth up to a sitting position. She tried to reassure Markie that Elizabeth would be all right, praising him for what he had done to staunch the blood flow. Telling Mr Laverstock to take her by the ankles, she put her arms under Elizabeth's armpits taking most of the weight, and together they staggered back to the house, resting a couple of times, before they managed to lay her on top of the bed, followed anxiously by the young Marky, wanting so much to be able to help somehow. Both he and Mr Laverstock were more or less pushed out of the bedroom while Mrs Spinner undressed Elizabeth, cleaned up her head and face and then covered her with a linen sheet and a heavy sheepskin.

Satisfied she was comfortable and that nothing more could be done until the master returned that evening, Mrs Spinner reluctantly allowed Marky to sit in the bedroom to keep watch, but warned him to keep quiet and to fetch her the moment Elizabeth came round.

Marky's anxious eyes did not leave her face for an instant, watching intently for the least sign of recovery. Eventually his vigil was rewarded with a slight groan from Elizabeth, who then turned her head to one side, slowly opened her eyes and looked directly at Marky. She wondered initially where she was and who was sitting there, as she was suffering from fuzzy vision and a splitting headache. Within a few seconds she was able to focus her eyes normally and smiled at Marky, stretching her hand out from under the covers so that he could hold it, surprised at the intensity of his emotion. His relief that she was conscious was plain to see as tears coursed down his cheeks, dropping onto her face when he leaned over to embrace and cuddle her, sobbing 'You're alive, you're alive!'

The commotion was heard by Mrs Spinner who hurried into the room, smiling broadly when she saw Elizabeth comforting the young Marky, patting him on the back, reassuring him that all was well and he had no need to worry any more. She led him gently outside, promising he could return as soon as she had cleaned and re-dressed the wound, and could stay there until Mr Paul returned, which was in fact where Paul found him later that evening.

From that time onwards, Marky was a different person in terms of his relationship with them both, particularly in the case of Elizabeth, who had now become almost a complete substitute for his dead mother. She too was able to rid herself of the earlier tensions, resulting in a long period of household harmony, in spite of Paul's prolonged absences as he gradually built up a thriving wool brogger's business. He was greatly helped by the early patronage of Canon Matthew and the surviving monks of Titchfield Abbey and was beginning to lay the foundations of a clothmaking dynasty that later generations would further develop.

Paul also made good his promise to teach Marky to ride. It was during a weekend excursion in the summer, by which time he had become relatively competent on a horse, that the youngster was reminded of fearful events that had led to his mother's death, which he then revealed to Paul, anxious to share the horror with someone he could trust and had grown to love. Elizabeth had reluctantly agreed to the two-day trip, understanding that for a young boy the prospect of camping in the open air was the event of the year, and had packed sufficient food and provisions for a week, as Paul had jokingly commented, to ensure that at least they wouldn't go hungry.

They had begun by riding towards Salesburye on the Saturday morning until they approached Fysherton where they swung northwards, following the River Avon. It was a beautiful day with a light breeze that fanned their faces refreshingly as the sun gradually increased its strength and rose slowly over the city on the right. They stopped to admire the impressive skyline of church towers, turrets and fine rooftops, dwarfed by the majestic spire and massive elegance of the cathedral, until Marky's attention was diverted by the squawking and clucking of ducks, paddling in groups up and down the river, expertly avoiding the occasional boat that came downstream. The river seemed to fascinate him and he plied Paul with questions when he spotted a water-wheel on the far bank, wanting to know its purpose, how it worked, to whom it belonged, and how to stop it when necessary, until Paul was forced to admit that he was not an expert on the subject, and they should perhaps continue their journey!

Since the road was extremely busy with travellers on the way to the market, Paul decided to move off the main track and they followed a small trail across fields of lush grass, passing several flocks of sheep under the watchful eye of their shepherds, whom Paul always courteously greeted, much to the surprise of Marky. At around midday, they stopped in the shade of a weeping willow tree by a large pond, and after making the horses secure, ate heartily from the bread and ham that Elizabeth had packed for them, enjoying the food and the idyllic surroundings.

Marky, however, was soon impatient to continue and shortly afterwards they came across a village that he recognised, telling Paul it was called *Littel* Amesburye and that he had once lived there. He immediately began to stutter, started to shiver, and refused to say more. After staring a moment in the direction of the village pond, he spurred Chestnut to a canter, leaving Paul behind him, wondering what had happened. After catching Marky up, they rode in silence for an hour or so along a track that gradually swung slightly towards the west, until Paul saw that the boy was reacting more normally and began to chat with him, careful not to ask any pointed questions.

By now they were out in very open countryside and could see in the distance a group of enormous stone pillars standing quite alone on the highest point of a large tract of moorland. Paul was fascinated to see that two of the pillars were supporting another massive block of stone, like a gateway, and he wondered who could possibly have constructed it and for what purpose in such a desolate area. It was an old shepherd who told them the place was called 'Stone Henge' and that nobody knew why it was there or who built it, but it was best to stay away from it at night, because there were a lot of stories about strange happenings out there.

In spite of the warning from the shepherd, Paul was determined to take a closer look, and although Marky appeared reluctant to go any closer, eventually he persuaded him to gallop with him in a race to the nearest pillar, making sure that he only just beat him, to the boy's intense delight. Making the two horses fast to a nearby bramble bush, they began to explore the whole area around the stone pillars and were disappointed to find, apart from rabbit- and sheep-droppings, nothing other than the traces of relatively large campfires in two or three places in the vicinity. Nevertheless, Paul experienced a strange tingling sensation in his back which he could not explain, making him sense that perhaps there was some element of truth in what the shepherd had said. Seeing that Marky was again extremely nervous, he decided they should leave and look for a comfortable, secluded place to camp for the night before it got dark.

It took them not much more than half an hour to ride down into a valley to the west and climb up a relatively steep hill shrouded with trees, following a small stream that gurgled and splashed its way downwards over a stony bed to the river below. They had the luck to find an opening in the rocky hillside, high enough to stand up in and about three paces deep. It was an excellent, dry, sheltered place to sleep for the night, with good tree cover all around them and within easy reach of the stream. Paul helped Marky to feed and water the horses, and tethered them in a nearby thicket, before beginning their own preparations. He showed Marky how to cut small branches and use them with moss to make a dry base on which they would later sleep with their sheepskin covers, and then began to prepare a fire outside.

Marky watched fascinated as Paul carefully selected the driest wood he could find, built up the branches making sure the thin, drier pieces were at the bottom of the pile, took a small handful of straw-like grass and ignited it with the flint and steel he always carried with him in a small, leather pouch while travelling. He blew the smoking grass gently until it burst into flame, carefully inserted it under the wood and within a few minutes the fire had taken hold. He then placed three thick branches over the fire, using them as a tripod and hung a cooking pot with a little water from the stream in it over the flames. He dropped in first small pieces of salted mutton that Elizabeth had prepared for them, letting them boil for some minutes before adding a selection of vegetables that had been separately packed in one of the saddle-bags. The two of them sat close to the fire, Paul stirring the broth from time to time while Marky, clasping his knees together with both arms, stared into the fire, his thoughts far away. Suddenly, he began to talk and it was then that Paul first heard from Marky the tale of horror that had been bottled up inside him for so long.

Once he started, it gushed out and Paul let him talk without interruption.

As Paul had suspected, Marky couldn't remember much about his father. He had been too young when he went off to the wars, and most of what he did remember was what his mother had told him later. His father had been killed somewhere abroad, Marky had forgotten where, but he remembered how sad his mother had been afterwards, and that there was never much food at home. Their little house was freezing cold in the winter, and he described how he had slept with his mother in front of the fire hearth where she cooked, to keep warm, covered with an old fleece a friendly neighbour had given them.

As he continued to pull out the memories that had been so firmly locked away, in spite of his young years and lack of education, it was a gripping tale, full of pathos. He described how hard his mother had to work, busy the whole day washing other people's clothes and repairing them from time to time. After they had eaten, and that was not every day, he added, she sat in the evenings by candlelight spinning bits of wool she had found in the fields, to make clothes for them both or something she could perhaps sell. She was often worried, he recollected, about how she was going to pay the church tithes and the taxes to the local lord, who seemed to like his mother, he commented innocently, even though she often told Marky how much she hated him.

From the warmth with which the young Marky talked about his mother, it was clear how he had worshipped her and that he had been happy most of the time with the simple, hard life they led together. When he was ill, he explained, his mother knew exactly which herbs to use to make him better, and she was often asked for help by other people in the village when somebody in the family was sick. Sometimes, when they were better, a grateful neighbour gave her a gift of clothing or food, and they all praised her for her knowledge, saying she knew more than any physician.

Then one day a crowd of people came to their little house – people he had never seen before, apart from the village priest who once before had visited them to talk with his mother. He could remember that one clearly, he remarked, because his mother had sent him to play outside while he was there, and she had been so upset later when he returned. They were all shouting at her, he recalled indignantly, calling her a 'witch' and all sorts of other things. She just stood there, not saying a word, not knowing what to do, and they dragged her out of the house. She screamed at them to leave her in peace, but they wouldn't listen, and tears came to his eyes as he tried to find the words to describe how he attempted to free her but was brutally pushed away. All he could do then was cry, he sobbed, and watched in fear and dread as they bound her hands behind her back, put a rope around her neck and led her to the village square, singing and chanting things he couldn't understand.

Paul tried to comfort Marky at this stage, but the boy pushed his arm away, crying, 'Let me finish, let me finish, I must finish it!' Reluctantly, Paul moved away a little and waited for Marky to recover and complete his horrific story. A few minutes passed, and Paul took the opportunity to stir the broth and put some more wood on the fire that had burnt down to glowing embers by this time, while Marky wiped his eyes and finally felt able to continue.

Paul listened aghast as Marky described how they had stripped his mother naked, laughing at her and doing other things to hurt her. How she screamed in pain, but they wouldn't stop, he said, and when he tried to pull one man away from her, he was picked up by another and held so that he couldn't move. They tied her to a stake in the ground near the pond, piled wood all around her, poured pitch onto the wood and set it on fire with a torch one of them was carrying. The priest, he remembered, held a cross tied to a stake in front of her as the flames sprang up, and she screamed in agony for a while until there was silence, apart from the crackling of the burning wood. She had looked at him for a moment before she died, he added, almost choking with emotion, and it was that look he had tried to forget.

They both sat there saying nothing, staring blankly at the fire. Paul did not know what to say or how best to comfort the young boy who had witnessed things no child should see; in fact, things that should never happen, evil deeds for which there was no excuse. Marky felt exhausted but in a way relieved that he had shared his nightmare with somebody else, and then, suddenly aware that he was famished, asked if the broth was ready, giving Paul the opportunity to move and busy himself with their supper.

It was good and in no time at all the cooking pot was empty. After building up the fire, Paul and Marky went over to the stream to wash and clean out the pot while there was still light enough to see what they were doing, and stood for a few minutes looking over the valley towards Stone Henge. The tops of the stone columns were just visible – a light mist was swirling gently over the moor obscuring the lower parts – giving the impression of an ominous presence hovering overhead in the distance. There was a chill in the night air and little resistance came from Marky at Paul's suggestion that he should settle down to sleep, since they were to make an early start the following morning. Covering him with the sheepskin, he watched him with the strongest feeling of affection he had experienced for the boy since he had been living with them, not moving until he was sound asleep, vowing silently to care for the child and protect him as if he were his own son, giving him every possible chance to make his way successfully in this hard and often cruel world. It had taken some time to gain fully the trust of the street urchin he had brought home months before, but now that Marky had unburdened himself of the greatest tragedy of his past, things would be different, he was sure. Ever since Elizabeth's accident in the stables, the relationship between his wife and Marky had been more like mother and child, but there had always seemed to be something preventing a really close tie in his case, for whatever reason. It had probably been as much his own fault as Marky's, he mused, trying to analyse his earlier prejudices and concerns, but that was all over now, and he lay down beside the child he had finally adopted as his son.

Later that night he awoke and saw that Marky was sleeping soundly in spite of the damp cold. He slipped outside to stir up the fire embers, laying sufficient branches over the hot ashes to last until morning, and then his attention was drawn to the other side of the valley by pinpricks of light coming from what he assumed were torches moving slowly around the area of Stone Henge. It was too dark to make out any detail, but it reminded him of a sort of procession. But why there, he thought, as he eased himself as quietly as possible back alongside Marky, wondering what it all could mean. However, sleep soon overcame his curiosity.

The following morning after a light breakfast, once everything was packed away in the saddlebags, they led the two horses down into the valley, mounted and rode alongside the river until they found a track swinging round to the south. Paul wanted to avoid Littel Amesburye at all costs and reckoned they would pass well west of it, needing then to continue for at least a further ten to fifteen miles before picking up the road home to Longeforde. Marky seemed to have completely recovered from the upset of the previous evening, and was reacting quite normally, clearly enjoying the long ride and constantly questioning Paul about everything they saw, hungry for knowledge.

They went through several hamlets and small villages but saw very few people, prompting Paul to describe his experiences of the pestilence in Titchfield and the terrible decimation of the population that resulted in most places. Marky was also able to remember that where he had lived earlier some of his friends had died but he hadn't known what had killed them. He supposed it had probably been the same thing, he added. Paul quickly changed the subject and asked him if he had any idea what he would like to do when he grew up, and was astonished to hear him say he wanted to make water-mills with such determination that he had to be careful not to show any amusement!

They arrived at The Willows by early afternoon – Paul had promised Elizabeth they wouldn't be late – and Paul let Marky describe the trip to her, bubbling over with enthusiasm and excitement, omitting however any mention of passing through Littel Amesburye. It was Paul who later told her when they were alone what he had learned about Marky's past and that he had decided, if she agreed, of course, that they should treat him like a son. She had noticed immediately when they came home that there was a subtle change in the relationship between them both, but had waited for some sort of explanation. Once Paul began to talk openly about it, she smiled, hugged him tenderly, and said that she had waited longingly for the day, and couldn't be happier.

Their life took another direction from then on. Paul continued to work extremely hard and although still frequently travelling to check carefully the wool quality before purchase or supervising the collection and transport to various warehouses that over several years he had had built or initially rented as the volume began to steadily grow, he spent as much time with Marky as he possibly could. His efforts were well rewarded. Although not academically inclined, Marky was very bright and particularly gifted with practical skills combined with a definite mechanical bent. He loved to watch the village blacksmith at work, willingly fetching nails, hammers and other tools for him while he was repairing carriage wheels and broken axles, or making farming implements. He continuously asked the blacksmith questions until he fully understood what he was doing.

If he was not at the blacksmith's, Elizabeth always knew where to find him – either at the cartwright and village carpenter's workshop or playing by the river nearby – and in spite of his protests she made him spend two hours each day learning to read and write. In the winter evenings his favourite occupation was to squat near the fireside and make model boats or carts and carriages with a concentration and skill that made both Paul and Elizabeth wonder. To encourage him, Paul regularly brought fine woodcarving tools, saws, drills, nails and other instruments home with him from his travels, marvelling at his dexterity as he worked steadily to produce at times beautiful models.

The months and the years sped by. Paul and Elizabeth had repeatedly been promising themselves to pay Tom and Jessica a visit, but there was always something to stop them. Elizabeth had managed to become pregnant twice but had unfortunately lost the child each time with miscarriages, to their great disappointment. However, the development of Marky more than compensated for their sad losses, and Elizabeth came to terms with the likelihood that she would never be able to bear a child.

One weekend in the summer of 1355 – Marky was by now thirteen as Paul and Elizabeth had agreed that it was his eighth birthday on that day they decided to adopt him five years earlier – they visited a watermill together near Salesburye. Marky insisted on staying there until he had drawn the various components, asking the miller sufficient questions to understand the wheel gearings and the other mechanisms. He could then hardly wait to get home to begin work on a model. Not more than a week later he proudly showed them both what he had made. He led them down to the river nearby, where he demonstrated to their astonishment that his model was mechanically perfect. One thing then led to another as they were talking, and Paul observed that probably one day other sorts of mechanical contraptions would be made for many of the tasks that required so much manual labour, thinking about his earlier experiences on the Castor and Titchfield demesnes, never dreaming what seed he had planted in the mind of the young Marky!

On 20 September 1355 the Prince of Wales landed at Bordeaux in the *Christopher* leading a fleet of more than two hundred ships carrying a small expeditionary force of less than 3,000 men, shortly to begin an epic *chevauchée* from the Atlantic to the Mediterranean and back. On that same day, Marky showed his father what he had secretly built in one of the garden outhouses. It was a working model of a **fulling mill**! The cornerstone of a future cloth empire had been laid.

On the same day, Elizabeth conceived a child that was to be born on 25 June the following year, a boy they called Simon, and Thomas Rollesby began to write the family chronicle.

30

Jessica

For both Tom and Jesssica, the journey back to Castor after they had taken leave of Paul and Elizabeth was a tense one. They were very much in love with each other but had some concerns for the immediate future. Would Jessica be content with the quiet life he had to offer in Castor, was Tom's main worry, and Jessica continuously wondered how his children would accept her as a replacement for the mother they had adored.

Since Jessica was far from being an accomplished horsewoman and snow was expected at any time, they headed for Southampton, and spent the first night together in a small inn near the quayside, hoping to catch a boat round to either Yermouth or Lowestoft if possible. During the evening meal Tom did his best to reassure Jessica that she was now safe and that she would find Castor a comfortable place to live, and she did her best to put on a brave face.

The decision as to whether they slept together or not was taken for them in that there was only one suitable room available when they arrived, and neither of them felt like searching for other possible accomodation at that time of night, particularly as it was bitterly cold. While they were eating, the innkeeper got a fire going in the bedroom and so it was pleasantly warm when they returned. Tom sat by the fireside while Jessica undressed, only making a move when he heard her slip into bed. He put his valuables in the wooden box at the foot of the bed, carefully placed sword and dagger on a perch within easy reach, hung his clothes on another one next to it, blew out the candle in the lantern the innkeeper had handed to him in the dining room and gently eased himself under the covers alongside her. Before he had time to say a word, Jessica, who had been lying on her back watching him intently as he got undressed, turned towards him, put an arm over his massive chest, and quietly said, with a smile he could just see from the light of the fire, words he would never forget.

'At last, Mr Rollesby, I have you all to myself! I have been waiting for this moment for such a long time!'

Whereas Tom had been a little apprehensive beforehand – he had not made love to anybody since Margaret had died – Jessica's openness, directness and hunger removed any uncertainty on his part. She moved over him, held his face firmly in her hands and kissed him repeatedly, her tongue searching his hungrily, squirming and writhing with passion as Tom caressed her back and buttocks. As he began to move his hands slowly around her she took hold of them and whispered in his ear, 'My turn first, Tom.' She placed his hands alongside his body and began to caress and kiss his chest, moving one hand slowly down over his stomach until her fingers found and closed around his stirring manhood. He had rarely been so sexually aroused as she gently explored his body, touching, soothing, rubbing and then kissing him until he felt he would burst with passion and excitement. At precisely the right moment, she rolled over onto her back, opened her legs slightly and drew his hand to one of her breasts, moaning softly as he stroked the swollen nipple. Tom fought the desire to take her immediately, enjoying instead the beauty and soft contours of her body. Jessica was by now trembling with anticipation, beginning to move her hips and pelvis expectantly, moaning with pleasure as he gently explored her growing dampness. He then pulled her legs apart and slowly penetrated her, thrusting gently until the moment she grasped his buttocks firmly, clearly signalling what she wanted, and they were soon lost in a sea of almost endless passion, pausing to rest briefly between each climax. Then, some time in the early hours of the morning, they tenderly kissed each other before dropping off into a contented sleep.

They slept until relatively late in the morning, and once awake, rekindled the passion of the previous night until Tom reluctantly extricated himself gently from Jessica's embrace, saying he must go down to the quayside and make enquiries for their return to Castor. Once dressed, he first talked with the innkeeper saying that his wife was not to be disturbed before walking the short distance down to the sea, looking out for suitable boats.

The quayside was a hive of activity. War supplies of all descriptions were being offloaded from waggons into large warehouses close to the quay and he stopped to watch cannon (the first he had seen), barrels of powder, lances, longbows, arrows, stones and sacks of quicklime for ballistae being carried or pushed into one or other of the stone buildings, supervised by several men-at-arms. He learned from one of them that three months previously a fleet of Spanish galleys had sailed up the Channel carrying merchandise to Flanders (France had recently concluded a naval treaty with

Castile) and had attacked, captured or sunk several English ships in the process. The king, he was told, was determined to destroy that fleet when it returned in early summer, and supplies were being built up in readiness at all the major ports along the coast. He also saw carpenters at work on at least two ships, building up high forecastles from which missiles would be thrown as well as housing groups of archers, reminding him of his first battle at Sluys, fifteen years before, so many years ago. His thoughts were disturbed by a ship's captain asking if he needed any help and from him he gathered that most of the moored ships were destined for Hythe, Dover and Colchester. However, a small brigantine was scheduled to ferry some horses to Lowestoft later in the day and Tom was able to arrange passage for their two horses and a small cabin for Jessica and himself, albeit at a high price of twenty-five marks, sailing promptly at high tide. As they sailed out of Southampton in the late afternoon, they passed a long line of military ships anchored in readiness, rolling gently in the swell and Tom pointed out some of the familiar landmarks to Jessica who stood at his side leaning on the rails, savouring the fresh breeze, not really listening but happy to have him so close, her body still tingling and glowing from earlier exertions. They were even able to see for an instant the battlements of Portchester Castle caught in the setting sun as the brigantine tacked around Southsea before taking a steady course past Selsey, hugging the coastline on its way round to the south-eastern port of Lowestoft, beginning to roll more strongly as the evening drew on. When the wind chilled, they made themselves comfortable in their small cabin, and slept well in spite of the cramped conditions.

By the following morning they had passed Dover and helped by favourable winds made fast progress. They made such good time that they reached Lowestoft in the early hours of the second morning. Jessica had enjoyed the trip and neither of them had suffered from seasickness, even though the sea had been quite choppy during the second night. Tom had jokingly commented they had been too busy to notice, laughing until Jessica blushingly told him not to be so shameless!

Once the horses were led ashore, clearly very happy to be on firm ground, they walked them out of the harbour area past the fishermen's cottages until they had settled down, stopping at an inn Tom knew well on the town outskirts, close to the Yermouth road. They were both famished, and the excellent meal of roasted rabbit, followed by cheese and chestnuts, washed down with a good claret, prepared them well for the final short journey to Castor manor.

The salty sea breeze kept the coast road clear of the few snowflakes that occasionally fell in the area, but the sun, shrouded by thick layers of cloud, had no chance to warm the air. It was bitterly cold but at least the riding helped to warm them a little as they headed north up towards Yermouth. The road wound its way through the flat countryside with its lush fields heavy with water around the many lakes and small, shallow streams they sometimes had to ford. Tom watched Jessica carefully when the going was hard, nevertheless pleased to see that she was riding much better now, seeming to have gained more self-confidence since they had left Paul's house only a few days previously.

After skirting around Yermouth, within two hours they were trotting through Castor village, only a few minutes from Tom's house. Jessica looked around her, taking in her first impressions of what was to be her new home and liking what she saw, particularly as they approached the house Tom indicated, saying, 'We've arrived at last, Jessica! Welcome, my love, to my simple house!'

It was in fact a beautiful house, and as they dismounted she could hardly wait to go inside and take a look, while Tom made the horses fast to a rail by the stable. Sensing her impatience, before seeing to the horses and their baggage he led her to the main door, unlocked it with a key hanging on a hook out of sight in the porchway, pushed it open and stepped inside. He quickly opened the shutters of all the rooms downstairs, allowing the afternoon light to flood in, and Jessica was able to get an impression of the quality and size of the house. During Tom's absence, servants had regularly cleaned and aired the house, so that although very cold, everything was in excellent condition. Fires had also been periodically lit to keep the dampness away, and while Jessica was excitedly exploring the kitchen and all the other rooms, Tom brought in some wood from a shed behind the house and quickly got a blazing fire going in the main room before settling the horses and carrying the luggage into the house.

Everything was in fact exactly as he had left it. Once the bedroom fire was lit, the house gradually began to warm up, bedding was aired, and all signs of tenseness left them both. Jessica prepared a broth from vegetables stored in the pantry, adding spices she found in one of the cupboards, and within three to four hours of arriving, as darkness began to fall, they both felt comfortable and relaxed as they sat by the fireside discussing what had to be done the next day. This included a visit to Sir William and Lady

Mortimer, to ensure that Jessica had everything she needed to run the household, and that arrangements were made as soon as possible for their wedding and how they could best handle the children – the only real concern of Jessica.

The following day began well. News of their arrival had quickly spread through the village and the manor house, and they were not long out of bed before servants sent by Lady Mortimer arrived, bringing some fresh food that was quickly stored in the pantry before they set-to with cleaning and dusting, anxious to catch a glimpse of the new 'mistress' rumoured to have accompanied Mr Thomas the previous day. They were not disappointed. Jessica handled the situation perfectly, seeking their help and sympathy but also able to direct them as to what should be done in such a way that they did it willingly.

In the meantime, Tom went to pay his respects to Sir William and Lady Mortimer, officially informing them that he wished to remarry and that his bride-to-be, Jessica, was already installed in his house, and that he would like to introduce her to them when it was convenient. He immediately received their blessings, Sir William insisting that the ceremony should be conducted by the chaplain in the village church as soon as possible, while Lady Mortimer raised the subject of the children and his plans for them.

It was a delicate situation in that during his frequent absences since Margaret had died, Lady Mortimer had acted like a mother to both Eric and particularly the young John, as well as giving his daughter Margaret regular tuition at the Dexters' home, where she currently lived, for which Tom was eternally grateful, and he respectfully said so. However, he added, once he was married, it was natural that his children should return home with him, but he would very much appreciate the regular contact of his ladyship, since they could only gain from her great qualities as a teacher and mentor. He was certain, he continued, that both she and Jessica would be able to share other common interests as well as her invaluable help with the children's education.

This seemed to satisfy Lady Mortimer, who then excused herself, allowing Tom to bring his lord up to date with the events in Calais, and Sir William to brief Tom on all the demesne affairs. He had a tremendous respect for Tom, and was clearly delighted to have him back not only as captain of his guard, but more as his right hand to supervise the everyday running of most of the demesne business, working closely with the reeve, John Dexter. This enabled him to pursue his major passions of hunting and jousting, with occasional visits to London for parliamentary and other political affairs, frequently sharing with his *protégé* a considerable amount of sensitive information and other details, seeking his views and opinions, trusting his judgement completely. Furthermore, he had very much a 'soft' spot for Tom's eldest son Eric, ensuring that he had begun the training and education to enable him eventually to become at least his steward or a clerk. This would not only guarrantee the boy's future well-being but also protect the later development of his own demesne at Castor and other family properties.

Before Tom left the manor house, Lady Mortimer returned, carrying the young John in her arms, followed by Eric who ran to his father to greet him, then stood awkwardly by him not quite sure what to do, until Tom tousled his hair affectionately, crouched down and hugged him closely. The ice was broken and tears of happiness trickled down his cheeks as he repeatedly sobbed, 'Daddy, daddy, at last you're back. Can I go home now, please?'

Tom looked at Lady Mortimer who nodded understandingly and after taking the toddler John from her for a moment, Tom cautiously asked her if she would keep looking after him for a little while longer until everything was settled. He said that Eric would visit the manor house daily for his tuition with her or the chaplain as usual, if that was in order. Taking young John back in her arms, she smiled, agreeing instantly to his suggestion, and Tom, after thanking her, took his leave, accompanied by Eric.

It was little more than a ten-minute walk, and Tom stopped to explain to his son that he was going to remarry and that his future wife, Jessica, was already at their house, impatiently waiting to see him, and that he should be on his best behaviour! Eric thought for a moment, grinned and then said, much to Tom's relief, 'Good! I'll have a real mummy again!'

Jessica hid her surprise well when Eric bounded into the house, whooping and shouting out her name with glee, running into her open arms, clasping her firmly round the waist, looking up at her face while she held him firmly to her. She smiled happily at Tom standing silently nearby and then looked down at his son.

'Eric, Eric, welcome home! I've heard so much about you. Tell me what you have been doing all the time your father was away. My, what a big boy you are!'

Tom excused himself and left them to get better acquainted with each other while he returned to the manor to check the guard and see for himself the status of everything and what needed to be done, before riding to the home of John Dexter and his wife Annie, to see his daughter Margaret.

She was only a little over seven years old, but had the maturity of a much older girl, and Tom wanted her desperately to accept Jessica, knowing that it was unlikely to be as easy as with Eric. When he arrived at the Dexters', he was not surprised to find that John was not at home and was able to have a few words with Annie alone before he saw Margaret. She had been delighted to hear that Tom was to remarry, fully understanding that in due course Margaret should return home, adding with her typical down-to-earth practicality that since their own son Robert clearly worshipped her, it was probably better she was not in the same house!

While Annie went to fetch Margaret, who was busy salting some meat in an outhouse, completely unaware that her father had returned, Tom tried to prepare himself, wondering how best to go about it. Even though she was wearing a simple work smock, his heart seemed to miss a beat when he saw her walking towards the house, deep in conversation with Annie, who hadn't told her who the visitor was. She was the spitting image of her mother and perhaps even more beautiful!

When she caught sight of her father, she sprinted the last few yards up the stone pathway, yelping and shouting in excitement, sounding more like a hound in pursuit of a hare rather than a young girl running to her father. Tom swung her off her feet, holding her as if she were a feather in front of him, before clasping her firmly to him, rocking her gently and patting her back, then lowering her to the ground. It was a joyous reception. She was full of questions and he promised her he would answer them all, but he had just got back and would give her all the news shortly, but had some things to do for Sir William first. However, before he went off, he added, there was something he had to tell her. He went on to explain the new situation.

She listened carefully, fixing her green eyes intently on his face, as Tom stumbled through the story of meeting Jessica in Salesburye, and how he was planning to remarry, and that they would then be able to live together as a complete family again, and that he was sure she would like Jessica.

Initially, when he had finished, there was hardly any reaction from Margaret. She simply stood there looking at him, neither approving or disapproving, making her father feel even more uncomfortable and not sure what he should say or do next. Fortunately it was Annie who broke the silence, saying how wonderful it was and how she would miss Margaret after the wedding took place, but would certainly visit her regularly, and other things in an effort to bridge the awkward atmosphere. Tom then excused himself, saying he would return the following day with Jessica so they could get to know each other better, mounted his horse, waved to them both, and rode off somewhat apprehensively to return home.

Later in the evening when Eric was in bed, Tom tried to describe to Jessica what had happened at the Dexters', saying that he wanted her to go with him to meet Margaret the next day. The complete acceptance of Eric had in the meantime built up her self-confidence, and she tried to reassure Tom that given a little time Margaret would come round to accepting her, as difficult as it would be, of course. She could never replace her mother but at least Margaret might come to like and hopefully love her for what she was. She then described what she had learnt from Eric and that she found him to be an extremely intelligent, sensitive and lovable boy, who hero-worshipped his father, but needed her affection also, and that he could well be proud of his son. Feeling they had exhausted the subject for the present, and since there was much to be done the following day, Tom led her upstairs to their bedroom where they undressed and slipped gratefully into bed, soon fast asleep in each other's arms.

Jessica's first encounter with Margaret proved to be much better than Tom had anticipated. Annie had clearly spent some time after Tom left the previous day persuading her to be more reasonable and to at least give Jessica a chance to prove herself. Although Margaret was somewhat reserved, she was polite and pleasant to Jessica and liked her more than she had thought possible. After that hurdle had been more or less cleared, they visited the chaplain to make arrangements for the marriage, agreeing a date ten days later to accomodate the wishes of Sir William and Lady Mortimer, and then attended to a host of other details that needed to be seen to for both the household and the wedding.

The days flew by. Tom was kept busy with demesne matters and Jessica needed all the available time for their private arrangements, spending nevertheless precious hours with Eric and visiting Margaret, who volunteered after a few days to return home with her, to both Jessica's and Tom's delight.

On the day of their marriage, the village church was packed. They had both wanted a quiet wedding, without fuss, but Tom's popularity made that impossible. When they arrived, they were greeted by at least two hundred villagers, many from outlying districts, who had not been able to find a seat in the church, all anxious to catch at least a glimpse of Tom and his bride and wish them the best possible luck. The manor guard provided an impressive greeting, lined up on both sides of the path leading to the church door and also helping to keep some semblance of order among the crowds milling around. Jessica was escorted by Sir William, splendidly attired as a leading knight of the realm, but the crowd only had eyes for the bride, whose jet-black hair contrasted perfectly with the slightly pink, exquisite damask dress that Lady Mortimer had given her which set off her natural beauty to perfection. For the occasion, Tom was wearing the white and green colours of the Black Prince that the Earl of Warwick had given him at Crécy, over a chain-mail hauberk, and was standing at the front of the church waiting impatiently for Jessica to come alongside him, having arrived a few minutes before her. Eric and Margaret were sitting with Lady Mortimer in the front row behind him, outwardly calm but excited nevertheless by the splendour and pomp of the ceremony as well as the almost mystical solemnity of the service.

Margaret began to daydream for a moment, capturing in her imagination a flash of her mother's smile and then looked intensely at Jessica as if for comparison, studying the happiness exuding from her smiling face as she glanced at her father standing contentedly by her side. She fingered the magnificent ring which had belonged to her mother, hanging on a chain around her neck like a talisman, tucked out of sight under her dress, and then silently vowed to be good to Jessica in the future, particularly now that her beloved father seemed to be so happy. She sighed and took hold of her brother's hand, looking forward to returning home.

She was not disappointed and rapidly came to love and respect Jessica who not only showed her how to bake delicious bread and sweetmeats but also taught her to think and reason objectively, a product of her earlier upbringing and education in Flanders. She also helped her with the French language that Lady Mortimer had begun to teach her in weekly sessions, and was always available to discuss the many problems facing a young girl rapidly approaching womanhood.

Similarly, Jessica gave Eric the affection and encouragement he needed to develop within the strenuous programme of academic learning imposed by the chaplain and the hard, practical demesne work supervised by John Dexter, both acting under the clear instructions of Sir William and the watchful eye of his proud father. On his twelfth birthday, Tom gave Eric a specially prepared longbow and on every free day Eric had for the following two years, he gave him unique tuition in the art of archery and the early stages of martial combat. He frequently reassured Jessica that it really was for his own good, even though it was quite certain, and Tom clearly saw this himself, that Eric would never be a warrior, taking much more after his uncle Paul.

A little over three years after his marriage to Jessica, Tom's youngest son John, although not quite five years old, was growing quickly into a very sturdy boy, giving every indication that he would be at least as large as his father and almost certainly would follow his footsteps. Given half a chance he followed him everywhere and became a common sight wandering around the armoury, feeding the horses, talking with the manor guard and playing at soldiers with a wooden sword one of them had given him. John watched Eric practising from time to time with his longbow and continually pestered him to let him have a go even though it was far too big for him. Seeing his interest, Tom eventually made him one, but with light arrows tipped with a small, wooden block for safety reasons. Jessica saw many of her husband's movements and mannerisms in the young child, and had to handle him relatively strictly initially to curb some aspects of his wildness and spirited behaviour, until he learnt how to behave. Although tempted at times, Tom never interfered in Jessica's disciplinary measures with John, whom she affectionately called 'the little rascal', but loved as if he were her own child.

By this time, Jessica was completely accepted by the manor staff and villagers as if she had always lived in Castor, and she herself had never been happier. She had a husband she adored and had developed a natural, warm relationship with the children whom she regarded as her own and who treated her in every way as if she were their natural mother. Eric, in the meantime, had become very friendly with the reeve's son Robert, in spite of the difference in years, and he became a familiar figure and visitor to their household. Jessica suspected that Robert's real interest lay with Margaret, and she carefully watched the situation as her stepdaughter developed into the early stages of womanhood. However, despite her youth, Margaret seemed to know exactly how to handle the young man.

Jessica was taken completely by surprise one day by Tom, who although he had taught himself to read, albeit somewhat stumblingly, was unable to write. He asked her to help him to learn. He explained that he knew he was missing something important, but had never had the chance earlier to learn and now wanted at least to catch up with his children in this respect.

It was not easy for her, even though Tom had the determination to succeed. He became frustrated and angry with himself when it took longer than expected to master the new skill, especially when he saw the ease with which Eric was able to write in Latin as well as English. However, he learnt and learnt well, and surprised Jessica further when he announced he intended to write the story of his family so that his children could understand how life had been in the past, so that they would perhaps better appreciate their standard of today and hopefully that of the future. Life has so much to offer, he added, but when you are not born into a noble family with all their privileges, it can be more difficult, especially in these days of disastrous weather, what with never-ending frosts, terrifying storms and now a drought.

'Nothing is automatic for people like us,' he had continued. 'You need to strive for success and that is far from guaranteed, particularly when there is so much jealousy, greed, evil and ignorance around us.' He concluded by remarking how lucky he had been, especially on the day he had first seen Jessica in Salesburye!

He began slowly, checking some dates and family entries in various churches around the demesne, talking with some of the older villagers he knew until he was satisfied that the data was as accurate as he could make it. He then began to write what he called his family chronicle. Most evenings for the following two years, when the children were in bed, he sat at a small table while Jessica busied herself with spinning or a little embroidery work, writing by candlelight what he hoped would be a worthwhile legacy for his children and the Rollesby name, perhaps to be continued by future generations, totally unaware what destiny had in store for him and his family.

31

Royal Celebrations and Gascony

An uneasy peace had reigned between England and France following the battle of Crécy, a peace that was frequently broken by both sides. Philippe VI was succeeded by his eldest son, Jean II, at his death in August 1350, and a series of truces were then signed and broken, boding ill for any long-standing peace. In early 1355, Edward III's wife, Philippa, gave birth to her thirteenth child and eighth son, Thomas of Woodstock, an event celebrated throughout England.

Tom was informed by Sir William, and somewhat reluctantly travelled with him to Windsor to participate in a series of tournaments set up by the Prince of Wales in honour of his mother and the birth of his brother. They were splendid affairs followed by sumptuous banquets, and Tom got to know several foreign knights in the process, as well as renewing his acquaintance and friendship with the Earl of Warwick. However, Tom was impatient to return home to his family, the more peaceful affairs of the demesne, and his chronicle, which had become a passion for him.

In recounting his experiences at Windsor to Jessica, he talked at length about some of the fine people he had met, including a certain Jean de Grailly, Captal de Buch, a renowned Gascon warrior. His concern, he recounted with some emotion, was that many of the knights he had met seemed only to be happy when they were fighting. They apparently had a passion for war, loving the excitement, risk, and of course, always looking out for booty to swell their personal coffers, and Tom reasoned (subsequent events proved him right) that it was only a matter of time before yet another campaign would be fought in France. Jessica shuddered at this and Tom reassured her that he would do everything possible to keep out of it, since he had more than enough to do at home. He confided that he was also sickened at the thought of yet more bloodshed, which never seemed to resolve anything permanently. The days had long passed when he had yearned for vengeance for the death of his parents, and what he had experienced at Sluys, then later at Crécy was more than enough killing for the rest of his life. He hoped that after the episode in Calais, his last *sortie*, his commitments in that respect were now over.

Meanwhile, the Prince of Wales, appointed as the king's lieutenant in Gascony, was assembling an expeditionary force of around 2,500 men, destined for France. Accompanied by the Earls of Oxford, Salesburye, Suffolke and Warwick and other leading knights, the Black Prince arrived with his fleet in Bordeaux in late September 1350. The Earl of Warwick later recounted with great pride to Tom the details of the highly successful 'Chevauchée' that in eight weeks created unprecedented havoc and desolation, as well as collecting massive quantities of booty, on the route from Bordeaux to Narbonne and back, from the Atlantic coast to the Mediterranean, returning to the Atlantic! It was a great humiliation for the French king, who in the eyes of his subjects was totally unable to protect them from the punitive raids of a relatively small English force.

Apparently, shortly after that exploit, so the earl described to Tom, winter quarters were set up in the neighbourhood of Bordeaux for the victorious English force until early in the following year, when skirmishing groups advanced more towards the north, *taming* the dissident population, the Earl euphemistically explained, in preparation for yet another major raid.

In spite of his good intentions and burning desire to stay at home with his family, Tom now found himself once again back in France in the early summer of 1356. A royal messenger had brought a letter to Castor in late spring, signed by the Black Prince and the Earl of Warwick 'repectfully requesting' him to proceed to Plymouth to take command of five hundred mounted archers being assembled there, together with large supplies of longbows, bowstrings, arrows, gunpowder, two large catapults and even a siege machine, as well as several boatloads of salted meat and fish, wheat, oats, several hundred barrels of ale and other provisions. After a tearful farewell from Jessica and his children, assuring them he would return as soon as possible, he sailed from Yermouth in a specially chartered boat to Plymouth to take up his command.

He reported to one of the marshals at the jetty, who led him to his quarters and took care of his weapons and horses. Boats of all descriptions were arriving from all directions at Plymouth, ranging in size from a mere forty tons to at least two hundred. Tom watched, fascinated, the activity around them. Some ships were being fitted out especially to take the many horses, while others were being loaded up with cartloads of supplies, including armour, shields, lances and other weapons.

It was almost three weeks before the fleet finally sailed out of the harbour and from nearby moorings towards Bordeaux. They arrived only four days later due to very stormy weather, disembarking in mid-June, extremely happy to have firm ground under their feet, but requiring a further two days for men and horses to recover from the strenuous journey, before proceeding in relatively good order to a garrison at Libourne where the Black Prince had established his headquarters.

Almost the first person Tom saw on arriving at Libourne was the Earl of Warwick, about to lead a patrol of men-at-arms off into the neighbourhood, on the permanent lookout for scouts or other soldiers loyal to the French king. They both dismounted and embraced each other.

'It's good to see you, my lord, but I can't say I'm particularly happy to be back in France again!' Tom exclaimed.

The Earl laughed and slapped him on the back. 'Yes, I can imagine Thomas, you would prefer to stay at home with, from what I have heard, that beautiful wife of yours, but you'll see, once back in action, you'll think differently. Mark my words, old friend!'

Although not at all convinced, Tom made no further comment on the subject, and listened to the earl's description of the '*Chevauchée*' of the previous winter, and how wonderfully successful it had all been. Then seeing that his men were getting impatient he excused himself, explaining he had to get his group of reinforcements and supplies organised, asking where they should set up camp. The earl commanded one of his lieutenants to lead Tom's group to the designated area, then rode off with his patrol.

Not much had been done in advance of Tom's arrival, apart from some flags placed by marshals marking off an extremely large field backing onto a hilly woodland area, about a mile to the southeast of Libourne, close to the River Dordogne. Halting the long column at the roadside, he called the centenars and vintenars to him to make it quite clear exactly what had to be done: where horses and waggons should be located temporarily; details needed to dig latrines, collect wood for the cooks, guard the supplies and weapons, erect tents, feed and water the horses, and a host of other items. He then moved to one side to ensure that his instructions were being carried out to the letter. He had taken stock of the five hundred or so longbowmen in the group, both in Plymouth and after landing in France, and was not particularly impressed with the quality of some of them, realising that a lot would have to be done to 'knock most of them into shape', as he had confided earlier to the centenars. However, the first priority had to be to settle the whole group, give them all a good meal, organise basic requirements and make the camp as secure as possible for the first night. Tomorrow would be another day, he mused, watching some form of order gradually emerging from the chaos.

As a clear signal to all, he spent most of the first night on guard himself, with one of the centenars, five of the vintenars and ten of the archers, all of whom were relieved of any duties the following day, apart from an emergency, of course.

Early the next morning, after briefing the centenars on what had to be done, he rode off to the headquarters in Libourne to report officially the arrival of his force and supplies, hoping to find out how much time they had before moving on, and see if there were any other instructions for him.

Libourne was a hive of activity. Waggons and carts of all types were hauling supplies to heavily guarded warehouses built especially for the purpose on the west side of the town, supervised and escorted by men-at-arms. He also saw a column of foot archers approaching the town from the direction of Bordeaux – yet more reinforcements, he mused. Let's hope we have enough food for them all, was his first thought! One of the men-at-arms directed him to a large, impressive tent erected not more than fifty paces from the main storage area, where he found several clerks busily engaged in carefully recording details of the supplies that were being stored nearby. Two or three knights and yeomen were also sitting on stools outside, enjoying the early morning sunshine of what promised to be a delightful summer's day, laughing and joking, without an apparent care in the world.

He recognised the Captal de Buch and walked over to greet him. The Gascon knight looked up and his face broke into an instant smile. He introduced Tom to the others, clearly pleased to see him again in spite of the fact that Tom had defeated him in a tournament at Windsor months earlier.

'Meet one of the greatest warriors I've ever had the privilege to fight. Praise God he is with us and not our enemies!'

Somewhat embarrassed, Tom shook hands with the others, immediately forgetting their names in his confusion, muttering words to the effect that Jean tended to exaggerate somewhat and that he was delighted to meet his friends.

One of the clerks stood up at the disturbance and walked over to the group, asking if he could help in any way, respectfully taking the supply and provision manifest Tom handed him, quickly glancing through it, and adding that he would return shortly with details of where the gunpowder and siege weapons should be stored. A few minutes later, the Earl of Warwick appeared and took Tom to one side, asking him if the campsite was in order and then if he would have room for a few more men. A 'few' turned out to be three hundred archers and one hundred pikemen that the earl confirmed would report to Tom's camp early the following morning. He also explained that further reinforcements and supplies were still on the way, and as far as he could see, it would take a good four weeks before the whole army would be ready to march. There was a large contingent of men-at-arms in Bordeaux and around Libourne, he added, as well as groups of pikemen, mounted and foot archers billeted in the neighbouring villages of Lussac, Branne and Castillon. Messengers would inform him two days in advance of the campaign start and should there be any problems, he was available most days somewhere in Libourne.

Before the earl left Tom, he arranged for one of the clerks and a messenger to accompany him back to his camp to handle the question of provisions and other necessary services, then wishing him 'God speed', mounted his horse held by a waiting squire and rode off with a small escort, leaving Tom to digest the new information and handle the obvious challenge of yet more, as he soon discovered, untrained and ill-disciplined soldiers.

Once back at camp, he left the clerk and messenger to supervise first the transport of the gunpowder and siege weapons to another location, before informing the centenars to prepare accommodation for a further four hundred men due to arrive the following day. He explained he had only just been informed, knew perfectly well the notice was too short, but they had to do it nevertheless, and woe betide any man he found not working within the next hour!

To lend weight to his words, he spent the entire day patrolling the area, making sure that he was very visible. He heard disgruntled comments from the perspiring men but chose to ignore them initially, providing they were working hard! Surprisingly, by late afternoon the temporary shelter of roofed huts – without walls of course – and rows of tents alongside them was almost complete, as well as more substantial paddocks for the horses. While the last details were arriving with more firewood, they were delighted to see that several oxen were already roasted and that clearly a very special meal was being prepared, not to mention the barrels of ale. The smell of the succulent meat and freshly-baked bread acted extremely effectively to counter possible complaints about the hard work – as Tom had calculated when he ordered the cooks to make a special effort for that day – and when the bugle call summoned the men for the meal, within minutes the whole contingent was ready to be served.

While the men were sitting back, having enjoyed what for most had been a banquet, and had drunk sufficient quantities of ale to adequately parch the thirst and mellow the spirit, Tom walked up to the front as arranged previously with the centenars and vintenars to address the whole group.

He began by congratulating and thanking them for the day's work – which took most completely by surprise – and then continued to explain about the additional troops due to arrive early the next day, finally adding that all those not delegated for guard duty or other necessary tasks would help to set up targets for archery practice for the day afterwards, under his personal supervision, beginning at first light. Some of the men grinned at the thought of archery supervision from Thomas Rollesby. They had never seen him in action and had little respect for the so-called officer class. They muttered to each other deprecatory comments about him, and who did he think he was to show them how to use a longbow!

Overhearing one of the not-so-subtle observations, Tom hauled one of the men he had earlier identified as a potential troublemaker up from the ground with one massive hand and sent him off with a pavise, walking towards some of the parked waggons that formed part of the camp's defensive ring to the east, telling him to keep going until he called him to stop and then take shelter behind it. He now had the attention of the total group. Once the soldier was underway, he took a longbow and ten arrows from one of the archers, checked the bowstring tension carefully, stuck the arrows into the ground just behind him and watched the progress of the now very nervous man. They all watched the soldier's progress, joking that he was already out of range, wondering what this big man, their leader, thought he was going to do or prove. It was at around three hundred and fifty yards that Tom bellowed out that he should stop, waiting until the man took shelter behind the pavise, tilting it slightly towards himself to protect his head should a 'lucky' arrow, he had reasoned, drop down in his direction.

The setting sun glinted on the brightly-painted pavise that looked in the distance little larger than a polished silver groat, making it, although clearly visible, extremely difficult to judge the range. The men's interest and excitement had steadily mounted as they watched the drama enfolding, and several of them had placed bets on the result. Few of them believed it was possible to hit anything at that range, even those with some campaign experience. There were two or three that had fought at Crécy and one of them had served with Tom, and knew how good he had been with the longbow, but decided to keep the knowledge to himself and make some money in the process!

They watched Tom check the wind direction carefully, select an arrow, take aim and fire. The arrow soared high and began to drop down towards the waiting soldier crouching fearfully behind the long, protective pavise. Before the first arrow dropped with a distinctive *thunk* plumb into the centre of the shield, Tom had already released another. The next eight went winging on their way in a flurry of movement and speed that none of them had ever seen before and the silenced group followed each one as they struck the target with a power and accuracy that left them breathless. No sooner had the last one found its place with all the others in the pavise, there was an almost simultaneous gasp followed by wild cheering as they expressed their admiration for a feat few thought was remotely possible. Tom then walked away to his quarters without saying a word, leaving them with a conversation topic that lasted most of the evening. He had made an enemy of the loudmouthed soldier who had been obliged to stand behind the pavise, but had gained the respect and admiration of every other single soldier – even those who had lost their first week's wages!

In the following days and weeks, by sheer hard work, stringent practice, discipline and good food, Tom and his centenars moulded a force to be contended with. They also practised a series of formations, both defensive and offensive, to ensure the best possible use of their firepower, effectively integrating the pikemen into Tom's various concepts. He made working parties cut long stakes about ten feet long and sharpened at each end, which groups of his archers were trained to use to strengthen defensive positions from the charges of mounted men-at-arms, in spite of initial complaints about exaggerated activity until they all began to see the value of his strategy. Tom knew, however, that no matter what he and his other commanders did, there would always be some lawless individuals among them that could not be fully trusted to obey their commands at all times, particularly within the last group of reinforcements, since his men came from such a variety of backgrounds and life experiences. One could never be totally sure how some of them might react when the going got very difficult, or when they were faced with other sorts of temptation. He therefore insisted on an iron discipline, but gave it a fairness and humanity mixed with a humour that was appreciated by almost all. The weeks passed quickly during this period of hectic, intensive training, drawing close to the fateful time when the whole English force was to set off for the second, famous '*Chevauchée*'.

Unknown to Tom, from the moment he left home *en route* for Bordeaux, a whole series of events took place that were to have a dramatic impact on the future development and fortunes of the Rollesby family. On the very day, 25 June 1356, that the Black Prince wrote to the Bishop of Hereford exhorting him to offer special prayers and organise other holy processions for the benefit of his troops in France, a son, Simon, was born to Paul and Elizabeth, a son who was to establish a cloth empire of enormous dimensions, building on the Polton family business and capitalising on Marky's invention: a fulling machine driven by a water-wheel. This invention proved to be a major factor contributing to the further expansion and wealth of the city of Salesburye and to the significant decline in the fortunes of Winchester during the following two centuries.

Subsequent generations of the Rollesby family, descending from both Paul and Tom, were later to establish liaisons with the famous Clopton family of Long Melforde (important benefactors of the magnificent Holy Trinity church that was finally completed more than a hundred years later in 1484), both in the cloth merchant business and on the battlefield of Agincourt in 1415. In addition, they helped found important wool and cloth enterprises in the Lavenham area, as well as producing craftsmen capable of building and carving the 'Angel' roof of the double hammerbeam type to be found in the beautiful church of St Mary's at Wulpet. But it was to prove to be a long, difficult and eventful development, that had its share of pain and tragedy on the way to success.

No sooner had Tom arrived in France when the beloved wife of his patron Sir William, fell ill from a type of consumption, which quickly led to her death some weeks later. His own family remained in perfect health while he was away, but following a quarrel between Jessica and his daughter, Margaret disappeared under somewhat mysterious circumstances and Tom never saw her again. These were all events of which Tom was totally unaware as he laboured with his large troop of archers and pikemen that were shortly to play yet again, as at Crécy, a major role in the annihilation of an infinitely larger French army, this time in the Battle of Poitiers.

32

The Second 'Chevauchée'

One afternoon in late July, the Captal de Buch rode out to Tom's encampment with a message from the Earl of Warwick that the army was to form in the vicinity of Bergerac, some fifty miles due east from Libourne and prepare to march on 4 August. There was not much time to load and prepare everything, but fortunately due to the rigorous training of previous weeks, the force left in good order and condition on the first day of August, following the course of the River Dordogne, reaching the appointed meeting place in the early afternoon of 3 August. After a briefing of all commanders, where the plans were discussed and the main objectives agreed, the English army of barely 6,000 men set off at dawn the following day.

In spite of the long days of hard training, Tom had managed to keep his chronicle reasonably up to date, sitting in his tent late at night writing by candlelight. For personal reasons, his brother Paul did not include everything that Tom had written when he later continued the family saga, but found the notes and comments written during the six weeks leading up to and including the battle of Poitiers so moving that he quoted most of them verbatim. As the army began to make its relentless and bloody journey northwards, it was clear that its purpose was one of terror and destruction, having little to do with what Tom considered to be the purpose for which he had been summoned to participate. He hated it and was never personally guilty of many of the atrocities committed before the great battle. He served the earl and his sovereign with the loyalty that was endemic to his character, going far beyond the bounds that anybody could expect when the 'moment of truth' dawned at Poitiers.

Extracts from the manuscript of Thomas Rollesby

4 August 1356

Moved out of Bergerac in set formation in three main groups. The vanguard is commanded by the Earls of Warwick and Oxford, the prince leads the central group, and the rearguard has the Earls of Salesburye and Suffolke as its commanders. The waggons and most of the footsoldiers are in the rearguard, protected by a contingent of men-at-arms. I and a large body of my mounted archers are in the vanguard. Two of my centenars are each commanding one hundred mounted archers deployed on each side of the vanguard supporting forces of five hundred men-at-arms split between the two groups, which have been ordered to fan out and devastate all the villages, communities or towns they come across for up to twenty miles on both sides of the main army column. Messengers will ensure they maintain regular contact. **May God have mercy on all the innocent people!**

We are moving slowly northwards and have not seen a soul all day. They know we are coming and are trying to keep out of the way. Our men have done nothing else but set fire to all the cornfields and destroy the vineyards we passed, looting the deserted farmhouses for food and any valuables they find.

After little more than ten miles we are now camping for the night, prepared to move on at first light.

7 August

It's a strange feeling to know you are being carefully watched from a distance. French scouts have been spotted several times observing our progress from the safety of distant hilltops, but they disappear as soon as we dispatch any of our men. No doubt we can expect an attack at any time, so at least we can keep the men alert.

We've only moved on about fifty miles in these first four days, and whenever I look back on the countryside behind us I see only smoke from the burning fields and farmhouses in a broad swath of destruction several miles on each side of us. Cows and sheep we couldn't take with us have been slaughtered and left to rot or be consumed by the fire all around them. I have stayed with the main body so far and can only hope that there were no people in those houses, because I shudder to think what may happen since we take no prisoners unless they are wealthy and can pay a ransom. This is no place for me!

Scouts have told us there is a town about three miles ahead, so we are camping here for the night and will attack it soon after daybreak. The Earl of Warwick has asked me to accompany him and some of his men to spy out the town first thing to decide the best way to approach it and check out any defences.

8 August

We easily captured and occupied the town of Périgueux as it was called, according to the earl, who seems to know the names of most places in this region. The prince agreed to spare the town from destruction since the mayor and a clergyman came out to meet us in peace, and gave us the keys of the main gates, in spite of what looked to me like good defences. It was surrounded by turreted walls with waterways on two sides which could only be crossed by narrow bridges from the direction we came, with wet marshland on the other side. If they had fought it would have cost us quite a few of our men, who were nevertheless disappointed because they couldn't look for their own booty. That's all they think about, the silly clods! That and their cocks of course, since given half the chance most of them will rape anything in a dress. They seem to forget it could cost them their life if they are caught at it, but some of them are little better than animals.

We left the rearguard and most of the waggons outside the town, and as we rode and marched slowly along the main approach, a narrow causeway passing over a bridge I believe they called St George, I shall never forget the strangest but extremely beautiful cathedral that rose majestically above the walls on our right side. It seemed to be made up of many small and large domes, which were all topped with what I later heard was called a cupola, looking like so many elegant chimney pots, supported by slender pillars. The building was dominated by one large, high tower, also crowned by a cupola, that I saw, when I got closer, was at the head of the cathedral, set out in a strange cross shape such as I had never seen before. I was glad that it would remain undisturbed, although we set guards at all doors just in case!

The townspeople watched us silently with hatred in their eyes as we made our way to what they called the 'amphitheatre', a huge, ancient circular building which serves as an excellent base for the men-at-arms, and most of the archers and pikemen, both in and around it. We then set up our headquarters in the nearby castle (the Chateau Barrière), and decided to rest there for two or three days.

Since the town has agreed to give us 50,000 gold crowns and provides us with food and as much wine as we can drink, they have been mainly spared the horror and humiliation that has accompanied our progress so far. **Please God it continues so!**

28 August

We have advanced about two hundred miles in the last two weeks and will stay to rest another day in this town, called Chateauroux, on the River Indre. From what I've seen so far, there seems to be a lot of clothmaking businesses here, so I'll look out for a nice dress or two for Jessica.

It has been a nightmare! An orgy of violence and destruction! Since we left Périgueux, no quarter had been given. Monks were beaten and humiliated in a pretty town called Brantome (at least the abbey and bell tower were more or less untouched) but everything else was laid waste. What could not be easily taken was simply destroyed; wine barrels smashed-in, crops and all other provisions burnt; furniture, all the possessions of the peasants and townspeople, simply everything was pillaged. We had to fight to control our own soldiers who ran wild like a pack of mad dogs.

The same thing happened in a place called Rochechouart and in Bellac, a small town standing up high on the edge of a rocky plateau about a hundred miles south-west of us. There a handful of people jumped to their deaths on the rocks below rather than surrender to our soldiers. The rest put up a strong resistance in spite of not having a chance, and I also had to kill one or two in more or less self-defence. **God, how I hate it!**

The earl has repeatedly told me we must do it to show the French King Jean that he won't have any peace until he accepts the claims of our own good King Edward. His own people will also reject him if he cannot defend them in their hour of need, or at least, that's what he says! I'm not so sure. When I look in their eyes I see only a burning hatred, and I know the day will soon come when they attack us in strength. I sometimes wonder if we shall survive here. I feel that time is running out against us. One thing is for sure. If I get out of this alive, I shall never return. Jessica, oh Jessica, if only you knew how much I love and miss you and the children!

31 August

We no sooner drew near to Vierzon than we were greeted by a hail of arrows and a charge of about a hundred men-at-arms. They smashed into the head of the vanguard, killing at least twenty of our men, capturing about a dozen or so, and made off with them under the protection of another hail of arrows and crossbow bolts fired by very determined soldiers. It took us completely by surprise, even though we were able to quickly counter-attack and take five or six of them as prisoners.

Sir John Chandos was furious since all the casualties were from his troop, and he vowed that that was the last time he would be caught unawares.

All the outlying groups were recalled and we charged into Vierzon in tight formation, brushing aside an attempted ambush – which nevertheless cost us another thirty men – and began to plunder the town. The prisoners we had taken were 'persuaded' to talk, and we gathered that the French king was approaching from the north with a large army that was about ten days' march away. Since we wanted to avoid a head-on battle with a probably much larger force, the prince commanded that we shall leave Vierzon at dawn, swinging west, before returning towards Bordeaux in the south.

1 September

We are following the River Cher, not far behind the French force we beat off yesterday that appears to be heading for the fortress town of Romorantin, a good day's march ahead of us. In spite of little rest, our men are eager to press forward, smelling a fight ahead and the promise of more booty before heading south for Gascony, Bordeaux, and then, hopefully home.

2 September

We have been in hot pursuit of the French knights that attacked us at Vierzon and they have clearly taken refuge in the fortress here at Romorantin. We are camped about two miles outside on the right-hand bank of the River Cher, waiting for the rearguard and waggons to catch up with us.

The prince, the earl tells me, is determined to raze the town and even take and destroy the castle, he is so angry. Nobody has asked me but I don't think this is a good idea. We are bound to lose a lot of men, and although we have a couple of assault belfries in the baggage train, we're not really properly equipped to lay siege to such a strong fortress. Not only that, there's a huge French army approaching from the north, and this is the last place we would want to meet them! Hopefully, better sense will prevail tomorrow!

3 September

The siege has begun. We have been lucky today, managing to break into the city in three places without too many losses. My archers broke up the groups of armed townspeople that tried to hold us back and the men-at-arms then rode them into the ground. It looks as if we'll have most of Romorantin under control by tomorrow. The rest of the baggage train arrived this afternoon and the foot soldiers have all been busy ransacking the place. We need to make sure they don't all get drunk tonight because we are planning to begin the attack on the castle tomorrow. In fact, work has already begun on tunnels in three places where our men have the best protection from enemy crossbowmen, although we have to keep a sharp lookout when they fire the big catapult they have up there on the top of the big tower.

4 September

We set up two 'trebuchets' this morning with a protective screen around them at the bottom to ward off bolts and arrows, and have been hurling large stones over the battlement walls and at the main tower for the last three or four hours, and it looks like some parts of the wall are beginning to crack and break away. We destroyed the wooden hoardings over most of the castle walls with fire arrows and my best archers make sure they keep their heads down below the battlement walls.

I see that two belfries have been built up now and the ground between them and the walls has been reinforced and smoothed so the wheels will not get bogged down when we push them forward. The prince seems to be everywhere, shouting encouragement to our soldiers and those poor souls digging the tunnels. Large numbers of props cut from the nearby forest have been brought in to support the mine tunnels and I hear that two of them will be completed by tomorrow morning.

Apparently they have to go very deep with the one under the corner of the main tower and so it will take at least an extra day to complete. The sappers are working in two-hour shifts and I've seen them staggering out a couple of times, coughing, covered in dirt, and totally exhausted with the exertion. I don't envy them their job! I hear that a couple were smothered to death by a roof section that caved-in under the tower. What a way to die in a war!

5 September

I'm writing this earlier today – hopefully I'll be around to finish it tonight! We're going to attack at midday, using the two belfries and scaling ladders on the west and south sides of the castle. They've already set fire to the props in the two mines under the walls, helped with barrels of pitch and some fat pigs added for good measure. We've got the formations ready for charging the walls when they collapse, *supported by archers and pikemen on each side, with a group of archers behind them to fire the initial volleys to clear the way. Men have been allocated to run up with the scaling ladders, followed closely by carefully selected men-at-arms and the best pikemen.*

I'm in charge of one of the belfries and I'm going over that wall with the second wave with axe and sword. I've no time for more – must make sure my men are well prepared and that the archers have enough arrows available. No doubt the priests will also want to bless us and reassure the men!

I survived. Just! My God, what a fight! I'm almost too tired to hold this pen, my hands are still trembling and I'm not sure I can describe how it really was.

It was nothing glorious. It was like a horrible nightmare. As I sit here in candlelight I am beginning to see again what I would like to forget.

At the sound of a trumpet, we pushed the siege tower close to the wall, and our men quickly climbed the ladders onto the three platforms while groups of our archers kept up a steady fire at the defenders above us. They nevertheless threw everything down on us they had; boiling pitch, quicklime, stones and even corpses. My left hand got a bit burnt, but it was nothing serious – not like some of the boys who lay screaming in agony on the ground as their flesh got burned off their bones, or were blinded and were stumbling about not able to see where they were. There was no time to think about them – we just had to leave them as they were and keep moving up and forward.

As I reached the second platform, the men above lowered the wall of the top one and with a shout stormed over the parapet with pike, sword and axe, screaming as they fell onto the already weakened defenders. I quickly scrambled up to join them followed by a swarm of others. There was no chance to organise anything – it was a free-for-all: groups just stabbing, slashing at each other until the opponent fell to the ground mortally wounded or was quickly finished off by the soldier behind.

After about twenty minutes of savage hand-to-hand, we heard the explosion and crashing of walls collapsing and our main forces started to pour inside the fotress from two other sides. It took the heart out of the rest of the French who then threw their arms down and surrendered. If I hadn't jumped in front of a group of them shouting at my men to stop and hold off, they would certainly have slaughtered them all as they stood there, filled with a hatred and killing lust that such a battle brings out in most of us.

We all stood there for a moment, panting with the exertion, leaning on our weapons for support, only then hearing the moans and screams of the dying and noticing for the first time the masses of bodies lying around us in every possible position, with blood everywhere. If there really is a 'Hell' then it cannot be any worse than that scene and what we lived through!

I managed to get some order, and we took the prisoners down a flight of stone steps and I ordered a group of pikemen to escort them to our command centre for later interrogation.

The resistance was virtually over at this stage; the remaining French knights had already surrendered or taken refuge in the main tower to fight another day. After posting guards in strategic positions within the castle, including the main gate and the breaches in the main walls, we returned to our positions outside to rest, wash and then try to eat something before falling down to sleep.

I can hardly keep my eyes open now and must sleep. There is much to be done early tomorrow, before we try to break into the main tower.

Jessica, my love, thinking of you helps me to maintain my senses in this mad world of violence and outrage, making me long to be back in your arms. Pray God I shall see the day!

It was during the night of 5 September that both Paul and Elizabeth were disturbed by the crying of their baby son Simon, not yet three months old, and while taking turns to hold and comfort him, Paul expressed his hidden concern for his brother. He told Elizabeth that he was sure Tom was suffering deep anguish somewhere away from home. He just knew, he repeatedly told her, and hoped he was not in danger or wounded. Come what may, he insisted, they would travel to Castor that year for Christmas.

6 September

When I woke up this morning I felt like an old man! God, how my body ached! It took me a while to get the stiffness out of my bones and feel fit to lead my men and face yet another day of bloodshed. But I forced myself to move and get on with it, and soon regained my old strength and spirit.

I sent out working parties to collect arrows, clean and store them in designated weapon waggons close to the castle main-gate, while I went to a briefing of the troop commanders.

The mine props under the big tower had been fired in the early morning, I learned, and we were told to be ready to launch the main attack at any time after midday. In the meantime, a trebuchet had been so positioned that it could easily hit the tower walls and as soon as sufficient larger stones had been gathered, it began the bombardment. A battering ram with protecting roof was also prepared for the massive tower gate – should it be necessary – after trying to blast it with a keg of gunpowder. I was commanded to select two hundred archers to support the attacking force of men-at-arms taken from the prince's own force and those of the Earl of Warwick. Early afternoon, we heard a loud crack followed by a deep rumbling and moments later the tower shook and suddenly one whole side began to break up until a large section of it fell to the ground with an almighty crash. Once the dust had settled we saw there was no need to go for the main door since most of one side was more or less opened up, exposing the surviving soldiers and knights on the floors above. The resistance didn't last long – we fired several volleys of arrows including some that had been set on fire and the survivors soon came down the stone steps to surrender, coughing and spluttering.

There were a couple of high-ranking nobles among the prisoners who agreed to pay a huge ransom – I think it must have been at least 30–40,000 gold crowns each – for their freedom, and the others surrendered their weapons and armour, of course, and whatever other valuables they had on them.

I couldn't help wondering if it was worth all the hardship, all the misery and killing involved for money many of us would never see or have the opportunity to enjoy. I have lost at least two hundred of my men so far, and I continuously wonder for what?

7 September

The day was spent in loading the waggons and burying our dead. Once that was done, I made sure my men got a good meal and spent time resting, since I expect we shall shortly be moving on. Some of them are in a pretty sorry state, and they are all tired.

It was depressing as far as the wounded were concerned. Many of the less serious arm or leg wounds could be treated and with luck most will survive – but the others! I tried to comfort some of them who were obviously going to die and the priests with us were kept very busy, giving absolution to the dying and offering prayers before earth was shovelled over the dead bodies in the mass graves.

I tried to find out when we planned to leave the city, but that is still not clear. I know the French army is not that far away, but apparently the prince is hoping reinforcements under the Duke of Lancaster will soon reach us, coming from the west.

8 September

We finally got the command to leave Romorantin by late morning and by early afternoon were at least five miles west of the city, making good progress along the valley of the Cher, heading towards the city of Tours, I was told. I still think we should make for the south while the going is good, and so do most of my men. They have only one main interest and that is to get back to Bordeaux intact with their booty, as soon as possible. I don't give a damn for all that. I only know that an avenging army moves quickly and the French will soon be on us if we are not careful, and from what I've heard, they have at least three times more men than we have. Also, they are not bogged down with carts and waggons carrying the spoils of war! But the prince seems to be obsessed with the hope of reinforcements.

11 September

This is the second night we've been camped close to Tours. Raiding parties have been attacking all the villages to the east and south of the city, while we prepared a strong position to counter any major sally from the French troops in the citadel. So far it has been very quiet, too quiet. I feel as if a strong storm is brewing up, and all my instincts tell me we should get out of here quickly before it's too late.

After setting up guard posts around us, I've got the rest of my men to stand down early and get some sleep while they can. I made sure we are well prepared to move out almost immediately if necessary.

I cannot sleep, and have just returned from a patrol around our position to check on the guard posts. They know me by now – not one of them was asleep!

I must stop. Somebody on horseback is approaching.

13 September

The hunt is on, and we are the hunted!

It was a messenger from the earl that came to my tent the night before last. We had to leave at dawn, the prince had commanded. According to the messenger, scouts had reported units of enemy troops on a broad front streaming towards us, and some were believed to have already entered Tours itself!

We have force-marched for two days now, heading due south. A heavy rain-shower has made it very heavy going for the waggon train and several have had to be left behind, including some of those loaded with booty! Fortunately most of my men don't know about that yet, since the baggage column is still a good five miles behind us.

Thank God the rain has stopped now and we found good shelter tonight in and around a small town called La Haye, which must be a good thirty miles south of Tours. Apparently, the main body of the French army is now about twenty miles to the north-west, so at least we have a little breathing space, unless they send on small groups to harry our rearguard.

One thing is for sure. We must be off at dawn tomorrow. We are in no position to fight a much larger army.

14 September

Yet another forced march! By the time we reached the outskirts of Chatellerault, I believe it's called, the foot soldiers were ready to drop and I shudder to think of the state of the rearguard. They won't arrive here before morning, and will certainly be good for nothing for at least half a day.

I was not too popular with the mounted archers when I told them they had to set up defensive positions around the camp, dig latrines and mark out the area for the rest of the waggons ready for their arrival, all before they got fed! But it had to be done, and I made sure there was plenty of ale and wine available for them later at suppertime as well as good portions of hot broth and freshly baked bread.

15 September

After a few hours of search we found a good place to face and fight the French – the prince is determined to fight their army – a large field on a plateau to the north-east of the town. We spent the day setting up our positions, using the stakes I had made earlier in the campaign to reinforce them. We also used some of our waggons to cover the ground behind us, but most of those from the rearguard were left under guard within the city walls.

It will be a long day tomorrow. I expect it will all be over one way or the other by nightfall.

16 September

I heard the prince and some of his men spent most of the night in a nearby priory. The earl told me he was hours in the church there (St Jacques) praying for our victory. I can only hope 'He' heard it!

We waited most of the day, expecting to hear them at any moment, but there was no trace of them. The men started to joke that they'd probably turned round and gone back home since they couldn't catch us, but I didn't believe that for one minute.

Late afternoon, we heard from the scouts that the French army was already south of us, passing along the valley of the Vienne. It looks as if they will try to cut off our route down to Bordeaux. My God, what a panic for a while! One thing was for sure – we couldn't stay here.

After a hectic couple of hours of loading the waggons and getting them in some sort of order onto the road to Poitiers before it got dark, we began to move out in formation heading south. We kept going the whole night, with small patrols constantly scouring the countryside in front of us and our flanks watching out for possible ambushes. There was nothing.

17 September

At daybreak we saw a large forest area on our left flank and since the ground was now dry, decided to move off the road, keeping close to its edge. We stopped and rested a while, waiting for further news from the scouts, and ate bread, cheese and whatever else was at hand, most of us wondering where it was all going to end, and then continued our way moving steadily closer to Poitiers which must only be a few miles to the south-west.

18 September

What a day this has turned out to be! Anything but a normal Sunday! I was leading a patrol ahead of the vanguard and we suddenly came upon a line of carts and waggons escorted by a group of French knights, just below us as we came out of the tree line. Fortunately we had a strong group which included some of my best archers and we made short work of most of them, although a couple managed to escape.

It turned out we had stumbled on stragglers from the French army rearguard, which we learned from one of the prisoners captured was now in Poitiers with the rest of their army. I sent the prisoners back with most of the patrol and joined by my old friend, the Captal de Buch and a few others, and we rode cautiously towards Poitiers to see if what we had been told was true and if so, where exactly the French were.

We soon saw them, massed all around the city, covering the whole countryside. It was difficult to judge how many men there were, with the sun more or less directly in our eyes, but there must have been something like 15–20,000 in all, swarming round like so many silver-coloured ants.

We raced back to the prince's group and reported all we had seen.

There is no time for too many details now. Our whole army is rushing forward over the road where we first came across those French stragglers and we are desperately looking for a good defensive position to the south of the city. My God, what a chaos we have! We shall need a miracle to come out of this in one piece!

33

The Battle

Sunday morning

After stumbling around several hamlets, farms and vineyards, close to a heavily wooded valley we managed to find a large, open field to the north of a village called Nouaillé, which looks like the only defensible position in the area. We have to make the best of it and there's not much time.

We quickly set up our front along a thick hedge that faced north-west and I got the archers to reinforce it with the long, pointed stakes as extra protection from cavalry, while the earl left some of the carts to protect the right flank and then he and his men laboured and sweated to push and haul the rest of the baggage train out of the way, lining them up in the woods behind us out of sight along a track that leads south.

By midday, we had managed to establish a reasonable position, but hoped we would have at least some respite before they attacked, since we all felt more or less exhausted. None of us have had much sleep in the last three days, and God knows how many miles we've covered, all on top of this frantic work!

He must have heard and took pity on us! We had just stood down for a meal, when a French cardinal in his red cap and a group of other churchmen galloped up to us with a flag of truce, and invited the prince to a 'peace conference', so the earl said to me later.

Anyway, while he was away negotiating with the French King Jean, we took the opportunity, after a rest, of improving our defences. We dug trenches in front of the hedge, on the flanks, and I set up groups of my foot archers in and around the carts on the right flank and around the hedge on the left flank, protected by pavises and a strong force of pikemen. Pages have been organised to keep the supply of arrows going from weapon carts behind the front line, and I allocated groups of mounted archers to positions well behind the hedge, so they could be used for flanking or other movements if and when necessary, close to strong groups of men-at-arms.

I'm not sure how many men we have now in total. We started out with around 6,000, and with the sick, wounded and those killed since we left Bergerac, I reckon we are down to about 4,000 fit men, including my 1,300 archers and pikemen. Certainly a lot less than we shall soon have to face! We had better rest while we can!

19 September Monday

Jessica, it's just before sunrise. I have already been up for a couple of hours – I couldn't sleep. I wanted to make sure my men got some hot grog and at least a piece of bread and ham this morning. They'll need every bit of strength they can muster shortly.

I hope to continue this tonight. Should it not be possible, I love you, as you well know. Come what may, somehow, I'll get back to you and the children. I promise! I hope and trust that you and the children are all well. Give my greetings to Paul and his dear wife if you should see them soon, and I should not be around.

By dusk the same day, the battle was over. Tom was badly wounded by a crossbow bolt in the final minutes of one of the most bloody encounters of the Middle Ages. More or less in front of the main gate of Poitiers, as he was trying to prevent the slaughter of French soldiers that had surrendered, somebody fired a bolt from the city walls into his back. He fell, pulled himself to his feet and some of his archers helped him back to his tent, where a surgeon was able to cut out the cruel barb and staunch the blood.

In spite of the pain and his weakness, and the protests of the earl and the Captal de Buch, he insisted on completing his diary, recording his experience and the horrors of that fateful day.

It all began when my Lord Warwick began to move off with the baggage train at daybreak, hoping to make it unobserved along the route to Gencay, and then escort it en route to Bordeaux as fast as possible. But it was not to be. He must have been spotted by a French patrol as he was crossing the River Miosson, because shortly afterwards we heard a lot of shouting from the hilly slopes on our eastern flank which minutes later was followed by a rumbling and drumming of the hooves of hundreds of horses quickly getting closer to our front line.

We could hear the chinking sound of chain-mail, the creaking and rattle of armour and the war cries of our enemy while I and the centenars were busy shouting orders to the archers to prepare to fire the first volley. Suddenly, two large groups of heavily armed cavalry emerged from the bushes and vineyards at the far end of the field and came thundering towards us, with lowered lances and drawn swords, screaming and shouting God knows what kind of abuse at us.

For a moment, it was fearful, but my men were magnificent. They waited with drawn bows until the commands came and then unleashed volley after volley into them. We downed most of the leading rank and from the flanks hit hundreds of their horses that either fell, or reared up in pain or terror, throwing the rider and frequently falling on to the other rows close behind them. One or two of the riders reached the hedge but were either impaled by concealed stakes or were picked out of the saddle by my pikemen. Lord Salesburye's supporting men-at-arms ran forward and finished off the fallen riders as they were struggling to stand up, or just lay helplessly on the ground. It was an absolute slaughter! Within minutes the attack was over. A couple of their leaders were taken prisoner and those knights that were not killed wheeled round and galloped back down the field onto their own men, causing complete chaos and confusion in the slowly advancing ranks of a massive body of dismounted men-at-arms.

We stopped firing and after more supplies of arrows were quickly distributed to my men and the archers on the right flank, we got our breath back and waited a few moments for the enemy to get a little closer, a solid mass of armour, flags and banners, gradually drawing nearer and nearer to the sound of pipes, clarions, tabours and a host of other instruments.

At just over two hundred yards, we began to fire as quickly as we could, and in spite of terrible casualties, by force of numbers they just kept on coming. I don't know how many brave men they lost, but the positions where men fell were almost immediately filled by other waves. The ground sloped down towards my position on the left flank, and I could see that the main thrust of the enemy was slowly being forced to turn towards us, and even with help from some of my mounted archers held in reserve, it was becoming almost impossible to hold our position much longer. Then a wonder occurred.

Apparently the prince had ordered the Earl of Warwick to return to help us, and at exactly the right moment – more by luck than good judgement he later admitted – he and his men came out of the woods on our left, and while the mounted archers deployed across marshland on the enemy's right flank, his cavalry charged them from the front. God, how we cheered, and the sight gave us renewed strength to fight on.

We were outnumbered by at least three or four to one, but after what seemed hours, their attack was beaten off with terrible losses for them. Not that we escaped lightly. They fought with such fury and determination that we also took a mauling, and lost at least two or three hundred men, not including the wounded.

When their broken force retreated, we saw to our complete surprise a very large reserve force just behind them, which turned round and rode off away from the battlefield! If they had only attacked us then, I'm not sure we would have been able to hold on. They left with heads hanging, apparently totally dispirited by the near annihilation of that second attack made on foot. I've never seen anything like it, even at Crécy. It must have been soul-destroying for the French king!

We all stood there panting, perspiration pouring off us, our clothes and armour spattered with blood. The dead or dying French covered the field before us, and our own dead or wounded were at our feet, or swaying shakily alongside us, hoping they would not lose an arm or a leg or later, their lives; nevertheless thankful that they had at least survived so far. But we also knew it was not yet over, and we had almost run out of arrows and spears. We were suddenly exhausted, our bodies trembling with fatigue.

I was proud to have them at my side. In the time when they were needed, they gave everything, prepared to die for what they had come to believe was their duty to England and their king. They carried the wounded back to the camp, trying to make them as comfortable as possible before hurrying back to the battlefield to recover arrows and other weapons lying around. I saw them tearing them out of still living enemy bodies, impervious it seemed to the cries and pain of those wounded or dying foes. It was a question of survival. There was no time or place for emotion or personal feelings – that would come later, I knew from previous experience.

Then in the middle of the afternoon, our enemies returned, filling the field like so many insects swarming around an open wound. I saw the colours and flag of the French king, and then saw him marching proudly with his nobles in the middle of the huge formation of men-at-arms, foot soldiers and crossbowmen. I tried to shout encouragement to the lads as the main division of the French army – they outnumbered us by at least two to one and were completely fresh – gradually but inexorably drew closer and closer. I took a longbow myself, sighted on one of their leaders and as I let fly, gave the command to fire at will. I hit him and as he sank to the ground, the first volley began to have its effect.

There was a slight pause, but after stepping over their fallen comrades, the march continued. Immediately following two short trumpet blasts, the whole group then veered to the right, the ranks of the right flank becoming the leading files, and headed straight towards my position, clearly intending to press round our central line and *outflank us simultaneously as they engaged Salesburye's front. Then all hell broke loose! Once at closer range, they used their crossbowmen to great effect on Salesburye's men-at-arms, also picking off some of our archers at the same time. I've never heard such a noise of clarions, trumpets and tambours before – it was almost deafening – as they began to surge towards us, throwing spears and shouting out war cries, scrambling across the trenches, straining to get at us between the wooden stakes and the bristling pikes. Somehow we managed to keep them at bay, summoning a strength and energy from somewhere deep within us, fighting for survival, knowing if we relaxed for a moment we would be swamped, overrun. I heard the prince shouting 'St George and England!' and thought I heard horsemen galloping behind me, but had no chance to look, I was too busy killing the attackers and urging the others on to keep at it. It had been bad enough at Romorantin but this was even worse. There we knew we would win in the end; here we were fighting for our lives, and as each minute passed, were weakening. Even though we had taken a terrible toll on our enemies they just kept coming on. As one fell in front of us, his place was immediately taken by another. We had no more men in reserve. We were the last.*

I just caught sight of what looked to be the French king, swinging a great axe, bearing down on us, surrounded by a group of knights and standard bearers, when a mounted body of archers and men-at-arms came swooping out of the high ground to our far left, bearing down on the rear of the attacking French. Almost at the same time, the prince swept round our front line leading Warwick's reserve men-at-arms and rode straight into the broadest front of the French division, smashing the leading ranks down to the ground like so many playthings crushed by a spoilt child.

You could see the sudden consternation in the faces of our enemies as they were so unexpectedly caught by cavalry on both sides, and we then knew victory was close at hand. We surged out from our defences, shouting like madmen, and must have looked like so many demons, covered in blood, stabbing and slashing them to pieces relentlessly. The survivors turned and ran, throwing their weapons to the ground, pursued by many of our men eager for revenge and any booty they could claim.

The Captal de Buch rode down towards me waving and shouting in exultation – he had led that charge from behind that demoralised King Jean's men. He dismounted, embracing me in his moment of triumph and understandable excitement.

He saw all the blood on me and couldn't believe I wasn't wounded. I was moved by his genuine expression of affection and delight that I had survived that final, terrible onslaught. Satisfied that I could manage, he rode off to look for the French king with some of his men, hoping to capture him alive before he fell into the wrong hands.

I then found a horse and went off towards Poitiers with two or three of my mounted archers to see what was happening and to bring the men back before things got out of hand. It took longer than I thought as we made our way slowly across the battlefield, hindered by the carnage that was everywhere. Words fail me. So many young men! Such a waste! God, will it never end? Has it really been worthwhile? I don't think I'll find out the answer to that question before I die.

When we finally reached the city gates, we saw that the townspeople had closed them even to their own retreating soldiers seeking refuge. Can you imagine that? Even those men that had risked their lives to fight us, the enemy! They just watched from the walls as our men took them prisoner or even worse.

You must know, Jessica, my love, in spite of what I said earlier, that I was wounded as I stood there at the gates, after the battle was over! I had wanted to make sure that nothing further happened to the surviving French soldiers, when somebody fired a crossbow from the city walls and as fate would have it, the damn bolt hit me from behind. I must rest soon since I'm feeling a little weak, but I wanted at least to finish this off before I sleep.

I promise never to leave Castor again.

Tom lay in his sickbed, unable to sleep from the pain in his back where the surgeon had cut out the deeply-embedded iron bolt. He had managed to staunch the flow of blood but was totally unaware and powerless to prevent the ensuing infection. Meanwhile the prince and his leading nobles were celebrating the resounding victory. They had managed to capture the French King Jean alive and had inflicted on the French one of the worst disasters in their history, and so one could understand their jubilation. It was almost comparable to Crécy in terms of the scale of destruction of the French army, but was perhaps even more remarkable in the way it was achieved.

However, in spite of the booty gained, the political humiliation of King Jean and his army commanders, the terrible loss of men, the suffering of the local population, and a subsequent truce that was signed in the following year, further bloody campaigns continued to be fought not only to the end of the so-called Hundred Years' War, but for many years afterwards. France eventually was able to reclaim her lost territories, and both the English and

French then went on to fight other campaigns and wars outside their own frontiers.

The Prince of Wales was anxious to return to Bordeaux as quickly as possible with the spoils of war and his important hostages, safely reaching the city without incident in early October. His soldiers could hardly wait to spend the fortunes they had picked up, and Tom, transported in an escorted waggon, was hoping to get back home alive. He had been badly troubled with an infection, and for days, at times in a delirium, had been suffering from a high fever, to the great concern of Jean de Graille, the Captal de Buch, who insisted on accompanying him.

The Black Prince sent a delegation on to England to take the French king's tunic and bassinet as proof of his capture to his father, and the ship, once clear of Portchester, continued on to Yermouth with Tom, a small escort and the Captal on board.

34

Epilogue

It was a miracle that Tom survived the journey back to Castor. He had been unconscious for much of the time, but frequently had mumbled Jessica's name and others that the Captal could not understand. It was his will-power and love for Jessica and the children that kept him alive. In his clearer moments, he knew that he was dying, and told the Captal so on several occasions, begging him to hurry before it was too late. The Gascon reassured him with tears in his eyes that they would soon be home with his family, he would live to see many more years, and should stop talking such nonsense.

It was if the villagers knew. As the waggon approached Castor, they stood outside the cottage doors silently and respectfully watching, recognising Tom's shield hooked on the side and his colours flapping on top. One of them guided the small cavalcade to Tom's house, then left immediately, leaving the Gascon noble at the gate moments before the heavy door swung open and Jessica appeared, her heart sinking as she took in the scene before her.

'It's Tom, isn't it?' she stuttered fearfully. 'Is he dead?'

'No, dear lady,' the Captal replied, 'but he's sorely wounded and I fear he will not survive much longer. Please try to be brave. I will help you all I can.'

His men carried Tom carefully into the house, laid him gently on the bed, paid their respects to Jessica and then went outside, leaving the Captal alone with her to explain what had happened. Once she had calmed a little, they left Tom a moment alone with young John – Eric was at the manor house unaware that his father had returned, and Margaret was still missing. The Gascon knight handed over all his belongings, including the gifts he had put aside for Jessica and the children. He also gave her a wooden chest filled with gold crowns, jewellery, beautifully engraved silver platters and other table ornaments, taking great care with Tom's diary, stressing the importance his dear friend attached to it. He then told her he would stay with Sir William for a few days, asking if there was anything else he could do for her in the meantime. She shook her head, not trusting herself to speak, and led him to the door.

In the meantime, Paul was already on his way to Castor. He had originally planned to visit his brother at Christmas, having been badly worried by a strong feeling that something was wrong. Before the ship carrying Tom had docked at Portchester, Paul had become impossible at home in Longeforde. He was moody, could not concentrate on his work and everything Elizabeth and Marky did seemed to irritate him. He even gave the impression of being no longer interested in his baby son Simon, far from the truth in fact, which led to a fierce quarrel one evening between him and Elizabeth. She knew something was disturbing him and had wondered if there was another woman in his life, he had become so difficult. However, on that fateful evening in early October, she stood her ground and insisted he explain what was bothering him so. In spite of his recent conduct, she chidingly stated, she still loved him and as his wife had a right to an explanation.

To her amazement, for the first time, she saw Paul in tears as he tried to reassure her that of course he loved her and the children, and he was sorry for his recent conduct, but couldn't help himself. For days he had been unable to get his brother Tom out of his mind, he had replied.

'He is suffering terribly, I can feel it,' he sobbed. 'It's been with me for days now. My back is aching, I cannot sleep properly, and I see horrible sights in my dreams. Elizabeth, please forgive me, but this feeling is so strong. I know we had agreed to go to Castor at Christmas, but I am certain I'm needed now!'

'Of course you must go immediately, my love,' Elizabeth retorted, putting her arms around him and hugging him tightly. 'I have never fully understood this uncanny relationship between you and Tom, but when I look at you I can see how important it must be, so please go with my blessing. I'll pack your things together and you must leave at daybreak.'

And as England began to celebrate the good news of the Black Prince's great victory at Poitiers, Paul Rollesby set off for Southampton, hoping against hope that his instincts were for once wrong.

Tom survived that first night at home, awaking early the next morning to find Jessica sitting by the bedside, looking down anxiously at him. He took her hand in his, squeezing it gently, and in a quiet voice said:

'You see, my love, in spite of everything, I kept my word. I'm home!'

Her eyes brimming with tears, she nodded, forcing a smile.

'I didn't expect anything else from you, Mr Thomas Rollesby! Welcome home, my darling!'

They both knew there was little time left, but neither wanted to think of it, both being anxious to use every available minute together. Tom called for the children and mussed John's hair, commenting how much he had grown. He took Eric by the hand and asked him how things were going with his apprenticeship at the manor house, and was pleased to learn he was doing well. Eric told him that Lady Mortimer had died while he was away, and that he believed Sir William was planning to marry a very young cousin of hers in the near future. Tom merely acknowledged this with a slight movement of his head and asked his son to convey his warmest and most respectful greetings to Sir William on his behalf, reminding him that they owed their lord so much.

It was then that he asked for his daughter Margaret, and listened carefully to Jessica as she described the day of the terrible scene between them both, when she flounced out of the house, riding off into the distance. Jessica explained how young Robert no sooner heard about it than he was off immediately in search of her, but nothing since had been heard of him, either. For a moment Tom said nothing. Then he told Jessica that he knew perfectly well how difficult Margaret could be, adding that she was more like an unbroken stallion than a teenage daughter. She, Jessica, should not blame herself in any way, he insisted.

'Margaret will return safely one day, I know it. If young Robert continues to grow up the way I remember him last, he will make her a fine husband. She needs a strong hand that one, believe me!' He smiled at some private memory, then began to speak of his brother Paul.

'Jessica,' he continued in an even weaker voice, 'Paul is going to arrive too late this time.' He put a finger to his lips to silence the protest he knew would be in vain. 'He is not far away. Give him my love when he arrives, and let him have my diary. He will know what to do with it. Trust him, all of you. He will help you through the future. John, obey your mother at all times, do you hear? Remember your father and try not to forget what I taught you. Eric, take good care of your mother and make sure you are a credit to the name of Rollesby. Serve Sir William well in my absence. You promise?'

Eric nodded immediately, and took hold of his father's feverish hand. Tom turned his head towards Jessica.

'Thank you for everything you have given me. I have never

stopped loving you from the moment we first met. Tell Margaret when she returns it's time she started to act more like her mother. And you all know how much I also loved her.'

He tried to say more, but suddenly there was no more to be heard. His hand closed on Eric's and then, gradually, his grip weakened. His arm dropped lifelessly to his side as he died.

The burial service was held two days later in the village church, where Tom was laid to rest alongside the mother of his children. Paul had indeed arrived too late, but only hours after Tom's death. Although deeply moved, he seemed to have anticipated what he found that afternoon in Tom's house, and was able quickly to help and make the necessary arrangements. Word had quickly spread and people from all quarters of the demesne packed the church, the graveyard and the whole village centre, all wanting to pay their respects to a man who had been idolised by the majority.

The eulogy was given by Paul, best acquainted with most facets of his brother's life. The congregation gasped when they learned that the man they had revered had been mortally wounded trying to save the lives of the enemy at Poitiers – people of the same race responsible for the slaughter of his parents! Paul quoted from some of Tom's diary entries and posed several questions concerning warfare, the sanctity of human life and ethical values, much of which passed over the heads of many but nevertheless gave some of them a great deal to think about. He ended on a note of hope for the future, following the example of his brother, vowing that he and the whole of the Rollesby family would endeavour to continue along the way of progress that Tom, in spite of numerous set-backs, had blazed for them all.

Once the family had recovered from the grievous loss of one of its greatest members, life gradually returned to normal, and as promised by Paul, successive generations not only continued to progress but left their distinctive and positive mark within the society in which they lived.

SOURCES

B. A. Seaby Ltd, *Coins of England*. B. A. Seaby Ltd, 1990.
Beaumont James, Tom, *Winchester*. B. T. Batsford, 1997.
Borg, Alan, *Arms and Armour in Britain*. HMSO, 1969.
Bradbury, Jim, *The Medieval Archer*. Boydell Press, 1985.
Chandler, John, *Salisbury: A History and Guide*. Alan Sutton Publishing, 1992.
Chaucer, Geoffrey, *The Canterbury Tales*, translated by David Wright. Oxford University Press, 1985.
Cole, Hubert, *The Black Prince*. Purnell Book Services Ltd, 1976.
Fry, Somerset, *Castles of Britain and Ireland – Plantagenet*. David & Charles, 1996.
Hammond, P. W., *Food and Feast in Medieval England*. Alan Sutton Publishing Ltd, 1993.
Hanawalt, Barbara A., *Chaucer's England: Literature in Historical Context*. University of Minnesota Press, 1992.
Harnett, Cynthia, *The Wool-Pack*. Puffin Books, 1961.
Hooper, Nicholas and Bennett, Matthew, *Cambridge Illustrated Atlas: Warfare – The Middle Ages 768–1487*. Cambridge University Press, 1996.
Huizinga, J., *The Waning of the Middle Ages*. Pelican Books, 1924.
Hunter, Judith and Hedges, Beryl, *Windsor: Castle, Town and Park*. FISA, 1989.
Labarge, Margaret Wade, *A Baronial Household of the Thirteenth Century*. Eyr & Spottiswoode, 1965.
Meyers, A. R., *England in the Late Middle Ages*. Penguin Books, 1952.
Miller, Edward and Hatcher, John, *Medieval England: Rural Society and Economic Change 1086–1348*. Longman, 1978.
Pitkin Guides, *City of Winchester*. Pitkin Guides, 1991.
Poston, M. M. *The Medieval Economy and Society*. Penguin Books, 1975.
Power, Eileen, *The Wool Trade in English Medieval History*. Oxford University Press, 1941.
Russell, Jeffrey Burton, *Witchcraft in the Middle Ages*. Cornell University Press, 1972.

Speed, John, *The Counties of Britain: A Tudor Atlas.* Pavilion Book, 1995.
Wall, Barry L. *Long Melford Through the Ages.* East Anglian Magazine Ltd, 1986.
Wright, Thomas, *The Homes of Other Days in England.* D. Appleton & Co., 1871).
Zeigler, Philip, *The Black Death.* Penguin Books, 1982.

GLOSSARY

ashlar   a facing made of squared stones on the front of buildings or hewn stone for such a facing.
aventail   a short cape of mail covering the lower part of the face and shoulders.
ballista   a special device like a huge crossbow for firing iron shafts and javelins.
ballock   a dagger. so called from the two lobes at the base of the grip.
baselard   a long dagger like a miniature sword with a long, flat guard and somewhat longer pommel.
basinet   a rounded helmet worn by knights when in armour.
Black Prince   the eldest son of Edward III.
brogger   fourteenth-century merchant or broker.
Captal de Buch   the title of a famous knight from Gascony, Jean de Grailly. (Reference: Hubert Cole's *The Black Prince*).
card   to comb, open and break wool, freeing it from the coarser parts and other extraneous matter. One of the processes in wool-making.
cellarer   usually a monastic officer responsible for the contents of a cellar, e.g., food and wine.
centenar   a mounted officer in charge of 100 archers.
chancel   that part of a choir in a church between the altar or communion table and the balustrade or railing that encloses it; or that part where the altar is placed.
chevauchée   originating from the French word *cheval* (horse), meaning a mounted skirmishing party designed to devastate property and the inhabitants to humiliate the local lord or, in this case, the French king.
'cuir bouilli'   leather hardened by a process involving boiling water.
demesne   an estate of land; the land adjacent to a manor house or mansion kept in the proprietor's (or lord's) hands, as distinguished from land held by tenants.
dulcimer   a medieval type of hand-organ.

fine   a tax.
flageolet   a musical instrument which is holed and keyed like the flute with a mouthpiece inserted in the bulb-shaped head of the pipe.
fletcher   arrow-maker.
Fuller's earth   a variety of clay or marl used in the 'fulling' process to scour and clean cloth.
fulling   the process of thickening and compressing the fibres of (woollen) cloth by wetting and beating. Also includes the bleaching or whitening operation.
gambeson   a padded tunic, tightly stuffed with wool worn underneath a chain-mail hauberk.
haberdasher   a dealer in drapery goods of various descriptions such as woollens, silks, linens, ribbons.
halberd   traditional weapon of Swiss infantry, adopted by the English. An axe blade with a spike on top and a rear fluke all mounted on a long staff.
hauberk   a protective garment made of leather covering the chest ('cuir bouilli') or chain-mail.
heriot   a chattel or payment, given to the lord, of a fee on the decease of the tenant or vassal.
hobelar   a mounted archer or horse infantry.
huckster   a travelling vendor of small articles; a hawker.
manumission   (charter or letter of) a document giving a serf his freedom.
marl   a mixture of lime and clay-like earth found at various depths under the soil, used extensively for land improvement. There are several varieties, e.g., clay marl, shell marl.
mercer   a merchant with a shop for silks, woollens, linens and cottons.
murrain   a cattle disease similar to foot-and-mouth disease.
nock   a device sometimes made of horn at each end of a longbow that holds the bowstring in place.
parlour   originates from *parloir*, the Anglo-Norman 'talking room'. In monastic houses the parlour was the room for receiving people who came to discuss business matters.
pavise   a long shield generally placed in front of a foot archer to give protection.
pike   long spear with a small blade which could be formed into a hedge-like defence against cavalry.
premonstratensian   an order of monks that wore white habits, occupying Titchfield Abbey for 300 years.

reeve the bailiff or steward of an estate.
ruddle reddish-coloured powder used to mark sheep.
sarpler a bale of clipped wool.
serf from the Latin *servus*, a slave. A forced labourer attached to an estate.
sortie of French origin, meaning here an expedition or campaign.
staple body of English merchants forming a quasi-monopoly of the wool trade.
tabor a type of drum, possibly of Arab origin.
tentering the process by which cloth is stretched on a wooden frame to make it set or dry even and square.
trebuchet a type of pivoted sling counterbalanced at the other end by a weight greater than the missiles, e.g., stone balls, lime, dead animals, etc.
trencher usually thickly cut bread acting as a plate.
vespers evening meal or evensong.
villein a feudal tenant of the lowest class.
vintenar the leader of 20 foot archers.
virgate an area of land varying between 20–30 acres.
windlass a winding machine with pulleys used to span a crossbow.